THE
INFILTRATOR

Also by Eileen MacDonald

Fiction:
The Sleeper
Non-Fiction:
Shoot the Women First
Brides for Sale

EILEEN MACDONALD

THE INFILTRATOR

SIMON & SCHUSTER
A VIACOM COMPANY

First published in Great Britain by Simon & Schuster Ltd, 1998
A Viacom Company

Copyright © Eileen MacDonald 1998

Simon & Schuster Ltd
West Garden Place
Kendal Street
London W2 2AQ

Simon & Schuster Australia
Sydney

A CIP catalogue record for this book is available
from the British Library

ISBN 0-684-81743-8

Typeset in Garamond by
Palimpsest Book Production Limited, Polmont, Stirlingshire
Printed and bound in Great Britain by
Butler & Tanner Ltd, Frome and London

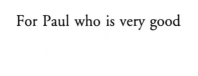

For Paul who is very good

Acknowledgements

Tessa Homfray, Senior Registrar of Clinical Genetics at St George's Hospital, London, inspired, guided and with commendable patience, corrected me and the various versions of the manuscript. I know that she will be relieved to (a) get it off her hands and (b) have it known that any errors that may have slipped in to the final text are mine and not hers.

Sue Gower's eldest son, David, has Duchenne Muscular Dystrophy. Sue's vitality, courage and realism were awe-inspiring. Without her generosity and openness, I would still have been stumbling in the dark about the many effects of Duchenne's on a family's life.

Very many thanks.

CHAPTER ONE

From a distance the van was almost invisible, just another dark shape in the night. Closer to and you could see it was moving, but so slowly that a cursory glance would miss it.

Midnight-blue in colour, windows blackened, lights off, it crept along the unmade road that ran like a peace-line between the woods and the high steel fencing. The noise of its engine, whining in low gear, would have given it away, but noise was not a problem. It was the cameras, tell-tale monkeys clinging to the fencing, their red eyes glaring and following, reporting back, that worried Gerry Winston.

Not that they were in range, he reminded himself for at least the fourth time since he had swung the van off the main road a few minutes before. Soon, but not yet. For now, as long as he kept to the far side of the track, hugging the undergrowth, the cameras could not reach them. In his head he knew it, but his hands still sweated on the steering-wheel and he could feel panic knotting at his insides. Get a grip, he swore at himself. This was only the beginning, and people were relying on him.

He grimaced and hunched forward in his seat, his eyes straining into the night, trying to keep the progress slow and steady, to avoid the ruts in the track. He thought that he'd memorised each one when he'd walked there that morning, head down, jacket-hood up. It had been a waste of time, he realised now. Nothing looked the same at night; nothing was the same.

In the morning he had even been able, on one level, to enjoy the walk. The barrenness of the trees and the cold, clear air had soothed him. Now the tension of the others was palpable, smothering him.

There was not a sound from any of them, no trace of their earlier hot air and bravado. The two sitting up front with him, the three in the back – each was as scared as himself. He reconsidered: they were *differently* scared. It was their first time, their first 'big' operation, whereas it was his eighth. Oh yes, he swore silently, compared to them he was the pro.

But only he knew what could happen if things went wrong. He knew what it was like to be thrown into the back of a police van, to hear friends turn against you to save their own skins; he knew how it felt when your bowels turned to water as the cell door slammed shut, locking you in, leaving no escape, no one to hear you.

The thin branches of a tree, witches' fingers, clawed at the windscreen, terrifying him. It would be just his bloody luck, he thought, to have a heart attack there at the wheel, to die on the job. He was not old, but six years of jail had left him supremely unfit, prone to panic attacks and claustrophobia. Face it, he told himself, you are a sad, burnt-out shell, and your 'comrades' – most of them at least twenty years your junior – would have been better off on their own. He'd told them that, but they hadn't wanted to hear it. He had knowledge that they wanted; he knew the ropes. How swiftly had the hero-worship and shining eyes been replaced by vicious threats and ugly promises. And so he had given in, craven and pathetic at the last.

He glanced at the luminous dial of his watch. Seven minutes to go. Seven minutes and he would be changing course, nosing out of the cover of the friendly trees, crossing to the other side, into the path of the camera lenses: cruel and cold and missing nothing.

He shivered. Of course, there was still time for things to go wrong. He found himself praying hard that they would.

With her next step, Mary Kennedy was out of the shadows and on her own – utterly exposed, every action clearly visible, indeed highlighted in the harsh sweep of the security lights. They were blinding her, they were so bright; she had to shield her eyes.

But in his sterile booth, he was not looking. Head bent, he was watching a screen, the TV probably. Bloody boring job, she thought, poor slob.

Her feet were bringing her closer. Gazing down at them encased in their black boots, she felt herself detached, viewing them as one would a stranger's, noticing the scuffing on the toe, the loss of an eyelet. Cheap, man-made shoes, but with plenty of good, solid tread on the soles. The sound of them hitting the tarmac, amplified by the high-walled buildings either side, was enormous to her. Surely it must penetrate even his Perspex, make him look up?

He kept watching his screen. He had nine screens to monitor, she remembered, nine moving pictures of the perimeter, plus his TV. It must be the TV that he was watching.

She kept her eyes fixed on him, trying to read his; she saw, yet somehow did not see, his brown, spiky hair, his rather fat, unappealing face. She was so close now that she fancied she could hear the sounds of his programme – gunfire and shouting – but her heart was hammering with such force that she couldn't be sure. Why did he stare like that – so absorbed? She bit her lip as a new thought occured to her. Was he seeing the van? Had that old man, Winston, moved out too early? Was the guard, even now, reaching for the alarm button, summoning half the police forces in Kent?

Mary's fingers closed around the cold black plastic in her pocket. She could end everything right now; the pressure of one finger would do it. She was not to hesitate, Winston had said – if she had the slightest doubt, she was to abort and return to base.

She swallowed. She would not be the one to ruin the operation. They had all worked too hard on it: weeks of planning, watching, following. She might be the baby (if only by a few months) of the group, the others might like to look down on her, but not after tonight, they wouldn't. They wouldn't be able to. They would have to admit that she had been brave, that she had proved herself the bravest of them all. For her part, there could be no mask.

No, she resolved, and her finger moved away from the plastic, the others would never know her doubts.

Directly ahead now, three metres and closing, was her target. It looked shiny and well cared for. She felt a pang of guilt, then from her poacher's pocket she pulled the canister.

She had come level. She stopped and looked over her shoulder. He still hadn't seen her. What did she have to do, dance? She wanted him to see her right now, to end the agony of waiting.

'Look at me,' she wanted to shout. 'Look what I'm doing.'

Something made Tim Dacre look up: an outside sound or movement. He peered down the approach road. With the floodlights on it was as bright as day out there. And there was nothing, but nothing, to be seen. Just the road, and beyond it the unmoving shadows of the buildings, and beyond them, the main road, with not even the headlights of a passing car to relieve the monotony.

He sighed and dropped his eyes. He was starting to imagine things. He resolved, not for the first time, to apply for another job. The boredom of this one was likely to kill him or drive him nuts, sitting there night after night, eating biscuits, staring at little screens. He was meant to do just that and only that for eight hours. Having a TV was of course absolutely against the rules. If the boss ever found out – and he did, it was rumoured, sometimes make spot-checks – Tim would be sacked on the spot.

In a way he hoped that would happen; at least it would force him to do something else. He was not stupid, just a little lazy. His school reports had always said the same thing. He had got two A levels, could have done better if he had applied himself, but he had never seen the point. He liked the easy life. Not much riled him. So long as he had enough money to pay his mum the bit of rent she wanted, go drinking with his mates and put petrol in his car, he was happy. He was not yet twenty; he had a bit of time – plenty of time – to chose a proper career.

He reached for another biscuit, let his eyes wander back to the spy movie he had been watching. He grinned. There was his own car, the hero driving it. He bent closer. This guy's car was new, and a much more powerful model, Tim had to admit, but it did show that his taste was impeccable. Not many lads his age owned a nearly vintage Austin Healey. He felt a warm surge of pride, and he glanced over to where his car sat – the love of his life, as a girlfriend had jealously referred to it – gleaming with polish in its customary place under the security lights.

He choked. Someone, some kid – a bloody girl!—was spraying paint on it! Just standing there calmly, raising her arm and dropping it, letting giant letters form and swoop in ugly black paint on his beautiful car. 'WANKE . . .' she had already written; she was on to the last letter now.

He rose, and let out a terrible sound that ended in a howl of rage and pain. Forgetting that he was ordered never to leave the booth unattended, that if he saw anything untoward he was to activate the alarm immediately, letting the police deal with any trouble, he tore open the door of the booth and rushed out. He was still roaring; she must have heard him, but she gave no sign.

'You fucking bitch!'

The girl had golden hair that shone brightly in the lights. She turned slowly towards him. Christ! She was only about fourteen!

'What the fuck are you doing?' He grabbed her by the arm, knocking away the spray-can, and flung her up against the ruined door. There were tears on his face; no expression but blankness on hers, two pale blue eyes watching his. He could hear himself gibbering with shock. He shoved his face into hers, spitting out his words. 'You bitch! Why'd you do—'

'That's enough!'

A man's voice, hard with anger. Dacre spun round, releasing his hold and feeling the girl suddenly slump, to see a figure the same height as himself but leaner, dressed in black – black trousers, black jacket, and – he raised his eyes in awful dawning fear – a black hood. He flicked a gaze, all that he dared, towards the dull metal implement in the man's gloved hand.

He moaned in terror. On the other side of the road his booth stood, door open, releasing its fuggy warmth into the dank November night air. He could hear the sounds of cars screeching, sirens waiting, from the TV. He tried to sniff back his fear.

'You all right?'

The man's eyes had travelled behind Tim to the girl. He heard her straighten herself up; she made a noise of assent in her throat. Thank God, he thought, he hadn't hit her.

'OK, you.' The gun came at him, connecting with the soft flesh of his stomach. What were they going to do? Shoot him? Leave his body lying bloody by his car? He wanted to be brave but he whimpered.

'We're not going to hurt you.' No discernible accent, but a nervousness that scared him more. Tim turned to appeal to the girl.

'Don't look at her!' The barrel pushed hard at his belly, knocking the breath out of him; the man's hooded face thrust into his own, breathing hard. Through the mesh of the black wool stitching he could see the flattened, pale flesh, grossly distorted. Had someone knitted that thing? Or had it been made in a factory? If so, for what purpose had the manufacturer envisaged its use? What, other than terror, could it be for?

'Face me!'

'Don't hurt me, please don't hurt me!' Tim was very afraid of peeing himself or fainting. 'I'll do anything you want!'

'Shut up!' The eyes were blinking fast. Tim heard rustling behind him, another indistinct noise from the girl, and suddenly the man relaxed, withdrawing the pressure on his stomach, regaining control.

'Just do as we say and no one'll get hurt. Turn around now. Go on.'

Turning, Tim saw the girl's bland face was gone, covered by another black hood. He tried to remember what she had looked like but failed. It was a good sign, wasn't it, that they wanted to hide themselves?

The man said, 'Give us the keys.'

Tim stared.

'The car keys. You got them on you? Or are they in there?' He jerked his head at the booth.

'No.' He felt the world slowing down. He patted his pocket, pulled them out. 'Here.' He gulped. 'Have them. Take her.'

A snort. 'We don't want the sodding car! Get in the back. Lie on your stomach. Don't look up.'

Tim hesitated, gazing down at the cloth upholstery. He kept it looking nice with his mum's Vax once a week. He hated the car to be untidy. Was it now to be his grave?

'Move it.' The gun prodded at his back.

He could not fit in the back, not all of him and his legs dangled off the end. He had to scrunch them up against the passenger seat. He hoped they wouldn't shoot him for that.

'Stay there. We're going to be watching you. Try anything

and you get this.' The gun jabbed once more, this time into his thigh, then they were gone. He heard them locking him in, their footsteps moving off, his television suddenly silenced. They were in the booth.

He didn't care. He should have had thoughts of flight and bravery, but none came. He didn't even open his eyes. He huddled down into the fabric, trying to be small, hoping they would forget about him, that they wouldn't come back.

He could smell the air-freshener that he had hung over the rear-view mirror that afternoon. Pine fresh or Spring Meadow – he couldn't remember, couldn't, in that state of mind, tell the difference.

His legs were cramping but he didn't dare move them. Tim began counting, trying to make the numbers pass slowly.

Cracks in the night, like tight pistol shots, as they cut into the fence. Four of them at it, tearing and pulling to make the hole larger. How long it was taking. Agonising minutes and seconds, knowing that the camera watched – the fourth camera, their marker – that it had picked them up, had them in its sights, transfixing them as it rotated on its axis, playing with them, teasing.

Impossible to believe it had been rendered powerless. Impossible not to believe that the transmitter had malfunctioned; that the others had been overpowered or had forgotten, in terror, to use it.

The rip of someone's jacket in the wild scramble through; a collision, a hand trampled underfoot, a scream of pain sharply cursed. Then the hill, foreboding in the night, rising up much more steeply than in daylight. It was hard not to fall; hard to see anyone else, everyone being in black, swallowed up by shadows.

On the ridge they paused. Below them, in the hollow, stood the buildings: single-storey golden brick, slanting slate roofs around a grassy courtyard; pathways of wood-chippings, lit by low beacon lights. A latter-day supermarket, merging in, using natural materials, upsetting no one. Over on the other side, out of sight beyond the rampart, were the heavy metal gates and the security barrier, set securely in its place by the entrance road, and the guard.

Thirty minutes was all they had given themselves. Six of them for the two main buildings and the smaller one, standing by itself, a little higher up the slope.

A last check that gloves were on, hoods down, and in two teams they fanned out. They saw the cameras under the eaves and by the doorways, knew that no one was watching now, that there was no one to hear, but still the smashing of the first window stopped them all. A collective holding of breath, the terror of discovery as they waited together in suspended time, then realisation and a snapping of the spell as the glass tinkled and fell.

They went in through the windows, helping each other, being careful not to leave clues behind on the jagged glass. Inside, accepting that they had made it, they heard only themselves, then as their ears adjusted they became aware of something else: a humming from nearby. The same sense of a dare gone too far, hot adrenalin and cold fear, as the lights went on. A long room with windows down one side, benches along the other, test-tubes and microscopes. On the walls, pinned or stuck up with tape, print-outs showing sharp black lines running up and down. Puzzling, unclear. Lie detector tests?

Tracking the hum, they moved out into the corridor, past some metal trolleys laden with cardboard boxes. Gerry opened one. It contained printer cartridges. Another was full of paper.

He moved on. The others had gone into the next room; he could hear their muffled voices as he approached. He could also hear the humming noise increasing and see a blue light. He felt a sudden drop in temperature. It was very cold in here, a giant, humming, cold room, its door wide open, its blue light making everything inside eerie and unreal. In front of him was a wall of metal shelving, filled stack upon stack with test-tubes, some in cardboard lids, others in little metal racks, most containing varied amounts of an unidentified liquid.

The slighter figure turned, holding up a tube. 'Look at this stuff!' Mike Pearson, sixteen, looking older in the hood but betrayed by his voice. 'What is this place?'

Gerry picked up another phial. 'I don't know,' he said slowly. A strange unease swept over him. These new buildings stood on an old MOD site; maybe it still was run by that Ministry. They used to do nerve gas experiments on animals here, but what were they doing now? He'd read all the stories: deadly monkey viruses for which there was no cure; airborne killers escaping into the environment, bacteriological warfare . . .

'Whatever it is, it's not what we're after, is it? Let's get on.' He stepped backwards into the corridor and was relieved when Mike and the other man, Chris Manyon, followed.

There were three more doors. The first was steel and locked; they tried the handle, it was useless. The next was open. Inside this room there were more fridges, and to one side several glass-fronted chambers – bathed in a soft, beguiling pink light – containing petri-dishes. Gerry extended a finger: the glass was faintly warm to the touch. Opposite, on a work-surface, was something like an overhead projector, but with a little mechanical metal arm, poised over yet more glass phials.

None of it made any sense. None of it was what he'd expected – what, reluctantly, he'd told the others would be there. He left the room.

Mike and Manyon were in the corridor beside a huge chest-freezer, heavily padlocked.

'Bet you there's something in here.'

Gerry wondered briefly if Manyon was being humorous, then he remembered the cut of the man. He frowned. 'Maybe, but I can't see how we can get into it. We haven't got the right tools.'

'And if anything's in there, it's too late, isn't it?' Mike said with a shrug.

The last room – their last hope. This one seemed purely for storage: piled to the ceiling with desks, chairs, crates.

'Looks like you've made a bit of a balls up, doesn't it?' Manyon's voice was scathing. 'All this for sod all,' he hissed.

Gerry felt his stomach sicken. Although he'd never wanted any of this, he prayed now that the others would have found something. Otherwise, out of spite, they might carry out their threats. In silence he led the way out, past the second building, which he could see through the windows was empty, and into the third.

The door was jammed open, the others standing just inside.

'Well?' They turned as he entered. The accusatory tone, the sniff from the woman, Caroline, told him everything he needed to know.

'Nothing?' he asked quaveringly.

'Offices,' Caroline whispered in disgust.

Manyon and Mike pushed past to take a look, but Gerry stayed where he was. He felt suddenly very tired.

'Why don't we trash the place anyway?' demanded another of the men, Lucas.

'What'd be the point of that?' Caroline, the leader of the strange crew, the coercer, turned on him.

'What d'you mean, "point"?'

'Yeah.' Manyon had come back. He liked to argue with her. 'This whole fucking raid's been a fucking disaster, right? So why don't we leave them something to remember us by?' He snorted. 'A calling card.'

'Yeah. Just 'cause these bastards have cleaned up their act, just 'cause there aren't any animals here—'

'Exactly.' She cut him off. 'We'll do something else at a later date, but we've worked too hard to throw it all away on pointless vandalism. Next time—' she stared at Winston in a way that he'd come to dread – 'we'll have to make really sure of our intelligence before we commit ourselves.'

'I still think . . .' Lucas's nasal voice began, and Caroline's eyes swung away from Gerry over to him.

'Well?' she demanded.

'This lot are up to something dodgy, aren't they? I mean, look at all the security out there! That's not for nothing is it?'

They argued on. Gerry was suddenly unbearably hot; he peeled off his balaclava, rubbed a hand over his face, looked at his watch, and realised that the others, down by the gate with the guard, would be waiting.

He cleared his throat, and they all turned to look at him. 'Caroline's right. It's not worth it. If they'd been abusing animals, sure, we'd rescue them and burn the joint. But what we've got here . . .' He hesitated, remembering those test-tubes, that warm pink glow in the first building. 'I don't know what we've got here. But it isn't worth going to prison over, I can tell you that. Not worth being locked up for six years, I can promise you.'

Someone yawned rudely but Winston carried on: 'Anyway, if we destroy things here, we don't know what sort of harm we might cause. Those test-tube samples—'

'What test-tubes?' Andrew, who hadn't yet spoken, suddenly demanded. He was Caroline's partner, a weak man. Gerry had been surprised to learn that he was a teacher.

He turned to him, described the wall of samples, what he

suspected they might be, and watched the effect hitting home, a sharp intake of breath running round the group like a snake.

'Caroline, he might be right,' Andrew said nervously. 'It could be viruses.' He clawed suddenly at his hand, scratching it clumsily through his gloves.

'OK,' Caroline said, and now no one argued. 'Mike?' she glanced about. 'Where did he go?'

'I'm here.' The boy emerged from a doorway, his hands held stiffly down by his sides.

'Come on.'

They went out quietly in single file, a sober, silent crew. Winston came last, paused to close the door behind them, but saw the wedge of paper keeping it open, and left it there.

Inside the empty building, the eyes of the hidden cameras, perfectly positioned to catch all angles, continued to record the scene before them. The microphones, voice-activated, switched themselves off as soon as the door closed behind the last intruder.

CHAPTER TWO

'. . . And, finally, police in Kent are denying reports that a retirement party ended in a naked midnight sprint along the High Street of the quiet market-town of—'

The sound died.

Sasha Downey groaned, rolled over and glowered at the radio-alarm clock beside her head. Then, wearily, she extended an arm and dealt the machine a sharp blow to the side. No response, so she did the same thing again. The sound spluttered back on with the weather forecast for north-west Scotland.

That, she muttered to herself as she snuggled back under the duvet, was it. Enough. For too long – more than a month now, ever since she had put the hour back – the radio had been tormenting her. In addition to playing hide-and-seek with its sound, it had been coming on half-way through, or even at the end of the seven o'clock news headlines, thus depriving her of her first daily fix of major stories. It wasn't as if, she thought morosely, she hadn't done her best to remedy matters. Although the manual had been lost long before, she'd spent an entire evening determinedly setting and resetting switches until, at after midnight, she'd discovered violence as a short-term solution.

She frowned. Bashing something as one's first waking act couldn't be good for the psyche. She folded back the duvet and sat up. She was a professional, she reminded herself, and she was earning more than enough for a new radio. A shocking pink Lady Penelope perhaps, like the one she'd seen in a recent Sunday supplement.

A faint sense of guilt, her father's voice, floated into her consciousness, telling her that she could always get her old one repaired.

She looked over at it again. It was so big that it took up most of her bedside cabinet. Its ridged aluminium casing was severely dented and the black paint on the buttons had flaked off. She hated it, she acknowledged calmly. She always had. But it had been a parental gift years before, just before her first term at Southampton. 'It may not be pretty,' her father had said, presenting it, 'but it'll last.' And, like a curse, it had. It had endured tremendously: through university; in Northampton for her first newspaper job; Bournemouth for the second, then Manchester – and it was still with her after five years and three moves in London.

But now, she thought, casting it an evil look, it would follow her around no more. That very day – if possible, that morning – she would go to the smart electrical shop in Mortimer Street and buy herself a Lady P.

Before she could change her mind she hopped out of bed, unplugged the machine and shoved it out of sight at the bottom of her wardrobe, thus saving her parents' feelings if they visited, and also avoiding the inevitable speech on being foolish with money.

Automatically she started pulling on her jogging clothes. Her parents hadn't been the only ones convinced that she'd been committing financial suicide when, eighteen months before, she'd quit her well-paid, prestigious job on a 'quality' national newspaper to go freelance. Many friends, including her then boyfriend, had told her that she was mad, as had several older colleagues on the paper. 'Keep your head down,' they'd counselled, and, 'Why not enjoy it while it lasts?' – but neither course had been possible for her.

She'd been at the paper for two years by then, having initially been taken on as an assistant to the investigations specialist, Ben Davies, a man who was generally regarded as a legend in the industry, and someone whom Sasha had hero-worshipped since her first days on the *Northampton Post*.

Almost half his age and with only four years' journalistic experience, Sasha had at first been very much in his shadow, but after bringing in two of her own exclusives she had gradually emerged in her own right. By the end of her first year, Davies had been referring to her as 'My Heir Apparent'.

They had had their own office, a budget that was independent of the newsroom, and were free within reason to pursue what they wanted. It had been a dream job, everyone had told her, especially at her age, and she'd readily agreed, without giving it much thought.

Then the Editor had changed, and with him so had the entire atmosphere on the paper. The new man had brought with him his own team, including a Managing Editor of news, whose brief was to give the paper a 'new edge', a more youthful and cohesive feel; to chop out the dead wood and, above all, to increase circulation. Within a few days, nearly a third of the paper's department heads had been dismissed, escorted from the building by security guards.

Sasha sighed, crossed over to her dressing-table and picked up a bobby-pin. With a practised head she scooped her long hair back into a pony-tail, at the same time pulling a face at herself in the mirror. It never made her feel very good about herself to remember that dreadful time.

They'd summoned Ben Davies at four-thirty, by which time he'd already transferred much of his paperwork into his car. 'Save those bastards the trouble,' he'd told her. He hadn't come back. When, on cue, the uniformed guards had entered with their black sacks, Sasha had pushed past them in tears. She'd been out on the newsfloor, part of a little numbed group, when the news editor had called over to her. He hadn't been able to meet her eyes.

'Uh, they want you upstairs, Sasha. I'm sorry.'

In a daze she'd presented herself outside the Managing Editor's door. What about my rent? she'd anguished. How am I going to live? And, most fervently she'd found herself praying. 'Please God, don't let me cry in front of them . . .'

Smiling, they'd welcomed her in and asked her to sit on the sofa. They were both great admirers of her work, she had heard them say; they loved her enthusiasm, tenacity and courageousness.

Biting her lip, she'd waited for the blow.

Then the Editor had started to talk about Davies.

'The trouble is, Sasha . . .' Something in the way that he'd spoken her name had made her flinch. '. . . he wouldn't, or perhaps more charitably, couldn't, move with the times. Long ago, he found what people wanted – or thought he did – and he stuck to it like a lawyer to an ambulance.'

The Managing Editor had laughed uproariously.

'It would be funny,' the editor had continued, and the other man's laughter had clicked off, 'except that he held you back.'

She'd stared dumbly.

'For instance . . .' The Editor had shuffled through the cuttings on the desk, and stabbed at one with his finger. 'This story he got you to do about young offenders . . .'

She'd come to slightly. The story had been one of their triumphs, the result of three weeks' painstaking research into the government's 'model' detention centre for twelve- to fifteen-year-old boys. Far from the 'happy, industrious environment' that a newly published report had boasted of, they'd found it to be a place of fear where bizarre and Draconian punishments were meted out by the staff to the inmates. As a result of the article, the governor had been suspended and an inquiry set up.

'The point that Davies failed to appreciate, my dear, is that the vast majority of the British public isn't in the least interested in what happens to these nasty little delinquents so long as they're off the streets and not stealing cars or vandalising people's homes.

'And to waste the talents and energies of a young high-flyer like yourself on such drivel is, in my book – ' his brows had come together – 'little short of criminal.'

'Most of the boys were on remand,' Sasha had pointed out faintly.

He hadn't appeared to hear her. 'You've been misdirected by a man who has, quite frankly, lost it.'

In future, the Editor had told her, she was to be the Investigations Unit. '"Sasha Downey, Investigator." Sounds rather catchy, doesn't it?'

To her shame, she recalled, she'd given a cheesy grin.

'Yes . . .' He'd warmed to his theme, his eyes lingering on her legs, then roving up her slim figure before coming to rest complacently on her face. 'I thought a series of "Sasha Downey Investigates" features – "Fearless Femme" style. Send you off with the Marines for a weekend or have you living rough on a mountain. Telling the readers what life is like in the raw.'

Sasha had gazed at him expressionlessly. She'd seen the end of her career as a serious journalist, and the start of Bimbo-hood. They'd produced a list of proposals for her: Sasha Downey Investigates the World of Female Mud Wrestlers; of Casino Croupiers; of Today's Mistresses; of girls who use male escort agencies; of girls who aren't afraid to be single. It had all been just short of soft porn, she realised now.

The only excuse that she allowed herself was that she'd been in shock. That, plus – and she grinned slightly – the speed with which she'd fallen quite so dramatically from grace.

Her first stumble had occurred almost immediately. Sent to interview the indulged, gossipy daughter of the paper's chairman about her venture into 'At Home Catering' (for a feature on Enterprise and the Single Girl), she'd come away with an exclusive on how some of the dinner guests – a junior minister among them – were misappropriating government grants to refurbish their country homes. The story had been shaping up for a front-page splash when the Editor had tapped Sasha on the shoulder and taken her into an empty side office. Was she not aware, he'd asked, that one of the diners was a non-executive director of the company that now owned the newspaper?

He'd been quite paternal over that one, Sasha recalled, telling her that perhaps one could hardly expect a young girl reporter to be acquainted with management matters. So he'd arranged a change of scene for her the next week. She smiled again, remembering just how disastrous she'd been as the 'danger girl'.

They'd tried to get her to abseil off the top of the newspaper offices. In spite of the instructor's assurances that the harness would hold someone three times her weight, she'd known, looking down, that nothing on earth would persuade her to leave the relative safety of that roof.

She ought to have mentioned to the Editor, she supposed, that she was a complete physical coward. She'd been so thankful when the army had turned down the request to stage a 'Challenge Sasha' on an assault course at Salisbury.

They'd probably been pretty desperate – she had, certainly – when they'd asked her to interview the newly elected female leader of a council in West London. Since her election, the woman had been very publicly engaged, much to the embarrassment of her party, in cleaning up a host of notoriously corrupt practices that had made the council a laughing stock for years.

Thank God, Sasha had thought, a serious piece of journalism at last, and proof that the editor wasn't really intent on changing the paper's middle-of-the-road-but-leftish stance to blatant right. Then the Managing Editor had told her what 'the Boss' actually wanted: Sasha was to ask the woman about her sixteen-year-old daughter's lesbianism.

'But I don't see what that's got to do with—'

'Come on, girl!' The man had rolled his eyes elaborately. 'What's happened to your news judgement? You don't really think the Boss is interested in Clean-up Clare's policies, do you? But her daughter being a dyke – and that's an exclusive, by the way – that's going to sell copies. See?'

Sasha had done the interview and it had gone well. The woman, although initially unforthcoming, had gradually thawed and emerged as humorous, fearsomely bright and very brave. It had probably been her bravery, Sasha admitted, that had finally inspired courage in herself. Back at the paper she'd written fast, the words and phrases coming easily. The finished product, the news editor had told her, looking uncharacteristically impressed, had displayed both maturity and wit. She'd been so pleased by his praise that when she'd been called up to the editor's office she'd gone with a light step, expecting further praise.

The Managing Editor had been with him. There'd been no smiles, no offer of a seat.

'What's this turgid crap?' The Managing Editor had slapped a copy of her article down on the desk. 'You were told what we wanted, and what do you deliver instead?'

Sasha, standing just inside the door, had felt curiously calm, able to return his stare without flinching. Out of the corner of her eye she'd seen that the Editor, having set his Rottweiler upon her, was now sitting back watchfully.

'Fucking wishy-washy, lettie-luvvie tripe! If we wanted a fucking political analysis we'd have got a political journalist to do it. And to do it *right*, by the way – not this pathetic hero-worship shite.' He'd paused to wipe his chin. 'Did you even *ask* this bitch about her fucking daughter? Or did you just decide not to bother? Why should you? It was only the editor that told you to do it, wasn't it? Or was it . . .' a gleam had entered his small eyes, 'that you're a lezzie too? Is that it? Couldn't bring yourself to shop a sister?'

There'd been quite a bit more along the same lines until, with a wave of one of those vast hands, he'd instructed her to get out of his 'fucking sight'. In the process of doing so, she'd seen the smile on the Editor's face and realised how much he'd been enjoying himself.

Back at her desk she'd worked on automatic pilot, buoyed up by a strange sensation of invincibility, of being someone else. She'd scarcely flinched when the Managing Editor had appeared and sat down beside her. She'd felt his eyes watching her as she'd typed on, heard his laboured breathing close to her own ears.

'You know this latest fashion fad,' he'd said eventually. 'The "Rubber Look". Used to be kinky but it isn't any more, right?'

She remembered that, very slowly, she'd pressed the Speller command on her keyboard.

'All the girls are wearing it, aren't they? Rubber dresses, rubber shorts, rubber shoes too . . . but who cares about the shoes? Eh, eh? Thing is . . .' He'd inched his chair nearer and his hot breath had rippled on her neck. 'The Editor's come up with another idea for you. He'd like you to get into one of those dresses and go for a walk through Soho at night. Tell the reader what it feels like. It'll be a great piece! We thought, "Solo in Soho – Sasha Downey shows how any girl with guts can go where she wants, when she wants, and dressed how she likes." You can do it sophisticated, funny – however you like. But you've got to do it on your own, he says. No hairy-arsed snappers looking out for you. We can do the pictures afterwards.'

She had taken her eyes off the screen then, and turned to stare at him.

He'd winked.

She'd stood up, noticing for the first time that he was only a couple of inches taller than she was. 'Excuse me,' she'd murmured, edging past him.

'Hang on, I haven't finished with you yet! Come back here!'

The whole newsroom had gone quiet, but Sasha had kept going. Behind her, the man's voice had risen: 'Don't walk off when I'm talking to you! You fucking little Prima Donna! Think you're untouchable, don't you?'

He'd caught up with her by the printer. Looking down, Sasha

had seen her copy emerge. She'd picked it up, torn it carefully along the perforations and handed half of it to him.

'What the fuck . . . ?'

'My resignation.' She'd watched his face go absolutely white.

After that, things had happened very quickly, making recall more difficult. She'd collected her bag – she had vague memories of people trying to talk to her – and left by the fire-escape, not waiting for the lift. By the time she'd reached home, a little after five o'clock, her feelings of euphoria were so strong that she'd felt light-headed.

She'd desperately wanted someone to talk to and celebrate with, so she'd been delighted on unlocking the front door to hear Edwin, her boyfriend, on the telephone. He'd been saying 'goodbye' to someone when she'd entered the room.

'Guess what I've done?' She'd bounced on the sofa beside him. 'I'm so happy, Ed! I mean I know it's mad, and I can't explain . . .' She'd trailed off, seeing his expression.

'I know exactly what you've done,' he'd said icily. 'That was your news editor on the phone. Have you gone completely off your head?'

He'd walked out of the apartment that afternoon and never came back. And so she'd lost her boyfriend and her job on the same day.

The morning after, waking and leaping out of bed before realising that she'd no work to go to, had been very strange. She'd been despondently checking through cupboards and drawers to see what else (apart from her favourite baseball cap, the cafetière and her spare set of keys) Edwin had taken when the phone had rung. It was the features editor of another newspaper. He'd heard about her departure and what had prompted it, and wanted a new version of her article on Clean-up Clare for his own paper the following day.

When it duly appeared she'd received another call from another commissioning editor, and gradually her workload had increased. Initially she had thought she would have to apply for another job, but after a few months she'd discovered that, not only could she stop worrying about the rent, but she was enjoying herself much more as a freelance journalist than as an employee.

She kept up some shift-work because it paid so well, and it was a good way to keep in touch with changing trends, not to mention sudden changes in personnel. The great difference was that now she could dip in and out, always able to move on, to remain unaffected by in-house politicking. She was in charge; she was at the beck and call of no one.

She was probably, it occurred to her now, unemployable. It was a vaguely scary feeling, she conceded thoughtfully; but also quite enjoyable.

'Prima Donna?' she murmured, catching sight of herself in the mirror. 'Probably.'

Apart from anything else, she was aware that she no longer fitted into a specific journalistic role. Freelancing had provided her with a much broader canvas and although her first love would always be investigative work, she'd developed a real liking for interviewing people in depth, particularly those in political life.

She zipped up her jogging jacket. Then, with a thumb and forefinger, tweaked open the window-blind. It was drizzling and dull outside. Growling, she dropped the slat and headed for the front door, indulging as she did so in her daily argument: she didn't *have* to go for a run. And too much routine could stifle a person's natural creativity and verve. She could relax in a hot bath, enjoy a leisurely and thorough read of the newspapers rather than take her usual canter. She could sort out some invoices . . . but no. Unless she went out now, she would feel sluggish for the rest of the day – and that, she told herself, would never do. Not if she bore in mind the calibre of the person whom she was due to be interviewing in less than three hours' time.

A nervous butterfly danced in her stomach. Reminding herself she'd done all the groundwork and only needed a quick look at her notes, slammed the front door and walked swiftly down the corridor towards the lift.

The new Health Minister had not given a full-length, one-to-one interview since being appointed six weeks before. Sasha, along with many other journalists, had applied to talk to her but, as time had passed and she'd heard nothing, she'd assumed that the prize had gone either to a medical journalist or a political heavyweight. Probably, she had reasoned, it being the Health Secretary's first cabinet role, her advisers would have opted for someone from one of the papers that backed the government.

Then, four days before, the press office had rung and told Sasha to report to their building in Whitehall at eleven o'clock on Friday morning. The Minister was prepared to grant her a forty-five-minute interview, on the understanding that the article appeared within seven days in either a daily or weekly publication with a circulation of not less than three hundred thousand.

Sasha had known exactly whom she'd wanted to pitch it to: Derek Hornby, the editor of *Comment*, a new, highly prestigious weekly news magazine. He'd commissioned her at once.

Feeling suddenly energetic, Sasha stepped into the lift. As she descended, she lifted herself up and down on her toes, flexing her calf muscles. Talk about luck, she thought, putting a hand out to touch the soft peach carpet that lined the walls. Was it true that the gods favoured some above others – and if so, why, and more specifically, why her? Sometimes she still had to remind herself that she wasn't an impostor: that she did truly live there, in Tanner's Court, Floral Street, where, wonderfully every morning, she was saluted by the uniformed concierge.

'Morning, Alexander,' she called out as she passed.

'Morning, miss. Don't you be overdoing it, now,' he said, as he usually did, before pressing the buzzer for the main door that let her out into the soft, grey rain.

CHAPTER THREE

It was only quarter to ten in the morning. Knowing this, seeing it clearly on his own wrist-watch, Colin Davenport still found it difficult to believe. Whole days seemed to have passed since he had been woken in the dark by the telephone call.

A break-in at the site. A security guard tied up; the fencing cut; signs of forced entry to two of the buildings, but no other obvious damage. In fact it appeared that nothing had been stolen. The intruders must have taken fright. However, owing to the nature of the work, the police had asked if Mr Davenport would please go in and check that everything was as it should be in his department.

He had been half-asleep – it was only a few minutes past four o'clock – and he had dressed, left the house and been half-way there before the thought had punctured his consciousness. With it had come sudden terror, a clawing nail in his flesh, the sense of his future falling away . . . Then he'd shaken himself properly awake. The site manager had said nothing had been taken.

The place, normally so quiet, had been an angry wasps' nest: police officers and incident tape everywhere and blue lights flashing on empty cars; radios talking to themselves, and people in white suits and soft boots like bee-keepers moving in slow motion; the blinding glare of arc-lights, making everything too white and hurting his eyes.

Then himself interrogated, his ID demanded, by two uniformed officers at the main gate.

Through the windows of the building figures had moved, trailing little posses of police. Coming towards him down the path, escorted by another officer, had been a young woman wearing a raincoat and yellow wellington boots over her pyjamas. Vaguely he'd remembered seeing her once before, coming out of one of the other buildings, but he hadn't known her name, and nor would he have expected to.

It was when he had got to his own building and seen the way the doors had been fully opened, leaving the wedge of paper exposed in a circle of yellow chalk, that the fear had returned, thudding in his chest. All he had wanted to do was run into his office and check, just to make sure . . .

'Good morning.' A man with short, greying hair, not in uniform, but wearing the rainproof jacket of a policeman, had emerged from Sophie's room. He had introduced himself and produced an identity card, but Davenport hadn't been listening or watching. His eyes had been fixed on his door, at the end of the corridor.

He'd taken a step towards it.

The policeman's voice had stopped him.

'And you are . . . ?'

'Colin Davenport. Unit supervisor.' His lips had been dry.

'Ah, yes. Thank you for coming so quickly, Mr Davenport. You're the most senior person in this block, I understand?'

He'd swallowed and nodded.

'I suspect that this may prove to have been a waste of time. There doesn't appear to be any sign of forced entry . . . but on that point, perhaps you could clear one thing up for me?'

His nervousness must have shown; he had always been bad at concealing things. The policeman had been suddenly watchful.

'I take it that this door was normally left open at night?'

'Open?'

'Wedged open, with that piece of paper.' And they had both stared at it.

Davenport had licked his lips. 'The . . . um, the secretary kept forgetting her pass card. So we, er . . . It's a very secure site – externally, I mean. There's never been a problem.' He had started blinking rapidly.

The policeman had said: 'Perhaps if you'd like to have a look round, see if anything's missing . . .'

Under that thoughtful gaze, Davenport had resisted the urge to bolt to his own room. Instead he'd led the man back into the general office, Sophie's domain. To him it had looked the same as ever: as if several other rooms – and none of them to do with work – had been emptied into this one. Mark's small room, cold and neat next door, had also appeared untouched.

Thank God, he'd thought, feeling the fear recede, and he had heard himself saying quite jauntily to the policeman behind him, 'I think you're right, Officer, a bit of a waste of time. Not that I'm complaining, I know you people have a job to do.'

Then he'd walked into his own office and seen that it was gone.

'Sir? Is something missing?'

He had felt himself falling through space.

'Mr Davenport, are you all right?'

'I . . . I . . . I'm feeling a bit dizzy.'

'Here, sit down.'

He had been trembling all over, unable to control it.

'Take it easy,' the policeman had ordered. 'Deep breaths. OK? So, what've they taken?'

'They . . .' In response to the authority in that voice he'd almost blurted it out. Then, snapping shut his mouth, he'd tried to pull himself together. 'N-no. No, noth-nothing's been taken. Nothing.'

The policeman had stared and frowned.

'I . . . I don't know what's wrong with me. Must be the flu. Yes, the flu. A virus . . .'

The policeman's eyes had slowly swept the desk: the telephone, the angle poise, the computer. 'Sure they've taken nothing?' he'd asked quietly.

'No! I mean – yes, I'm sure.'

'This is a serious incident, sir. I don't know if you've realised that yet. A firearm was used to threaten a young man's life, and that man is now not in very good shape – heavily traumatised, could suffer permanent psychological damage. We're looking at aggravated burglary here. Ten to fifteen years. It looks to me as if whoever's responsible knew exactly what they were after.'

'No.'

They had stared at each other. Finally the policeman had produced a card. 'If you want to change your mind, you can get me on this number.'

Colin Davenport had been left sitting, staring at the card. Detective Chief Inspector Tony Holland, an Ashford telephone number. He had stayed like that for nearly an hour, and in that time if he had thought anything he had not been aware of it. When he had finally started to think coherently his mind had raced, weaving in and out of a maze like a blind man in panic, finding no solution. In the end he had done what he should have done at the beginning – called John Stockart at his London number – only to discover that he was already on his way.

He had seen Stockart twice that morning. Once, briefly, just after he had arrived, and then again an hour later, when he had finished with the police. Now Stockart had gone again, saying that he had a visitor to meet, but that he would be back. And Davenport wasn't to think of going anywhere.

Davenport groaned out loud. Going where? Where *could* he go? Wherever he went Stockart would hunt him down; those pale, pitiless eyes would seek him out, close in for the kill.

He jerked himself awake, ran cold fingers through his hair, felt the start of stubble on his chin. For the first time he noticed what he was wearing: a jumper he had spilt something down, and his old jeans, the clothes he had been wearing last night, that had been lying on the floor by his bed. He ought to have a shower, he thought woodenly, make himself more presentable and less easy to intimidate. He ought at least to move from the plastic chair that the policeman had given him, move round to his proper place behind his own desk, but that, he reminded himself with a shudder, was where Stockart had been sitting.

He had always been afraid of Stockart, he realised now. Even when the man had been wooing him, promising him all things, he had been a little scared, had known by instinct to keep his distance, that something essential in the other man was lacking. Now he could understand Stockart's power, his astounding success in the pursuit of what others said was the impossible. The man didn't care about anyone. He was a monster. His voice that morning had been level and quiet as always, but utterly devoid of humanity.

How had Davenport not noticed that dead tone before? And how had Stockart ever been able to convince anyone that he cared about others' suffering?

'You're telling me, then, that this laptop contained everything?'

'Oh no, not everything. No, no, John. Not by any means.' How Davenport had hated his own cravenness, even as he had uttered the words, his desperate attempts to propitiate. 'O-only the rewritten material. I'm sure of that . . . pretty sure. I erase things a-as I go along, you see,' and he'd gulped, not because he was lying – he wasn't – but because Stockart simply terrified him and made him not quite sure of things.

'Why did you leave this . . . critically sensitive information lying around in an unlocked building?'

'I know. I know I've been stupid, but—'

'Stupid? I'd put it a little more strongly than that.' How those eyes had bored into him, full beam on a hapless rabbit in a country lane. 'You've never spoken about what you do to an outsider, have you, Colin?'

'No! I swear it! Really, never!'

'I think I pay you well, Colin. Very well. Enough to ensure loyalty, I'd have hoped.'

Davenport had started trembling again, so violently that he could not speak, could only listen to the awful honey of the other man's voice.

'The inspector knows you're lying, of course. He knows something's gone from in here.'

'H-he does?'

'Yes, Colin, he does. He asked me if you were happy here, if you could've been tempted by a rival. Unlikely, I'd have thought, given everything – but one can never be entirely sure of human nature. And it's . . . peculiar, isn't it, that your laptop's the only thing they took?'

'John, look, I swear, I know nothing about this! You've got to believe me!'

Colin had seen nothing to show that Stockart had even heard the appeal; just those eyes, hard instruments, holding him down, dissecting him . . .

He shuddered at the memory. Outside, someone walked along the gravel path by his window, but he couldn't see who it was; the blinds were closed. He wondered what was happening elsewhere on the site. The police must have largely gone by now. Much earlier they'd moved round him, brushing bits of carpet, putting dust on the door – dusting for fingerprints, he supposed. He hadn't really watched very carefully.

Was everyone else back at work? Perhaps the other two were in, sitting in the neighbouring rooms. The thought gave him comfort: Sophie in one of her mini-skirts, and Mark, who fancied her and whose idea it had been to jam open the front door, and who'd gone ahead and done it anyway, in spite of Davenport's weak protests, the same way that he'd overruled him on the volume of Sophie's music or her time-keeping.

'Davenport.'

He jumped. He hadn't heard the door open.

Stockart re-entered. In his beautiful suit, white shirt, dark tie, he didn't look like a man who'd been up since dawn. He was even wearing cuff-links, Davenport noticed now, small silver knots, discreet but expensive-looking.

'This is Mr Hall.'

Davenport's attention switched slowly. The visitor had already taken his seat behind the desk. He too wore a suit, but less elegantly, and there were circles under his already dark eyes. They studied him impassively.

Stockart leant against the wall, his long legs crossed, arms folded. 'Mr Hall's a security expert. Nothing to do with the company. He works for me, on a contractual basis. He wanted to meet you.'

Davenport tried smiling, but it set his facial muscles twitching, and anyway, Hall made no attempt to smile back.

'It's just possible,' Stockart went on, 'that Mr Hall's going to be able to salvage the appalling position that your crass negligence – if nothing more sinister – has placed us in.'

'John, please!' Davenport's knuckles gripped the plastic sides of the chair. 'I've told you, it was sheer oversight on my part. Nothing else, nothing sinister!'

They both watched him: Hall, brooding and dark, the finger and thumb of his right hand playing with a signet ring on his left; Stockart, the ceiling light bright on his fair head, his thin lips drawn straight across the colourless face. Davenport swallowed noisily. It was difficult to say who was the more menacing.

Stockart spoke again. 'On first sight, it does seem that you're telling the truth. Either that or you're a bloody good actor, which we'll find out soon enough.

'However, to return to the facts: by the end of today, Mr Hall assures me, we'll know the identity of at least one of the culprits, if not more.'

'You will?' Davenport gazed in hope at the visitor. 'So the police've found something?'

A faint smile touched Hall's face. 'The police? No, forget about the police.' His voice was low and there was the trace of a foreign accent, although Davenport couldn't place it. 'I would suggest,' Hall continued, addressing his words to the desk-top, 'that the police are going to find it difficult to proceed with their investigations. The perpetrators took elementary but sufficient precautions in respect of fingerprints.' He cleared his throat quietly. 'These sort of people generally do,' he said.

'These sort . . . ? You know who they are?' Davenport blinked rapidly. 'But how? I mean, if the police don't—'

'He's already told you to forget the police, hasn't he?' Against the wall, Stockart moved impatiently. 'The perpetrators,' he lingered over the word, 'appear to be animal rights activists. Animal lib.'

'Animal lib?' Davenport felt dazed. 'But they don't steal computers.'

Stockart raised an eyebrow. 'No? Possibly not as a general rule. But I think in this instance your laptop was a temptation too far.'

'A temptation . . .' Davenport echoed, then tried pulling himself together. 'I'm sorry, John, but . . . animal rights? We don't *use* animals here.'

'No, I think they gathered that in the end. Quite a quarrel they had about it. The leader got so hot and cross he took his balaclava off. And started talking about his prison record. Given that information, it's likely that we'll know his name and address within an hour or so.'

'I beg your pardon?' Stockart wasn't making any sense.

A gleam came into the man's eyes. 'You've heard of the Police National Computer? Where criminals are listed? Mr Hall assures me that it shouldn't take his people very long.'

'No, no, I didn't mean that.' Davenport's brow puckered. 'I

meant, I mean – I don't see how you can know. If . . . if you take my—'

'Surveillance, in a word, Davenport.'

Davenport stared. 'But the police said the cameras—'

'Oh yes, they knocked out the compound's cameras by taking out the guard, then trashing the film. Mr Hall told you that they took some precautions. But one could hardly expect them to see the other cameras.' One corner of his mouth went down. 'Or the microphones. Any more than you could.'

'The . . . I'm sorry, I really don't understand.' He blinked from one man to the other, caught the amused look on Stockart's face. 'You were watching me?' he whispered.

'Yes, and listening to you too.' Stockart's expression grew more animated. 'Oh, I didn't have everything installed just for you. The system was already here, courtesy of Mr Hall.'

Davenport glanced again at Hall, saw how intently he was still being watched and looked swiftly away again. My God, he thought, chewing at his cheek, what had he said out loud as he'd worked away on his own? What had Sophie and Mark said? Or done?

'I had it put in several years ago,' Stockart went on, sounding, for him, almost conversational. 'Just in case, you know . . . and just as well, as it's turned out, isn't it? I always have it reactivated when I've got something going on down here. Once a week the tapes are sent up to me for viewing. But I've got out of the habit of looking at them nowadays. Rather boring, don't you know. So I suppose I ought to take part of the blame myself for this. If I'd bothered to look, I would've seen your slovenly habits myself. However, one learns from one's mistakes. You'll work from home in future.'

Davenport gulped. This was the first real indication that they didn't believe he was guilty, that he'd have a future. 'Sure, John, sure. I mean, I'll have to come in a bit; I'll have to reaccess the data . . .' He nodded at the computer on his desk.

'We'll discuss that later. In the meantime, you're to say nothing about what's been taken to anyone. Do you understand?'

'Absolutely! Absolutely, John. I'm just so relieved, so . . .' He swallowed again and grinned weakly in Hall's direction. 'Excellent work. Excellent, yes . . .'

Hall blinked once, slowly, as if for him even that automatic action was deliberate.

Davenport shook his head. He felt so much more relaxed now, as if a great weight had been rolled away. 'Animal rights, eh? Who'd have thought it?' He chuckled. 'They won't know what they've got, will they? Be double-Dutch to them! You know, I almost wonder if it's *worth* retrieving it. If you go and grab it, they might get the wind up, don't you think? Put out some kind of statement, you know how they do . . .'

He stopped suddenly, aware that there was a different degree, almost audible, in the way that both men were now staring at him.

Stockart moved quickly to stand in front of him. 'What're you suggesting?' he hissed into his face. 'That we let them keep the computer? Are you *sure* you're not involved with them?'

'J-John! You know I'm not! You can't believe that!' He shifted sideways. 'Mr Hall, p-please tell him, I'm, I'm—'

'Tell me what, Colin?' Stockart's hand, ice-cold through the thin fibres of Davenport's jumper, came down like a vice on his shoulder. 'I think I know you pretty well. That you can be bought and sold like the rest of your breed, that you've got the scruples of an alley-cat . . .'

'John, please!' His collar-bone was being crushed. 'You're hurting me!'

'Am I?' The grip got harder. 'You think you're indispensable – don't you? – because of one skill in one area.'

Davenport tried to squirm away. Out of the corner of his eye he could see the other man just watching, doing nothing. The smell of Stockart's after-shave assaulted his nostrils. He was going to be sick, he thought, and felt a blackness rush up at him. He was going to faint . . .

'Get out.'

Davenport blinked and came round, his hand seeking out his shoulder, rubbing at it. Stockart had retreated to the desk beside Hall.

Shakily, Davenport rose to his feet. 'I'm not in league with them, John. I never was. I want you to know that. I'll be on my way now.' He turned. All he wanted to do was get away, back to the house where he lived, distance himself from Stockart and those eyes. A thought struck him, and without meaning to, he shot a swift glance around the room. There was nothing obvious, no wires or lenses.

Were there any back at the house? 'I'll . . . I'll just say goodbye to the others,' he said, his hand on the door.

'The site's been shut for the day,' Stockart said. His voice had returned to normal; no trace of the terrifying anger was left. The whole incident might never have happened.

'Oh – Davenport?'

He trembled again.

'Just before you go, let me have the business card, will you?'

'The . . . ?'

'The card that Mr Holland gave you. The policeman – you remember him? You put it in your jeans, the back pocket. Thanks. It'd never do if you changed your mind and decided to give him a ring, would it?'

CHAPTER FOUR

Philippa Tyler was impatient to give her first interview. As the new Secretary of State for Health, she had seen the wisdom of obeying her PPS and keeping a low profile – of smiling charmingly at the cameras and answering questions with, 'I've yet to master my brief on that one!' – during her first month in office. None the less, the settling-in period had irked her. She was keen to be in the public eye, to have her opinions aired; to make her mark.

She was a clever woman, a voracious reader and absorber of facts, and she also had the ability to be all things to all people. After six weeks of briefings and meetings, days and some nights of argument and careful manoeuvring, she felt supremely confident in herself and her new role. The media, correctly handled, could only enhance it. At forty-three years old she was youngish for her elevation to the cabinet but not remarkably so, and her grey hair made her look older.

She picked a loose thread from the pale yellow sofa that she was sitting on, and plumped up one of the scatter cushions with the butterfly picked out in gold. The decor of the room, her office, had been chosen by her and was chiefly yellows and white. It was her statement: feminine, bright and clean.

There was no dirt in her past that had not been dealt with; she had always been most meticulous in that respect. Let any reporter, however investigative, she thought with a smile, try to trip her up.

It had been her PPS's suggestion to award Sasha Downey the first interview, and Philippa had concurred. She had read and liked a recent interview by Sasha with the deputy leader of the opposition – a woman whom Philippa privately admired, recognising in her a similar astuteness to her own – and had been flattered by a phrase in Sasha's fax, describing her as a politician who was 'clearly not afraid to break the mould'. That observation, Philippa felt, deserved encouragement.

Plus, according to the press office, Sasha was a rising star. 'Very definitely hot,' her PPS had said, 'but still hungry. She'll get you good coverage – probably not in one of our usual organs, but that will provide even more impact. Catch the others on the hop. Shake them up a bit.'

Philippa spent a few moments practising sitting down graciously, her legs to one side, making sure her skirt modestly covered her knees. She was a largish woman; thus she had to be careful of what she wore and how she wore it, especially in front of a younger woman. On the beech coffee-table in front of her, slightly to the left of the pile of that morning's newspapers, stood the wooden-framed photograph of her husband and her two daughters. The girls had arrived exactly as she had planned, two years apart. Everything in its place, she told herself as she moved the photo fractionally closer to the armchair opposite, where Sasha would be sitting.

It was nearly time. She rose and checked her appearance in the golden-framed mirror in the alcove, approving of what she saw: brown eyes with some lines (that could be from either worry or laughter); a carefully made-up face, showing just the right amount of female vanity; and her grey, wavy hair.

There was a discreet knock and Sebastian, her secretary, put his head around the door. 'Miss Downey's arrived, Philippa.'

'Good. Show her in. Oh, and coffee at half past, with biscuits.'

Her heart was beating a little faster than normal, taking her by surprise. She must be nervous, she realised. A good thing, she had always thought – it made one that much sharper. Probably Miss Downey was nervous too, although from what she had been told Sasha was quite the – she searched momentarily for the word – intrepid reporter. Not that she had to be fearless this morning:

everything was about to be handed to her on a plate. Philippa smiled slightly. It made one feel quite magnanimous, spoon-feeding journalists.

Mentally she reviewed the file photograph. Sasha Downey was an arresting-looking girl, with that long dark hair and those legs. Philippa had once longed to be leggy, before she had learned to appreciate the far greater attraction of power.

'Minister? Miss Downey to see you.'

The sort of girl who would go far. Philippa smiled again, remembering the first time she had been told that.

The door opened and she raised herself up. Warm, intelligent and welcoming . . . but, after all, caring.

The clinic occupied the top two floors of the Mistletoe private hospital on the north side of the Thames, a stone's throw from Lambeth Bridge and within easy walking distance of Parliament. Negotiations were underway urgently for its expansion downwards, but space was short in the building. Promises of the fifth floor becoming available had not materialised, and there had been talk of a new building entirely for the clinic, but there was no nearby land available and it seemed foolish to banish the most outstandingly successful department of the hospital to Docklands. However, no one disputed that fresh arrangements would have to be made, and sooner rather than later.

Sixteen months before, when news of the breakthrough had first appeared in *Science and Discovery* magazine, the world, it seemed, had come calling on the hospital. At the beginning they had received a hundred or more prospective patients a day, most of them turning up without an appointment: people from overseas; people willing to pay double to jump the queue; people bringing with them stories of heartbreak and despair; women lying about their age in order to be allowed treatment . . . Even now there were still sometimes hundreds of calls a week. Every time the name of the clinic was mentioned on television or the radio, or quoted in a newspaper, the phone lines jammed – in spite of the new twelve-line switchboard, complete with automatic queuing system and pleasant jingles, that had been a priority acquisition the previous autumn.

The new drug had transformed their modest IVF clinic into a Mecca for the childless. Before, their 'Take Home Baby' rate had been 12.4 per cent. Now it had soared to 89.4, all thanks to the discovery of the 'wonder' drug Infutopin, taken either in tablet form or in a short course of injections. Truly, the medical world had agreed, a stunning success. People called it a miracle. Infertile couples spoke the hospital's name reverently, the answer to their prayers.

Infutopin owed its existence to the discovery of a gene, Human Receptor Gene A1007LQ, also referred to in the media as the 'Octo-pus' Gene, by researchers at Branium Pharma (Pharmaceuticals) UK Inc. Having been identified, the gene's DNA had been sequenced and its protein engineered into the drug that had catapulted the whole IVF process out of the primary time-warp in which it had been mired since 1979. Infutopin, it had been explained countless times to journalists and patients, simply made embryos stick. 'Like an octopus, Daddy?' the son of one of the doctors had asked, and so the more media-friendly term had been born.

'Think of the gene as possessing special receptive powers,' the clinic's PR man would say with practised ease to the camera or microphone. 'Before, no matter how skilful the sur-geon – and we think ours were as skilful as any – the fact was that a great proportion of test-tube embryos failed to implant in the womb. Why, is a mystery, and might remain so for some considerable time, because quite frankly, we no longer need to know.

'Now Infutopin, with its unique abilities, does the job for us. It stops the womb rejecting the embryos; it's easy to take; it has no adverse side-effects. It is – ' and he would give a short laugh to show that he was joking – 'almost too good to be true. Thousands, eventually millions of people are going to benefit because of what we are doing here.'

The media had lionised the team, and the team loved it. It suited them all to forget that they were merely the instruments for the miracle, that the real magicians were the backroom boys and girls, the research scientists who'd discovered the drug.

They hadn't even been researching into IVF. They'd been working on something else entirely and had found the gene by accident. Thus it was by another miracle that Infutopin had actually made it to the market-place.

Once there, of course, any medical team could administer it. The only reason that the Mistletoe clinic had got the drug first, three months ahead of anyone else, was because the hospital was owned in its entirety by Branium Pharma.

A slight fear – that once the drug was generally available the Mistletoe would cease to enjoy such prominence – had proved groundless. Of course, as soon as it had been launched other IVF clinics had bought their own supplies of the drug. But initially there had been delivery delays – and profuse apologies from Branium when clinics ran out of stock – a state of affairs that tended to persist, leaving other clinics and their patients in a state of uncertainty.

The Mistletoe had never suffered from such problems. In the public mind the cure and the clinic were firmly linked. It was where the drug had been pioneered, and where the TV crews were regularly allowed access. It was where everyone who needed IVF wanted to go, irrespective of the extra cost – roughly twenty per cent higher than elsewhere – on top of the already expensive Infutopin treatment.

But it wasn't really that expensive, Branium argued. Not if one took into account that, without Infutopin, a woman might have to undergo several cycles of treatment – five were not unknown – and then may still be unsuccessful. Whereas the Mistletoe could virtually guarantee one treatment per baby. Look at the fact, the accounts department said, that the clinic had stopped the practice of re-implanting three embryos (the legal maximum, and the norm in conventional IVF treatment, where rejection of at least one was more or less expected) because of the likelihood of triplets. Why risk multiple births, with all their associated problems, when one could have a single healthy child from one treatment? The clinic would do twins, if specifically requested, at no extra charge.

All in all, the hospital felt their fees were justified if not actually good value for money. It certainly wasn't being greedy, not when one bore in mind the desperation behind each case history.

And as much as the patients wanted treatment at the Mistletoe, a great many young doctors wanted to work there. There was something very special about being able to look into the eyes of a desperate couple and tell them: 'Yes, we can do it. We can give you a baby.' It was heady stuff, being a god. The number of times that a member of staff was asked to be a godparent, or to be present at the birth – difficult to refuse that last request when the couples opted, as many of them did, to have the baby in the maternity wing on the second floor. Thank

God, the doctors would mutter among themselves, the wing was so small.

The main board directors of Branium were, of course, delighted. Infutopin was a blockbuster drug; it was going to make them millions. And the publicity generated by the clinic was exactly what they had hoped for; people had begun to link the miraculous success at the Mistletoe with their other products. Why buy ordinary aspirin, cold remedies or mosquito repellant, when you could buy Branium's? Profits for the forthcoming year looked even better than for the previous twelve months, and those had been record-breaking. In the new year there were to be bonuses for all.

'The Feel-Good Factor', the clinic's resident psychologist called it, trying but failing to remain professionally detached.

Sasha sat frowning at the middle-aged businessman opposite her. The man tried to ignore her unwinking stare, tried to convince himself that, on the one hand, the girl was a looker (and as she was looking right at him she must fancy him) and, on the other, that she might be one of the nutters the government had decided to let wander the streets, and that she was about to stab him through the heart with a knife from that big shoulder-bag of hers. In the end, so unnerved was he, he got off the bus a stop early.

Sasha was unaware of him, or anyone else. She was utterly immersed in her thoughts, mentally reviewing the meeting she had just had with Philippa Tyler, trying to eliminate the sense of disquiet, the awful feeling that she'd missed something vital or failed to ask an essential question.

But the interview, she reassured herself again, had gone well – in fact, extremely well. She ought to be delighted; she *was* delighted. In most respects she had got far more than she had expected. Having spoken to political journalist friends she'd been quite prepared for a 'soft' interview: the new minister using her first in-depth media opportunity to talk about herself without giving very much away.

Instead, Sasha had been given the 'Agenda for the Nation's Health'. It constituted a scoop.

Tyler had called it her 'Blueprint for care'. For the elderly it would involve the setting-up of community homes and drop-in centres, where the emphasis would be on family-style care – on 'getting to really know Mrs Brown', on 'remembering that she likes her tea with two sugars', on 'these little things that cost so little, but show that we care very much'.

Tyler had gone on to describe a whole programme on the prevention of stress in the workplace; schemes to promote healthy lifestyles; awards to companies that introduced healthcare programmes for their employees, including perhaps an extra day or two's holiday a year, to 'give people time to smell the roses; to be glad that they're alive. So important, Sasha. I hope you take time for yourself each day?' She had proposed a far greater acceptance of alternative medicine generally, and promised more funding for two NHS homeopathic hospitals.

Sasha had felt breathless, and not just at the speed with which the agenda was being delivered. The proposals seemed to fly so totally in the face of current government thinking. It was well known that the Prime Minister considered alternative medicine 'quackery', that to increase productivity, employers were coming under increasing pressure to cut back on 'nannying tendencies' such as sick-pay for the first year of service and the provision of canteens in the workplace. And as for old people, the attitude emanating from Whitehall seemed to be that there were too many of them and that, unless they had sorted themselves out with pension schemes, they ought to have the decency to die as quickly and quietly as possible.

'Er, Minister, could I ask . . . ?'

'One moment, dear.' Tyler had raised a manicured hand and repositioned herself slightly on the sofa. The low winter sun had glinted behind her head, making her grey hair gold. And then she'd dropped her bombshell.

The leasing of four floors of the recently closed St Peter's NHS hospital to the Mistletoe private hospital – or, more specifically, the Mistletoe Infertility Clinic. 'In addition, NHS funding for five hundred places a year at the clinic. You seem surprised . . .' Mrs Tyler, settling back against her butterfly cushions, had looked warmly amused.

Surprised, Sasha thought, was putting it mildly. Aware that she'd been goggling, she'd tried to rearrange her features more professionally. 'I am! I mean wasn't St Peter's shut to save costs? And now you're effectively selling it off to the private sector.'

'No, no, you weren't listening. The Mistletoe will be paying the market rent; it will, in effect, be paying for the NHS places. Don't you see? It's a plan which, I think, benefits all parties. The Mistletoe needs the space; we have it. The Mistletoe has the best track-record in the world for treating infertility; and that's what we want for our patients.'

'But wouldn't you be better off . . . I mean, wouldn't it be fairer to fund an NHS infertility team?'

'Why? Why shouldn't NHS patients have the best? I'm not saying that, in time, other clinics won't catch up with the Mistletoe, but they're at the top of the league-tables now, and why should people who can't afford private medicine have to wait for years? Why can't they go to the best place in the world when it's right here in their own country? Especially for people who are at their most desperate . . .' She'd paused, her gaze straying to the framed photograph on the table between them.

'Yours?' Sasha had asked obligingly.

'Yes, mine. Katie's eight and Samantha's six.' A long, lingering look, a gentle smile playing around the mouth, before she'd resumed. 'I'm sorry, my dear. But I've been so lucky, and I know this is what all mothers say, but I cannot imagine life without them. I can only guess at the heartache of people who find themselves infertile.'

'Yes.' But Sasha's mind had been elsewhere. 'Surely the Mistletoe's owned by a drugs company? Branium?'

'Yes, that's right.' Mrs Tyler had nodded.

'Well, doesn't that make it even more peculiar . . . that you're being seen to help a huge company like that?'

The sorrowful look, magnified, had returned. 'What is peculiar, Sasha, in my department seeking to bring the best medical care to the nation? Thanks to Branium, Britain now leads the world in infertility treatment. You do know about Infutopin, I take it?'

'Um, yes. I mean, I've read about it . . . Yes, of course.'

'So you'll be aware that it's a genetically engineered drug?' Tyler had sat forward on the sofa. She hadn't waited for Sasha to answer, 'Branium, along with several of the other major pharmaceutical companies in the world, has been investing millions in the research and development of such drugs. Do you know what the next century is going to be known as in the medical world?'

Sasha had shaken her head. She'd been more intent on watching the transformation taking place than in fully attending to what was being said. The tape recorder could catch Tyler's words but not the illumined eyes, the eager expression that had lifted the whole face, making her suddenly seem young.

'The Age of the Gene. There are projects underway at the moment, Sasha, that quite honestly, boggle the mind! The Human Genome Project, for example. By 2010, every gene in the human body will have been identified. Amazing, isn't it? One of my briefing papers described it as being of greater significance to mankind than landing a man on the moon. And once the genes are identified, the potential benefits to medicine are enormous. Staggering! We'll be able to tell good genes from bad ones; we'll live in an age where the scourges of Aids and cancer and Alzheimer's – all the horrors of modern times – are vanquished!'

There'd been a glow to her cheeks, a flame in her eyes. 'The speed of development in this field is quite staggering. You're aware that they can already tell whether a test-tube embryo will develop cancer in later life? It's not going to be so far in the future when they'll find the gene that switches off the various cancers! Now . . .' She'd edged so far forward on the low sofa that she had appeared perched, ready to spring. 'I, for one, want to see British drugs companies right out there in the forefront of this field. And if offering Branium a few hundred cubic metres of space is seen as favouritism, then so be it. I nail my colours to the mast!

'And let me also say, if Branium come up with more superb drugs or therapies I shall continue to look favourably upon them. There's another three and a half towers going spare at St Peter's, and the Mistletoe is only on the other side of the river, a bare five minutes' walk. What could be more convenient for the doctors, I ask you?' She'd waved a hand vaguely. 'Or more symbolic – representing the bridge I intend to see built between private and NHS medicine?

'It's time that we in this country stopped running ourselves down and started patting ourselves, and others, on the back. Especially our scientists and doctors. Let's reverse the brain-drain, I say! Make this country such a centre of excellence that the Americans will be queuing up to come and work here!'

It had been quite a speech, Sasha mused; quite a performance. Or had that part at least been genuine? That was her problem, she realised: she simply didn't know whether Tyler had been acting from start to finish. Was it possible that all that zeal had been faked? *Could* someone fake that glow? Had it been as much a part of the act as the sorrowful looks, or the fond, maternal glances at the little girls? Or had everything been genuine, and Sasha was doing the woman a huge disservice?

She rubbed her forehead. What had happened to her antennae, she wondered, normally so sensitive, that enabled her to read people quickly and accurately? She closed her eyes and concentrated hard. Mrs Tyler simply didn't look like a scheming politician. The grey hair and crinkling brown eyes, the soft yellow twin-set and elegant tweedy skirt; she looked like someone's mother – fundamentally sincere, a good person. The kind of person who wouldn't mind criticism that she was aiding a drugs company, so long as the childless were being helped.

Sasha shook herself. *All* politicians acted. The trouble was that Tyler was so good at it that Sasha couldn't get a true reading. She'd been outsmarted. That explained her disquiet.

The bus gave a sudden lurch forward, nearly sending her sprawling into the aisle. What did it really matter? she thought, regaining her seat. She had an excellent news story and Hornby would be delighted. She ought to be flattered that the minister had selected her to deliver the goods.

Later that afternoon, she decided, she'd give the photographer a call – he'd arrived as she had departed – and compare notes.

She fished the evening paper out of her bag and leafed through it. A headline caught her eye: 'Research Company Raided'.

'Armed raiders left a security guard bound and gagged this morning after breaking into laboratories in Kent . . .' She scanned the rest of the story, automatically looking for a line that might be developed: the guard tied up but not hurt; the police not commenting; investigations continuing . . . No, it was only worth the few paragraphs it had already got.

She looked up. The bus was in the Aldwych; her stop had been the last one, and it had started to rain again.

'Oh bugger!' she yelped, leaping up.

'Really!' An old man sitting opposite her, who'd been thinking how wistful she was, looked quite upset.

'Sorry! Daydreaming!' And she turned on him such a dazzling smile that he felt quite young again.

'Charming girl,' he told himself, eyeing her legs as she slipped off the bus and into the traffic, 'A spirited filly, oh yes!' And he sank into his own daydream as the bus rounded the crescent into Fleet Street.

CHAPTER FIVE

The GP went out of the room.

Melanie glanced sideways at her husband. His face was white and set and he didn't look back.

'Patrick?'

He said nothing.

'Are you OK?'

'Mm. Fine.'

But he'd only said it, she knew, to shut her up. He didn't want to talk to her. She'd tried again that morning before they'd left for the surgery. 'There's nothing more to be said,' he'd told her brusquely, then risen quickly from the breakfast table and gone to join Ludo in front of the TV set. He hated morning television, and only allowed it as a bribe to Ludo to be ready in time for the school bus. Anything not to be alone with her.

She resumed the destruction of the tissue in her lap. The silence from Patrick was much, much harder to bear than the terrible rage that had engulfed him when she'd broken the news three days before. On his return from work, she'd followed him into their bedroom.

'What?' he'd said at first, his head stuck inside the wardrobe, and genuinely not having heard her.

She'd repeated it.

He'd been in the process of removing his tie and stopped, one hand clutching at the knot. He'd turned and stared, not at her but through her. He's in shock, she'd thought, and gone forward with a hand held out to touch him, and had felt him tense against her.

'Patrick, darling . . .'

'How long?'

'How . . . ?'

'How many weeks?'

'I, well . . .' He'd never spoken to her in such a way before, so sharp and cold. He'd always been gentle, understanding, her best friend. Her voice had quavered, 'I'm not absolutely sure.'

He'd shot her a look of pure loathing.

'About nine, maybe ten. I . . . I can't be more specific, Patrick. I can't remember exactly.'

'Can't remember exactly?' He'd echoed incredulously, mocking her, making the words sound high and silly. He'd slammed the wardrobe door and the floor had shaken. 'Can't remember *exactly* when you forgot to use the cap? Can't remember *exactly* when you decided to go ahead and get pregnant without telling me? You bitch! You scheming little bitch!'

She'd felt sick. It hadn't been Patrick at all, but a stranger who'd invaded his body. 'No, don't,' she'd whispered, backing away from him, her legs finding the bed and sitting down hard upon it.

'Don't what? What else would you call it? We agreed, I seem to recall, that we were going to give it another year, save up some cash and go for IVF again. Hadn't we? Well, *hadn't* we?'

Transfixed, she'd nodded. Then, taking a deep breath, she'd slowly shaken her head.

'What d' you mean, no?'

'Patrick! Don't shout at me!'

He'd snatched her hands away from her ears. 'I'll do more than bloody shout at you!'

From the floor below had come a faint cry. In an instant Patrick had been on the landing, his voice a lullaby, calling down the stairwell that it was all right, that he and mummy were 'just messing around.' Then he'd closed the door and turned back to her, and the look on his face had chilled her.

'You're telling me, are you, that we didn't discuss this?' His voice had hissed low, hot breath in cold air. 'You'll have to forgive me, my memory must be playing tricks, because I remember you saying—'

'I didn't say anything much. I only agreed because you were so keen.'

He'd rocked back as if she'd struck him. She'd been tempted not to go on, but had known that it was then or never. 'I told you that I didn't know if I could go through with the whole thing again.'

'But you know it wouldn't be the same as last time! Not with this new drug they've got! It's as near as dammit guaranteed!'

'But we can't afford it. We can't even afford the ordinary IVF.'

'That's why we're waiting the year, remember?'

'Oh Patrick!' She'd buried her face in her hands. Did he believe that it was only to do with money? Had he no intimation, though he had murmured the right things, how she'd really felt during the IVF process? Discarding male embryos simply because of their sex, because there was a fifty per cent chance that they too would be born like Ludo? But what if they'd been unaffected? That was the question that had haunted her.

'"Oh Patrick" what? It's better this way, then? Deliberately deceiving me—'

'It wasn't like that!'

'What *was* it like then?' He'd stepped away from her. 'Talk about a *fait accompli*! "Darling, there's something I've got to tell you." My God!' He'd broken into an ugly laugh. 'What d'you expect me to do? Celebrate? Break open a bottle of Bolly? Let's drink a toast to the birth of another son who's going to end up in a wheelchair.'

'Don't, Patrick,' she'd whispered.

'A cripple by the time he's eight, dead before he's twenty.'

She'd felt a sudden lurch inside, like the baby moving – but it couldn't have been, it was far too early. When she'd miscarried her two test-tube girls at eleven weeks, she'd felt that she'd deserved it, that it had been her fault, that she'd done it to them. She'd been manipulating nature, rejecting the babies that should naturally have been born to her.

Patrick's eyes had narrowed. 'So we're going to go through the whole thing again, are we? See him take his first few steps. Thank God, we'll say. He was a bit late walking but he's all right now. OK, so he plods along – but that's just his personality. Like the way he talks. That's a little slow too. Nothing's wrong though, he's just a laid-back kid, that's the way we like him.

'Then when he starts bumping into things, we'll try convincing ourselves that that's fine too, he's just a bit clumsy. Lots of kids are, it's nothing to worry about. How long should we leave it this time, Mel, before we take him to a specialist? Till he's three? Four?'

He'd bent down to meet her at eye-level. 'Or should we wait "just a bit longer"?'

She'd gasped. That had been her plea, begging for more time for Ludo, trying to make herself believe that in another week or two, another month maybe, he'd get over his funny, awkward patch, he wouldn't take so long to get his words out, he'd remember how to walk properly, the way he once had, how to climb the stairs without falling. 'You'll see, you'll see,' she'd said brightly, too brightly, to everyone.

Patrick hadn't finished. 'Should we wait till he's at school, in the playground? When the other kids are laughing at him because he can't run and jump and hop like them, or—'

'Stop it, please!' To listen to him, she'd thought, anyone would have thought he hated his son, not loved him so much that he could deny him nothing, that he cried out Ludo's name in his sleep, for the things he'd never have or be, for the perfect son that might have been.

'At least this time we'll know the kind of thing to say to him, won't we? We won't need counselling to prepare him. When he asks why he's not like his little friends we'll have it off pat, won't we? We'll tell him that he's got a bit of a problem with his muscles, that they're trying to find a cure for it, and meanwhile the most important thing is to try and keep him as supple and healthy as possible, so he's got to be a good boy about his exercises and his special diet, and wearing his splints . . .'

He'd trailed off, and looking up she'd seen tears in his eyes. She'd made a move to comfort him but he'd pushed her away and wiped his eyes himself. 'Of course, it's going to be difficult for the little fellow, keeping his spirits up when all he has to do is look over at Big Brother Ludo in his wheelchair and know what's in store for him when he's ten – or eight, or whatever godamned age it's going to be.'

'Darling, don't torture yourself.'

He'd looked straight at her. 'No, you're right. It's not my fault, is it, darling? It's *your* fucking gene.'

He'd never said such a thing before, not even at the beginning, in those very dark days immediately after the diagnosis. Duchenne's Muscular Dystrophy. It had meant little to them then, but they'd soon learned. Oh yes, she thought bitterly, they were experts now.

Except in very rare cases DMD affected only boys, about one in every four thousand in the UK. Caused by a mutation on the X-chromosome, one third of DMD cases occurred spontaneously, but the majority were genetically inherited via the mother. She was nearly always a symptomless carrier, but if she had the DMD gene her sons stood a one in two chance of being affected.

Ludo had been a month short of his fourth birthday when Melanie had finally given in and taken him to the GP. She'd tried to make light of the symptoms, but she'd seen the way that the doctor's face had changed from kindly reassurance to open concern as he'd watched Ludo stand up from where he'd flopped down on to the floor: first by resting on his knees and hands, then pushing himself up into a crab position, before finally, and painfully slowly, gaining full height by using his hands to climb up his legs.

The Gower's Sign, it was called, a definite Duchenne's trait, caused by weakening of the hip muscles. She knew all about it now, of course, but back then . . . How could any mother have known? Even if she had noticed it, how could it have sent out alarm signals?

'When did he start doing that?' the doctor had asked quietly.

'That? Oh, you mean that!' She'd reached out and pulled Ludo protectively towards her. 'It's just his way. Just the way Ludo stands up. Isn't it, darling?'

'Can I see his calves, Mrs Alder?'

She'd swallowed hard. They'd always thought that Ludo's calf muscles were big – but what was wrong with that? Patrick was quite a muscular man. ('Look at that,' he'd said, proudly prodding the tubby legs when Ludo was still tiny. 'He'll be playing rugby for England in eighteen years.') And more recently, trying to counterbalance her unacknowledged doubts, she'd drawn comfort from those sturdy calves: they showed, surely, that Ludo was a strong, healthy little boy?

Enlargement of the calf muscles was another Duchenne's indicator. The GP had taken a blood test which revealed that Ludo had a very high level of a muscle enzyme, creatine kinase. In DMD cases, the enzyme leaked into the bloodstream. The diagnosis was fairly definite by then, but not officially confirmed for another five months until the muscle biopsy.

DMD, Melanie remembered the specialist saying, was a progressive disease. Progressive: the word had spun in her head like a sycamore seed falling to earth as the woman talked on. Everything was progressive, wasn't it? she'd thought. Babies grow in the womb, progressing month by month, first just a bundle of cells, then a funny little blob, then the head and arms and legs . . . they are born, they open their eyes, they cry, they grow up to become children, teenagers, mums and dads themselves in the end . . .

Ludo's DNA test had shown the missing parts of the Dystrophin gene quite clearly. It looked, Mel had thought, staring at the photographic record that she'd held in her hand, like a tower of pound coins neatly stacked up, one on top of the other, only with some coins just not there. Crucial coins, without which the tower would eventually tumble, essential parts. The parts that in a normal person produce the dystrophin protein which is essential for muscle development and maintenance. Lack of it resulting in weakness that, in time, affects almost every muscle in the body, sends that body tumbling like a flimsy tower of coins to the ground.

But the eyes were always spared, the consultant had said – and Mel, suddenly focusing her attention, hadn't been able to bear it. Ludo's gorgeous blue-grey eyes, his long, sweeping lashes. Far too pretty for a boy, they'd always said, secretly congratulating themselves. The prospect of those eyes watching his own decline . . . Very quietly, like a sigh, Mel had felt something inside herself die.

Patrick had asked a question and the counsellor, dropping her eyes, had softly said, 'Yes.'

'What?' Mel had demanded.

'It's always fatal,' Patrick had croaked and sought her hand. They'd clung tight. Not their little boy. He was so good; he was innocent and beautiful, and only a baby still, really. He had hair the colour of corn and a slow, deep-throated, infectious chuckle that made you want to scoop him up and cuddle him and never, ever let him go.

'When? I mean, how long?' Mel had asked in tears.

'It's really not possible to say at this stage.'

Patrick's voice had gone small and hard. 'We need to know,' he'd insisted.

'Much can be done to delay the onset of deformities, through exercises, physiotherapy . . .'

'Just tell us.'

'We have some DMD sufferers who are in their twenties, even early thirties. Some are married, you know.'

'The worst.'

'I really can't—'

'Will he be a teenager?' Mel had blurted suddenly.

'Oh, Mrs Alder!' For a second the professional mask had slipped and Mel had seen her own horror reflected in that other face. Then the woman had gathered herself together again. 'Certainly we can expect him to make his teens. Maybe, probably, early twenties – although, as I've said, every case is different.'

'But,' Patrick wouldn't let her go, 'you've already told us that the weakening in his hips is quite pronounced. "Earlier than usual," I believe were your words.'

'That doesn't necessarily mean—'

'Christ! D'you think we're stupid? D'you think we can't read between the lines?'

'All I was going to say, Mr Alder, is that the condition doesn't follow any set path. Also – and I know this may come as a shock to you right now – it's beginning to appear that the boys who go into wheelchairs earlier . . .'

Mel had shut her eyes.

'. . . tend to live longer.'

More than likely, she'd heard the woman say, Ludo's deterioration would be a gradual thing. He'd weaken, but then there'd be a plateau. There was no reason why, at least for the first few years, he shouldn't go to a normal school. Games would always be difficult. But children were so adaptable, the counsellor, back in her stride, had continued. Ludo could get a friend to run for him in rounders, for instance. And she'd smiled brightly. Football – ah, well, football was really out of the question. It was a good idea to encourage sedentary hobbies: trainspotting, for instance, or bird-watching.

Crash, crash, crash. All their normal, ordinary little hopes had come tumbling down. No cricket for Ludo, then. No team games or sports days. Would they take him in the cubs? Mel had wondered suddenly. Suppose he wanted to go sailing? They lived near a reservoir, and Ludo had always been captivated by the brightly coloured dinghies on the water. Would they let a little crippled boy sail?

From about seven years onwards, the counsellor had continued, Ludo would probably wear splints while he slept. That was a measure to stop the muscles contracting and to keep him 'on his feet' as long as possible. Also, from about nine years old, there was the possibility of surgery and callipers to support the weakened muscles. And then, ultimately, there was the wheelchair.

'Often it's quite a relief for them, getting into a wheelchair. Walking becomes such a struggle, and the chair gives them mobility again, you see.'

Ludo was six and a half now, and already in splints. It was possible, the last consultant had admitted, that he would need a wheelchair 'sooner rather than later'. Pushed again by Patrick, he'd estimated another year perhaps, although Ludo was a determined little boy and he might stay on his feet a bit longer than that, if they were lucky.

If they were lucky. Ludo wasn't lucky; it wasn't in his genes. Mel scrunched the tissue up in her hands. She and luck had parted company long before: at her conception, in fact. Her own DNA test had uncovered the defective gene. She hadn't known that she was a carrier. She was one of two girls, her mother an only child, but apparently there'd been an uncle who'd always been 'weakly' and had died of pneumonia at the age of fourteen. Back then, very little had been known about DMD and Mel's great-uncle had never been diagnosed. But the gene had lain in waiting. Mel imagined it as doing just that, crouching like a great, evil toad in the roots of her family tree, jumping from generation to generation, biding its time until she and Patrick had met and fallen in love, and in making love had shaken the tree, waking the toad, giving it its chance.

They'd both wanted several children, three or four at least; it had been one of their favourite topics of conversation from the early days of their relationship. But that desire, like so many others, had changed after Ludo was born. One option, the genetic counsellor had told them, was sterilisation.

'What else?' they'd each echoed, and then had smiled wanly, the only smile of that bleak interview.

There was the possibility of egg donation, but it was a long wait. No, they'd both shaken their heads to that. Thank God, Mel had thought. If Patrick had wanted that she couldn't have accepted it, not another woman's egg inside her because her own were no good.

But with the suggestion of IVF Patrick had been so keen, so hopeful, that in spite of her misgivings she'd gone ahead. When she'd told him that she didn't want to try again he'd kissed her and said no, of course not. He understood. But then Infutopin had come along, and he'd stopped understanding. He'd kept quoting percentages at her – how she had come to dread those iron statistics; they'd seemed to be everywhere, on the news, in the papers – and had talked about a 'little sister for Ludo'.

Mel shuddered. She'd been trapped, cornered, increasingly so as the months had gone on, and Patrick had opened a savings account for the treatment and started putting in a set amount each month. Then, in late September, he'd told her that he'd put their name on a waiting list at the IVF centre in the city, the private one that had an Infutopin programme. He'd expected her to be pleased; he either hadn't been aware of her fears or had chosen not to see them. She knew that she ought to have said something, to have told him what she really felt. Many times she had been on the verge, only to pull back, terrified that he'd reject her.

When she was twenty-two Mel had had an abortion. It was a late one – a baby girl – but she had been determined to be 'mature' about it. The sense of guilt and grief, hitting her weeks later, had nearly unhinged her. For months she'd been on tranquillisers and anti-depressants. Two years afterwards, when she'd met Patrick, she'd been over the worst of it; and although a part of her had always meant to tell him – they were proud that they had no secrets from each other – another part had shied away from upsetting his image of her.

After Ludo, that piece of her past had faded away. She hadn't really thought about it until the day when the IVF doctor had mentioned with dizzying casualness that they'd be 'discarding' the male embryos. Then all those buried feelings had come flooding back. She would be murdering those tiny specks of life, she'd thought, in the same way that she had murdered her daughter all those years ago.

She studied her hands. Patrick was wrong. She hadn't set out to deliberately deceive him by getting pregnant. There'd been nothing 'deliberate' about it, nothing premeditated. Oh, he was right in one way, she supposed – she'd stopped using contraception. But she hadn't *meant*, hadn't actually thought through the consequences, not in cold blood, not deliberately.

She shook her head to dislodge the fuzziness that was there. It was as if, she thought slowly, her subconscious had acted independently, seeking a way out of the trap, taking the 'alternative route' as the genetics counsellor had put it, by going ahead with another pregnancy and having the fetus tested at about ten weeks of age.

'Tested?' Mel had asked fearfully.

'Yes. You'd undergo chorionic sampling, or CVS. It's quite a simple procedure: a catheter is inserted into the chorion – that's the membrane surrounding the fetus – and a small part is removed for analysis, to see if it's a boy and carrying the defective gene.'

'And then? If it is?'

She swallowed. In the almost silent days since the row with Patrick she'd had plenty of time to berate herself. What had she imagined Patrick's reaction would be?

'How would it be,' she'd asked him shakily, when he'd seemed to have calmed down a bit, 'if we didn't have the CVS?'

He'd simply stared at her.

'I mean, there's a one-in-four chance that the baby'll be all right . . . a girl or an unaffected boy.'

He'd started shaking his head, very slowly, from side to side.

'That's what the counsellor said, d'you remember?'

'She also said,' Patrick had addressed the carpet, 'that most parents with one DMD boy wouldn't chose to have another.'

'But you're crazy about Ludo!'

'Yes, I am,' he'd said quietly. 'But I wouldn't wish him on my worst enemy. I'm like all those other parents, Melanie. I don't want another one like him. I couldn't. And if you don't agree to have this CVS test . . .' He hadn't completed the sentence; he hadn't needed to. The meaning was clear: have the test; if the fetus had the gene, terminate; refuse either the test or the termination, and lose Patrick.

Mel's eyes swam. She'd hardly slept over the last two nights. Then, the previous evening, she'd made her decision, and steeling herself had told Patrick that she'd have the CVS test. Have it as fast as she could, so they'd know.

'It's the waiting I can't bear the thought of,' she'd told the GP twenty minutes before. 'The hanging about, not knowing.'

The doctor had nodded sympathetically. He was new to the practice, quite young and keen to be helpful. He'd glanced over at Patrick and then back to her. He knows we're not speaking, she'd thought, and blushed, then had been disgusted at herself for caring about such a thing at such a time.

'The waiting period isn't long,' he'd told her gently. 'Three days is the norm.'

She'd felt the colour drain from her face. 'But . . . but I've read that they can do it in twenty-four hours.' She'd been banking on that, she'd realised; that had been part of the deal that she'd done with herself.

The doctor had sighed. 'Technically, yes, they can. But in practice it's another matter. Labs gets busy. Three days is really the minimum, sometimes it can take up to a week, even in the private sector.'

She'd go insane. She'd have to say she'd made a mistake, changed her mind. She'd looked up. The doctor had been staring into the mid-distance. 'Although I do believe . . .' and he'd stopped abruptly. There was something he wanted to check, he'd said, and excused himself.

Mel looked at her watch. He'd been gone a long time. She felt Patrick watching her, but when she turned he looked away immediately. Please God, help us, she begged, forgetting all the other prayers she'd ever uttered, how she'd vowed never to pray again – because God, if he existed, didn't answer her.

The door opened and the GP re-entered, beaming. 'Well, Mrs Alder, Mr Alder, a bit of good news.' He sat down, placing the notepad he'd taken in front of him, and the smile faded. 'I'm sorry. Perhaps that's not the best phrase in the circumstances. It's just that I remembered there is a hospital that's offering a much shorter waiting period for CVS in cases such as yours.'

'Oh yes?' Mel swallowed. 'How much shorter?'

'Guaranteed overnight.' Then he beamed again. 'Is that better?'

'Oh, much!' Mel felt suddenly light. 'That's wonderful.'

'It doesn't change the outcome,' Patrick said stonily.

She and the GP turned to stare at him. Those had been the first words he'd spoken.

'Well, no,' the doctor admitted after a moment, 'but Mrs Alder did say it was the waiting that bothered her.'

'It was. It is.' Mel felt she had to apologise. She gabbled on, 'We're really very grateful, doctor.'

'Not at all. I'm pleased that I remembered about it. The hospital has developed a really advanced technique with the testing – I think they've got it down to twelve hours. There was some literature about it somewhere . . .' He flicked through a stack of papers on his desk, then shrugged disarmingly.

Mel smiled back. She daren't look at Patrick; she could feel him glowering.

'Well. . .' The GP gave up. 'They didn't want to be flooded with people wanting the quick test. You can imagine.'

'Oh yes,' Mel murmured.

'So they chose a minority group who were likely to want the test. And that group – ' he smiled triumphantly again – 'was DMD. They sent a sort of Round Robin to GPs at the beginning of the year, asking us to refer people who fitted the bill, so to speak . . . Anyway, the important thing is that the study's still running. I wasn't sure; that's what I wanted to check on before telling you about it. Didn't want to get your hopes up.'

'Thank you,' Mel whispered.

'Not at all. Now, it does mean you'll have to travel to London.'

'That isn't a problem.'

He consulted his notepad. 'And they wanted me to tell you that they will require a blood sample from you, Mrs Alder.'

She almost laughed. 'Neither's that.'

'I'm sure it isn't.' They smiled together. 'They'll explain every-thing to you there. But eventually, so I understand, they're hoping to do away with CVS altogether, just analyse the fetal cells within the mother's blood to give a definitive diagnosis.'

'How wonderful,' she smiled. 'But not yet?'

'No. Several centres are trying it, this hospital being one of them. It's a place with an excellent reputation – private, although they're offering this test free, of course, for their study. The

Mistletoe. Where Infutopin was launched. You'll have heard of it?'

Mel's heart jumped. 'Yes,' she said softly.

'Oh indeed,' Patrick snarled.

'A real centre of excellence. I'll write you a referral letter, and you can take it with you. The doctor's name is . . .' He glanced down again at his notepad. 'Dr West. Dr Will West, Genetics. Fifth floor at the Mistletoe.'

CHAPTER SIX

Thanking her caller profusely, Sasha hung up.

She would have to accept it, she thought. Philippa Tyler had
an impeccable background: a perfect political record, no sniff of
anything untoward in her private life, and now Sasha had received
final confirmation that Tyler was not, and never had been, a
director of Branium Pharma (Pharmaceuticals) UK Inc. or any
of its subsidiary companies (of which there were apparently dozens
world-wide). Nor had her husband, brother or parents.

'Of course,' her informer had told her in his New England
drawl, 'the available information only goes so far. She could be
using anyone as a cipher.'

'Yes, you're absolutely right.' Sasha had laughed. 'It was a bit
of a long shot, too obvious really. But sometimes it's the obvious
. . .' She'd broken off, staring down at the rows of kisses her pen
had drawn, seemingly of its own accord, along the lines of her
notebook.

'It's the obvious that you overlook? Sure.'

There'd been a pause.

'Well, thank you so much, Charlie. I'd better let you—'

'D'you want me to do a run on some other big drug companies
against her name?'

She'd gulped. He was so kind. 'Oh, would you? That'd be really great. So long as it's not too much trouble.'

'Not a bit of it. I've told you, the day shift at this place is a dawdle.' He worked as the London bureau chief for an American news corporation. 'Unless a bomb drops, New York doesn't even think about me till three o'clock most afternoons. All I was doing was sitting here reading the papers and twiddling my thumbs.'

'Well, if you're certain . . .'

'Certain. I'll call you right back.'

Sasha sighed, got up and wandered over to the window that looked down into an alleyway. She mustn't imagine things. Charlie Page was simply a very kind, caring, warm human being, who was probably lonely now that his very glamorous, beautiful and petite TV-presenter girlfriend had just departed for the States, no doubt on holiday.

The previous week Sasha had seen her standing in the lobby chatting to Alexander, who clearly considered her to be ravishing – as indeed she was. Her ash-blonde hair hung in a luxuriant, thick plait over one shoulder, and she'd been wearing a three-quarter-length, honey-coloured sheepskin coat in which she'd looked fabulous.

Sasha had been returning from her run, hot and sweaty. She'd almost knocked Tamarin flying as she'd come in.

'Sorry!'

To give her credit, Tamarin had recovered quickly, unflattening herself from the wall and assuring Alexander (who'd leaped to her aid, shooting Sasha a reproachful look) that she was absolutely fine and wasn't hurt, no, not one little bit. Then she'd smiled up at Sasha and replied that, yes, all those suitcases were hers. There'd been four, ranging in size from an enormous trunk to a round cosmetics bag looped over Tamarin's arm, all in a distinctive brown and tan pattern that didn't look fake.

'Going home for Thanksgiving?' Sasha had ventured, pleased that she'd remembered the American holiday, and hoping that it made her sound cosmopolitan.

'Yes,' the woman had answered, still smiling and showing her small, milky-white teeth. Her taxi had arrived.

'Well, see you when you get back,' Sasha had called.

Tamarin had been putting up the hood of her gorgeous coat. It framed her small face perfectly, setting off her expressive almond eyes. 'Or sometime,' she'd said quietly, and gone out through the opened door.

In spite of her best intentions, Sasha had read deeply into that last remark. The pause before Tamarin had replied; the sad yet determined look, the upward tilt of the chin as she had marched resolutely, irrevocably, out of Charlie's life for ever . . .

Stop it, Sasha told herself. Tamarin had been gone for less than a week. And the previous evening, when Sasha had bumped into Charlie, he'd seemed perfectly cheerful, not in the least like someone suffering from a broken heart. He'd been eager to talk, wanting to know what she'd been doing, and so she'd told him. Then he'd asked her if she'd like him to do a run through on the Internet to see what it might throw up on Tyler.

She made a low, growling noise in her throat. Remember how Charlie and Tamarin look together, she reminded herself, turning away from the window and going into her galley kitchen to make a coffee.

Charlie: at least six feet two inches tall, dark, curly hair, wonderful, earnest eyes and a boy's cheeky grin. Beside him, Tamarin was like a little golden angel. And he was so protective of her, always opening doors, shielding her from the traffic as they walked down the street. They were the radiant, made-for-each-other American couple.

Or had been, murmured another voice at the back of her head. Apart from the previous Tuesday's encounter she hadn't seen Tamarin for weeks. Nine weeks to be specific.

It was the evening of September the twenty-ninth, Sasha's birthday.

She'd been celebrating with friends in the basement of an American restaurant in Covent Garden, trying very hard to have a good time and demonstrate what fun it was being single, when she'd caught sight of Charlie and Tamarin four tables away. Tamarin had had her back to her, giving Sasha a good view of Charlie's face, and he hadn't looked very happy at all. He'd spoken little; judging by the way Tamarin's head had been moving, she'd not given him much of a chance. Charlie had occasionally shrugged, played with his food and generally looked miserable.

'Hey! What's the big attraction?' one of her girlfriends had asked, craning her neck. 'Oh, I see! He *is* nice, isn't he?'

'Who?'

'What d'you mean, who? Hunkie over there, that's *who*. The one with the come-to-bed eyes. The one you've been ogling for the last ten minutes.'

'I have not!'

'Liar. Oh, he's getting up. Well . . . he's a big boy, isn't he?' She'd nudged her. 'Just right for you, wouldn't you say?'

'I don't know what you're talking—'

'He's coming this way. Oh!'

'What?' Sasha had kept her head down, concentrating hard on her plate of rigatoni, wishing her friend would shut up and yet dying to know what was happening.

'He's got a girl with him. God, she's pretty! Little bitch.'

'Honestly!' Sasha, suddenly deciding that she ought to play it straight, had looked up and laughed lightly. 'He's a neighbour, and she's his girlfriend. Hi, Tamarin!'

But Tamarin, by then level with Sasha's table, had passed by without acknowledgement. Charlie, following behind, had looked distracted then, recognising Sasha, had smiled. 'Celebrating something?' he'd asked.

'Um, not really. Well, only—'

'It's her birthday,' her friend had put in.

'Many happy returns.'

Smiling up at him, thinking how much she fancied him and praying that it didn't show, Sasha had seen the wretched look in his eyes and forgotten everything else. 'Are you OK?' she'd asked.

'I'm . . .' He'd glanced over to where Tamarin stood waiting stiffly by the door. 'I'm just fine. Thanks for asking, you're sweet.' Then he'd bent down, swiftly kissed her and gone.

Only on the cheek, Sasha told herself for the umpteenth time – but it had been more than a peck; he'd squeezed her shoulder too, and called her 'sweet'.

'God, Sasha Downey, you're pathetic,' she said out loud and carried her coffee back to the red velvet sofa that was too large for the room (did in fact dwarf it, but was wonderfully soft and engulfing). 'Always blowing things out of proportion. Imagining what isn't there.' She sipped at the drink. A lover's tiff, that was what she'd witnessed. And the kiss had been merely platonic, the squeeze an acknowledgement of her concern. Nor did the fact that she hadn't seen Tamarin since signify anything. There were eighteen flats in the building, two lifts and a flight of stairs (not that either Tamarin or Charlie were likely, being in the penthouse on the sixth floor, to use the stairs); Tamarin, like Charlie, worked shifts. It was perfectly feasible for Sasha not to have seen her for nine weeks.

She looked at her watch. It was after twelve, and she would have to start on her final version of the Tyler article or it wouldn't be ready for the following morning's deadline. Which would, she reminded herself, be sheer madness, as she'd spent most of the weekend writing the first draft. The trouble was that, since the recent encounter with Charlie, and now the two telephone conversations, she was finding it very difficult to concentrate.

'You'd have thought,' she told herself sternly, 'you'd have learnt your lesson with Charlie Page last year.'

It had been about two months after Edwin had walked out following the terrible row over her resignation. Although she was aware that they'd never been the most compatible of couples, she'd missed him. Living on her own and working on her own, she'd quickly realised, was not much fun at all. She'd begun to dread weekends especially, and therefore had been quite pleased when, one Friday morning, a features editor had called, close to tears, to beg her, if it was at all possible, to produce her piece on child labour a week early – on Monday morning. The 'bastard' lawyers had just pulled a scheduled piece, leaving her with a yawning hole.

Sasha had worked all weekend. By Sunday night she'd finished, and was very pleased with her efforts. The article was a long one, five thousand words, but nicely put together. She had been humming to herself, wondering if the features editor would keep her promise about a bonus, when she'd swung round in her chair and knocked over her mug of hot coffee. The liquid had seeped straight into the grille at the back of her computer. For a moment she'd stared, then with a yelp she'd jumped up, snatched up the nearest thing at hand – her sweatshirt – and started mopping furiously. As she did a desperate staccato prayer had emerged – 'Please, God, Please, God' – but her eyes, fixed on the screen, had seen it was no use. The letters on the lines had started to fall from their words, somersaulting, imbued with a life of their own, dropping down the screen and out of sight.

'Oh God.'

She'd hit a key, any key. More letters had run amok, whole words now joining them. Then there'd been a flash, a hissing sound, and the screen had gone blank.

Sasha had gone into shock. She'd stood rocking herself and moaning for some time before she'd switched the machine off at the mains. Then, with a terrible sense of foreboding, she had switched it on again. Still blank. Dead.

Not only the article she'd just finished, but all her others, including two lengthy investigations that had been in semi-note form, another article that had to be ready the following week, and on top of all that her precious files of contacts, had been on that computer.

'It can't be, it can't . . .' she'd whimpered, feeling the tears roll down her cheeks. It was Sunday night; nothing would be open. But there had to be an emergency number somewhere . . .

She'd grabbed the computer's manual from the shelf. Its index had swum before her eyes, forcing her to focus hard. 'Using the System Setup Programme'; 'Performing a Memory Upgrade'; 'Installed Software Support Facilities' . . . She'd flicked wildly through. None of it had meant anything to her. She'd never understood the machine's internal workings or had any desire to learn . . . 'Where to get help'.

'Oh thank God!'

She'd turned to the page. There'd been two telephone numbers: one for Basel in Switzerland, the other for Dallas. Fighting down hysteria, she'd tried both. Basel appeared to have been disconnected and there was a recorded message on the other, advising that the offices were now closed and callers should 'try again later'.

The rest of that night had passed in a blur. She must have slept eventually because she remembered waking and thinking it had been a nightmare, before stumbling through into the main room and discovering it hadn't.

At nine she'd telephoned the shop where she'd bought it. They didn't stock those computers any more. She'd nearly screamed, but the assistant told her there was a place called 'Compu-docs' in Brixton. The number she was given had been answered by a harassed-sounding man, 'Dr Data', who'd cut her short by telling her to get the hardware in before ten if she wanted any results that day.

It was half-past nine. She didn't have a car. A taxi was her only option, and it was the rush hour. She'd called the front desk and gibbered at Alexander, then, hoisting up the machine, she'd staggered to the lift and down to the lobby. There Alexander had gravely informed her that he'd summoned a cab, but they hadn't been able to give him an ETA.

Her head had been spinning. 'A what?'

'Estimated time of arrival, miss. Now, why don't you put that great thing down for a minute? Do yourself an injury.'

'I've got to get to Brixton!'

'Well you won't get there any faster by holding that, will you? Careful now, miss. You're going to go flying over that flex.'

'But . . . What's that?' From the street had come the distinctive chug of a diesel engine. 'It's a taxi!' she'd shrieked, leaping up. Her foot had caught in a loop of the trailing cable and she'd hit the revolving doors with a smack. Looking up, she'd seen a figure in a raincoat paying the cab driver and stepping back on to the pavement, and before she could scramble to her feet the cab had gone.

She'd lain on the carpet and sobbed. She'd hardly been sensible of where she was, let alone that she'd been blocking the entrance . . . And that had been how, tear-stained, battered and barely coherent, she'd first encountered Charlie Page. He'd come through the revolving doors and by necessity had stopped in front of her.

She sighed and ran a finger around the rim of the mug that she held. Since that night she'd not drunk anything, or allowed liquid in any form, near the computer. Now she took proper coffee breaks at safe distances.

She glanced over at the machine, imagined it tapping its own keys, waiting for her. Let it, she thought defiantly. This was her time, and one of her best memories. She'd examined it a hundred times. That morning, she was now convinced, had been when she'd first fallen in love with Charlie Page. Not that she'd known it then; she'd been too desperate, too blind with panic to interpret the signs.

He'd asked her if she was OK, simply that, and her heart had jumped up into her mouth. She smiled, luxuriating again in that moment, marvelling at how someone's voice could do that to another person, how it could contain a secret ingredient that only that person could hear.

She tucked her legs under her. Was it really possible for someone to fall in love on the basis of three words? For she was sure that it had been right then when it happened, not later, after she'd had so much to thank him for, or when she'd started to love all the other things about him.

Back then, lying on the carpet, she'd turned and looked up at him. He was taller than herself. (No matter what, she always noticed men's heights. It was a throwback to when she'd been thirteen and first shot vertically, leaving everyone else in the class, boys briefly included, behind.)

'I . . . I think so,' she'd said in response to his question.

'I told you to watch that cable, miss.'

'Steady,' Charlie had said, taking her arm, the one that didn't hurt, and she'd had the strangest sensation. Strong heat, it had felt like, shocking her but drawing her in. She'd seen reflected in the pupils of his eyes two images of herself, staring back but swaying slightly. She'd muttered, 'My computer . . .'

His grip had tightened. 'That's quite a crack you got. I heard it from outside. Maybe you ought to sit down.'

'No.' She'd shaken her head. 'I haven't got time. I've got to get—'

'You're in no fit state to go anywhere,' Alexander had said reprovingly. 'You do what Mr Page says and sit down for a bit.'

'Where d'you have to get to?' Charlie had asked, and she'd focused blearily on him. He had longish hair; then (and many times since) she'd imagined herself touching it, feeling it under her hand . . .

'Um, Brixton.'

'South London, right? Drugs, Yardies, riots?'

'Right.' In spite of everything, she'd had to smile. 'Amongst other things.'

'Tourist short-hand, huh?'

She'd indicated the computer on the floor. 'I've got to take that to Brixton, to get it fixed.'

'It's sick?'

'Um, you could say that.'

'Your taxi's here, miss,' Alexander had called out.

'D'you think you could . . . ?' She'd suddenly felt shy. She didn't even know his name.

'Give you a hand with this stuff? Sure.' And in an easy movement he'd scooped it up, cables and all, and started towards the doors. 'What's wrong with it?' he'd asked over his shoulder.

She'd felt herself redden. It was such a stupid thing to have done. 'Oh, I . . . um, spilt my coffee on it.'

'Ah, Wet Computer Syndrome.'

'You've heard of it?'

'Oh, sure – a common complaint. But it's a real pain, too. Drying didn't help, then?' He'd been in a segment of the revolving door by then.

'Drying?' she'd echoed, following him out to the pavement.

'Where to, sir?' asked the cabbie.

'Ah, Brixton. It's not for me; it's for the young lady.' He'd turned to her. 'D'you want to get in first, and I'll put—'

'How d'you mean, drying? With a towel or what?'

He'd looked startled. She hadn't meant to shout. 'I'm sorry, I—.'

'That's OK. When did you spill the coffee?'

'Last night.'

'D'you have a hair-dryer?'

'A what?'

'Look, mate,' said the cabbie, leaning over. 'Are you getting in or what? Only, the clock's running and—'

'Oh God, the time! What's the time?'

'Er, I'm sorry but I can't quite see at the moment . . .'

'Nine forty-seven,' the cabbie had put in, 'precisely.'

'But that's . . . that's nearly ten to!'

'Correct.'

'I can't get to Brixton before ten, can I?'

'Not an 'ope. Unless you're plannin' to sprout wings and fly.'

'Oh God!' She'd started crying again.

'Why not at least try the hair-dryer? Give it a chance, anyway.'

Sasha got up to stand and warm herself against the radiator, surveying the mess that was her flat. That's what came of working all weekend, she thought drearily. A year on, she was still working most of them, as well as every day in the week. No time to clear up. No one to clear up for . . .

'Oh, don't be so pathetic,' she hissed. The place had been a tip, she remembered, when she'd shown Charlie in. But if he'd noticed the piles of newspapers and cardboard boxes of cuttings everywhere, he hadn't said a word. The embodiment of tact, she thought – and whoever said Americans weren't polite?

On the journey up in the lift they'd discovered their shared profession. 'Deadlines, huh?' he'd said, depositing the computer on the desk. 'You got a screwdriver anywhere about?'

'Oh! Are you going to take it apart?'

'I've got to get at the guts of it if we're going to dry it.'

The tiny intestines of the machine, the bright wires and miniature metal parts, had amazed her, also scared her. It'd been like opening up a brain. The liquid, Charlie had told her, had permeated the motherboard. Was that, she'd asked fearfully, peering over and trying to see what he meant, particularly bad? But he'd had the hair-dryer on by then and hadn't heard her. She'd imagined all the thousands of precious words being blasted away by that hot wind, and unable to bear it any longer had retreated to the kitchen to make coffee.

Before the percolator had finished its job, he'd called her. 'It's dry now.'

'Oh God.'

He'd given her a quizzical look. 'Aren't you pleased?'

'Oh, yes. It's not that. It's just . . .'

'Now's the moment of reckoning?'

'Right. Are you positive it's dry?'

'Positive.'

He hadn't reassembled it. The open chassis had reminded her of Sunday mornings spent miserably huddled inside one of her old cars, while her father pulled out bits from the engine and told her to try the ignition again. She'd averted her eyes and switched on – and data had appeared on screen.

'You've done it! You've *done* it!' She'd flung her arms round his neck. 'Oh God, you're wonderful! Oh, thank you so much! How utterly, utterly, fantastic!'

'Glad to be of service.' He'd laughed and submitted briefly to her hug before drawing away. He hadn't wanted to touch her again, she realised that now. But she'd been so happy she hadn't noticed.

'I thought I'd lost the lot, you see. You've no idea.' She'd found a tissue and wiped her eyes.

'Oh, but I have.'

She'd stopped in her tracks. 'You mean, it's happened to you?'

'Yes. About three years ago.'

'God, I'm glad! That it's not just me who does stupid things. Oops!' She'd made a face. 'There I go, insulting my rescuer.'

'Feel free.' He'd grinned, once more at ease. and it had been then, with the removal of terror, that it had dawned on her just how attractive he was: the bright eyes and generous mouth; the way his chin curved; the easy manner and warm smile . . .

Suddenly she'd remembered something. 'Hey, I've got a better idea than coffee! How about some champagne? I want to celebrate.'

'Sure! Sounds good.'

She'd opened the fridge door. 'And I can offer you eggs, bacon, peppers . . .'

'Oh. Ah – no, nothing to eat for me, thanks.'

She'd remembered what he'd told her in the lift: that he'd just got off night-duty. 'God, yes,' she'd prattled on, taking the bottle and the champagne flutes that Edwin (surprisingly) had left behind, into the other room, 'when I do nights it turns my whole system upside down. I want breakfast at four in the afternoon . . .'

'It's not that.' He'd been standing with his back to the window, arms crossed, suddenly awkward. She'd felt her stomach flutter. Her body had known, she realised, before her mind had.

'Actually, I'm going out for brunch.'

'Oh.' She'd swallowed. 'Anywhere nice?'

He hadn't known. His girlfriend was choosing the venue that day. When he was working nights she took her lunch-break early . . .

Of course he'd have a girlfriend! She'd told herself that it didn't matter. How could it? They'd only just met. But she could still remember how her hand had closed around the glass stems, how let down she'd felt. She'd gone through the right motions, though: opening the bottle of champagne, pouring and sipping and chatting politely, until he'd looked at his watch and said he'd better be going and she'd thanked him again and he'd gone.

She stared across at the place where he'd sat. She'd expected to get over him immediately, and had been taken by surprise to find herself thinking so much about him, noticing things in retrospect: how he'd looked at her, what he'd said, his voice, the effect of his touch. A late-onset schoolgirl crush, she'd decided, trying to make light of it . . . but the attraction, instead of diminishing, had grown stronger, fuelled by the knowledge that he was so near to her, that at any moment she might see him.

But three weeks had passed before she had, and then – she pulled a face – there he'd been with Tamarin, both of them standing in the lobby, waiting for the lift. Charlie had introduced her and everyone had been charming, and Sasha had gone out into the street and cried, and people passing had stared – but she hadn't cared, her heart had been breaking.

She'd tried to hate him but it hadn't worked; he hadn't done anything wrong. He may have been attracted to her but he loved Tamarin. He was living with her, for God's sake, she'd told herself over and over again. And he'd let Sasha down at once, as quickly and gently as he could. After that meeting she'd seen him periodically, most often with Tamarin on his arm, and he'd always been pleasant, asking after her computer (Tamarin too, which had made it worse), and with a great effort Sasha had come round to looking on him as a friend, a fantastic neighbour who'd appeared in the nick of time to rescue her.

By putting him in that category, and only taking him out for daydreams, she'd managed to get on with her life. She'd gone out with a couple of people, developed a fairly active social life, and worked like mad. When her body reacted – as it was still wont to do on seeing Charlie, thankfully with butterflies rather than blushing – she would calm herself down, tell herself that it wasn't to be. Eventually she'd meet someone else who'd do all those things to her that Charlie had done effortlessly, but who'd also be available.

Which was why, she thought now, frowning down at the carpet, it was so confusing, with Tamarin vanishing and Charlie being so eager to help with Tyler. At the end of that last call, when he'd asked how long she thought the Tyler article would take her, had he been about to ask her whether she would be free later on? And why the hell had she answered: 'Till midnight, probably, knowing me'? He might have been summoning his courage, and she'd rebuffed him.

Exasperated, she got up, marched over to the desk, and sat down. She'd wasted enough time dreaming; at her current rate of progress she'd be up all night, which would wreck her for other work the following day.

'Philippa Tyler is an intriguing woman,' she read on the screen. She stared at the line, unable to remember why she'd written it.

'Concentrate, concentrate,' she muttered. She was a professional journalist writing her first article for *Comment,* not a lovesick teenager. She pulled her notebook nearer, flicking back a page. On it she'd jotted down Tyler's history: middle-class home, scholarship education, place at Oxford, marriage, children, career . . . immaculate, challengingly so. She shook herself. She hadn't been commissioned to dig dirt on Tyler; there probably wasn't any anyway.

Her eye fell on an underlined note. 'That's right,' she murmured, scrolling up to the paragraph she wanted and inserting: 'Mrs Tyler's first job was as a public relations officer for the embryonic nuclear industry . . .'

CHAPTER SEVEN

In death, the man managed to achieve a look of deep inner peace that had eluded him all his life. His eyes were open and appeared calmly accepting, his lips set together but slightly askew, as if in the end he might have been amused, might never have experienced betrayal or prison, or the terror of his last few hours on earth.

Gerry Winston had not been long in the water. It had not yet bloated or distorted him; the waves had only brought him to the shore and there, after nudging him around a little, had receded. He had lain on his side, his head resting on the fine sand, until at 8.25 a.m. an elderly woman out exercising her dog had found him. She had not been as horrified as one might have expected, perhaps because of that aura of peace.

There was nothing on the body to identify him – no papers, wallet or credit cards in his pockets – and in the car park there was no abandoned car. How he'd arrived at the beach was to remain a mystery. No one had reported him missing, and there were no obvious signs of violence. The young constable who had answered the 999 call was convinced, upon glancing into those quiet eyes, that he was looking at a natural death. 'Heart-attack, most probably,' he told the old lady, who had waited out of the sense that she owed the dead man something.

'But he looks too young for that, surely.'

'Or a brain haemorrhage,' the policeman suggested, warming to his theme. He had been reading up on the subject. 'You go just like that. He wouldn't have known what hit him, no time to feel anything.'

Later, at the post-mortem, the pathologist confirmed the constable's initial diagnosis: the deceased (they still didn't know his name) had suffered a massive heart-attack. There were a few bruises on the body, a rather nasty one in the genital area, but they signified nothing; the man could easily have sustained them just prior to death, in his dying fall perhaps. He had been dead before he had gone into the water. The pathologist hazarded a guess that he had been walking along the shore when the first pain struck, and had lain where he fell until the tide came up and carried him out to sea, depositing him a few hours later back on land, some way from his home. That would explain why no one had yet come forward to claim him. There would be no inquest; it was judged a death by natural causes.

The local news agency at Aldeburgh did their best to provoke the nationals' interest, but the news desks in London proved characteristically hard-hearted towards the unknown corpse. Then, a day after the body's discovery, the fingerprints made a match on the national index at Scotland Yard and the *Wealden Press and Star* prepared the story for its front page.

'Kent man found dead on beach at Sizewell B nuclear reactor in Suffolk.'

For decency's sake the reporter had left the fact of Gerry's previous conviction until fairly low down in the story. 'Mr Winston, 46, an animal rights activist, was released from prison seven months ago after serving six years of a nine-year sentence for fire-bombing department stores. "He was not the type to have enemies," his ex-wife, Penny, told the *Press and Star* last week. "Gerry never liked rows," said Mrs Winston, 41, of Norman Rise, Cranbrook, who is due to marry again next Spring. "Any stuffing he did have got knocked out of him in Ashford [prison]. I don't know if he was still into animal rights. I haven't seen him in years."

'Mrs Winston added that she thought it "unlikely" that her former husband had gone to the beach at Sizewell to protest against the nuclear power station. "What would he want to go all the way up there for, when he had Dungeness down the road? Anyway, he was never interested in nuclear things. He was never interested in anything much, except animals.'"

The *Wealden Press and Star* came out on Thursdays. That Thursday morning at eight-thirty, seven days after the raid, Chris Manyon stood on the pavement outside the newsagent's shop in Tenterden, shaking. He stared at the photograph of the much younger Gerry on the front page, then read the story, every word. The shaking intensified.

He glanced right and left, then took off across the road, running for his car. He scrambled in, started the ignition and pulled out without looking, nearly crashing into another car. He didn't want to be in a traffic jam, sitting there like a target so he swung the car clumsily in a wide circle, mounting the pavement on the other side of the road and smashing the offside rear into a telephone box. He kept going, bouncing back on to the road, seeing in his rear-view mirror the horrified faces staring after him.

One woman raced to the telephone box and came to a dead stop, staring open-mouthed at the wreckage. Manyon saw another writing down his number and dashing into the newsagents, and moaned out loud. He had to dump the car; he had to get away from there.

The sign for the leisure centre appeared and a picture flashed into his head of the little minicab office beside it. It wasn't always manned. Would it be open? He turned right, slamming his foot down hard on the gas and cursing the car for its slow acceleration. It was going at fifty miles an hour now.

He checked the mirror again. A couple of other cars had turned into the road, but no police. He tried to calm himself, tried to remember how the police dealt with reports of dangerous drivers. He hadn't even *been* dangerous, not really – he hadn't killed anyone, had he? He hadn't even hit anyone! And it helped, he reassured himself, that it was a woman who had reported him; the police always regarded women as a bit hysterical, didn't they?

Another quick check. A woman was driving the car behind him. Bloody nice car, a new BMW. Probably – he sneered – some Tenterden housewife, trying to look cool in her sunglasses, on her way home after dropping hubby at the station. Quiet, safe lives.

Well, not for him. He had always known something better was waiting for him.

He'd get a minicab, get to the nearest station with the fastest train to London – minicab drivers knew such things – and then he'd vanish.

He felt his heart slow down a fraction. They'd never find him; they might look, but he was a smart man. Not like Winston. He had the sense to see that he had to get out, not sit about waiting for them to come looking.

In the BMW the woman talked quietly into the microphone clipped to the sun-visor.

'He's directly in front of me now. He's slowing down a bit. Looks like he's pulling into the leisure centre . . . No, he's stopped by a minicab office. I'm going past. If you'll take over, McMahon, please . . .'

Thursday was also publication day for *Comment.* Sasha had got up at seven – even before the alarm had gone off on her new, bright pink, perfectly reliable radio – and jogged up to the newsagents on the corner of Neal Street. There she'd bought four copies of the magazine: one to send to her parents (because they expected it and would have been offended otherwise) and three for herself, for her cuttings file, although she doubted she would be cutting the article up. It looked too good whole.

She had got the lead story. Tyler's face smiled gently up at her from the cover. The headline ran in white lettering across her grey waves: TYLER BRIDGES THE GAP: ST PETER'S TO BE REOPENED FOR PRIVATE IVF. EXCLUSIVE FIRST INTERVIEW WITH HEALTH MINISTER. Inside, Hornby had let her run over four pages. There were two photographs of the minister: one sitting neatly on the sofa, head tilted towards her daughters' picture, wearing that soft, loving expression; the other a courageous figure braving the wind and rain on Lambeth Bridge, the tower of St Peter's peeking behind her shoulder. It was a terrific show. Very little that Sasha had written had been changed, and the phrase she'd invented – 'Queen of the Genes' – had been been used in bold for a cross-heading.

When she'd sent over the piece, Hornby had called to say how much he liked it, which had been gratifying – but there was nothing like seeing it in print. Or hearing it followed up on the radio, first on the news headlines and later in an interview. Soon the evening paper would be picking up the story, then the rest of the media. Undoubtedly during Prime Minister's Questions the opposition would have a go at Tyler; and by the end of the day the story would have changed out of all recognition. Most people would have forgotten that *Comment* had carried her interview in the first place, but that didn't matter. The ones who counted, the news and features editors, would know it had been hers, which could only mean more commissions, more work.

Her doorbell rang, just one short buzz. She frowned. It had to be internal. Alexander let no one pass who hadn't first gained entry via the external intercom system. Perhaps it was the commissionaire himself with a parcel, or maintenance – although it was very early for either.

She put her eye to the spy-hole. Charlie Page stood outside, seeming to stare straight at her, though of course he couldn't see her through the convex glass. She hadn't heard from him since his last call about Tyler, four days before. Further proof, she'd told herself resolutely, that he viewed her simply as a friend and colleague.

He made a sudden movement, his face looming large and grotesquely out of focus, and there came another sharp buzz.

She pulled open the door. 'Hi, Charlie!'

'Oh, hi.' He looked startled. 'Sorry, I didn't know if you were in.'

'Yes. I was just, um . . .'

'Great piece.' He pointed at her hand.

'Sorry?' She looked down and saw that she was still clutching *Comment.* She stuffed it behind her back. 'Oh, thanks. Please don't think I walk around the flat parading my stuff! I was only—'

'I don't,' he said quickly.

He looked a funny colour, she thought, greenish.

'Thanks again for all your help with it.'

'Oh, it was nothing.'

There was a pause. He made no move to go, as though he was waiting for something.

She shook herself. 'God, I'm sorry!' She took a step back. 'Come in. I was just making some fresh coffee.'

'Ah, I'm on my way to work, actually.'

'Oh.' Of course, now that she looked properly, she saw that he was wearing a very respectable suit and tie under the raincoat that he always seemed to wear (and that made him look so American).

'I just stopped by to say congratulations.'

'Well, thank you again.'

There was another pause, more awkward than the first. What, she wondered, was she supposed to do next? Back off and shut the door? Make conversation about the weather? 'So,' she began brightly, 'how's—'

'D'you think . . .' he said suddenly.

'Yes?'

'I was thinking, maybe – ' he glanced at her nervously – 'we could meet up for a drink.'

Tamarin, she thought. Oh, sod it. 'Oh I do! I mean, I'd really like to.'

'You would?'

She nodded.

'One night after work? Say, over the road at the hotel bar?'

'The Heathman? Yes, sure. I go there quite a bit on my own, actually.' She blinked, realising she sounded like a lush. 'I mean, just to read. It's got such a relaxed atmosphere,' she ended lamely.

'Yeah, you're right. I like the way it feels too. So . . . maybe tomorrow night?'

Her face fell. Tomorrow was a girls' night out. They happened infrequently, but the rule was that you never let the others down, no matter how tempting another offer might be. 'I'm sorry, I can't.'

'Oh.'

'I'm already going out – with some girlfriends. To the cinema.'

'Right.'

'How about next week?'

'I'm working nights.'

She suddenly felt desperate.

'I guess you're busy tonight.'

'Tonight? Um . . . Not particularly, as it happens.'

'How about eight o'clock? Is that OK?'

'Yeah.' She smiled at him, he looked so pleased. 'Great.'

'I'll see you then, then.'

She shut the door then leaned against it, hugging the magazine to herself. Then she started singing – very loudly and very off-key, but it didn't matter, there was no one else to hear. And anyway, she told herself, she could do what she wanted today.

In the lower half of her abdomen, Melanie Alder felt the punch of the long, thin needle. She gasped.

Patrick's grip on her hand tightened. 'What?' he demanded. 'What is it?'

'It's the needle entering your wife's uterus, Mr Alder.' The nurse, stationed on Melanie's other side, spoke calmly. 'Doctor will now be guiding the needle towards the membrane surrounding Baby . . .'

Melanie swallowed. She wished the woman wouldn't refer to it that way. Mel wasn't allowing herself to; by an act of dedicated, fierce concentration, she was viewing it as nothing more than a conglomeration of cells, a large, pink, unshelled prawn. And Mel hated shellfish. It wasn't a baby, she repeated again silently. Not yet. Not until it had passed the test and proved it wasn't a carrier.

'Doctor will next be removing a small amount of tissue . . .'

Don't think about it, Mel told herself. Don't listen. She looked at the clock. Not long now, she promised herself. It was 3.28 p.m. By eight o'clock the next morning there would be a telephone call and they would know. If it was bad news, then it – that bunch of faulty, unwanted cells, that ugly prawn – would be quickly disposed of. Only if the news was good could it be called a baby.

'Ow!' The needle suddenly stabbed inside her.

'Don't jump,' the nurse ordered sharply.

Mel glared. What a sensible, plain face, she thought, and what a vinegary little mouth, painted pearly-pink to match the pink-and-white-striped candyfloss uniform and frilly cap. The women was at least fifty; had she no idea what she looked like? Mel cast a cold eye downwards. What she could see of the nurse's body looked shapeless, no proper figure to speak of. Most likely sterile, or never married. 'I'm married to my job', Mel could imagine her saying prissily, all the while bitterly envying women with husbands and children.

She looked up again.

The nurse was smiling down at her: a kindly smile, a motherly, concerned face. Mel blushed scarlet. She felt dreadful for being so dismissive. It was the strain, she told herself, that was making her so hateful – the strain of not dwelling on what was really happening, what Dr West was doing with that needle, what they were all there for.

She raised her head slightly. She could see the white-coated figure at work at the end of the bed. When he'd first entered the room, sliding quickly down to her feet, she'd thought him a terribly washed-out, featureless sort of person.

'Ah, Dr West,' the nurse had said, beaming proudly – but West hadn't replied, either to that or to Mel's own timid 'Hello, Doctor'.

Perhaps he was deaf, she'd thought, deaf and bald, as well as nearly chinless, with NHS spectacles. Now, needing a new focus, it occurred to her how rude he'd been. He could have asked her how she was, couldn't he? He could have spared a word to calm her fears. Instead he seemed deliberately not to see her, as if, beyond her womb, she didn't exist. Was he too grand to talk to her? Did he only talk to his private patients? My God, she thought, freshly aggrieved. Am I not a person too?

He turned slightly and the needle moved again within her. Sweat poured down her body. Oh, I didn't mean it, she prayed. I didn't mean to criticise. Please don't be angry with me, please don't . . .

But he wasn't looking at her; he hadn't heard her thoughts. His gaze had become fixed again to the ultrasound screen.

'Melly?'

She turned and smiled at Patrick.

'All right, darling?' He stroked her hand. 'The nurse says Doctor won't be much longer.'

It was catching, she thought, suddenly in the mood to be amused, the way people called him 'Doctor' so reverently, in hushed tones, with capitals. What had happened to the definite article beforehand? No other profession merited that, did it? she asked herself. Take herself: would anyone ever say, 'Ask Receptionist for an appointment'? Or Patrick: 'You need Maintenance Engineer.' Not, she hastily and silently assured Dr West, that she was being critical. He could be addressed any way he liked.

But if only he would get on with it. It was difficult to keep thinking of distractions, pleasant or otherwise. She felt as though she'd spent hours in that small, hot operating room, propped up on the gurney, the hospital gown ignominiously bunched up, exposing everything below.

A trickle of sweat ran down her cheek. Patrick leaned forward and wiped it with a tissue. She smiled. What had happened to the 'crucial' departmental meeting he'd had to attend that day? He'd turned up at noon, just after she'd had the blood-test, and had apologised humbly for being such a bastard. It hadn't been until she'd left that morning, he'd said, that he'd realised. He'd got there as fast as he could.

She was glad he was there. Of course she was; they could share jokes about Nurse later. But in a sense, having to find the strength to face the day on her own, the whole thing had become very much her battle. Hers and – she felt her logic wobble – its. The baby's.

Had Patrick changed his mind about other things too? If there was something wrong, would he still insist on a termination? Don't, she told herself, turning her head away. Don't think about it. Don't assume the worst.

She thought of Ludo, that morning as she'd been rushing out, crying because one of his splints had rubbed during the night (though there'd been no mark on his leg when she'd looked), telling her something about Paul, his best friend, calling him names.

'What names, darling?' She'd been rummaging in her handbag for the car key. Patrick, thank God, had at least said she could take the car to the station, that he, grudgingly, would take the bus.

'Bad names.'

'Oh, I wouldn't take any notice. You call him some back.'

'No. Don't talk to him any more.'

'Oh?' She'd stood up. 'I've got to go now, Ludi.'

His face had crumpled. 'You don't care! You don't care what he called me!'

Her heart had caught in her throat. 'Oh, I do. Of course I do.' She'd tried to hug him but he'd fought her off. 'Ludi, I've got to go. Mummy's got to go to London, you see. Darling?'

He'd howled louder, starting to work himself into a gasping rage. They had to be careful of those tantrums, the doctor had warned; Ludo's lungs weren't good, he could quickly get into real trouble. 'Go away!' he'd screamed. 'I want my daddy. Daddeee!'

And Patrick had materialised in an instant – he must have been listening – all soothing and tender. And Ludo had let himself be lifted on to his lap and comforted.

'You'd better get going,' Patrick had told her stiffly over the golden head. 'You don't want to miss your train.'

Mel looked once more at the clock: 3.33. What was the doctor doing? She ran her tongue over her dry lips. A one-in-two chance that it would be a girl; one-in-four – was that right? – that it would be a healthy boy. How did that compare to the lottery? And did such comparisons work for her or against her?

'That's it.' The nurse patted her shoulder. She was smiling. 'All done. Good girl.'

'Great,' Patrick said weakly. 'OK, Melly?'

She nodded, looked down, and saw Dr West set down a test-tube of watery red stuff. Her baby's fluid, she thought numbly. Her eyes travelled to the doctor's face and saw for the first time that he was really quite an old man with a careworn face, that his eyes were tired behind the spectacles, that there was sweat on his brow. Why, he's nervous, she thought, surprised.

He looked up and their eyes met.

'Thank you,' she said humbly. 'Thank you very much.'

He stared at her as if seeing her for the first time, and his gaze didn't drop. He was really peering at her. She felt quite embarrassed.

He coughed, seeming to collect himself. 'Er, n-not at all.'

He's only shy, she thought, and felt emboldened herself. 'You'll call us in the morning, will you?'

The question seemed to floor him.

The nurse took charge. 'Ooh, I shouldn't think Doctor'll be in at that time! It'll be his secretary. Won't it, Doctor?'

He blinked slowly, first over at the nurse, then down at Mel again. 'No.' He spoke more firmly now, in a fluting, well-modulated voice. '*I'll* call you. At eight o'clock.'

CHAPTER EIGHT

Caroline Henshaw had told everyone to be at the house by seven that evening. Now it was quarter-past and only Clive Lucas and Stuart Richley had turned up. Andrew was there of course, but he lived there so he didn't count. That left three unaccounted for: Mike Pearce, Mary Kennedy and Chris Manyon.

Caroline had had a terrible day. She'd heard about Gerry Winston during the morning break at the library. The secretary and the chief librarian had been discussing him, passing the newspaper between them, when she'd come in. It had been a shock.

'Are you all right there, Caroline?'

They'd been full of concern, urging her to lie down, slyly insinuating that she might be pregnant, that she must be careful, that she might have caught the virus 'going round'.

Virus. The word had taken her straight back to that night, to that stupid, botched raid that had been all Winston's fault. Andrew had been imagining rashes ever since, irritating her with his symptoms . . . But suppose he wasn't imagining things? Suppose Gerry Winston had got infected and it had been that that had killed him? Suppose he'd passed on the virus to the rest of them? They'd all been together in the van, breathing the same air on that journey back. Suppose Andrew wasn't simply being a hypochondriac?

She'd nipped out to the telephone-box in the high street to call him. He'd been on his break too, hadn't heard about Winston, had whimpered when she'd told him. He'd said, 'I've got an itch on my wrist, you know Caroline. D'you think—'

'Of course not!' Then she'd checked herself and said more kindly, 'I'm sure it's nothing. Don't worry about it.' She'd told him to tell Mary about the meeting, and that Mary was to tell Mike.

So where were they now? she wondered. They knew the address. She chewed her cheek. Mary adored belonging to the group, and Mike was a quiet boy; Caroline had never had any trouble with him before.

And then there was Chris Manyon. she chewed harder. He'd skived off, his supervisor had said bitterly – not bothered to phone in or even switch on his mobile. There'd been no reply at Manyon's home, though she'd called three times. In the end, telling the chief librarian that she thought maybe she *was* getting the flu, she'd left work and driven over to Manyon's maisonette and shoved a note quickly through the letterbox. 'Our house at seven.' Just that, no address, the simplest message.

She'd tried throughout the rest of the long afternoon to keep herself busy, not to let her mind dwell on imagined viruses that got into people's brains, made them drive off to odd, out-of-the-way places and die of heart-attacks on beaches. But where had Manyon gone? Had he handled the test-tubes in that lab? Had the airborne killer got him too?

The doorbell rang.

She was on her feet at once. 'That'll be them now, I'll get it.' She dashed along the hallway. Through the glass in the front-door she saw Mary's face, and presumed that the others must be behind her. She opened it. 'Where've you all . . . ?' Then she saw that the girl was unaccompanied. 'Where've you *been*, Mary?'

'At Mike's.'

'Isn't he coming?'

A shrug and a sniff.

Caroline pushed the girl in front of her into the sitting room. 'So what happened to Mike?'

Mary took the chair next to the gas-fire and studied her finger-nails. 'He's not coming,' she muttered.

Andrew piped up. 'Did he say why?'

She ignored him, addressing her words to Caroline. 'I went round there like he – ' she jerked a thumb in Andrew's direction – 'said. He didn't know about Gerry, so I told him, and he went all funny.'

'Funny?' Caroline demanded. 'In what way?'

'Shaking. Really bad. He scared me. I thought he was having a fit or something. Then he said,' she looked slowly round the room, 'how it was his fault.'

'What?' Lucas frowned. He'd never had much time for the younger members of the group. 'What's he on about?'

She didn't answer him. To Caroline she said, 'He said he'd show me. Then he went off to his room and brought back a laptop. He said that was what it was all about.'

'What did he mean?' Caroline demanded sharply

'He said he'd nicked it out of that lab.'

'He did *what?*' Andrew butted in.

'He'd seen it in a magazine. Cost thousands. He really wanted one, he said, but he'd never be able to afford it. So when he saw it there he went back and pinched it.'

'Pinched it?' Andrew asked dazedly. 'On his own?'

She gave him a lengthy look.

Caroline laid a hand on her arm. 'Mary, why did he say it was his fault? About Gerry's death?'

'Oh. Oh yeah. He started feeling bad about taking it. So he went up to Winston's to tell him, and he saw him going off with some people in a car.'

Caroline felt her head spinning. 'When was this?'

'Saturday morning. He couldn't sleep, so he got up when it was light and walked over there.'

'But why,' Andrew said, gazing at Caroline, 'didn't he tell us?'

Caroline frowned. 'Did he think it was the police?'

'Yeah, that's what he said. He kept thinking they'd come for him.'

Stuart rose suddenly. 'I'm going to see him. She only knows hearsay.'

'He's not there,' Mary said in a small voice.

'Where is he, then?'

'Dunno.' She gazed at the carpet.

'Mary,' Caroline glared, 'don't try my patience.'

'I told you! I dunno where he is. All he said was that he'd had an idea, but he knew if he told you lot you'd try to stop him. He wanted me to go with him.' She glanced fleetingly at Stuart. 'But I said no way. I've got my GCSEs to think of.'

'Did he go on foot?' Stuart demanded.

She went pink. 'I dunno, Stu. Honest. He just asked me not to say anything for two hours, so you wouldn't be able to come after him. So I didn't. I walked round and round.'

'Silly little bitch,' Lucas hissed from the other side of the room. 'What d'you think this is, a game?'

'All right.' Caroline said calmly. 'Mike lives near the station, doesn't he? So he could be in London by now, or . . .'

'Ashford. Or on his way to France.'

Caroline nodded. 'Did he take the computer with him, Mary?'

'Yeah. He wrapped it in his sweatshirt.'

Caroline got up, simply for the sake of moving, hoping that the motion might restart her thought processes and give her a plan. She walked over to the large picture window that looked out on to farmland. Was there someone out there, watching them even now? Or at the front – was a car waiting, its engine idling?

Andrew said, 'We mustn't panic.'

Caroline turned round. Everyone but Mary had visibly tensed.

'And we mustn't jump to conclusions.' Andrew swallowed. 'Must we, Caroline?'

Appealed to directly, she remembered her position, that the others would be looking to her for guidance. 'Absolutely not. It's possible that these people Gerry went off with were friends.'

Lucas and Stuart both snorted.

'It's *possible*, I said. It's also possible they were the police.'

'I think I might've heard,' Stuart interrupted loftily.

'Yes. But it may've been some sort of unofficial talk. They might've been Special Branch – because of his record – just trying to see what he knew about the raid.' That sounded quite feasible, even to herself. 'Yes, and he was so disturbed by it that he took himself off to Suffolk.'

'Why?' Lucas asked. 'Why Suffolk?'

'A relative?' she suggested.

Lucas eyed her disparagingly. She'd had trouble with him before.

'Or else they were from the government,' she said, and was

annoyed at the slight quaver in her voice. 'REDEV's built on an MOD site, isn't it?'

No one said anything. Caroline went on: 'It's where the MOD used to experiment with gas and—'

'Germ warfare,' Lucas put in.

'Quite.' Voicing her fears made Caroline feel a bit better. She took a deep breath and told them about Manyon's absence from work that day. A strained silence greeted her announcement. Andrew made odd gulping sounds in his throat until she frowned at him and he stopped.

Mary said after a moment, 'Mike's going to put it right.' She looked round at them. 'That's what he said,' she added falteringly.

'That little fucker!' Lucas exploded. 'He's probably right! He's probably the reason Winston's dead! Can't we report him missing to the police?'

Stuart opened his mouth to speak but Caroline was too quick. 'Suppose the police've got instructions to hand over anyone connected with the raid to . . .' She paused. '. . . government people? We can't risk that.'

'And we can't risk turning ourselves in, either,' Andrew said suddenly.

There was another silence. Then Lucas said, too belligerently, 'So? What're we going to do?'

Andrew licked his lips. 'Maybe we all ought to do what Mike's done and take off for a bit.'

'What, go on the lam?' Lucas laughed, but no one else did, and Caroline wondered if Andrew was right. He was sometimes.

She cleared her throat. 'Maybe not immediately, but we've got to be prepared, and we must all keep in touch very closely. If anyone wants to stay here tonight . . .' She caught Lucas's incredulous look. 'At the very least I must ask everyone to call me first thing tomorrow morning. At eight, shall we say?'

Lucas shook his head slowly. 'You've got it wrong. There'll be an explanation.' He pulled on his bomber-jacket. 'It's just a series of coincidences. Mike's only a kid. He got freaked out, imagined things and took off, but he'll be back. And Chris'll have gone on the piss in Ashford or somewhere.'

'I do most fervently hope so,' said Andrew, scratching again.

'You'll see,' Lucas promised. 'This time tomorrow they'll be back and we'll all be pissing ourselves about it.'

The telephone-booth stank of urine and was very cold. Upon hearing the answering-machine message, Mike Pearce clunked down the handset. He wanted to talk to *her*, not her bloody machine. He checked the time. Maybe she was still working. Out on assignment, or else – and he frowned – on holiday. Or perhaps she used the answerphone to vet her messages.

He studied the card in his hand. 'Sasha Downey, Investigative Journalist', and the telephone number. That was all. But he remembered her clearly. Very tall and slim, with lots of dark hair and a great smile. He'd been in awe of her, the glamorous national journalist, but she'd been all right. She'd listened to him properly, asked him some decent questions, not treated him like a kid the way some of the other journalists had. For eighteen months, chiefly for show, he'd kept her card in his plastic credit card holder.

He rubbed the heel of his hand over his eyes. So much to think of, so much to plan, and he was tired, dead-tired with the strain. It had almost been a relief when Mary had told him about Gerry – confirmation that he hadn't imagined it, that he hadn't gone mad.

That morning . . .

Gerry's face, chalk-white but set; the big man's hand coming down on top of his head as he'd folded him into the back seat; another slighter man, no more than a shadow in the passenger seat; and then the driver. It was the driver's face that haunted Mike's dreams, causing him to start up in terror, making him so afraid that he now feared to sleep.

She was beautiful, he acknowledged that, though she was probably as old as his mother – maybe older, he thought generously, but very . . . different looking. Her dark hair was lifted high off her face, her skin tanned and unlined, her eyes large, dark, slightly slanting. She'd been staring into her rear-view mirror so she hadn't noticed Mike appear from around the corner, hadn't seen him stop and stare.

Then the car had started moving and suddenly, unsure of what he'd been doing, only knowing that he had to do something, he'd stepped forward. The woman's eyes had fixed upon him, and suddenly he hadn't been able to move, though he'd known that that was what he had to do. He had to run.

His heart thundered. Around him, through the smeared glass of the booth, the traffic of South London roared and glared: the white lights of the cars and the softer amber sodium of the street-lights. You could get lost in London; you were harder to find. He took a deep breath . . .

Gerry, in the back seat, had jerked forward, and the woman's glare had snapped off Mike and on to him. Then she'd pulled down her sunglasses and the car had gathered speed. Just for a split second, as the car had passed, Mike had caught Gerry's eye before he'd turned, slowly and deliberately, away.

Gerry had saved his life! And it was his fault that Gerry was dead. A sudden faintness came over him, and he closed his eyes, steadying himself against the shelf by the phone. The rucksack, resting on the ground, leaned heavily against his knees. He shivered. Deep down, he'd always known that those people – that woman – couldn't have been from the police.

He picked up the handset and dialled Sasha's number again.

The bar of the Heathman Hotel was three-quarters full, yet it did not feel crowded, and neither was it too noisy. The chairs and sofas, deeply upholstered, elegantly mismatched, were widely spaced in semi-circles and quarters, encouraging small groups and low voices.

Sasha and Charlie had been there nearly forty minutes, discussing work in the nervous way that people do, she considered, when they don't know each other very well and are afraid to let a silence fall. A great deal of the conversation had centred around Tyler, who during the day had been accused by a back-bencher of deliberately seeking to undermine the Prime Minister.

Charlie had obviously been monitoring all developments, which was sweet of him, and very flattering. But there'd been nothing so far, Sasha thought in frustration, to indicate the status of the evening. Date or drink? And, if a date, how about Tamarin?

She glanced up and caught his eye.

'Great place, this,' he said. 'It always surprises me that it's not busier.'

'It's probably because it hasn't been written up yet. Most

people don't know it exists. Or they think it's for hotel guests only.'

'That's right. I'd no idea. It was only when Tamarin had some friends staying here . . .'

Hold it, Sasha instructed herself. Hold that intent, listening expression, don't slump like a let-down balloon.

'. . . that we discovered it.' He paused.

'How is Tamarin?' Now, where, she wondered, had that come from? And so warmly and sincerely put. Just like Tyler.

'Tamarin? She's fine. Fine.'

'Good. I saw her in the lobby last week. With all her cases.' Oh no, she thought numbly. She reached for her glass.

'You did? Yeah, she's gone back to the States.'

'For Thanksgiving.'

'Right. Well – for a bit longer than that, as it happens.' He picked up his glass and applied the swizzle stick vigorously. 'We split up. A few weeks back. She was collecting her things.'

She felt lit up like a pinball machine. 'Oh, I'm sorry,' she murmured.

'You are?'

'Well . . . you were so close.'

'*Were*, yeah. I guess we were, one time – you tend to forget. It hadn't been working out for some time. We tried to patch it up. You know how you do.'

'Oh yes.'

He looked up. 'You've, uh, you've gone through it?'

She nodded.

'Recently? I mean, are you still, ah . . . ?'

'No, it was over a long time ago.'

'Oh.' His relief was clear. As an actor, he didn't touch her, she thought. On that score, she hadn't quite realised the extent of her own abilities.

'I'd have told you about Tamarin the other night, you know, when we met in the elevator. But I didn't want you to think . . .' He fingered his collar. (What a truly gorgeous mouth he had, she noticed suddenly. Slightly wide – but she loved wide mouths on men, they hinted at generosity. And he'd well-defined lips, not in the least bit fleshy, but soft-looking) '. . . to think that I was, you know, saying that I was, or asking if you were free . . . Oh Christ.'

'It's OK,' she said gently and smiled. Acting was such hard work.

'It is? I mean, you're so . . .' He made a vague gesture. 'And you seem to go out so much.'

'I do?'

'Yeah.' He took a swig of his Bloody Mary, almost choked. 'So, there isn't anyone special, so to speak?'

'So to speak – no.'

He grinned widely. 'Wow. I mean, that's good. Um, if it's not being too forward, d'you fancy something to eat?'

She grinned back. 'I'd love it.'

'Now? I don't know if they do food here, or—'

'Only bar-snacks.' They were mouth-watering – she'd had them before – but they'd be over far too quickly, and suddenly it was important for the evening to last as long as possible.

'Oh. Well in that case, if you're prepared to wait another half-hour,' he shot her a sheepish look, 'we'll be able to get a table at Birds.'

She smiled but shook her head. 'Oh, I shouldn't think so. It's one of those places that you have to book weeks in advance, you know. You can't just walk in.'

'I know. I've booked.'

'What?' She stared. 'Weeks ago?'

'No.' He smiled. 'Only this morning, after you'd said yes. I booked on the off-chance. We're pretty good customers of theirs. I mean, AGN are. Um . . . you don't mind?' The worried look had suddenly returned.

'Oh no, not a bit.' The restaurant served delicious food, but the service was notoriously slow. She met his eyes. 'I think it sounds perfect.'

CHAPTER NINE

At 6.18 the following morning, the fire brigade succeeded in cutting Christopher Manyon's body free from the wreckage. It had not been an easy task; the front of the car, on impact with the wall, had concertinaed in upon itself, leaving the torso embedded in the steering-wheel and nothing very much remaining of the head.

A real mess, was the verdict of the chief fire officer, but there'd been little sympathy in his voice. The fumes inside the car had been quite overwhelming, even after the roof had been cut away. As if further proof were needed, shards of a broken whisky bottle lay on the floor on the passenger's side, while on the back seat rolled an empty but otherwise intact vodka bottle.

The miracle, the emergency services agreed, was that no one else had been hurt. They could thank the early hour for that. Manyon had gone racing down the hill in Hastings shortly before five o'clock – residents had woken to the sound of him smashing and banging into their cars – then, entering the bend, he'd lost control and crashed into the reinforced concrete wall at the bottom.

In spite of the mess, identification was speedy. An envelope with his name and address was found in his jeans' back pocket, and the details checked perfectly against those of the registered owner of the vehicle. By seven-thirty a policeman and woman were on their way to his next of kin. Each was dreading what lay ahead. The Manyons had lived locally for years; Christopher was an only son, years younger than his three sisters. How to break the news to a woman of sixty-three, a widow, that her boy, the light of her eyes, was dead?

The previous summer, when it became obvious that Ludo was finding the stairs too difficult, they'd moved him down to the ground floor into what had been the dining room. It was far from ideal: the room was linked by dividing doors to the sitting room, which meant that in the evenings Mel and Patrick either had to sit in the kitchen or talk in whispers, and having friends round was impossible. Ludo woke easily, making watching television a trial, the volume had to be kept so low. In the end they'd given up, put the main set in his room and bought a small portable for themselves, for their bedroom.

He moved now in his sleep, his head turning on the pillow, one hand lazily attempting to scratch his ear. Mel watched him. She had slept little the previous night. On each of the two occasions that he'd called – they had an intercom system rigged up between the bedrooms – it had been Mel who'd got up and seen to him, even though Patrick had volunteered. The second time, at a little before five, she'd stayed up.

She preferred to be doing something, even if it was only sitting. It was better to be there in case Ludo needed her. And he had seemed so very needy in the night: on the first occasion whimpering to be turned over; on the second, wanting the potty, one of the 'make-do' arrangements in use at night.

Imagine what it's going to be like in a year's time, or two years, Mel thought. Ludo off his feet and into his first wheelchair. She gazed about the room. Soon they'd have to start thinking about a proper extension – a purpose-built bedroom and bathroom; an electronically controlled bed, so that, at the press of a button, Ludo could be sat up, or have his knees bent, or his feet elevated. He would get heavier with the inactivity that the disease brought on; he'd need pulleys to pick him up and run him on gliders into the bathroom. And a computer with a hands-off facility, for when the muscles in his hands no longer had the power to operate a keyboard. She felt her throat constrict. She kept thinking that she'd got used to it –

she'd seen the older boys in the DMD support group – but still, all the paraphernalia of handicap . . . It drove it home.

Was it any wonder that they spoiled him, she and Patrick both – now, while they could, while he was still with them? Materially, within reason, Ludo had every toy and book and video he wanted; and emotionally, as much as (and probably more than) they ought to give. At the support group Mel had heard some of the other mothers complain that the burden of care was dumped on them. The fathers distanced themselves, staying late at work, claiming they needed the overtime to pay for additional expenses, but really seeking excuses not to spend time with their sons. Mel could never level such a charge against Patrick. They vied to spend time with Ludo, to play with him, talk to him, take him where he wanted and when. Holidays for the previous two years had been Ludo's choices: Disneyland both times, France when he was five and Florida last summer. 'Where are you going to take him next?' Mel's mother had asked. 'The moon?' And Mel had answered, 'If he wants it,' defiantly, like a spoilt child herself. She gazed down at the wondrous fringes of his eyelashes, so dark and perfect against his pale skin. They mustn't ruin him, she thought urgently, no matter how tempting it was.

For the countless time she looked at her watch. It was very nearly time. Perhaps she ought to go into the kitchen, where the telephone was? Or should she wake Ludo now, be fully engaged when the phone rang, so that she wouldn't be able to take the call? But she wanted to hear it first-hand; she couldn't bear to hear the phone ringing and to know that Patrick knew before her, to wait even a few seconds for his paraphrase, good or bad. Her mind felt gluey. She didn't know what she wanted, didn't know what to do with herself.

Ludo would wake any moment and need the lavatory. If she woke him now, she thought suddenly, she would just have time to whisk him upstairs to the bathroom – though 'whisk' was optimistic; he weighed twenty-five kilos – so that she could use the extension in the hall.

He stretched but didn't open his eyes.

She jiggled his arm gently. 'Come on, sleepy-head.'

''lo, Mummy.' But he wasn't awake yet. Slowly he yawned and smiled. 'Love you . . .' It was his old greeting, had been his first acclaimed declaration as a toddler, though lately not much in use. Her heart melted. She put out a hand and touched his hair, her still-asleep angel.

He opened his eyes.

'All right, darling?'

The perfect brows came together in a knot. 'Phone, Mummy.'

Her heart jumped. She hadn't heard it ring, but even now Patrick's voice was coming clearly through the thin wall, saying that, yes, this was Mr Alder speaking.

She rose and ran. Behind her Ludo bellowed, 'Mummy, Daddy's got it! Mummy? Are you deaf?'

Patrick was standing over the kitchen table, both hands clutching the handset. 'Yes?' he was saying tightly.

She ducked under his arm and came up against his chest, forcing her head between his and the phone. Through the instrument she could hear the reedy voice of the doctor.

'. . . the Dystrophin gene is present.'

She couldn't make sense of the words. Was that good news or bad? 'Patrick?' she whispered, terrified.

'And that means . . . ?' he asked, swallowing hard. She inched closer in.

There was a pause at the other end of the line. 'I'm sorry?' said the doctor, and Mel saw again the scholarly, remote face, and remembered how he'd looked at her without seeing a person there.

'In plain English,' said Patrick.

'Well . . .' A cough. 'It means that the fetus is producing the Dystrophin protein, which in turn—'

'Is that OK or not?'

'Oh, I see.' Another cough. 'The fetus is in fact normal.'

'Normal?' They both echoed the word.

'He doesn't have it?' Mel whispered. Her hands flew to her stomach, touched and cradled. We've passed, she thought wonderingly. He could be a baby now; he was going to be allowed to live.

Against her, Patrick trembled and the phone fell from his grasp.

Mel caught it. 'Dr West? Thank you so much. Oh God, thank you!'

'Oh! Er . . . not at all.' He actually sounded embarrassed.

A lump came to Mel's throat. That dear, modest, brilliant man. 'You've no idea what you've done,' she gulped. 'No idea what this means to us.' She dropped the phone, turned to Patrick and held him fast. He was sobbing as hard as she.

'Oh, you clever girl,' he whispered. 'You clever, clever girl.'

'It's going to be all right.' She raised her head, wiping away her tears, then his. 'Everything's going to be all right.'

'Mummy!' Ludo suddenly roared. 'What're you doing?'

'I'm just . . .' She made a move to go to him, but Patrick held on to her.

'We'll be in in a minute, darling,' he called over her shoulder.

'Now!'

'Oh, Ludi! Use the potty if you need it.'

'No! You've got to come now!'

'Don't yell at us like that,' Patrick called mildly, and catching Mel's eye, grinned. They were rewarded with an absolute, stunned silence, and suddenly found themselves laughing.

At the other end of the line, Dr West listened. He heard the laughter, then the husband say, 'It's all right, Ludi. We're not laughing at you,' and the mother: 'I'm coming, angel,' and then, sounding startled: 'Oops, I didn't hang up,' then more giggling before finally the line went dead.

For several minutes afterwards West continued holding the handset against his ear, hoping that one of them might pick it up again so that he could hear more. It never occurred to him to replace the receiver himself. He needed to eavesdrop, to discover what ingredient they possessed that had made him – his brow puckered – not *care*, exactly, but certainly be curious about them.

After they'd gone the previous day he'd re-read their notes. It was a brief history: names, ages, the DNA print-out, the genetic 'marker' of the son, showing the deletion in his gene so that West would know what to look for in the fetus. (If it was affected, the deletion would be the same.) Then the DNA studies of the mother, her blood tests showing elevated levels of CPK. Nothing out of the ordinary; nothing that he hadn't seen many times before. No clue to explain why, when he'd looked into that woman's eyes, he'd seen something that had made him feel physically punched. Or stuck with a needle – penetrated, invaded, as if it were she who'd punctured his membranes and not the other way around.

He was only thankful that when it happened the procedure had been concluded; he wasn't sure that he'd have been in a fit state, afterwards, to have performed it.

He knew that people found him cold and arrogant. He'd heard it said often enough, sometimes to his face. Not that they were characteristics he particularly sought to change, both being built into his personality, genetic in origin, and nurtured, he had no doubt, by his upbringing – older parents, neither given to displays of great affection, only pleased that he did well academically. A cold fish, they'd called him at school, and left him alone, which might have initially hurt, but he'd no memory of it doing so. Even his wife had called him cold. After three years of marriage she'd suddenly announced that she was divorcing him on grounds of mental cruelty, citing all the instances when he'd failed her emotionally. That had hurt, very much, especially when he learnt that she'd been having an affair. He'd hoped for some time that she'd come back, but she never had, and although he'd still been a young man, not yet thirty, he'd never married again.

In time, however, he'd found that he enjoyed the single life; work, as it had done at school, had quickly absorbed him. With no home life he could work as long as he wanted; it was nothing for him to sleep at the lab. In his field such behaviour hadn't been that unusual, and apart from a few wilderness years his dedication had paid off.

He'd certainly always earned enough to have a housekeeper – in the last few years, more than enough. Branium paid him a fortune. They needn't have – money had never mattered much to him, and most of it sat uselessly in the bank. So long as they let him do what he wanted, left him alone, gave him the facilities he needed, he was happy. And they'd always done that: provided him with excellent laboratories, equipment and material, plus direct, unhindered access to one of the top men (he hated red tape, had a dread of speaking in public) as well as a highly motivated staff, if and when he needed them, to perform the more menial and sometimes distasteful tasks.

He remembered his first time with a human subject. The young, dark-skinned woman had been too terrified even to look at him. And, of course, the language barrier had helped. In that remote part of the world, a mountainous region in northern Albania, not many people spoke English, and West had known only the barest rudiments of the language – please, thank you, God willing – not enough for a conversation, even had he wanted one.

Those first subjects had been as far removed from him as laboratory animals, as the mice and rats he had previously used. By the time he'd started work in the UK, there in the Mistletoe hospital, he'd acquired enough experience in dealing with human patients not to be afraid of involvement. He'd devised a system whereby the nurses did all the talking, explaining, reassuring – in most cases he'd found them only too willing to do that – leaving him free to concentrate. A quick hello and goodbye from himself, sometimes not even that, sufficed.

Until the previous day, with Mrs Melanie Alder, the last patient in the study. Was that it? he wondered. A subliminal release of tension, knowing that with the removal of the needle from her abdomen, his work was, for the moment, complete? Eighteen of them – eighteen male fetuses of DMD mothers. It had taken much longer than they'd expected to get a decent number; they'd hoped for twenty, but it wasn't Albania, where lack of contraception coupled with the strict Muslim prohibition on abortion had provided him with more DMD families than he had needed. In the UK, after a promising start – six suitable candidates in the first ten weeks – it had been an uphill struggle.

He scratched at the back of his hand. He'd seen the desperation in Mrs Alder's face and been moved by it. But others, he realised now, mentally reviewing, had looked just as desperate, without provoking any reaction in himself. He'd never addressed a patient directly before, and when he'd heard himself saying that he would call her he'd been astonished. What had possessed him?

The previous evening he'd pulled up her full medical record on his computer. He knew about her abortion, her depression, the birth of her doomed son and her unsuccessful attempt at IVF treatment. It hadn't satisfied him, any more than listening to her conversation just now. He didn't even know what he was looking for, he realised, perplexed.

There was a noise outside his door. One of the cleaners, or – he checked the time – his secretary arriving for work. It was nearly ten o'clock. He gave himself a mental shake. He'd been sitting idle for nearly two hours, letting his mind wander. Most unlike himself.

He switched on the computer, keyed in his password, waited a few moments, and selected 'Follow-up' from the index. Five names appeared on screen: the names of the baby boys so far born to the mothers in his pilot study. The babies ranged in age from sixteen days to nine weeks old. Two of the names were highlighted, which meant that in the previous twenty-four hours they had received medical attention.

He felt no alarm. He checked the infants daily on DAMR, the Direct Access to Medical Records, a computer network system that had been launched two years before. He saw that Subject Three was due for his regulation six-week-old check-up; the other, the second subject, was the son of a highly-strung woman who'd already taken her baby to her GP four times, and the child was scarcely eight weeks old. She'd been to the surgery once before that week, on Monday morning. Then the complaint had been of a 'sniffle'. The GP, a woman who seemed imbued with saintly patience, had carefully examined the infant, noted that everything was normal, and told the mother once more than her son was perfectly healthy, but to bring him back again if she was worried.

He checked first on the six-week-old. The examination had been completed twenty minutes before, and everything – he quickly scanned – looked entirely normal. He glanced at the time again. He had a meeting in two hours' time, and there was data on Melanie Alder to be processed before that; because of his daydreaming he was running late. It was tempting to skip Subject Two's diagnosis altogether. But he sighed and ran the cursor up anyway.

The baby's name appeared, and his date of birth. His mother had taken him to the previous evening's surgery. She'd complained that the baby's cold had seemed no better, and that although he was eating properly he seemed unusually irritable and unresponsive. West frowned. Then, seeing what came next, he raised an eyebrow and frowned harder. The baby had been referred to hospital for a blood-test.

His eyes widened on the words. 'Blood-test?' he muttered, aware that his heart was thumping a tattoo in his chest. His hands on the keyboard felt suddenly sweaty, and he rubbed them hurriedly on the desk-top. 'It'll be nothing,' he murmured to himself; the GP's patience had finally snapped, that was all. She must have told the mother that she'd done every check she could; there was nothing wrong with the boy, but to be on the safe side, to finally assuage any concern . . . His eyelids flickered.

He jumped out of the notes and entered the name of the referring hospital. He'd never heard of it before; it was located somewhere in Somerset. With such a young baby they'd have done the tests straight away, probably kept him in for the night, so he'd be there when the results came through. Tiny babies could 'go off' so quickly – he chewed his cheek – one minute they were healthy, but the next . . . You only had to look at them sideways and they were half-dead. 'Unusually irritable.' That didn't sound good. Babies didn't have many ways to show that they weren't well; they couldn't tell you, they couldn't point. If they were irritable, unresponsive . . . He chewed harder. Hadn't one of the mother's complaints been that the baby seemed unusually pale? West remembered something else: hadn't the mother reported a little bruise on his leg? That could mean, it could indicate . . .

The hospital's directory was on the screen. West requested the Haematology Lab, then tapped in the baby's name. The results were there, if only just: they'd been entered twenty minutes before. West's eyes flickered wildly again, then stilled. There wasn't any point in panic, nor in false hope. With these sorts of results he knew that the hospital would immediately repeat the test – they were probably doing so right now, hoping that there'd been an error, a clot in the sample – it was notoriously difficult to get a decent sample out of a tiny baby, their veins were so little.

But he knew there'd been no error, he'd seen that blood picture before: the high white-cell count, abnormal lymphocytes; the haemoglobin low, the whole picture confusing. He re-read the pathologist's comment at the bottom: 'Query Leukaemoid reaction. Query Leukaemia?'

He put his head in his hands. His fingers felt cold. He felt strange, disconnected, as if he'd been sucked out of the normal course of things and spat out on the rim. When his hand reached out for the telephone it seemed like a stranger's hand; he couldn't remember having instructed his brain to move those muscles.

The direct line started to ring. He didn't know if he'd be able to speak. The secretary answered and he cleared his throat.

'Could I speak to John, please?' He was surprised at how calm he sounded.

'I'm sorry,' she said. 'He's in a meeting at the moment. Can I—'

'Get him!' His voice broke. 'It's an emergency!' he shrieked.

CHAPTER TEN

Glancing round the table, John Stockart could see that he'd got to them. As with the executive directors two years before, so again it had been the mention of money that had done it: his reference, right at the end, to a 'Super Blockbuster'.

There was a reverent pause as the six non-executive directors of Branium Pharma absorbed those words for the first time. Then one of them, the merchant banker with the gingery, wispy hair, asked cautiously, 'As big as Infutopin?'

'Infutopin? Sure!'

'Infutopin's in the gutter compared to this baby!'

It wasn't Stockart who'd answered, but the finance director and the deputy managing director, speaking together. They laughed, but neither yielded.

'We're talking billions.'

'. . . billions. Millions of billions – we don't know exactly how much, do we, John?'

Stockart smiled at the bright, shining eyes turned upon him. 'No,' he admitted modestly. 'It is a previously untapped well.'

'We've struck bloody oil though, haven't we?'

'Bloody oilfield, more like!'

'Only the size of Texas!'

He sat back and watched them – his five fellow executive directors, chief executive included – do his work for him. It was utterly pleasurable to hear them use his phrases: 'a greater breakthrough than landing a man on the moon'; 'a modern-day miracle'; 'it's going to take us into the stratosphere.' It put the burglary, and its consequences, not in context exactly – the computer was still missing, although only that morning Hall had assured him it couldn't be much longer, they had the names now – but at least for a short while Stockart could push that whole sorry mess to the back of his mind and indulge himself in the appreciation he so richly deserved.

It had been he who, ten years before, whilst on a trawling exercise at a conference, had first come across Will West. West, he'd previously discovered, had pioneered new biotechnology techniques to isolate and clone a human growth hormone. The resulting drug had made his company several million. But then other companies, including Branium, had copied the drug and marketed it for less. When Stockart had met him, West was working on techniques for gene therapy. Stockart had contrived to 'bump into him' in the hotel bar. After a few drinks he'd managed to steer the conversation round to West's work, and to what was now being so eagerly, greedily discussed around the table: the Infiltrator Technique.

The reason, West had said, that current attempts at gene therapy were failing, was that they were trying to incorporate the 'good' gene into the muscle of the sufferer too late.

Stockart had nodded, concentrating hard.

The 'good' gene, West had told him, had to be taken up by the body of the sufferer, where it would start producing the protein whose absence causes the disease. The problem was that, after birth, muscle ceased to be a dividing cell, therefore it was not able to absorb the good gene. Now, West's idea – Stockart had smiled expectantly – was to put the good gene into the sufferer *before* birth, when the muscle was a rapidly dividing cell.

'My God,' Stockart had breathed. 'Is that possible?'

'Of course it's possible!'

'You've done it?'

'I've . . .' West had hesitated for the first time, darting a look at Stockart's lapel to see whom he was talking to.

But Stockart had removed his badge earlier. He'd smiled into the doctor's eyes. 'It's only an idea at the moment, then, Will?'

The high brow had folded down. It was more than that. At first he'd achieved outstanding success but then there'd been a couple of hitches. It had been a bit expensive, admittedly, but West had viewed that as part of his learning curve. Not so his company. Since then they'd side-tracked him, brought in new men, expecting him to work under them.

So how far had his research got? Stockart had pushed gently.

West had paused before answering. He'd done some preliminary stuff on mice – at his lab at home, because those bastards wouldn't give him time.

The results? Stockart had been unable to keep the edge out of his voice.

West had blinked. It had worked.

Stockart had felt his blood pounding. He'd asked if West had mentioned this to anyone at his company. West had slowly shaken his head. No one would listen. He'd been scheduled to present an outline a month before, but they'd postponed the meeting. They weren't interested, didn't care.

Stockart, staring at the bent, self-pitying head, had thought quickly. If there was any possibility of this technique working . . . He'd taken out his card – Director of Special Projects – and slid it under the man's nose. 'I'm interested, Will,' he'd said softly.

West's eyes had goggled as he read; the rivalry between his own company and Branium was legendary.

'They don't care; I do.' Stockart had assured him, deciding that this was the moment to pinion him down. 'Take me through the nuts and bolts of the thing – just simply.'

Simplicity was clearly a problem, but by making West stop and repeat where necessary, Stockart had got the gist. First, a healthy copy of a specific gene – say the Cystic Fibrosis gene, or the very large Dystrophin gene – had to be genetically engineered in a laboratory. Then, with its 'promoter' – a sequence of DNA that ensures the gene is 'turned on' in the appropriate tissue – it would be cloned to make millions of copies, before being inserted into a type of virus (known as a 'retrovirus'), which would then be introduced into the DNA of a sufferer.

'The sufferer being the fetus in the womb?' Stockart had queried.

'Precisely.' West, in the telling, had sobered somewhat. 'Of course, the retrovirus would have been rendered non-pathogenic.' He'd sighed heavily. 'In layman's language, that means harmless. It's a virus; if it isn't disarmed it could cause problems. But, disarmed, it's incorporated into the host, along with the good gene.'

'Thus overriding the effects of the bad gene?'

'Crudely speaking, yes.'

Stockart had swallowed, almost afraid to pose the next question. 'D'you think it could work in humans?' He could feel himself clinging on to West's papery lips, forcing them to speak.

The slightly protruding eyes had met his. 'Yes,' West had said quietly.

Get him, the chief executive had ordered. Give him whatever he wants – labs, his own team, a fat salary – give him six months, and then they'd know. It was worth it, wasn't it, if this thing, this Infiltrator Technique (Stockart had thought up the name – much easier to handle than grappling with all that scientific jargon), was going to work?

Stockart, studying the highly polished surface of the board table, smiled to himself. The technique had worked all right. On mice, on rats and dogs, and then on human embryos. Along the way one of West's teams had discovered Infutopin. In deciding to go ahead with the development and launch of the new drug, utmost care had been taken to ensure that there could be no connection between it and West's work. No one wanted anyone – particularly from West's first company – to put two and two together, to be reminded of West and his crazy notion about gene therapy.

West himself, engrossed in the next stage of the Infiltrator trials, had seemed unperturbed by the fuss surrounding Infutopin. It didn't concern his field of research; therefore it was of no interest to him. He'd become pretty grand by then, and very remote, locked away in his labs, relating only to his team-leaders (and only when he had to), never presenting reports or attending meetings or doing anything at all, in fact, that he didn't want to do. Quite a brat, if a sixty-year-old man could be called a brat.

Stockart smiled again. He didn't mind pampering the old bastard. It was worth it. He wondered what the company would offer him next. His salary, coupled with bonuses, already made him the third highest paid in the company. But why not the second? Why not more than the chief executive? They owed it to him. They'd pay if they wanted him to stay . . .

'John?'

He snapped to. Everyone was looking at him.

'I think that's yours.'

'What?' He became aware of a bleeping sound. 'Oh – I'm sorry.' He pulled the pager out of his pocket. On the digital read-out was an internal number that he knew well.

'Something urgent?' there was a touch of frostiness in the voice. It was a rule that board meetings were never interrupted except in cases of dire emergency; the deputy MD was also insanely jealous of Stockart.

'It'll be nothing.' He smiled apologetically. It would be West panicking about something again. Sometimes, he thought, the old man went too far: calling him up day or night – he seemed to have no sense of time – gabbling science at him, expecting him to understand, to be there instantly with the solution for any little problem. He took a deep breath. Remember the money, he told himself. Remember the glory.

He switched the bleeper off and turned his attention back to the meeting.

'New genes are being discovered all the time,' the financial director was saying excitedly. 'Genes for the colour of eyes, colour of hair, height . . . and there's lots of work being done on intelligence.'

The merchant banker swallowed. 'You're saying that this Infiltrator Technique will be able to deliver all that?'

'In the future, we don't see why not. It's just a matter of identifying the gene. The technique would be the same.'

'Blond-haired, blue-eyed son, IQ of a hundred and eighty?' another director put in gleefully. 'Certainly, Mr and Mrs Jones, no problem!'

Now *that*, Stockart thought (though his expression betrayed nothing), would have been better left unsaid. On cue, from the other side of the table came a discreet but audible cough.

'May I, ah, say,' It was the bishop, appointed prior to Infutopin's launch, to forestall criticism of meddling with life, and kept on, Stockart and others considered, long past his sell-by date. 'May I say . . .' The elderly cleric had a particularly twittery habit of speech, like a sparrow's jabbering. '. . . that it sounds a trifle – I don't wish to be melodramatic, or to throw a spanner in the works, but . . . dare I say it, um, hum – Brave-New-Worldish?'

Before Stockart could open his mouth the human resources director pounced. She was a tough woman in her early forties, with a penchant for wearing red lipstick and culottes. 'We're talking of being able to cure the great scourges of mankind. In the future – though, as John says, not-too-distant future – ' she sparkled across at him – 'cancer, heart disease, strokes. The Biggies. As it is, right now we can cure – we *have* cured, for God's . . . sorry, goodness sake – how many cases of Duchennes, John? Well, over twenty, anyway. That's twenty little boys who're going to grow up strong and healthy; twenty babies whose mothers will never know the heartbreak of watching them waste and sicken; twenty less young, innocent, beautiful lives cut tragically short . . .'

Stockart thought she was overdoing it. So too, from the looks being exchanged around the room, did several others. But it was having exactly the right effect upon the bishop. A pink flush spread across his pallid face; his mouth was opening and shutting like a baby bird desperate to be let back into the nest.

'Don't you think that in this case we could be God's instruments?' she asked sorrowfully.

'Oh, well – yes! Yes, indeed, but—'

'That it's possible that He's given Dr West this great ability, this miraculous power – that He's *inspired* him with it – to save these little ones?'

'My dear! Please don't misunderstand me. It wasn't diseases I was talking about. It was the – you mentioned it yourself, I think, just now – the "super-babies". It smacks to me of . . . It's what the Nazis were trying to do, wasn't it? Create the super-race? I was thinking how appalling it would be, truly appalling, should a great good – a God-given good, as you say . . . should that be traduced, misused for commercial gain.'

A soft chuckle interrupted him. Everyone, including Stockart, turned. At the top of the table the chief executive sat smiling.

'My dear Bishop.' He laughed gently again. 'I think you've entirely misunderstood the tone of those remarks. Light-hearted banter only. Was it not?' And he fixed human resources with a look, and she mumbled and nodded. Around the table came other murmurs of assent. The chief executive continued. 'I can assure you that we are years, *light-years* away from being able to find the intelligence genes, or the beauty genes or the longevity ones – or any of the ones that the public fondly imagines we're on the brink of discovering and using for our own evil ends.'

There was a ripple of laughter.

'B-but the Human Genome P-project . . .' the bishop whispered.

'The Human Genome Project – you are perfectly right – will, by 2010 or thereabouts, have mapped every gene in the human DNA. An outstanding achievement. Even so, how possible is it, really, to discover the genetic make-up for intelligence? The best geneticists, ours included, have been working away on this for a long time, and what've they discovered? That there's not one gene for intelligence but many – only some of which have been located, and some which might never be. So, the problem is going to be, which *combination* produces intelligence? And does one conglomeration of intelligence genes in one individual have the same effect in others, or is each person uniquely different? One must not forget upbringing, environment. Surely we're all agreed that intelligence is a combination of genes and environment?

'However,' he went on firmly as the churchman raised a fluttery hand, 'I may tell you, Bishop, that even were it possible, even if I had before me the blueprint for beauty, for the creation of men and women of genius who would live to be a hundred, I wouldn't use it.'

'No?' The cleric's eyes popped open, a smile trembling on his lips. 'Oh, I'm so glad to hear you say that!'

'Absolutely not.' The chief executive solemnly shook his head. 'No. If we were to set foot on that path it would indeed, as you so rightly pointed out, be the first step on a terrible, terrifying road – that of eugenics. Be assured, Branium will *never* take that step, neither now nor in the future. We are devoted, Bishop, solely to the relief of human suffering. To that end we dedicate ourselves, mind, body and soul.'

There was a soft round of applause, in which the bishop, eyes now watering, joined in most loudly. Stockart, clapping too, looked over at the transformed, rather other-worldly face, the scraggy neck above the dog-collar, the shock of white, too long hair, and thought, not for the first time, how much he despised so-called men of conscience, who sat high on their golden clouds, and yet whose judgments were so malleable, like clay in a potter's hands.

There was a knock on the door.

'Come!' called out the chief executive, frowning.

His secretary peeped nervously in. 'I'm so sorry to disturb you. It's a message for Mr Stockart.'

Stockart's stomach tightened. He rose and crossed swiftly to the door. 'What is it?' he whispered.

'It's from your secretary, Mr Stockart.' Her breath tickled his ear. 'Dr West says he's got to talk to you right now.'

West, Stockart considered again, needed a staff to look after him – but that was impossible; he'd blab about something vital.

'John? Shall we adjourn for a few moments?' The chief executive asked.

'No, no.' West could wait; it would do him good.

Stockart turned back to the room. 'Sorry about that.' He resumed his seat.

Someone was being asked to repeat something. 'I said, it's all quite legal, of course?'

Stockart blinked. He stared at the speaker; the Professor of Venereology from a red-brick, south-coast university.

'Legal?' queried the legal director, and Stockart started to doodle on his sketch pad: a jagged pattern cutting up and down like a heart monitor.

'Yes, well . . .' A note of nervousness had crept into the professor's voice. He was a Seventies hippy who liked to be a rebel, even though Branium made healthy contributions to the running costs of his research laboratories. 'Legal' wasn't what he'd actually meant – of course not – but when John had said in his presentation that 'silent' trials were being conducted in Britain . . .

'Yes?'

'I just wondered if we were covering ourselves properly. In case of anything untoward occurring, and . . . and involving us in expenditure.'

The legal director consulted a document in front of him. He let a silence fall before looking up. 'This – ' he thumbed through the papers, making them whir like a fan – 'is the paperwork relating to our initial request to begin trials into Dr West's technique.'

'In Albania?' the professor quipped, and the jags on Stockart's page grew closer in and sharper, like spikes of hair.

'In Albania,' the lawyer agreed. 'I assure you that the legal requirements in Albania are every bit as stringent as our own. If you would care to have a look . . .' And he swivelled the file around and pushed it across the polished surface to face the professor.

'I don't speak Albanian, actually.'

'It's been translated.'

'Oh.' The professor shrugged. He flipped over a couple of pages. 'It all seems to be in order. Of course, one cursory look at it, like this—'

'You're quite at liberty to remain behind afterwards and read it. As is anyone else. You'll understand that we can't let it leave the premises, for reasons of security . . .'

'Absolutely,' the bishop echoed. 'Quite right. Most proper, if I may say so.'

'But it's here to be read by any of you at any time.'

Any interest – Stockart had seen it flicker on the faces of one or two of them – immediately died. There was nothing more likely to kill curiosity, he reminded himself, than allowing people open access. His doodle took on the appearance of waves.

The professor, seeing himself stranded, shoved the hair back out of his eyes and pronounced himself satisfied.

The lawyer smiled. 'Now, the Albanian system of controls concerning medical experimentation is, in fact, modelled exactly on our own. One of the most stringent – if not *the* most – in the world. As we're all aware, the research and development of a drug or treatment can take seven years or more . . .'

'Or considerably more,' the sales director grumbled.

'. . . and at any stage during that process a rival company can step in and pip us to the post, costing us millions, in terms of both R and D costs and lost revenue. Which is one of the reasons that the clinic in Albania was chosen for Dr West's pilot studies into the technique: its remoteness. It's a very long way from anywhere. I can personally vouchsafe for that.'

He cleared his throat. 'Now, as John briefly mentioned in his excellent presentation, the Infiltrator could not be patented here in the UK – it's a technique, not a drug, and UK patenting laws don't cover genetic techniques. So, while we were not – and are still not – aware that any of our rivals are on our trail, we didn't want to risk it.' He looked up. 'And the same holds true today, concerning the pilot study now underway at the Mistletoe. If we went through the customary channels, Dr West would have to present his findings before not one, but two regulatory bodies – one government and one local to the centre where the experiments were being conducted. Multi-disciplinary bodies, ladies and gentlemen, comprising of lawyers, ethicists, and,' he paused, 'geneticists from rival drugs companies.'

There were general noises of understanding. 'I see,' Stockart heard the woman on his left, a city analyst, murmur.

'No one is disputing the fact that Dr West is a brilliant scientist,' the legal director continued, 'but I think it's fair to say that he is not at his most confident in front of an audience, particularly when we have reason to believe that at least two of the members of the governmental body are, in the colloquial phrase, gunning for Dr West.'

'Professional jealousy?' the analyst asked.

'Exactly.' The lawyer beamed upon her. 'Our good fortune regarding Infutopin is, of course, our rivals' misfortune. Dr West's previous employer has shown particular bitterness, and one of the geneticists on the government regulatory body comes from that company.'

There was a general murmur of understanding.

'Plus – ' the lawyer steepled his fingers – 'I don't know how many of you are aware that there was a break-in at the Westminster premises of the government regulatory body last summer?'

Stockart studied his pen-nib.

'In the course of which,' the lawyer went on, 'data relating to the genetic experiments of two of our main rivals was stolen. That we find terribly worrying, especially when one considers the high likelihood that the break-in was orchestrated by another rival . . .'

'Surely not!'

'I'm afraid so, Bishop.' The lawyer nodded sadly. 'When our competitors cannot gain the information they require by fair means, they turn to foul. Do we really want to deliver Dr West's brilliant innovation into their hands?'

'Oh come on!' the analyst exclaimed. 'If they've had a break-in they'll be pretty hot on security now.'

'But why risk it when we don't have to? When we know that the technique works, that use of it fulfils every statutory regulation in the book, and that book exactly mirrors our own? You must know that we'd never go against the law of the land. When all that we're doing with the "silent" pilot study underway at the Mistletoe is allowing Dr West the extra time he wanted to re-run his technique, here, where he can closely monitor the babies' progress, and produce more data for the authorities when we do go public in the spring.'

'Won't these regulatory bodies come down on you – us,' the analyst corrected herself drily, 'like a ton of bricks for not getting permission from them in the first place?'

Stockart felt his stomach knot.

'Oh, I hardly think they'll be too harsh,' the lawyer said smoothly. 'Not when we can produce perfectly healthy baby boys as evidence.'

'I see.' The analyst cleared her throat. Stockart tensed. The rest of the room went suddenly quiet, awaiting her lead. 'You plan to use the children as proof of your pudding?'

'If necessary, yes.' The lawyer sounded bland. 'Why not? If, when we go public, we face criticism from the regulators or from anyone else, all we need do is show the before and after pictures of the Dystrophin production in the fetuses: before the treatment, the faulty gene that would've caused Duchenne's; afterwards, the perfect one. Who's going to complain? The parents?'

He paused for breath. No one spoke. Silently, Stockart came the closest he ever had to prayer.

'Of course not!' The lawyer suddenly thundered. 'They're going to say, "Thank you, Dr West!" And, "Thank God for Branium!"'

People were exchanging looks around the table. Stockart, catching a couple, kept his eyes down. He heard, for the first time and very loudly, the ticking of the clock on the wall above the fireplace.

'By doing it this way,' the lawyer continued more gently, 'we're not only accommodating Dr West's request, but we're guaranteeing the technique's security.'

'On that score . . .' The voice was not one that had been heard before. It belonged, Stockart saw in a sideways glance, to the other merchant banker, the one with silvery hair. 'Isn't it rather risky to have told us about the UK trials at all? I appreciate that you'd have had to have told us in the end, but why now?' He bent forward to see the lawyer better. Stockart saw him frown.

'Ah ha. I'm being thick, aren't I?' The banker nodded his head. 'Of course I am. You've waited till this stage because it's too late if we were going to complain, isn't it? Five babies have already been born, I think you said, Mr Stockart?'

He opened his mouth to agree, but the man had already moved on.

'So now, if our reaction to what you've told us was to go public, you'd handle things in the way you've just described, wouldn't you? Yes, it's true, bad babies made good, and here's the proof.' He cracked his knuckles and Stockart flinched. 'You've manipulated us in exactly the same way that you intend to manipulate the government regulatory bodies, the public, and even the parents, should they dare to complain.'

Stockart gazed at the man, saw the scars that long-ago acne had etched in his face. Could such an ugly man, even at this late stage, ruin everything?

'Manipulating?' The chief executive at the other end of the table sounded genuinely shocked. 'No one's manipulating you! You've been informed at the earliest opportunity, I assure you. You must appreciate the very high levels of security that have surrounded this project from day one. Why, until very recently most of my main board directors knew nothing about it. Only myself and two others were fully informed at every stage. I'm sorry if you feel ignored, but with a breakthrough like this—'

'The parents,' the banker interrupted. 'The ones in the Mistle-toe study. They're in the dark too, aren't they?' When he delivered a salvo, Stockart saw, he sat forward, rocking gleefully on his hands.

The chief executive was responding again in a troubled voice. 'Regrettably, yes. It was felt,' he pulled down his cuffs, 'that in order for Dr West to be allowed to work in privacy, and also to prevent him being deluged with pregnant DMD carriers, it was better to conduct the study silently . . .'

'Telling the parents that they were having the ordinary test for DMD, only that the results were much faster than normal?'

'Quite.'

'And that, for the purposes of research, would they mind having a blood-test . . .'

'Yes.' The chief executive's tone made it quite clear that he wished to move on now.

'. . . whereas in fact this blood-test was how Dr West discovered which fetuses were affected, which ones to go for with this Infiltrator thing.' The banker waved an impatient hand, and suddenly Stockart hated him full-throttle. 'And the parents, of course, are expecting CVS – so they're not the least bit suspicious, are they?'

Nineteen months before, one of West's research teams had make a breakthrough in pre-natal testing. They had discovered how to detect fetal abnormalities by means of a simple blood-test taken from the mother. It cut out the need for the intrusive and sometimes risky CVS and amniocentesis tests, and it had come at exactly the right moment for West: with it, he could secretly sample the mother's blood to see if she was carrying a DMD boy, then perform the 'mock' CVS, during which he inserted the Infiltrator. But the existence of the blood-test had to remain a secret.

Something snapped, and Stockart's head jerked up to see what it was. The chief executive set down two halves of his pencil. He closed his eyes as if in pain. 'I don't know what you want,' he said slowly. 'We've given these children, who would otherwise have been born with this awful disease, perfect life.' He opened his eyes and sighed. 'I admit it's unfortunate that we can't be upfront with the parents . . .'

The banker inhaled noisily.

'. . . for reasons that've already been explained to you. I don't actually see what we've got to apologise for.'

'Nor do I,' put in the bishop stoutly. Stockart blinked over at him. 'As our, er, friends say: a modern-day miracle. Yes. Quite.' He licked his dry lips. 'One does not question the provenance of miracles.'

'Let not the right hand . . . eh, Bishop?' asked the analyst.

'Quite.'

'This report that Mr Stockart mentioned,' the banker said.

'Yes?' murmured the lawyer.

'It sets everything out, I presume? It goes into detail about the trials in Albania?'

'Oh, yes. A great deal of detail. Isn't there, John?'

With an effort, Stockart pulled himself together. 'Indeed. One could even say too much.' His voice felt tight, as though a sharp stone had lodged in his throat. He swallowed carefully. 'All the scientific and medical data is there in appendices – rather inaccessible to the non-scientist like myself, I'm afraid . . .' He smiled deprecatingly. He felt steadier now that he was speaking. 'But you'll find the main body of the report very clear. It hasn't been written by Dr West.'

Several people laughed.

The banker said, 'In that case, I'm looking forward to reading it.'

Stockart stared. The man sounded quite mild.

The banker looked past him, fixing his gaze on the chief executive. 'As you say, it's a shame that the parents can't be informed, but,' he shrugged, 'quite understandable in the circumstances.'

There was a visible relaxing of tension, quite a babble of conversation, and Stockart heard the chief executive ask if they should have a show of hands. He did a double-take. The banker was chatting to the sales director, taking a sip of water, smiling round. What had happened to the suspicion, all that aggression? At that moment, the banker, raising his hand to vote, caught his eye. 'Great stuff, John boy,' he said.

'John, are you planning to vote?' The chief executive was smiling too, beaming from ear to ear. 'Good. That makes it a unanimous agreement by the full board for the UK trials.'

Everyone was smiling now. All the games had been played; the ordeal was suddenly over.

Stockart couldn't believe it.

'So when can we expect the report? I know there's been a bit of a delay.' The chief executive slid Stockart a glance. 'Typesetters or something . . .'

'Two or three weeks.' Stockart's mouth felt cold and numb. It was as if he was in shock, he thought – after all those months of preparing for this meeting, perfecting his presentation. 'At the latest.'

'Excellent. We look forward to it. Well, you'd better go and deal with whatever dire emergency awaits you.'

'Emergency?'

'Someone wanted you rather desperately, remember? One of your girlfriends, no doubt.'

On the way out, closing the door, he heard the chief executive say, 'John? Oh yes, he's completely brilliant, isn't he? We're so jolly luck to have him.'

And the numbness melted away, leaving him basking again in a warm glow as he descended the stairs to his office, to find out what Will West wanted now.

CHAPTER ELEVEN

Sasha stood in the white-tiled cubicle, letting the hot water drum down upon her head. She lifted her face to the shower-head. She adored power-showers, it was one of the best things the Americans had ever invented.

She grinned. She couldn't help herself. She felt the way she had when she was in the fifth form and the head-boy had phoned her up one evening and asked her out to dinner. She'd gone, even though she'd already eaten, and ordered the lightest thing on the menu – fish, which he'd been embarrassed by because it was also the cheapest – but hadn't been able to swallow a mouthful, neither then nor for days afterwards, because she hadn't needed food any more, she'd been so full up with him.

Of course it hadn't quite been like that with Charlie. The night before she'd managed three courses with ease, plus petit-fours and quite a quantity of wine. God, she thought, he must think me a pig – and she glanced down at her stomach, still reassuringly flat – but he hadn't seemed put off by her appetite in the least. Far from it, he'd been as reluctant as she to have the night end. After the meal they'd dawdled back through the covered market, lingering over shop windows; and it had been in front of the twee bookshop, with its bow-fronted windows and the permanent display of Dickens, that she'd felt his arm rest on her shoulders, so lightly that if she'd shown the slightest hesitation he'd have known instantly. But of course she hadn't. She'd moved closer in, and his touch had got surer, and by the time they had finally reached Floral Street they'd establish a rhythm, loping along like a pair of long-legged teenagers, not shying away when they touched but not yet daring to hold hands.

'Mush,' she muttered, finding the soap by touch and starting to use it vigorously. She was working a shift that day, starting at noon, and she was already on schedule to be late. 'Your brain's gone to mush. Mushy, sentimental . . .'

At the main door they'd both stopped. The lobby had been bathed in a golden glow, most welcoming. But once through that door, she'd thought, once into the lift, and there would come the questions of coffee or not, and whose apartment, if either, and was it too soon, and if she didn't, would he think she wasn't interested? And the whole terrifying prospect of saying or doing the wrong thing and wrecking everything.

'The Heathman does terrific nightcaps.'

'It does?' She'd glanced eagerly up – he was a good four inches taller, such bliss – to find him looking anxious.

'If you'd like one. Or maybe you'd rather—'

'Oh no. Let's.'

A brandy and several coffees later – and it had been much later – he'd taken her to her door, waited till she'd fished out her key, and kissed her on the mouth so gently, not much more than a brush of his lips against hers; not demanding, not expecting anything more. But the sensation – her body shivered at the memory and her fingers strayed to her mouth – had shot to the core of her: the urgent, hot need for him, sudden unbearable excitement, almost too much, followed immediately by a feeling, like a sigh, of deep physical contentment, a glimpse of the land of milk and honey.

That's the only thing she felt like eating, she thought dreamily now: milk and honey, the food of the gods. If she could hold that feeling for ever . . .

'Oh, hell.'

The telephone was ringing. How long it had been ringing she'd no idea; she only knew that with the bathroom door shut and the shower running she frequently didn't hear it at all.

'Hang on, hang on,' she called, leaping out of the cubicle and grabbing a towel as she ran. It would probably be the news editor, telling her to go straight to a job rather than come in – and if he didn't catch her he'd assume she was on her way, so when she turned up half an hour late he'd notice and think she was acting the grand dame. He was a sensitive soul, that news editor, and she was working for him again the next day . . .

It was still ringing. She snatched up the nearest extension, the one in the hallway.

'Yes?'

'Is that Sasha Downey?' A young voice, male, very nervous: no one that she knew. If this was some American Express promotion . . .

'I don't know if you'll remember me. I was at the demo at Shoreham.'

Shoreham, she thought wildly. Then she got it: live animal exports, someone dead under a lorry. A year or more ago, she'd covered a huge demonstration held to mark one of the anniversaries of the death. Little old ladies, bank managers, schoolchildren, and the police getting heavy-handed, dragging people off by the hair. Oh no, not now, she thought, she couldn't deal with a protester now. Why, in the first flush of freelance enthusiasm, had she been so profligate with her business cards?

'Look, this isn't a good time for me to talk. Give me your number and I'll call you back.'

'No.'

She did a double-take. 'What?'

'I'm in a phone-box.'

'Well . . .' She glanced at the clock on the wall; it was later than she'd thought. 'I can't talk to you now. I've got to go to work.'

'What, now?'

'Yes, I start at twelve o'clock.' If it's any business of yours, she added silently.

'But you've got to talk to me!'

She laughed indignantly. 'No I haven't!'

'But I tried you all last night!'

'Oh, it was you, was it?' In the early hours, after she'd floated back into the flat, closed the door and peered through the spy-hole, feeling a silly stab of disappointment that Charlie had already gone, she'd gone into the sitting room to find the answerphone flashing madly at her. Something wrong at home, she'd thought, her brain instantly clearing, or a problem with a story, or a fantastic assignment half-way across the world. But all the machine had yielded was a series of clicks, interspersed with the sounds of sniffs and sighing. 'You jammed up my machine, d'you know that?'

'I'm sorry, I didn't mean to.' He sounded very contrite.

'Well, OK.'

'And I meant to call you first thing, but I slept in.'

You and me both, she thought. The minute hand jumped again, and she remembered that she also had to iron a shirt. 'I'll give you a number where I'm going to be later.' Unless she got sent out. 'Or they'll certainly be able to get a message to me.'

'Please! Please don't go. You've got to help me!' He suddenly sounded so scared and young.

She sighed. She'd call in late, risk the sarcasm, the allocation of the dullest job on the schedule. 'Who *is* this? Hello? Are you still there?'

'Yes, I . . .' She realised he was trying not to cry. 'I'm . . . My name's Mike Pearce. From Tenterden. You interviewed me.'

She'd interviewed dozens of people at Shoreham, and had got some excellent interviews. The German magazine that had commissioned her had been very pleased. But a year later, to try and remember one face from among that crowd . . . She shivered and wrapped the towel more tightly around her, flicking wet hair out of her eyes. She'd wouldn't have time to dry it properly, she thought.

'I'm sorry, I can't quite place you.'

'You . . . you said I talked sense. It was me that told you about it all being down to economics. How it was cheaper for the farmers to export live lambs. How it was all down to profit margins, and how sick it was that we sent thousands of our own lambs to slaughter in terrible conditions and imported New Zealand lamb for the home market. Remember?'

Vaguely now, she recalled an earnest young boy spouting figures at her, enjoying showing-off. She frowned: he'd been *very* young. 'You were with a school, weren't you, Mike?'

'Yeah.' He sniffed. 'You know who I am now, right? I've got to talk to you about something . . . something, really . . . I dunno. I've got to meet you.' His voice was going all over the place; it couldn't have been long broken.

'OK. How about Monday morning? say about—'

'No! It's got to be today!'

'It can't be!' Her voice had risen too. Calm down, she told herself. 'I've just told you, I'm on my way to work.'

'You don't understand . . .'

He broke off again. Why, she asked herself, had she started this?

'They're going to kill me!'

'Hang on. No one's going to—'

'They've already killed Winston!' He took a shuddering breath. 'And I dunno about the others cause I left . . .'

'OK, take it easy.' She saw the minute hand of the clock move again. 'Who's Winston?'

Only gulping sounds came from the phone.

'Hello?'

'He's . . . We broke into these labs. He said it was research labs, you know, experimenting on animals. But it wasn't. I nicked this computer, a laptop. And now he's dead.'

Her head reeled. 'What did he die of?'

'Heart attack, the paper said.'

She counted to ten, exhaled slowly. 'How old was your friend, Mike?'

She heard the rustle of a newspaper. 'Forty-six, it says here.' Another pause. 'He looked older. He'd done time.'

'Ah.' Her hand was cramping. She swapped sides, took a handful of towel and started rubbing at her hair. 'Look, I know it's upsetting when a friend dies—'

'He didn't *just* die! I saw him being taken away!'

'Who by?'

No reply.

'Mike?'

'Two men and a woman. She . . .' Another pause. 'She looked at me. Her face . . . she's . . . She was the driver.'

Obviously the police. 'Did your friend know you'd taken the computer?'

'No.'

'OK. If he didn't know, he couldn't have told them, could he? So there's no way his heart attack could be related to what you'd done, could it?'

He made a non-committal sound.

'You've still got the computer, have you?'

'Yeah.'

'Well, maybe you ought to give it back. It might make you feel less guilty.' Sometimes she sounded like such a social worker. She pulled a face. Journalism could do that to a person.

'But s'pose they *did* kill him? They might kill me too!'

'Oh, come on.'

'You didn't see her. You didn't see what she was like. Mary said Andrew was really spooked too.'

Somewhere she'd lost the place. 'Who're they?'

'She's this girl, a kid really, in our group. Andrew's a teacher at her school. Kingsmere. He told her to go to his house for a meeting. He was really jumpy, she said. Weird.'

'He went on the raid?'

'Yeah.'

A school-teacher leading a band of pupils on animal rights raids? She raised an eyebrow. The tabloids would love that. Not that she was tempted – she knew how they'd treat the story – but sensitively handled, an interview with a young protester turned raider, from schoolboy to law-breaker . . . The teacher angle could be brought in too, but anonymously, no need to mention the man's name or the school. Yes, she thought, she could place that.

'You live in Tenterden, do you, Mike?'

'Near it.'

'Right. Well, I would like to talk to you. I'll have to hire a car . . .'

'I'm not there now.'

'Oh, where are you?'

'Brixton.'

Charlie, she thought automatically: that first meeting, the tingle when he'd touched her.

'What're you doing there?'

'I told you, I left.'

She closed her eyes. He'd run away from home. 'Er, Mike, how old are you?'

A pause to match her own. 'Eighteen.'

'Do your parents know where you are?'

'My mum does.'

'Oh, good.' That had sounded sincere enough at least. She didn't need to worry about him, she told herself, and Brixton was much easier. She wasn't even sure where Tenterden was. 'Look, Mike, how'd it be if we met up on Sunday afternoon?'

'Not today?' He only sounded disappointed now, not desperate. 'Or tomorrow?'

'No. I'm working.'

'Tonight? Or tomorrow night?'

'I'm going out tonight, and . . .' She caught herself. He didn't need to know that she was hoping to see Charlie the following night. 'Let's say two o'clock on Sunday,' she said briskly.

A heavy sigh. 'OK, then.'

'Where'd you know in Brixton?' Where did she know, come to that? 'How about the tube station?'

'Yeah. It's just down the road.'

'Good. I'll meet you at the entrance. What d'you look like?'

'Don't you remember?' He sounded hurt.

'Um, kind of. You've got brown hair, haven't you?' Generally the best bet, brown.

'Yeah.'

'And you're quite tall?'

'Yeah.'

'I'll be wearing a red jacket,' she said, 'and I've got long—'

'Dark brown hair. I remember you,' he said with emphasis.

'Oh. Good. I'll see you there, then. Two o'clock.'

She replaced the handset. Ten minutes had passed. The bits of hair that she'd towel-dried, she saw in the mirror as she passed, were sticking up in clumps. Growling, she grabbed her shirt and made for the kitchen and the ironing board. Crazy, she told herself, to have spent all that time talking to the boy. He was probably insane, had made up the whole story, or he wouldn't show on Sunday and she'd waste the afternoon finding it out. An afternoon which – who knows – she could have spent walking hand in hand with Charlie through Hyde Park.

The red light on the iron blinked off and she stamped it down on her collar. Immediately there was an angry hiss and a burning smell. Her only clean shirt now resembled an onion skin around the collar.

Swearing horribly, she stomped off to get dressed.

*   *   *

The story of Christopher Manyon's death was the lead item on West Kent Radio's *News at Noon*.

'A man who was being hunted by Tenterden police yesterday for dangerous driving, died in a car crash in Hastings early today.

'According to the police, Christopher Manyon, twenty-two, a rep for an agricultural feed company, had been found to have over four times the legal limit of alcohol in his blood . . .'

The radio was on in the office at the library, where Caroline Henshaw was eating her sandwiches when she heard it. Fortunately she was on her own, and fortunately her way of coping with shock was to become fiercely practical.

She telephoned the school to be told that Andrew was teaching and couldn't be disturbed. She lied easily, and they fetched him at once.

'M-m-mother?' He broke down. 'Oh God, Caroline, what happened?'

Sorry, she explained brusquely: his mother's death had been the first thought that had entered her head. She cut short his protestations by telling him about Chris.

'No, no, no,' he moaned. 'No, no—'

'Look, Andrew, we haven't got time for you to crack up. Tell the Head you've got to go home. She'll let you.'

'But, Caroline!'

'Andrew,' she hissed. 'D'you want to end up dead too?'

She could see that she would be better off on her own. Telling him to meet her at the leisure centre café at one o'clock, she scribbled a note for the senior librarian that she'd been called away – there was no point in bothering with excuses – and slipped out of the door unnoticed. On the pavement she hesitated. She needed to go home for their passports, but suppose the house was being watched? She saw the telephone box, stepped in and dialled her neighbour, then waited agonising minutes as the old lady shuffled off to check.

'No, dear. There's no strange cars outside. Were you expecting one?'

'No, no. Thank you.'

She slammed down the receiver and set off resolutely for home.

Through the rear-view mirror the driver could see all approaches to the house, and had still parked sufficiently far away not to arouse suspicion. She switched off the car's engine and prepared to wait.

The job was proving to be a messy one. She'd expected the first man to have given her the information, but he'd died too soon. The second one, the blubbering rep, had proved more cooperative, and she now had names and addresses. She hadn't been lying that morning when she'd told Bernard Hall that it wouldn't be long now.

There was movement in the street. Reflected in the mirror, someone was walking swiftly up to the house. Now they were opening the door. She had been right to think that some of them might go home for lunch.

'Okay,' she said quietly to the two men in the back seat.

Caroline had promised herself that she would be in and out of the house in a minute. She knew exactly where the passports were – in the middle drawer of the bureau in the hall. But having stuffed them into her bag, she thought that she must take something else, something valuable that she could sell if necessary.

The house seemed very empty, waiting for her to decide. The door to the main reception room stood open, and she remembered the previous night's meeting: Lucas saying how Manyon had probably just gone on the piss. How horribly right he had been! She bit her lip; she did not have time to dwell on such matters.

Her mother's wedding ring, gold, and portable. It was in her jewellery box upstairs. It wouldn't take her a moment.

She actually had her hand on the ring when the doorbell rang. She twitched open the net curtain but could see no strange car outside. It would be her neighbour, of course; she must have seen her come in. Shoving the ring into her bag, Caroline galloped downstairs. She wouldn't give the old woman a chance to detain her. Ready for her dash past, not even bothering to check through the frosted glass, she pulled open the front door.

Andrew Henshaw had bought himself a cup of instant tomato soup from the vending machine. Now he regretted his choice. When he'd arrived he'd felt like soup, something warm and soothing, but the first sip had burnt his mouth. He told himself that he could always get something else, but he felt too apathetic to move.

He wrinkled his nose. The café was steamy and stank of chlorine. It doubled up as the spectator's gallery for the swimming pool below, but at lunchtime during term-time, there were few people viewing. Nothing for him to look at, to take his mind off things.

He glanced at his watch: five minutes to one. Only a little longer and Caroline would be there and everything would be all right. She had said she had things to do. What things? he wondered suddenly. He had the car outside; they both carried credit cards. What could she be doing? A terrible thought came to him: that she had decided to leave him, that she was less visible on her own. He could imagine her thinking it, carefully weighing up the pros and cons of staying with him – they'd been married twelve years; he knew what she thought of him – and suddenly he was sure that was what she had done.

Or else . . . or else she'd been caught by the three people that Mike had seen take Gerry: government people, he was sure of it now. He trembled. My God, why hadn't they run the previous night? But that morning, when everyone had called the house at eight as planned, it had seemed that everything was going to be all right. He'd thought they'd been overreacting, feeding off each other's fears. Even his virus scare had struck him as rather unlikely.

That had been then. Now he felt very peculiar, floaty, his forehead clammy, his pulse racing. Was it symptoms or shock? He moaned. He couldn't cope with it all on his own.

One o'clock. Caroline had not told him what to do if she failed to appear. He moaned again, slightly louder, but no one heard him. He stared straight ahead at the stairs and at that exact moment he saw a head appear, looking right and left, searching. Caroline! He could have wept. He half-stood, raising a hand like a flag, then he saw that she was not alone, that a man came half a pace behind her.

Before signalling right on to the Dungeness road, the woman

checked her rear-view mirror. On the back seat, her passenger sat still as death between the two men.

It was strange, she mused, how most of the time, after minimal struggle, people came quietly. Was it a hope that by obeying orders they would not be harmed? Or was it despair, knowing that there could be no escape? Or was it – she smiled slightly – simply the English trait of not wanting to cause a fuss? My God, if it was her, how she would fight! How she would scream and kick.

The road through the marsh was nearly empty: a few farm trucks and vans; no tourists this late in the year. In the last week she had come to know the area quite well. A bleak place, with its flatness below the road and the endless sheep grazing on the boggy land. But it had a beauty too, owed largely to that very bleakness, and a sort of strength, it being an act of defiance that it existed at all, strained as it was from the sea, the canals and little dykes rimming the fields like Holland.

The turning lay just up ahead. This one – she glanced in the mirror again – should not be too difficult. This one, she could tell from the eyes, thought that her presence betokened mercy: a woman, a mother-figure, a nurturer and protector of life.

'Is there any need to kill them all?' the client had demanded of Hall that morning. And he'd only sounded half-convinced, Hall had told her, when he'd said yes, that his team needed to protect themselves, not leave witnesses to go running off to the police.

The client wanted his computer back, not a trail of dead bodies littering the countryside. 'Someone might put two and two together. Ever thought of that?'

Just leave it to his people, Hall had soothed, they were professionals. The best.

The sign appeared, and she signalled right once more, on to the track that led to the disused military buildings.

'They've got Lucas.'

Andrew stared at Caroline's white face, at the small green eyes boring into his. Very determined she looked, and rather fierce. Sometimes he wished she was a bit softer, more girlie.

'Did you hear what I said?'

He nodded, aware that she expected more of him, but not sure what. He felt confused and rather put out. He had held himself together, as she had told him, had waited there patiently for her to arrive – and then she had walked in, late, with Stuart Richley.

Stuart looked glazed. 'Lucas called me. He'd heard about Chris on the radio at work. He said he was going home and I should get everyone round to his place. I tried the library first, but they told me Caroline had gone home so I went round. She said we'd better ring Lucas to tell him to meet here instead.' He paused, this big son of a policeman who had his own gun and knew how to use it, and wiped the moisture from his face, running it back into his hair. 'So I did. I called. He answered, and then the doorbell went.'

A shudder shook him. 'I had this feeling. I shouted, "Don't answer it!" but he'd already gone. They . . . I could hear . . .'

Watching curiously, Andrew saw the big shoulders start to shake, then the head dropped forward and the whole top half slumped as Stuart was racked with sobs.

'It's all right, Stu.' Caroline patted his shoulder. She looked round. 'Sssh. Come on, we've got to be strong.' She shot Andrew a look over his head. 'We've got to get Mary.'

'Why?'

'Don't be stupid. They know who we are. They went to Clive's home. Chris must've given them his name and address, and we've got to assume he's told them everyone's. It was just Clive's bad luck that they got to him first.' She took a deep breath. 'So – what's the best way to get her out of school?'

Andrew frowned, unprepared for this sudden demand. There was so much he didn't want to think about. 'Get her out of . . . ?' he echoed.

'God, Andrew, you're hopeless.' Caroline got up. 'Look after him. I'm going to phone.'

The afternoon secretary was not exactly pleased to have her routine disrupted – but then, she reasoned, she was a mother herself, and she could hear the worry in the other woman's voice. She consulted the timetable on the notice-board.

'She's in double-French, dear. I can get a message to her to call you . . . Oh, I see.' Ridiculous, she thought, how in this day and age employers still wouldn't let their staff receive incoming calls.

The mother babbled on. She really did sound upset. The secretary sighed. The classroom was at the other end of the building.

'Very well, dear. If you wait, I'll fetch her.'

CHAPTER TWELVE

It felt, Stockart thought, as if an ice-worm had got into his intestines and was now working its way down to the pit of his stomach.

'Are you absolutely sure?' he asked Will West quietly.

'Of course I'm sure.' A long, trembling sigh. 'What do you take me for?'

You don't really want to know, Stockart thought, surveying the bowed, shaking figure in the chair opposite.

Leukaemia. Leukaemoid picture. Those words should never have been uttered. Never. Especially not there, in his office, on the same day, within the same hour that he'd won the full backing of the Board.

'I did everything right, everything,' West was saying now. 'I just can't understand. He was fine at six weeks. It doesn't make sense!'

The worm twisted inside Stockart. 'You said the pathologist's comment was "query Leukaemia"?'

A tremor shook West's frame. 'Yes.'

'Then there's still the possibility—'

'No, there fucking isn't!'

West didn't normally swear. Ridiculously, for a moment, Stockart was shocked.

'I know what I'm looking at.' West's face was pink. Of course,

Stockart reminded himself, the doctor wasn't actually the timid creature his appearance suggested. He wanted to be another Einstein.

'The hospital's already rerun the tests. They're the same. Haemoglobin's eight, and the white cell count . . .' he quavered. 'You can look if you like, it's on DAMR.'

The worm twisted again. 'Is there any possibility,' Stockart said slowly, 'that this is a coincidence? You said yourself he's older than the other kids.'

West looked up and stared, but said nothing.

'I know that any suggestion of Leukaemia would automatically lead us to suppose—'

'He's two weeks older, and the symptoms are the same.' West spoke dully. His eyes had taken on a faraway expression. 'The incidence of Acute Lymphoblastic Leukaemia in babies this young is extremely rare. And in light of our previous experience . . .'

The worm froze.

In the mountains of the northernmost part of Albania, where that country adjoins Montenegro, seventy miles from the Albanian capital, was an excellently endowed medical centre, the Same World Hospital. As with the Mistletoe in London, so the Same World was owned and run by Branium Pharma UK.

It was the only modern building within miles. Beside it was a small airstrip and a landing pad for a helicopter, but no roads led to it, only tracks running to the surrounding scattered villages. Branium had bought the land in 1991 when the country was still, just, under communist control. A year later, when that regime fell and inflation soared to one hundred and fifty per cent, the hospital had become a lifeline to the thousand or so inhabitants – no one knew exactly how many – of the mountains. From it they received food-packages, vitamins and medicines, free of charge, as well as medical treatment.

The mountain people, the poorest of the poor, many of them illiterate, their lifestyles unchanged for centuries, could only marvel at the Western bounty. They walked for days to reach the place, and the hospital became firmly established in the local minds as a haven, as well as their only medical centre. The people were pleased, indeed proud, when asked to supply details of their extended family trees, to describe the illnesses that they or their relatives had suffered from, to undergo a few routine tests. And that had been how, within three months of the hospital opening its doors, the database had been formed.

It exceeded the team's expectations, confirming all the preliminary studies – which, in their turn, gave credence to a strange little paper, written by an Albanian doctor in the fifties and presented to a conference of Eastern bloc scientists. In it he'd referred to the 'mountain people' of northern Albania, who produced an abnormally high number of physically handicapped children, all of whom died before adulthood. The paper was quickly suppressed and the doctor and his family dispatched to work in the mines for bringing shame to the nation – officially, there were no handicapped children in Albania.

The paper subsequently lay unread for over thirty years until, with the collapse of communism across Europe, the medical archives were opened up for the first time. A Branium researcher trawling through the records in Berlin had selected the paper, from among hundreds of others, as being of potential interest, and sent a photocopy of it back to the UK. There, one of the company's doctors became quite excited; she was convinced that the symptoms sketchily described by the Albanian doctor, were identifiable as the blood disease Thalassaemia, and Duchenne's Muscular Dystrophy – both genetically inherited, life-shortening conditions. If she was right, she insisted, then a study of the mountain people might provide invaluable research material for the company. She was immediately given the go-ahead to conduct a preliminary field study, and the evidence of her eyes – the waddling gait of the little boys, the weak, anaemic toddlers – was quickly confirmed by blood-tests. How many DMD and Thalassaemia cases there were, she couldn't tell, but in one village alone there'd been eleven affected families.

That study had been conducted at the beginning of 1991. By then Will West had been with the company for three years. He'd done a great deal of work in his research laboratories, he'd perfected the technique – now he needed to put it into practice. Stockart had consulted with the chief executive and the legal director. To conduct clinical trials in the UK would mean a massive amount of red tape coupled with the ever-present risk of espionage – unnecessary, surely, when there was Albania waiting for them.

The latest statistics revealed that, within the region, the incidence of DMD was one in every twenty-eight boys; of Thalassaemia, one in thirty-seven children. Staggering figures when placed alongside the average: DMD, one in 4,000 boys; Thalassaemia one in 4,000 births.

'I'd call it a heaven-sent opportunity,' the legal director had said.

'I couldn't agree more.' The chief executive had smiled. 'You've got the green light, John. Go ahead.'

The hospital was built in four months. The team already knew the families they wanted. In the unrest of 1992, the twice-weekly · delivery of food-parcels ensured that those families were contacted, and so the database was established. When West had arrived there towards the end of that year, there were twenty-six women of child-bearing age, known DMD carriers, waiting for him.

When the first batch didn't work, when the embryos had all miscarried within days of treatment, West had been shaken. But almost at once he'd announced that he knew where he'd gone wrong, and he wanted to have another go. This time, instead of injecting into the chorion, he'd try the umbilical cord directly.

'Whatever you say,' Stockart had said.

There had been fewer miscarriages that time, and those that had occurred, had been later on. Most of the babies had gone full-term. Two had been stillborn, but the others had been live at birth. Some had looked fine, had even briefly thrived, but between the ages of four to six weeks, all had developed Leukaemia.

SWii Syndrome, they'd called it. SW for Same World, ii for the second trial. The Leukaemia had galloped through the tiny bodies, and within twelve weeks all the children had died. The Albanian parents had trusted the medical team to the end, pathetically grateful for the reassurances that their sons had not suffered unduly. The whole project had been put on hold. West himself had retreated into the suite of laboratories that formed the entire upper floor of the hospital.

Two years later he had emerged like a butterfly. He had identified the problem. Stockart still remembered that telephone call. All that West had done was to misplace the Infiltrator by a fraction.

'You see, rather than placing it into DNA junk . . .'

'Sorry?'

West had tutted, then laughed. Stockart hadn't remembered

ever having heard him laugh before. He'd sounded like a young man. 'Sorry, I forgot. Ninety per cent of the human DNA is rubbish, junk. I've told you that before, haven't I? That's where the Infiltrator's got to go, so it doesn't interfere with anything else, and that's obviously where I thought I'd put it, but I made a mistake. I put it into the beginning of another gene.'

Hence the havoc and disintegration. But now, West had assured him, he knew better. One more try – and Stockart, noting the sudden hint of pleading, and pleased to hear it, had agreed.

The babies had been born – perfect.

At four weeks, at eight – perfect.

Those nine Albanian boys were now aged between a year and fourteen months. The good gene was present and functioning well, they had no health problems, and they were continuing to develop absolutely normally.

Stockart's worm twisted. Because of those children he'd convinced himself and the chief executive and the legal director to go ahead with the Mistletoe study. The three of them had been the first to get excited by the before-and-after DNA story, the perfect child produced by the Infiltrator – by Branium – from imperfect material.

Stockart gazed into the mid-distance. The plans they'd had! Each egging the other on. Babies to order; babies by Branium. Babies that parents would pay anything for. Babies whose genetic print-out had been pre-planned – 'bad' genes excised, 'good' ones put in. Children who'd never have cancer, who could live without that fear; children whose intelligence had been genetically enhanced; whose beauty, height – weight, even – had been pre-programmed before they'd even been born.

In retrospect, he thought suddenly, there'd been warning signs with the Mistletoe study. There'd been two fairly recent miscarriages, Subjects Eleven and Fifteen. West had tried to dismiss them, saying such things occurred naturally, but he'd sounded a fraction too confident, Stockart thought now, as if he'd been trying to convince himself.

But then, nine weeks and two days before, the first boy had been born and he was perfect, then the second, the third . . . They'd held their breath – or at least Stockart had – as the first one had entered the danger-zone of between four weeks and six weeks old, but he'd emerged with flying colours on the other side.

Stockart and West had actually got drunk together that night, in the same office where they sat now, not on the upright desk chairs but lounging on the two leather sofas at the other end of the room, feet up on the table, topping up each other's glasses like two good old drinking buddies.

'The dreamers of dreams,' Stockart remembered himself saying, and West, 'the realiser of dreams'. He'd been feeling quite emotional.

'It's a bloody miracle, Will. You're a bloody genius.'

'Thanks.' West had been slurring his words by then. They both had. 'Give me the genes and I'll give you the babies.'

The chief executive had been almost beside himself. He'd seized Stockart by the hand and pumped hard. There'd been tears in his eyes. 'John, I've got to hand it to you. There were times when I thought this thing wasn't going to come off. But you've proved me wrong. My warmest congratulations, my very deepest thanks – and please convey the same to Will West.'

'Bloody nice one, John,' the legal director had echoed.

Then the chief executive had cleared his throat. 'We'll need a report for the Board. No mention, of course, of any of the unfortunate events.'

'Absolutely.' The legal director had nodded somberly. 'All references to SWii Syndrome to be removed.'

'And a sanitised version of the first trial as well. Say, just a couple of the miscarriages?'

'Sure,' Stockart had agreed. 'Two sounds about right.'

'And then lots and lots of emphasis on the lovely Swii batch.'

The chief executive had picked up a slim folder, and out had come several large black and white photographs of the healthy Albanian boys. He'd selected two and handed them to Stockart. 'We'll put these in. Nothing like pictures of bouncing babies to warm the cockles of the heart.'

He'd paused. 'While we're at it, we'd better get someone to rewrite West's notes as well. I don't suppose he'd do it himself?'

Stockart had shaken his head. 'Afraid not.'

'What – on ethical grounds?'

'Not so much that.' Stockart had smiled. 'It's the way he operates.

Very meticulous; everything has to be exact. He wouldn't be able to invent them.'

'Tiresome of him. But you can find someone who would?'

'Not within the company,' the lawyer had interjected.

'No, indeed.' The chief executive had cracked his knuckles.

'Someone, obviously, that we can trust.'

Stockart had nodded seriously. 'There *is* someone I've heard of. He's—'

'Fine, fine.' The lawyer had broken in. 'Keep the name to yourself, eh? Let not the right hand . . . Remember?'

And so Stockart had instructed Colin Davenport, a man whom, in fact, he'd hired two months before in expectation of giving him that very task. Davenport was a rewrite man, a consummate camouflager who went under the title of 'management consultant', and who was known as possessing the freshest, fastest, most exciting talent in the business, as well as being extremely discreet.

Davenport was only twenty-nine years old. His earnings had shot up overnight. One might have expected fast cars, penthouses, girls, a potentially dangerous, flashy lifestyle – but no. The sole outlet for his newfound wealth was a seventy-nine-year-old woman who lived in a damp basement flat, an old woman who walked painfully on two sticks, whom Davenport visited every other day, plus an outing on Sunday: his grandmother.

An unusual young man, Bernard Hall had reported back, and Stockart had agreed – most odd. But any security threat?

'None, in so far as one can say that about anyone.'

Davenport had been bought. His talent was at Stockart's disposal; his expense justified. Certainly the rewrite he'd done on West's notes had been excellent: seamless, and far easier to understand than the original. He'd been allegedly within two days of finishing the report itself, well ahead of schedule, when he'd gone home without even shutting the door, leaving it all behind him on that desirable, portable little computer.

All that, and now this. Stockart felt briefly sick. He knew the chances were now good for the computer to be found, but in light of West's latest news that particular nightmare seemed to have receded. Probably, he thought, Davenport had been right all along: no one would be able to get past the security system that he'd programmed into the software. A different system for every job, Davenport had told him on the day he'd hired him, and he'd given him a demonstration, there and then, on the screen.

Amazing, Stockart had thought. What an amazing mind.

The owner of the other amazing mind was still mumbling away to himself like a wino on the Embankment '. . . in her voice? No. It was something in the eyes . . .'

No help from that quarter, Stockart told himself grimly.

The worm, that had seemed to die, woke suddenly and bit like steel, bringing Stockart's mind back to the present. He gasped.

'What did you say?' West raised his head wearily.

'Nothing.'

It was all going to be left up to him to sort out, as it always was. He'd barely got half a sentence out about the burglary before the legal director had silenced him.

'We're sure you can sort it out, John.'

'We're relying on you,' the chief executive had added with a steely smile. 'We know you won't let us down.'

They didn't want to know; they'd dumped it all on him and washed their hands, not letting their right hands know . . . Stockart's stomach twisted and he felt his strength drain.

He took a slow, deep breath, fought his way back to the surface. He needed to prioritise, to assemble the facts.

If the SWii Syndrome ran its normal course, the baby could die at any moment; it would almost certainly be dead by January, which was when the next full board meeting was scheduled. At that meeting he'd be handing out copies of Davenport's report – the man was working on it night and day; it would undoubtedly be ready by then – nicely printed, neatly bound. He could see it in his mind's eye: the photographs, the medical data, the appendices and footnotes and not one single mention of Leukaemia. So that when, sadly, he announced the death of one of the Mistletoe boys, no alarms would sound. It would be a tragedy, especially for the parents – he could hear himself saying the words – a bitter blow indeed . . .

'This is a tragic coincidence,' he said out loud. It sounded good, most convincing. Suddenly he believed it himself.

'What?' West blinked up.

'A one-off.'

'But, John—'

'You said it yourself. Leukaemia in babies this age is very rare. We've been unfortunate, that's all.'

'But he's one of the oldest! You know the others will develop—'

'I don't know that!' Stockart felt a shot of anger. He'd sorted things out, and now West was complaining. 'And neither do you! We can handle one out of eighteen, OK?'

West's head wobbled on his thin neck. He reminded Stockart of a dandelion clock, ready to be blown away.

'We'll monitor the others, cross that bridge if and when we come to it. OK?'

The old man trembled. His silence, his presence, was abruptly more than Stockart could bear.

He stood up. 'I've got things to be getting on with, Will, as I'm sure you have.'

West rose slowly. He seemed unable to take his eyes off Stockart. 'I'll let you know when . . . if there's any more,' he whispered, his hand on the door.

'You do that.' Stockart pulled a pile of papers towards him, picked up the top one, and busied himself with it until he heard the click of the closing door.

The large cameraman stepped back heavily on to Sasha's foot.

'Ow!'

'Sorry, love, I didn't see you there.' But the words had a practised ring, and he made no attempt to let her back in. She glared at his vast frame for a moment, then resentfully moved herself.

From her new position to the side of the cramped media enclosure she had a view of a great deal of mould spreading out along one wall, and a long, dark corridor signposted: 'X-Ray', 'Pathology', 'Physiotherapy'.

This, she told herself, had to be the down-side to being a freelance journalist. One agreed to do a couple of shifts to help out a short-staffed news editor – because one had heard that he was about to be appointed as features editor to the Sunday supplement and, in spite of being a moody bastard, the supplement had loads of space to fill and the rates were brilliant – and due to an unforeseen hold-up one arrived late and took the brunt of the man's warped sense of humour. He'd been grinning as he'd given her the assignment: Philippa Tyler going walkabout inside St Peter's

Hospital, showing the media the empty wards that would soon be filled with happy, grateful IVF/Infutopin patients.

'We've got it marked down as a picture caption only,' the news editor had told her. 'But I know that someone of your calibre, with your insights into the Minister, will be able to produce something much better than that. Oh, and by the way,' he'd paused and pointed at her collar, 'you've burned your blouse. Did you know?'

Sasha grimaced. He'd be lucky to get his picture caption, she thought. The term 'walkabout' had been optimistic. St Peter's, having stood empty for almost a year and not having been properly maintained for several years prior to that, was not in any state to receive visitors. Windows had been smashed, the roof leaked and some floors were in a state of collapse. The whole place reeked of damp and decay. The press, on their arrival, had found themselves coralled into a small roped-off space between the elevators and the padlocked entrance to a ward.

Philippa stood there now, along with the Mistletoe's administrative officer and a surly-looking man in a hard hat who was in some way connected with the proposed renovation.

To give her her due, Sasha thought, craning her neck to see, Philippa was conducting the sad little affair with aplomb.

'One can just see, one can imagine all too clearly what this place is going to look like in three months' time.'

'Sure can,' murmured a photographer beside Sasha.

'Bomb-site,' muttered someone else, a little too loudly.

Philippa didn't appear to hear. She turned, smiling, to the Mistletoe's administrative officer. 'Now, I know that you've already got some great ideas for this floor. You were telling me about a carpeted reception area here, with some nice potted plants . . .'

Sasha realised she was coming her way.

'. . . and here there will be consultation rooms, with a small side-ward, and then what was the phsyio department could be knocked through into the pathology labs, creating at least two theatres and providing a spacious working environment for the embryologists.'

The administrative officer looked dazed, but he managed a nod.

'Most exciting,' Philippa went on. 'Terrific potential.' She was winding up. 'Thank you all so much for coming.'

Philippa smiled in the general direction of the pack, then her eyes alighted on Sasha. She stepped forward.

'My dear!'

Oh no, Sasha thought, feeling herself redden. Around her, people who'd been starting to pack up, stopped.

'What a terrific piece in *Comment!* Such a gifted young writer. You must be so pleased.' Her brown eyes were sparkling with what looked like pleasure. Perhaps she *is* totally genuine, Sasha thought, confused.

'And I absolutely adored "Queen of the Genes". A bit cheeky, but so eye-catching! Who thought it up?'

'Um . . .' Sasha gazed down at her boots. 'I did actually.'

'*You* did? What a clever girl you are!'

Behind her, someone sniggered.

'But what are you doing here? I didn't realise they sent writers to cover these little affairs.'

Careful, Philipppa, Sasha thought. These people can be vicious if slighted.

'I was keen to see the practical side of your plan,' she said. Weak, she thought, but Philippa didn't seem to think so.

She nodded, beaming. 'Were you? Perhaps you'll come back when it's finished. So nice to meet a dedicated journalist. Keep up the good work,' and she turned away.

'Minister?' A boy's voice piped up. Sasha looked round at the young radio journalist who'd been standing next to her.

'Yes, dear?'

'I . . . I wonder if I could just have a few words with you, in a sort of one-to-one . . .'

'But I've finished now, dear.'

'But you see I'm . . . I'm from Inner London Youth radio . . .' His voice suddenly broke with nerves, and Philippa took pity.

'Very well, just a couple of minutes,' and she launched again into the speech about Branium's brilliance, the Age of the Gene, and how exciting it all was, like landing a man on the moon.

She could have been hearing it all for the first time, Sasha thought, preparing to go.

'Or when nuclear power was first discovered,' suggested the boy, greatly daring.

'I–I'm sorry, Minister. I didn't mean to interrupt.'

Sasha stared. Something in Philippa's face had slipped. There was a look on it now, something raw – the way that she was looking at the boy, as if she was actually afraid. But that made no sense, Sasha thought, none at all.

Philippa regained her composure quickly. 'Yes, I suppose so. Now, I want to show how much we in Britain appreciate a company like Branium . . .'

Sasha caught up with the others on the staircase.

'Hullo, it's Tyler's pet.'

'Who's a clever girl, then?'

But she wasn't listening. Her mind was replaying what had just occurred. Then, for no reason she could think of, she heard again Mike Pearce's voice in her head, breaking – as that other boy's just had – when he'd begged her to see him that day.

It was four o'clock on Friday afternoon. Sunday afternoon seemed a long time ahead – and suddenly, irrationally, she knew she was afraid for him.

CHAPTER THIRTEEN

'Police.'

'I can see that. What d'you want?'

'It's about Michael, Mrs Pearce.'

'Mikey!' Liz Pearce clutched her cardigan about her. 'What about him? Is he all right?'

'He's fine as far as we know. But we'd like to talk to him. May we come in?'

'No you may not.'

That stopped them in their tracks, she saw with satisfaction. Eighteen months before, Liz Pearce would have described herself as a supporter of the police. She would probably even have subscribed, she admitted, to the notion of the local bobby administering a clip round the ear to young vandals. But that was before Mikey had come back from Shoreham with a gash over one eye, black and blue from where they'd hit and kicked him. And him only a kid of fifteen!

They stood there on her doormat, the big heavy man and the pretty woman officer, looking at each other. Then the woman said, 'We only want to talk to him, Mrs Pearce. If you could tell us where he is . . .'

'What d'you want to talk to him for?'

The woman cleared her throat daintily. She really was lovely to look at, Liz thought: big, dark eyes, nicely made-up. Hard to imagine someone like that beating up kids, but the WPCs had been some of the worst, Mikey had told her. 'We believe that your son may have been involved in a burglary.'

'Burglary!' She laughed out loud. Then her face grew hard. 'Mikey's never been involved in any trouble in his life, I'll have you know. He's a good lad. Even after what you lot did to him at that rally!'

'Rally?' the man queried.

'The memorial rally at Shoreham. You remember! Don't play the innocent with me! Thirty people taken to hospital.'

'The animal export demo?' he hazarded.

'Oh, clap clap! Hole in one!' She saw that her neighbour – an elderly, fussy man, washing his car as he always did on Saturday mornings – had stopped to stare at the scene on her doorstep. Let him, she thought defiantly.

She glowered at the two before her. 'So, you're going to trump up some charge against my Mikey, are you? He told me that's what you did. Worked your way through the protesters, trying to pin something on each one. Taken you this long with my son, has it?'

'Mrs Pearce . . .' The woman smiled sorrowfully. 'Truly, this has nothing to do with that rally. We have reason to believe that your son may have been part of the group that's gone missing.'

'What group?'

They looked at each other, then carefully at her. 'You haven't heard the news? It's been on the local radio this morning. About the school-teacher and the girl. There's four of them that've gone missing.'

'No I haven't! I've only just got up. I work nights, see.' She frowned. 'You're saying that this group's done a burglary? A school-teacher? Likely isn't it?' She laughed again, loudly. 'Don't suppose this school-teacher was at Shoreham too, was he?'

'Now, now, Mrs Pearce. The burglary was a very serious one, and there's strong evidence to link this group—'

'Like hell!' she hissed. 'I've wasted enough time on you two and your accusations. Mike's not gone off with any group, if it's any business of yours! He's staying in Brixton with his brother!'

'When are you expecting him back?'

'When he's bloody good and ready to come home, that's when!'
Liz felt the blood rush up into her face. She had a legendary temper,
and if these two weren't careful . . . She took a step towards them.
'I want you both off my doorstep this minute!'

They stepped back, but the woman said, 'If you'd just let us
have an address for him . . .'

'Piss off out of it!' She looked up. Her neighbour's eyes were out
on stalks. 'And that goes for you too, you old git!'

She slammed the door so hard that the flimsy frame shook, then
leaned against it, fighting to control herself. How dare they! As
if life wasn't hard enough, and as if Mikey wasn't a son that any
mother would be proud of! A burglary! She snorted and moved
down the hall into the kitchen.

His note lay on the side where he had left it on Thursday night.
'Gone up to see Dave. I'll call tomorrow.' And he had, yesterday
morning, to say that he was fine and he had just felt the need to
see his brother. He did that sometimes – took off to spend a couple
of days with Dave. Liz didn't mind. On the contrary, she thought
it was nice that the boys got on so well. It meant Mikey losing a
day's college, but they all did that at his age; it was nothing to
worry about.

She took a cigarette out of the box and lit it. Then she switched
on the radio.

'The fifteen-year-old girl went missing yesterday afternoon after
a woman, posing as her mother, lured her from Kingsmere school
in Tenterden. Mary Kennedy of Hazledene Avenue . . .'

Mary Kennedy! Liz gasped. She knew Mary! Mike had been
trying to summon up courage to ask her out for over a year. Not,
Liz thought privately, that Mary was much to write home about –
undersized and pinched. But if Mikey liked her . . .

She blinked. Why, Mary had been there to see Mike only a
couple of nights ago! She remembered the girl coming in, sitting
at the kitchen table, and Mike making her coffee; neither of them
saying much, obviously waiting for her to leave for work.

She sat down suddenly. Could there be any connection with the
girl's disappearance and Mike going off? But no – the radio was
saying that Mary had last been seen yesterday afternoon, a day after
Mike had gone.

She inhaled deeply and blew out a smoke ring in relief. The girl's poor parents! She didn't know them – they lived in Tenterden – but she could imagine what they must be going through. And Mike – if he knew, he'd be worried sick about her.

She wondered if he'd heard the news up there in Brixton, if it had reached the national networks. If it had, surely he'd call her about it – and then, Liz thought, she could warn him about the police being after him. She chewed a nail. If only she could call him. But Dave had no phone in his flat. She remembered stories about people being framed, sent to prison and left rotting for years. Perhaps Mike ought to have a solicitor.

She stood up and made herself a cup of coffee. There was no use worrying about things, she thought, sighing. Mike would be back by the following night – he wouldn't miss a second day's college on Monday – and she could discuss it with him then. With any luck, Mary Kennedy would have turned up by then too. Safe and well, Liz prayed suddenly, closing her eyes and crossing herself.

People did such terrible things to kids nowadays.

'What d'you think?' McMahon asked.

'She was telling the truth.'

They'd removed their caps and jackets as they'd got into the car. (The woman's blouse was not immediately identifiable as being part of a police uniform.) As they turned out of the Pearces' road, McMahon took off his tie and undid the top button of his shirt.

'She's not going to tell us any more.'

'Not willingly, no.'

She took the main road back to town. On the outskirts they passed a large brick building in front of which were several marked police cars. 'That's the school,' McMahon said.

She drove into Waitrose's car park and stopped. It was almost noon on Saturday and the place was teeming with families and trolleys. They were of interest to no one, but as a precaution she pulled on a jumper over the blouse.

'We're going to need someone watching the house to see when she goes out.'

'Right. What about the neighbour? The old man she shouted at?'

She considered briefly. 'No. Too much of a risk. There's too many uniforms about.'

Earlier that morning, on their way through the town, they'd seen
a house-to-house in progress. All their efforts must now be centred
on finding the boy.

'We'll give her a couple of hours. If she hasn't gone out by then
we'll think again.'

Mike sat alone in his brother's flat, trying hard to concentrate on
the football on television. But he couldn't; life had become too
unpredictable for relaxation. He felt hot and sweaty. He gazed
around the room where he had spent the previous two nights.
It was sparsely furnished, the carpet worn through in places.
Along one wall there were book-shelves supporting a few CDs,
no books.

Dave didn't have much money, but he was a great elder brother:
no questions asked when Mike had turned up late on Thursday
night; no telling him what to do while he was at work. There'd
scarcely been time for that anyway. Dave was employed in a video
store near Marble Arch; he was gone early and came home late six
days a week. Since his arrival Mike hadn't seen him for more than
a few minutes at a time, and he'd needed to see someone, to have
someone to talk to.

After getting through to Sasha the morning before he'd found
a vegetarian shop in the high street, had bought some food, a
newspaper and a phone-card. Back at the flat he'd scoured the
paper, but there'd been nothing in it about Winston, nor on the
lunchtime news, nor the evening.

In the evening he'd taken the computer out of his rucksack
and switched it on. He'd got the menu up and double-clicked
on the item marked 'Colin's files'. A short directory of three
files had appeared. He'd selected the first, C:\WPDOCS\SWi,
and the screen had gone red; then, slowly, starting from the
bottom, a picture had appeared of a city skyline. He'd examined
it painstakingly, as he had done several times over the previous
week. What did the graphic mean? What was it trying to say? As
far as he could tell there was no instruction, no clue telling him
what to do next. So, was that it? he'd wondered in despair. Had
Winston died for a few pictures – there were two more of them
– or was he missing a vital clue?

He'd switched it off in disgust and, watching television, had fallen into an uneasy sleep. He hadn't heard Dave come in, but knew that he had because of a note in the kitchen that morning saying, 'Might be late again tonight. Sorry. Buy yourself a pizza.' And next to it there'd been a five-pound note – welcome because Mike's own resources were dwindling fast, but not as welcome as having Dave there in person.

He chewed his nail. When he was on his own his imagination started working overtime; he thought he saw things and heard things that weren't there, imagined that there were footsteps behind him, that people in the street watched him too closely, that at a corner or in a doorway they were waiting, she was waiting.

He sniffed. If Dave had been around he'd have never done what he had that morning, would never have been so stupid. But he'd been fed up and lonely, and a part of him had felt excited at the prospect. He'd gone to the telephone-box and dialled Directory Enquiries; then, quickly, before he could change his mind, called the number he'd been given.

It had rung only twice before a pleasant female voice had answered, 'REDEV. May I help you?'

He'd hung up, his heart pounding. It was Saturday; he hadn't really expected his call to be answered. He'd bitten his nails, told himself not to do it, then rung again. This second time, before he could stop himself, he'd gabbled, 'I want to speak to someone about the break-in.'

'One moment, please.'

God, how that had fazed him! She hadn't shown the slightest surprise, not even a moment's pause. He'd clung on, fascinated and horrified, making the handset wet with his sweat. There'd been a few clicks, then a man's voice had said smoothly, 'Good morning. I believe you'd like to discuss . . .'

He'd listened, his blood thundering in his ears until he couldn't hear anything else, then he'd slammed the phone down and run for his life. He'd bumped into people in the street. Someone had tried to grab hold of him, but he'd bulldozed his way through, not stopping until he had got back to the house, raced up the front steps, opened the front door and run up more stairs before reaching Dave's flat and safety at last. He'd flung himself down on the sofa, shaking like a crazy thing.

His great plan to tell REDEV that he had the computer – to

bargain with them for its return, threatening them with exposure if they didn't comply – had failed. He hadn't possessed the courage to go through with it. An hour had passed, and then another, and the need, like a craving, for someone to talk to had come upon him again. He'd gone back to the phone box and dialled the Henshaws' number. He had a duty to phone, he'd told himself, to let Caroline know he was all right – and, in passing, perhaps, to mention that a journalist wanted to interview him the following day.

There'd been no reply.

Preparing a short speech in his head, he'd then called Mary. A woman had answered, not her mother, and had wanted to know who was calling. An officious-sounding woman. The kind of woman who might have very dark eyes, who might watch and stare and coolly drive people away to their deaths . . .

On the TV, someone scored. Had they got Andrew and Mary and the rest? he wondered, suddenly frantic. He felt himself start to tremble again. Were more deaths to be laid at his door? Was he, just by being there, endangering his own brother? And if he went home, his mother? He remembered being in the laboratory, how scared Gerry and Andrew had been about viruses; he felt now like a virus himself, contaminating whoever he touched.

A whimper escaped from his mouth and a salty tear ran down his cheek. He was only sixteen years old and very scared. And Sasha had not remembered him at all, although he had had fantasies about her for months. He started to cry in earnest.

Smiling distracted thanks as someone held open the door for her, Rose Gilbert negotiated her way out of the crowded surgery and on to the street. A cold wind whipped at her face, making her eyes water, and she quickened her pace, hugging the baby closer to herself.

She could hardly believe what the doctor had just told her. To think that her own flesh and blood, her daughters . . .

Her son snuffled in his sleep, causing her to glance down, and at once her face softened. He was so beautiful, so pale, like a little china doll, with a miniature cleft in his chin and a perfect rosebud mouth. Even now that he was nine weeks old she still found herself occasionally having to check that he was real. She touched his cheek gently, marvelling at his warmth and softness.

She couldn't remember the girls ever being quite like this. Her face hardened.

'It's really quite common, Mrs Gilbert,' the doctor had told her. 'Children can get very jealous of the new arrival. These little bruises . . .' There was one on his leg, another on his back; she'd noticed them the evening before when she'd been changing him. '. . . look very much like pinch-marks.'

'Pinch . . . ?' In a sense it was a relief, assuaging the horrors she'd imagined the whole night long, but she wasn't yet ready to admit that. 'Are you sure?'

'Pretty certain that's all it is. Now, my advice is don't make a big thing about this. Spend some time with your daughters, show them how important they are to you, and don't leap to your feet every time this young man whimpers.' And he'd prodded Jeremy's stomach before handing him back to her, his snow-suit rebuttoned wrongly. 'Remember, babies are resilient. They can take a few bumps and bruises.'

Rose saw the car parked up ahead and increased her speed; she didn't like the idea of Jeremy being out too long in such cold weather. For herself, she felt quite warm – hot with rage, she shouldn't wonder. Exactly what was the doctor advocating? Wholesale attack? That she should stand back while Jeremy was pinched, thumped and kicked? Was the man insane?

Which one of them was it? she asked herself, reaching the pavement and unlocking the car's passenger door. Charlotte, aged six, who seemed to have taken Jeremy so much in her stride, or Lucy, three and a quarter, who, now she thought about it, had become more demanding, more clingy, since his arrival? Or was it both of them? she thought wildly. Taking it in turns to torment their helpless brother? God knew what Edward, her husband, was going to say. He'd also doted on the girls, Lucy especially. But now . . .

Rose was a DMD carrier. She'd been tested twelve years before, in the same year that her brother, aged nineteen, had died of the disease. His cruel deterioration had marked her childhood. Never, she'd told her fiancé, did she want to give birth to such a child. When the test result had come through she'd given him the option of breaking their engagement, but he'd brushed that aside. They could always opt for IVF, he'd said, ensuring they only had girls.

And that was what they'd done. After one unsuccessful attempt she'd become pregnant with Charlotte, then Lucy. Two was enough, they'd agreed – and then something must have gone wrong with her coil, because she'd found herself pregnant again.

Rose checked in the mirror before moving out. Jeremy's eyes suddenly opened, he yawned mightily, then fell immediately back to sleep. She paused, watching his breathing. It had been fifty-fifty that the CVS test would have shown DMD, and if it had – she took a breath – then she wouldn't have hesitated. He would never have been born.

She'd had to wait four terrible weeks for the test – they wouldn't do CVS before ten weeks, in case it damaged the developing fetal organs – but the results had come through quickly, the fastest available. She was in luck, her GP had told her, the Mistletoe hospital in London was conducting a pilot study . . .

She waited for a gap in the traffic. With the news that she'd been carrying a healthy male fetus, she and Edward had realised that they wanted another child very much indeed – that their plans to build a conservatory on to the back of the house, to take more expensive holidays, could wait. And her mother, Rose remembered, smiling, had said that she could always help out financially – she had her savings – and, of course, with any babysitting. She'd never been that helpful with the girls.

Rose moved out into the busy road. Jeremy James Gilbert, they'd named him James after her brother, whom she'd adored. Five years younger than her, when he could no longer walk, when he couldn't feed himself any longer, she had wept.

How *could* Charlotte and Lucy? Her anger bobbed up again. She wouldn't tell her husband, she decided. He might lose his temper. She'd tackle the girls herself, as soon as she got home – and if it resulted in a slap, then so be it. They had to understand how naughty they'd been. They had to accept that Jeremy was here to stay.

The Gilberts' doctor kept his note-taking to a minimum. Minor bruises, he'd written, on left thigh and middle back. Suggested sibling rivalry.

Ten minutes later the details appeared on DAMR.

Walking up her road, Liz Pearce saw that the two water company men had replaced the manhole cover outside her house and gone. They'd been quick, she thought, whatever they'd been doing.

Inside, she dumped two of her shopping bags on the mat and carried the rest through to the kitchen. She badly wanted to sit down, have a coffee and a cigarette, but she made herself unpack first. While she was reaching up to a shelf she felt something wind itself about her legs and she jumped.

'Oh! Hello.' Looking down, she felt silly at her fright. It was only one of the cats. 'Are you hungry then?'

The animal, a thin grey one, was a newcomer. It had appeared earlier in the week, emerging from Mike's room when she'd just got home from her night-shift – and giving her a fright then too. She'd seen a movement only, had briefly thought it must be burglars.

She should have known better. Mike was forever collecting stray animals; he'd done it since he was small, in the way that other children collect comics or (in David's case) beer-mats. In the back garden was a row of hutches, built by the boys' father, currently containing several rabbits and guinea-pigs. The grey cat was the third in the house; they already had a plump tortoiseshell and a neurotic, fluffy creature that spent much of its time hiding behind the washing machine.

The grey cat meowed.

'What? There's food there if you want it.'

She'd already fed the outside animals that morning, had put the old blankets around their cages to keep out the worst of the wind, as per instructions. A great deal of her conversation with Mike the day before had centred on those mangy guinea-pigs – if it got any colder she was to bring them inside, he'd told her, or at least put them in the garden shed.

The cat jumped up on to the breakfast bar and meowed again.

'What?' She stroked it, and it started purring deeply, pushing its head up against her hand. 'You just want some attention, do you?' Although the action was soothing, she couldn't stop worrying about Mike. It had been the same all morning, even since the police had come. In the supermarket she'd bought some organic apples, then gone to the health food shop for a tub of the chocolate-flavoured Tofu ice cream he loved so much. They were treats that she could ill afford, but she wanted to tempt him home. She wished so very much that he would phone.

She told herself she was being foolish, giving into unfounded fears, but none the less, each time she glanced over at the phone by the kitchen door she willed it to ring.

It was while she was refilling the tea-bag tin that she noticed the telephone flex was the wrong way round. She was left-handed; whenever she replaced the receiver, the flex fell to the left. Now it was on the right, and a loop of it had got caught on the knob of the little drawer under the telephone shelf, the way it always did when right-handed people used the phone.

'Mike?'

There was no answer. Of course not. She bit her lip, then slowly picked up the receiver and uncurled the flex. She opened the little drawer; it contained only stamps and string. She looked around the kitchen. From its vantage point the cat watched her, its green eyes boring into hers. Nothing else seemed to be out of place: Mike's note was on the side; her magazine lay open at the page she had been reading; on the shelf above the breakfast bar, Mike's animal magazines served as usual as a book-end for her cookbooks, his vegetarian ones, their photograph albums and her address book.

She looked again at the telephone and the flex now hanging where it should have been, and she tried very hard to convince herself that, for once and without noticing, she had used the phone with her right hand.

The day had turned grey and darkness had come early. By the time they reached the London outskirts it was night. Using a pencil-torch, McMahon was giving directions from the London street atlas. They were in slow traffic descending Brixton Hill. It took them ten minutes to crawl from the tube station down the High Street, with its glaring Christmas decorations, to the railway bridge. But the woman was a patient driver, an excellent driver, one who could not be a passenger – which was why, even though she was in charge of the entire operation, she was behind the wheel.

She'd changed her surname many times, but her first name had remained the same: Anna. She couldn't answer to anything else. She'd tried, and had quickly arrived at the conclusion that the failure to respond to a false name was far riskier than keeping her own.

She was English, though she'd neither been born there nor lived in the country for longer than a few months at a time. She preferred the climate of the Mediterranean; with her dark colouring, it suited her better, she blended in more easily. Whenever there was a break in her work she retreated to Greece or, in winter, Cyprus. In England, cold home of her father, she never felt at home.

She worked sometimes directly for a client, and sometimes for someone like Hall. She was expensive, but then she was recognised as being close to the top of her profession – certainly the best woman, and for some jobs that was invaluable. People still found it hard to suspect a woman; a businessman seeing an attractive, unknown woman on his doorstep would generally open the door. And for surveillance work a woman was far less noticeable than a man. Besides, some people – Hall included – simply liked her way of doing things, her style. She was thorough, clean, and she produced results. She'd worked for him before to their mutual satisfaction, and for a week's work, two at the outside, the fee for the current project had been generous.

By that night, she estimated, it would be over and she could return to her villa. They had the address now, and the boy's photograph, a recent one, conveniently dated, from the album. As soon as she'd seen it, she'd recognised him, although it had taken her a few moments to remember exactly where from. He was the boy who'd appeared from out of nowhere as they had been taking the first man, Winston, away. She'd assumed at the time that he'd come from one of the cottages further down the hill.

She took the next left, then the second on the right. The road they sought ran across the next junction. She began looking for somewhere to park.

'Mike?'

David Pearce stuck his head around the door of the sitting room, but his brother was not there, and neither was his rucksack. David frowned. He'd managed to get off work early, in time to race back to the flat, collect Mike and take him to a party that night, that was supposed to last through until Monday morning. He'd debated whether he wanted his kid brother tagging along, but his conscience had smitten him: he could not leave Mike on his own for two days – longer if he got lucky. Now he pulled a face. It looked like wasted effort.

He went into the tiny kitchen and saw the note on the cooker: 'Thanks for letting me stay and for the cash. Gone to stay with mates. Mike.' David picked up the piece of paper. As far as he knew, Mike didn't have any mates in London. Then he shrugged. He didn't know Mike very well any more. Besides, he hadn't said where his friends were; they might be back at home. He wandered back into the living room and saw a small pile of clothes at one end of the sofa; Mike must have been repacking and forgotten them. He frowned again as he recognised a baseball shirt that had once been his own and which was now one of Mike's favourite garments. Mike was very careful with his possessions; it was odd that he had left it behind. Should he, David wondered, phone his mother to pass on a message that it was safe?

He looked at his watch. The party was on the other side of town. He'd call his mother at some point during the weekend. He picked up the beers he'd brought home and went out, keeping his eyes down, the way people did in London – and when a couple barged into him as he turned the corner, he didn't bother to look up or apologise.

CHAPTER FOURTEEN

Sasha stood at the entrance to Brixton tube station. It was already fifteen minutes past two, but she was trying not to worry; public transport, she assured herself, was notoriously unreliable. However, she had gained the impression from Mike Pearce that he was staying within walking distance of the tube. 'It's just down the road,' she remembered him saying now, quite clearly. So he wouldn't be travelling by bus or tube, which meant that he was late without a reason. Face it, she thought glumly, he was probably not coming at all.

She shivered; it was cold standing still. She tried to huddle down inside her red jacket but it did not offer much protection; it was a fashion item, not made for warmth. She had a full-length wool overcoat at home, but it was black, and she'd told him that she would be wearing red. She didn't want him to miss her.

She pulled a face. How the tables had turned since he'd called her on Friday. When she'd agreed to meet him it had been partly out of the sense of doing him a favour. True, she'd hoped there would be a story in him; but remembering, during a long, dull shift at a press conference the day before, how obsessed he'd sounded, her heart had sunk. Brixton on a Sunday afternoon with an unhinged boy? No thanks. But then, that morning . . .

Every newspaper had run the story. Two of the tabloids had splashed it with 'EXCLUSIVE!' tags.

'Teacher Runs with Schoolgirl.'

'Girl, 15, Kidnapped from French Class.'

'Policeman's son plotted with kidnap pair in the Swimming Baths.'

Sasha hadn't immediately made the connection. What a tabloid godsend, she'd thought, scanning the articles. Then the names had started to hit her memory like a hammer on a bell. Tenterden; a girl called Mary; a teacher called Andrew, Kingsmere School.

'Oh no!' she'd howled. And just then the phone had rung. It had been Charlie (she'd told him about Mike the previous evening), wanting to know if she'd seen the papers that morning.

'Yes!'

'Ah. Anything I can do?'

'No! Sorry, I didn't mean to shout.'

'Its OK, I know how you feel. I'll let you get on.'

To think, she'd tormented herself, that she could have spoken to Mike on Friday, had his story ready to present the next morning to any of the newsdesks. The boy who'd known the victim and her kidnapper, who'd known that they were both animal rights extremists. None of the papers or news services had made any mention of that, nor, obviously, their participation in the laboratory raid. She'd lay bets that Mike knew the other two referred to in the articles. If he'd known Henshaw he'd have known his librarian wife, who'd been seen apparently 'plotting' with the policeman's son in a leisure centre. Mike held the key to the whole affair.

She'd groaned. The broadsheets as well as the tabloids would have snapped up her story and paid her handsomely. Her credibility as a hard-news, finger-on-the-pulse journalist would have jumped up several notches.

She blew into her cupped hands. She supposed that she could still try to follow up the animal rights line, but it wouldn't be easy without any evidence or witnesses. She could try talking to the runaways' relatives and friends about it, but that could be very tricky with the amount of police and media attention they'd be receiving.

People were oozing out of the tube. Although she knew Mike would not be among them, she examined each figure as it appeared, watched as some paused, doing up coats and jackets, grimacing against the cold before setting off.

She shifted her weight from one foot to the other. Where *was* Mike? It was possible that he'd decided not to come. That he had realised his fears were unfounded, or that he'd returned the computer and gone home. It was equally possible that, spurned by her, he'd called another journalist. That made sense too, she thought, pulling a face. If he was the sort of kid who'd kept her card for over a year, he would have kept others'. And if that was the case, she told herself stoically, she might as well forget about trying to salvage the animal rights line: it would be all over one or all of the papers in the morning.

The cold seeped into her, making her eyes water. She glanced at her watch. Thirty seconds left, then she'd go home.

A pair of black shoes entered her field of vision.

'Uh . . .' A tall, thin boy wearing black stood before her. His face was thin and chalk-white, and his eyes were red-rimmed.

'Sorry I'm late,' croaked Mike Pearce.

The note in the brother's kitchen proved that the boy had been there, Hall said. His operatives estimated that they'd missed Pearce or his brother by mere minutes. The electric fire had been still warm; the sofa dented . . .

'I'm not interested in their bloody estimates,' Stockart interrupted. 'They lost him, didn't they? That's all I'm interested in.' He glared at the other man. He'd called him that morning as soon as he'd seen the story in the newspapers. Hall had told him the facts the day before, but to see it in black and white, especially the photographs . . . Stockart had stared incredulously at the teacher and the schoolgirl. Were *those* his enemies? Those two and a spotty-faced boy? His stomach had knotted into a tight ball. He was being made a laughing stock.

With an effort he'd reminded himself of the good news: that he'd heard nothing further from West over the weekend, which meant that they were going to get away with it; that he'd been right, the Leukaemia in one infant was nothing more than a nasty coincidence, unrelated to the Syndrome. That was indeed good news. The best. He must concentrate on that, he'd told himself.

Hall continued: 'It's unfortunate, I agree, that the boy got away, but these things happen. One cannot predict every move that a target is going to make, especially—'

'Doesn't look as if your bloody operatives can predict the time of day.'

'Especially when one is dealing with a young, frightened boy like this.'

Stockart, on the edge of his chair, snatched up the paper on the table. 'You're sure, are you, that it's the boy who's got it? You're not going to catch him and find that it's Henshaw you wanted after all?'

'No.'

'Or Stuart Richley, the policeman's son? Jesus Christ!' He threw the paper down and it skittered across the table-top. 'That's all I needed, isn't it? A bloody copper's kid, with your lot after him!'

'We're not after him. I've told you. The last informant—'

'Another fucking body, I suppose. Christ!' He glared again, but Hall was studying his hands.

Hall resumed quietly: 'He was well-informed and co-operative. We can forget about the others.'

'And if they're caught? If they talk?'

'About what?' Hall looked up, his face bland. 'They'll sound like hysterical fools.' He nodded at the paper. 'They already do, don't they? Teacher chasing around after a schoolgirl, his own wife aiding and abetting. And then they tell the police that someone's been killing their friends, that someone's trying to kill them . . .'

'They're right there, aren't they?'

Hall shrugged. 'A heart-attack; a drunken driver.'

Stockart's eyes gleamed. 'But how about number three? The last one?'

Hall held his gaze. 'Let me worry about him.'

He's a true professional, Stockart thought, completely unperturbed, and he felt a surge of admiration. 'Go on,' he muttered under his breath.

Pearce's two known addresses had been searched, nothing had been found, and they were now being watched, Hall said. In addition, there was a phone-tap at his home. He was just a kid from the sticks; it would only be a matter of time before he resurfaced or tried contacting the site directly again.

Hall stretched out his hands. 'We find that, once they've done that once, they do it again. And now we've got our equipment in place—'

'Pity it wasn't there when he called.'

'. . . We'll be able to keep him talking and get a fix on him. I'd say we're looking at a very short timetable now.'

Stockart opened his mouth for another remark, but saw that Hall was expecting it and shut it again. He sank back in his chair instead, studied the centre rose on the ceiling, and said quite pleasantly, 'But in the meantime you've no idea where he is?'

'No.'

'Or what he's doing?' For the first time since Hall had arrived Stockart felt a twinge in his stomach. The pain-killers were wearing off.

'No.'

'Has it occurred to you,' he pressed his finger-tips together, 'that now might be the time for a change of leadership?'

Hall said nothing.

'To sack your head of operations?'

'For what purpose?' There was an edge to the man's voice – very slight, but noticeable.

Stockart said airily, 'Oh, just a gesture. Shake your operatives up a bit. Cut off the head, see the body jump.'

'But I have every confidence in the person I have chosen.'

A definite edge, Stockart told himself triumphantly. What was it, favouritism? Or something murkier than that? 'Well,' he took a deep breath, 'I don't. I want him sacked.'

The atmosphere thickened perceptibly. 'I'm afraid that's not possible at this stage.'

'What?' Stockart lowered his gaze. 'I'm the client, and if I'm not satisfied—'

'But the person in charge is exceptionally good.'

'I want to see him.'

Hall studied him briefly. 'It's a her, not a him.'

'A woman?' Stockart gave a short laugh. 'You're kidding!'

'No.'

'How can a woman—'

'She has personally supervised each interrogation in this instance.'

Stockart stared. Hall had previously told him some details of the techniques used. A woman? How extraordinary! And how exciting too. 'I insist on meeting her.'

'For reasons of security—'

'Otherwise, you're gone.' He couldn't sack him of course, not in the middle of a job, not with Hall knowing all he did – but he felt reckless. The man was watching him again, as he always did. Like a lizard, Stockart suddenly thought, regarding a fly.

'Very well.' Hall shrugged, as if it were of no account. 'If the laptop's not back in your possession within the next forty-eight hours, I'll ask—'

Ask! But Hall was in charge, surely? Stockart felt a prickle of desire. 'Order, you mean, don't you?'

'*Arrange* for you to meet. But I really think it won't be necessary. We'll have the boy long before then.'

CHAPTER FIFTEEN

As soon as Sasha had seen him, she'd realised that Mike Pearce had been sleeping rough; although on closer inspection of his white face and pinkish eyes, she doubted if he'd done much sleeping at all.

He'd walked a long way, he'd told her shakily, and got lost; he'd been sure that she would have gone. And then he'd started to sway on his feet, and she'd grabbed hold of him and taken him into a café, where she now sat watching him devour egg and chips.

At least he wasn't a vegan, she thought, preoccupied. The look he'd given her when at first she'd suggested a bacon sandwich . . . Stupid of her, but she'd only been concerned with getting food into him quickly before he fainted.

She saw that some colour was beginning to creep back into his thin cheeks, and wondered when he'd last eaten. She'd asked no questions yet; she was unsure now whether she would. Once he had finished eating, she considered, that she might simply put him on a train home to his mother.

He was all eyes and nerves, his features too big for his face, with long limbs that wouldn't fold away tidily. And he kept shivering, head-to-toe shudders that he didn't seem able to control. He must have caught a chill, she thought, then sighed: he was bringing out the worst of her social-worker tendencies. But she honestly couldn't bring herself to pump a young boy in such a state. The story could wait – or even, she conceded ruefully, not get told. It had never really been her type of thing, anyway.

'None of it's true,' he blurted suddenly, startling her.

'Sorry?'

'What they're saying in the papers.' He set down his eggy fork and fixed her with those dark, haunted eyes. 'About Andrew, and—' he blushed scarlet – 'Mary.'

'Oh.' She'd forgotten that Mike might have different ideas, that this particular lost boy was unlikely to go quietly. 'No,' she said carefully, 'I didn't think it was.'

From his rucksack on the chair beside him he pulled a battered Sunday paper. It was one that she recognised, bearing the 'Gymslip Temptress' headline. 'It's a pile of crap,' he mumbled, and coughed hard.

'Ah. Papers do sometimes get hold of the wrong end of the stick. Or exaggerate.' She watched him carefully. 'You know all of the people in the story?'

He nodded.

'All of them went on the raid you told me about?'

Another nod. He'd taken up his mug in both hands, his long fingers overlapping, his eyes studying her.

She glanced over her shoulder. The café was almost full. She and Mike were sitting at the back, nearest the kitchen, where no one could overhear them. She looked back and saw that Mike's eyes had filled with tears. She felt a lump rise in her own throat. 'Hey . . .' She touched his hand gently.

He snatched it away, scarlet again. She'd forgotten how young he was. Levelly she said, 'Come on, Mike. Nothing's that bad.'

'Yes it is.' He wiped his eyes with the heel of his hand, leaving a smear. 'I told you on Friday and you didn't believe me.'

She sighed. This wasn't what she wanted to hear. 'Your dead friend on the beach?'

His voice shot up. 'Yeah! Why won't you believe me?'

'Ssh. It's not that. But if you look at it logically, one of you, out of six—'

'There was eight.'

'Oh? That reduces the odds still further, doesn't it?'

He shook his head. 'Chris and Lucas . . .' He coughed again. 'They've gone too.'

'Oh?' She felt herself switch gear into proper listening mode. 'I didn't see anything about another two anywhere.'

He shrugged and rubbed at a mark on the table-top. 'I dunno if they've gone with the others. Chris isn't on the phone. I tried Lucas this morning but his mates said he wasn't home.'

'They didn't sound concerned?'

He chewed his thumbnail. 'Not really. They said he was probably at his girlfriend's.'

Her interest level dropped again. 'That sounds reasonable, don't you think?'

'Yeah, I know.' He looked up suddenly, catching the expression on her face. His shoulders sagged. 'You don't believe me, do you? You think I'm crazy.'

'No—'

'I told you about Winston being taken away.' He stared down at the formica top. 'I told you about the . . .' he shuddered, finally getting the word out: 'woman who was driving.'

'The police?'

He shook his head hopelessly.

'Mike.' She leant forward. 'Your friend had a criminal record. They took him in for questioning. When he got home—'

'He didn't.'

'What?'

'He never came home.' He glanced up. His face was flushed pink again; she wondered if he was feverish. 'Least, I'm pretty sure he didn't. But they came back.'

'They?'

'The ones who took him away. I saw them. I was watching.'

The man had been in the back of the van since eight o'clock that morning. He'd made himself as comfortable as he could on the foam rubber mattress, but he was a big fellow and by necessity a good proportion of the available space was taken up with equipment: telescopic and recording gear, as well as the camera. His muscles now were cramped and aching – even small movements like stretching had to be kept to a minimum – and the enforced inactivity made them cold. It was also stuffy, it being considered too great a risk to open a window in a supposedly empty van. He had to make do with the air filtering through the dozens of pin-prick holes in the van's rusty exterior.

It had been considered a good vehicle for the job – too old and wrecked-looking to provoke interest – but a gang of local boys had already visited. They'd tried the front and rear door handles, balanced on the bumpers, peered in through the opaque glass, unaware that they could be seen quite clearly. They had all looked about twelve years old.

'Can't see nothin'.'

'Yeah? So? Could be full of stuff.'

'Nah,' someone else had ruled. 'We got other stuff to do. Come back t'night, maybe.'

David Pearce's flat was on the opposite side of the street, three car-lengths away. It had been dead all day: no movement, no visitors. In the man's opinion, it was empty.

Boredom was the hardest part of the job; not the discomfort or the danger or the dirty stuff, but the minutes dragging into hours of sitting still, watching, listening, doing nothing. It could drive a man mad. He counted the minutes, then the seconds, until three o'clock, the time when he had promised himself a ten-minute break.

Now he put his hand on the door handle. He opened it cautiously and crawled out backwards, the way a heavy workman would. No one was watching; no one was about. He walked to the end of the road and quickly into the main thoroughfare. It was good to be moving. He wanted a coffee and the toilet; he'd never got used to pissing into a bottle the way that the others did.

He stopped on the pavement, looking around. Opposite was the tube station and – he squinted – a supermarket, several foodstores, a couple of hairdressers and . . . he took a step closer – yes, a café, further down on the left. He set out for it at once.

On top of whatever virus Mike had caught, Sasha wondered if he was anaemic. He looked so pale. She studied him as he talked. His hair was spiky on top and long at the back, a very dark brown, almost black; it emphasised his white complexion, the darkness about his eyes – which didn't look healthy at all, the whites pink. But perhaps he always looked like that, she told herself. He shivered again, and she thought, no, she ought to be taking him to the station right now, phoning his mother to make sure someone was waiting for him at the other end.

But she was surprised at what he was saying. 'You went back to Winston's house on your own? At night?'

'Yeah. Sunday night – well, Monday morning. About two.'

'Two in the morning?' She tried to keep the disbelief out of her voice.

'My mum works nights. In a minicab office.'

'Oh.' Occasionally she felt the confines of her middle-class upbringing.

'I couldn't sleep, and . . .' He coughed again in that painful way. 'I was worried about Smokey. Gerry's cat. I thought, if Gerry had been taken away . . .' He gulped. 'Well, there'd be no one to feed Smokey. There aren't any next-door neighbours or anything. Gerry doesn't . . . didn't know many people. So I went back.'

'And?'

'There was a car outside, and the lights were on upstairs. The curtains were closed, but I could see people moving about.'

'What made you think it wasn't Gerry?'

A triumphant look entered his eyes. 'He never went upstairs. He lived in the kitchen and the back room. He told me it was after being in prison – he didn't like big places any more. Anyway, I saw them come out.'

'It was the same people?'

He gave a jerky nod.

'But not the woman?'

She saw his pupils contract. 'Mike? The woman wasn't there?'

He shook his head slowly. 'No, it was only the men.'

'You recognised them, you're sure?'

He nodded again, more emphatically. 'Gerry's got this security light. Anyway,' he glanced at her accusingly, 'I remember faces.'

'How did you see them without being seen?'

'I hid in the bushes by Gerry's front door. It's all overgrown there, and,' he gazed at her, 'they weren't expecting anyone to be there.'

Touché. She silently congratulated him.

'I waited till they drove off, then I got out and went to round to the back door. Gerry never locked it.' He bit his lip. 'They'd switched the lights off and opened the curtains, so you'd never have known they'd been there. There was no sign of forced entry, no smashed windows—'

'You'd know all about that, of course.'

He gave her the ghost of a smile. 'But you know what it meant?'

'Uh . . .' He was smarter than he looked, she thought.

'They had his key, or they knew about the back door.'

It could still have been the police, she told herself. It was an odd time to search someone's house, agreed – but suppose the suspect, or perhaps another informant, had just revealed the whereabouts of something at his home, and the police had been eager to check it out at once?

Mike coughed again, more loudly than before, and a man who'd been heading for their table, a plate of food balancing on a mug, veered sharply away. Mike took a gulp of tea. 'They were searching for something,' he muttered, 'only it wasn't there. It'd never been there.'

His eyes darted about her face and, although logic dictated otherwise, she felt caught up again. 'You've got it with you?' she asked quietly.

His hand went protectively to the rucksack. He pulled it towards him. 'Yeah. D'you want to see?' He stopped and stared past her, and she heard the ring of the bell as the door opened.

Standing at the front, the man scanned the café for a Toilet sign. All he could see, right at the back, was a door to the kitchen. He could go and ask at the counter, but time was short and the woman serving had a customer. Besides, it was stuffy and busy and he had seen, just as he'd opened the door, another bigger, brighter-looking place on the other side of the street.

He turned to go, felt suddenly that he was being watched, and cast a glance around him, to the end of the café, where he saw a dark-haired girl in a red jacket flick round at the sound of the bell or the draught, and away again. No, there was nothing. But better always to be sure: methodical, thorough stagecraft. He went out.

*　　　*　　　*

'Mike?'

'I thought I saw someone . . .' He shrugged. 'Sorry.' From the battered rucksack he withdrew a slim laptop computer, encased in grey plastic. 'Here it is,' he said proudly, and in spite of herself Sasha could feel her pulse thumping.

'Light, isn't it?' she said, taking it. About the same weight as her bulging old Filofax, too heavy now to be carted around, which of course she was well aware totally defeated its purpose. She set down the small machine in front of her. 'How d'you open it?' she asked.

'Here.' He pressed the side and the lid came up, revealing the screen. 'You turn it on here.' He pushed another button and the start-up data appeared. It was about ten times faster than hers, she estimated. If ever she was to replace it, she'd be tempted by something like this. Charlie would be delighted, she thought.

'Who's Colin?' she asked, reading from the screen. 'It says "Colin's Files".'

'Yeah, I know. Bloke who owns it, I s'pose.'

Oh yes, she reminded herself guiltily. She was handling stolen goods. 'Mike?' she began tentatively. 'You'll have to return this, you know. It could be really important to someone.' The owner, for instance, she added to herself.

'Hang on.' His head was touching hers as he tried to use the computer upside-down. He double-clicked twice on the mouse.

'You know you way around this,' she commented, watching data appear and disappear.

'Mm. Look at this.'

She looked. The screen went blank for a second, then, starting from the top, a graphic appeared, working its way slowly down. It was a man dressed like Robin Hood carrying a bow and a quiverful of arrows. He was yawning.

'What is it?' she asked.

He sighed. 'I dunno. It's all I can get. That and two other pictures.'

'And that's all?'

He nodded and sank back into his seat. He coughed, but it sounded less severe now. 'I think it's like a password, sort of security thing, like a system gate.'

'I've got to tell you, Mike, my level of computer literacy – well . . .' She grinned suddenly, remembering Charlie's phrase. 'It's been described as Jurassic.'

'Huh?'

'Never mind. It means I haven't a clue about cracking computer codes. Sorry.'

He slumped in his chair, chin on chest. He didn't look like a thief, she thought. His hands as they rested on the table seemed still unformed, childish, somehow gentle. They belonged to a kind boy. 'Did you find Smokey?' she asked.

He blinked up. 'Yeah. She was under Gerry's bed.'

'Ah. Good.'

'I took her home. I was going to leave a note, you know, in case Gerry . . .' He trailed off.

Sasha stared at his bent head. Why would an animal lover, she wondered suddenly, go off without arranging for someone to look after his cat? It was odd.

'She wouldn't eat at my house for three days,' Mike continued. 'Just hid under my duvet. Gerry had her from a kitten; he got her the first week he got out of prison. He said she was his best friend. He'd wanted a black one, but she was the runt of the litter so he had her, even though she was grey. He was nuts about her.'

Was it possible the man had been abducted? 'Mike? These labs you broke into . . .'

'Yeah?' He pushed his mug to one side.

'Tell me about them. What was in them?'

'Nothing, really. I told you.'

'Who'd they belong to?'

He sniffed. 'REDEV. Research place. But Gerry said . . .' He stopped deliberately.

'Yes?'

'He said it had once been MOD.'

The adrenalin surged through her again. 'Once been?'

'Yeah. During the war. He said they used to test nerve gas there. On animals.' He shuddered. 'They put them in rooms and gassed them. Disgusting, isn't it?'

'Horrible. So it's not MOD any more?'

He sighed. 'No, it's REDEV. I just told you.' He flicked a

fingernail against the thick white china. 'But when we were in there that night, there were these test-tubes.' He hesitated.

'And?' she prompted.

'The others got the willies about what was in them.' He paused again. 'Thought it might be nerve gas or something.'

'But not you, huh?'

'Nah!' He looked scornful. 'Course not.'

But he was willing to believe much wilder theories. For the first time she put her own mug to her lips and took a sip. Or were they so wild?

A story was taking shape inside her, nibbling away, gathering strength, demanding to be heard. Activists, breaking into secret government labs, see something or are exposed to something they shouldn't . . . She felt a frisson of excitement and fear. Had the government, desperate to get their computer back, authorised the abduction of Gerry Winston? Had their interrogation gone too far, ending in the dumping of the body on the beach at the nuclear power station? If she was right, there would have had to have been a cover-up over Winston involving the police, the pathologist who'd examined the body, even the coroner. Or had the government people arranged everything themselves, including a carefully worded press release? She would have to find out more about how Winston had died; see if the two other animal rights people that Mike had mentioned would talk to her.

'Mike?'

'Uh?' His head jerked up as if he'd fallen asleep.

'Your group. How long've you been together?'

At once his expression grew guarded. 'Why?'

She glanced around. The table behind had emptied. 'Only that the police are pretty clued-up about animal rights people. They have an index that monitors activists—'

'ARNI, you mean?'

She was surprised. She knew about the Animal Rights National Index, which kept track of activists around the country, through her story on the live-exports protesters, but she hadn't expected him to. 'Yes. I'd have thought you and the others would've been on it, wouldn't you?'

He shrugged but was watching her carefully.

'I'd have thought that, after your raid, the first thing the police would've done would be to visit known animal activists. That didn't happen.' She left a gap for him, which after a moment she filled herself. 'Which means you're not on it. In fact,' she prodded his newspaper with a finger, 'the police don't seem to be aware that any of you were involved in animal rights.'

He smirked.

'How come?' she asked simply.

He studied her a few moments longer before finally making up his mind. Then he said very clearly, 'Group policy.'

'I'm not with you.'

He gave an elaborate sigh. 'We have no structure, no group meetings, no history. We come together only to perform one task, then we disband.'

Word-perfect, she thought, slightly stunned.

'There's no connection between us except the obvious: the teacher – pupil thing; friendship – ' he blushed, becoming a schoolboy again – 'between pupils; girlfriend, boyfriend. Apart from that there's nothing to link us. Some of the others,' he made a face, 'even eat meat.'

'Ah.' She still felt taken aback. She glanced down at the newspaper photograph of the school-teacher. 'Who thought this up?'

'Caroline. And it worked too. The police never had a clue.'

'They knew about Winston. He had a criminal record.'

Their eyes locked. 'It *wasn't* the police,' he said finally, wearily, and looked away.

She glanced down at the computer again. She saw the way the huntsman stood, one foot resting on a hillock. He was looking straight at her, she thought, as if he was trying to tell her something. Of course, she thought.

'OK,' she said.

'What?'

She swivelled the machine round to face him. 'You'd better switch this thing off.'

He looked startled. 'Why? What're you going to do?'

'You think this picture's some kind of security mechanism?'

'Uh, yeah.'

'We need to know how to get past it, and I happen to know someone who's very clever with computers.'

His hands went protectively around the machine, pulling it towards himself. 'Who?'

'A friend.'

He regarded her suspiciously.

'Another journalist – much more computer literate than me. It's worth a try, isn't it?' She warmed to her theme, telling herself it was true – Charlie was brilliant with computers – and besides, she suddenly longed for a second journalistic opinion, specifically his. 'We could have a look at the news services; see what else the police – or whoever – are saying about the others.'

'We're going to a newspaper office?'

'Sort of. It's a news bureau. It's got a TV studio as well. It's where he works.'

'Your boyfriend?' Mike blushed violently. 'Sorry,' he mumbled. 'Didn't mean to be nosy.'

'Oh, um . . .' She stuffed her notebook (she hadn't written anything, she saw) back into her handbag. 'That's OK. Shall we go?'

He didn't move, wouldn't look at her.

'What's wrong?' she asked gently, thinking, oh no, after all this he's going to do a runner. 'You do want me to investigate this, don't you?'

'Yeah, but . . .' He chewed his thumb. 'This other journal-ist—'

'He's trustworthy, Mike. I promise.'

'Yeah? It's just that,' he dropped his gaze again, 'it's important it gets done right. These people . . . You didn't see her.' He shuddered.

She glanced round. The café was filling up again; two families at the front, an old man two tables away, and two young women by the counter.

'Sasha?' Mike's eyes were terrified again. 'That's why I can't go home, see?' Tears traced their way down his cheeks. 'That's why I left my brother's. I was scared they were going to find me.'

She nodded, wanting suddenly to be gone. Deep breaths, she thought; they were safe there, among other people. She said quietly, 'Let's go and sort a few things out – one way or another, huh?'

He took a long, quivering breath, wiped his cheeks with his sleeve, and nodded once.

She kept her voice light. 'I can't have you wandering round London scared half to death.'

'I'm not imagining it.'

'I never said you were.' She stood up, waited for him to do likewise. 'You've got me thinking the same way. Well, nearly.'

'Yeah?' He cheered up at once. 'So you're taking me on?'

She smiled. 'In a manner of speaking. Come on.'

Chapter Sixteen

Dimly, Will West became aware of a noise outside. Before he could identify it, the door opened.

'Oh, I beg your pardon, sir.' It was a hospital security guard. 'I didn't realise you were still here.'

West gazed at the man. He didn't think he'd ever seen him before, although the guard was smiling amiably as if he knew him. He pondered the words he'd uttered. They made little sense. Where else would he be, he wondered?

'Are you all right, sir?' There was concern in the guard's voice.

West collected himself. 'Perfecly.'

'Don't overdo it,' the man smiled. 'No one ever thanks you for it, in my experience.'

West stared after him as the door closed. He supposed he was what they called a well-meaning fellow. He probably wasn't used to finding people working on a Sunday afternoon.

His eyes strayed back to the computer screen. In the preceeding hours he'd grown accustomed to what was there. He could look at it, absorb it without flinching, without that sickening jolt to the system that had threatened initially to unhinge him.

A one-off. West remembered Stockart saying it, so long ago it seemed, cutting West off, leaving him stranded while he sailed on, impervious to the facts, blind because he chose to be. Not so himself. Though he'd dreaded what he would see, he'd craved it too, like a drug that he knew would harm him. He'd come back to his office straight away on Friday, shutting himself in and the world out, to wait. DAMR had not kept him long.

First had come the results of the second blood-test. If anything, the baby's blood-film was worse: the white blood cell count higher than before; the haemoglobin, eight; the platelet count abnormally low. Still 'Query Leukaemia?', but only queried, West knew, because the incidence of the condition in such tiny babies was extremely rare. In the haematology laboratories of the general district hospital where Subject Two had been taken, they wouldn't be expecting Leukaemia; it wouldn't seriously be on their list. In spite of what it looked like they'd be toying with more mundane explanations. West remembered, from his early days, a clinician telling him that, when you hear hoof-beats, you look for horses, not zebras.

He ought to be looking at this, West told him silently, suddenly spiteful. What would he call this? Forget zebras – this was Pegasus, bloody centaurs, the apocalypse. No, he'd whispered, it isn't simply a weird blood-film, the sort of thing one might expect in babies so young, and no, there isn't a clot in the sample, any more than there had been in the first. Nor is it the blood of a Downs Syndrome baby. It's what it looks like, he'd hissed to the man from his past whose face he'd long forgotten, and to those unknown clinicians and doctors now scratching their heads in the district hospital. It's Acute Lymphoblastic Leukaemia. Do a bone marrow biopsy and see. What're you waiting for, fools?

They were simply waiting, according to the baby's case notes – incredulously read by West an hour later – to see if the picture would clear. He'd actually laughed out loud then, a high, dry sound that had got too loud, bringing a knock at his door and a muffled inquiry, rendering him quickly silent. They were hoping, those fools, that the unusual counts would adjust themselves, that whatever infection had produced them would sort itself out in a day or two. The parents had been reassured, West had read, that this would probably happen. So it was better to wait rather than plunge in at once with a bone marrow biopsy – the only definitive way of determining Leukaemia, but a traumatic procedure for such a small baby. It was better to give it a few days, maybe a week.

Wait and see. West had sucked his teeth in fury. They could wait until Doomsday and it wouldn't get any better.

Then, as quickly as it had come, his anger had evaporated, and with it much of his energy. His eyelids had drooped, his head felt heavy, every movement became a huge effort. What did it matter what they did? Biopsy or not, treatment or not, the result would be the same. Death due to infection or haemorrhage would occur at any time now; in West's experience sooner rather than later. Remission? Forget it. Not in the cases he'd dealt with.

So what had gone wrong? Over and over again he'd forced his mind round the same circuit, until finally it had slowed and he'd fallen asleep at his desk, slept for hours, all through that night, waking only when the weekend cleaners reached his floor at eleven o'clock on Saturday morning.

The cursor on his screen began to move and his eyes were at once riveted to it. Subject Two was being transferred to a specialist children's hospital in Bristol. Prior to the journey they'd taken his temperature – it showed no change. West shrugged. Give him time, he thought, sinking back once more into his reverie.

After his rude awakening the previous morning he'd at once checked on the baby. Then, as now, there'd been no change. That, plus the deep, dreamless sleep from which he'd just emerged, had combined to make him feel suddenly optimistic. It was possible that Stockart was right, that Subject Two was no more than an unfortunate blip in his statistics. A horrible, cruel coincidence sent to test him. He'd left the baby, his parents and the medical team, exiting all the way back to the index. It was Saturday, he reminded himself, a bright, clear winter's day outside. He'd go home, have something to eat, listen to some classical music, perhaps even go to the countryside for a bracing, head-clearing walk. And then he'd reached his list of names again, his babies, and seen that another one was highlighted: Jeremy James Gilbert, Subject One.

His hands had been trembling so much that he'd scarcely been able to key in the commands, but it had been there waiting for him when he had: bruising. A Leukaemoid symptom. He'd scarcely acknowledged the GP's foolish diagnosis; his mind had been on a roller-coaster, veering out of control. But he'd made no sound, no movement, not even blinking his eyes until they'd hurt, stuck like that on the screen.

He'd always known. That had been the first thought to emerge from his subconscious when he'd come out of whatever catonic state the shock had induced in him.

It had been mid-afternoon. He'd got up, feeling like an old, old man, gone to the sink in the corner and drunk cup after cup of musty water. In a way he'd felt relief. He'd been right all along. He was the doctor; what had Stockart ever known but what he'd taught him? Both the first and the second subjects had Leukaemia.

Slowly he'd returned to his machine. Everything felt slow, dragged down: history rerunning, going back on itself; himself unravelling.

He'd called up the list once more, staring at it, waiting for the next one, and at seven o'clock in the evening it had come. Subject Four, three weeks and three days old, from Northampton. His parents had noticed a rash, had feared Meningitis, and rushed him to Casualty. Not the Meningitis rash, West had told them – numbly now, with no trace of his former anger at their innocence – it was the purplish-red rash showing Thrombocytopenic purpura: low blood platelet count. Leukaemia. Subject Four's blood-film two hours after admission was as he'd expected, but again the hospital was playing it cautiously, even more so than Subject Three's: 'Query, query Leukaemia?' Two queries, clinician's shorthand for: 'This is what it looks like, but surely not . . . ? We can't believe it.'

Throughout the night and into that day he'd continued to monitor the subjects. In the morning he'd followed the progress of Four as another blood-test had been taken, a bone marrow biopsy mooted, and then put on hold for a week. A week! He'd be surprised if the infant lasted that long.

Unwillingly, he remembered one of the Albanian boys from the second trial. His parents had brought him into the clinic, and they'd arrived on his floor where, for some reason, there'd been no one else around. They'd actually walked into his office, the father carrying the child, the mother trailing behind. Four of the babies had already succumbed to the disease. There'd been no interpreter, but there'd been no need of one. Wordlessly, the father had handed him the child – he'd been at the door, trying to edge them out – and he'd had to take it. The face had been very pale, the breathing laboured.

'I'm going to call another doctor,' he had said loudly, hoping to make them take it back. 'Hold him while I phone.' But they wouldn't, and the father had begun pulling at his sleeve, pointing at the baby, shouting in his face. And then, suddenly, the child had convulsed – once, twice – and the laboured sound had stopped, snuffed out, and the child had been dead in his arms. More out of shock than anything, he'd tried resuscitation. Futile, of course. All the while the father had been at him, his incomprehensible language jabbering at his brain, until finally, looking up, West had shaken his head, and the noise had sharply ceased, replaced by silence.

'I'm sorry,' West had said. 'I've done everything I can,' and the truth of that bald statement had abruptly jabbed at him, causing him to look down. So when, a moment later, someone had said in clear English, 'Thank you. Thank you very much,' he'd glanced up expecting to see someone else, one of the team members there in the room. But it had been the mother, speaking the only English words she knew, her eyes fixed unwaveringly on his.

He winced – not at that picture but at another, far more recent: Melanie Alder. The crisis had banished her from his conscious mind – though not, he realised now, from his subconscious. His long sleep hadn't been dreamless; she'd been there. In his dreams her eyes had held his, not letting them go, telling him something. But what? He shivered again, and his mouth dropped as the words came back. She'd been thanking him in the same way, with the same words, that that Albanian mother had used, that she herself had used the previous week when he'd just withdrawn the catheter from her womb, carefully setting down the syringe so that, if she looked, she'd be fooled into thinking she'd undergone CVS rather than . . .

She'd thanked him humbly for her son.

He'd never cared before. There were only subjects, like mice or dogs in the labs. But now . . . He stared sightlessly ahead. He could see her clearly: dark hair, cut short; small features, a full lower lip, eyes that worried too much. He frowned. How did he know that? He didn't, of course – he was just imagining it – but that wasn't like him, to put himself inside other people's heads. He didn't know how to do it. Except in her case, he found that he did. Her voice, thanking him again, shaking as she'd spoken the words, praising him like a god for what he'd done.

He blinked. In seven months' time she was going to give birth to a son who'd contract cancer of the blood and die within a few weeks. That's what he'd done for her – and, he knew, for the others in the study, but they didn't matter. He felt a sudden constriction in his throat. He'd no idea why. He only knew that, for whatever reason, she mattered to him in a fundamental way. She'd spoken to him, and he was changed.

He knew that she was strong. She'd overcome much in her life and still had her first son's death to bear, but her unborn baby's as well? The tight feeling intensified, spreading up into his nose and eyes. She could only take so much, and then she'd break like a butterfly on a wheel. Was he the one who was going to do that?

The tightness burst. He put a hand up to his face, withdrew it and stared. His hand was wet; he was crying. He couldn't think when he'd last cried – if ever. Now he let the tears bathe him, not bothering to wipe them away, but watching as they dripped on to his desk, until the flow ceased of its own accord. He was going to protect her. The resolve came out of nowhere, but hardened at once into steel. How, he didn't at that stage know, but he'd do it. He'd examine the tissue from the infants that would soon be dead, he'd work out why it had happened, and he'd save her and her unborn child. He'd do it; he knew he would. He was a genius, wasn't he? He could hear himself being called that again, see the champagne corks popping, Stockart beaming upon him . . .

He took a sharp breath. Stockart – who'd decided that there wasn't any connection with the SWii Syndrome; that there wasn't any need for action. How chillingly he'd spoken. The power, West had thought, of even the average mind to deceive itself. He brought his eyes back to the screen, to the three names highlighted there. If Stockart saw this . . . His eyes flickered. The whole project would be abandoned. Loose ends tidied up, everything shut down. No help for Melanie then; there'd be nothing that he could do for her.

Stockart mustn't know, then. The idea was beautifully simple. He knew Stockart; he was a man who expected his orders to be carried out. He'd told him to monitor the babies and it wouldn't occur to him that West wouldn't, or that he would conceal the truth.

Very vaguely, at the back of his head, a note of alarm sounded, the knowledge that he couldn't keep such data secret. But the thought was an irritating beggar and he shook it off. True, he cautioned himself, standing up, he didn't have much time. Melanie (he smiled – such a pretty name) needed his help. He'd get into his lab straight away; he always did his best thinking there.

His heart thumped with the prospect of what he was about to discover, and with his own bravery in the face of that madman, Stockart. He'd keep quiet about the two new cases. He wouldn't look to see if there were any more, or hang around waiting for the fools to carry out the biopsies, for a GP who'd diagnosed sibling rivalry to come to his senses.

He sneered down at the computer. He didn't have any more time to waste. He had work to do.

Lucy Gilbert was three and a quarter years old. She could remember when she'd been the baby, but now her place had been usurped. She gazed in at her brother, fast asleep in the cradle where she used to sleep, and wished that he'd never been born. Ever since they'd brought him home from the hospital things had changed. Her father said they hadn't, but Lucy knew they had. Her mother didn't love her any more.

The day before, her mother had led her and Charlotte into the playroom and firmly shut the door. She needed to talk to them, she'd said, about something very serious. She wasn't angry, she'd said – at once Lucy had sensed that wasn't true – she simply needed to know which one of them had done it.

Lucy peered closer. Jeremy was so small, and with his eyes closed tight he looked like a doll. At first she'd thought that was what he had been and had wanted to play with him, until her mother had snapped at her not to jiggle him about so. She was to leave him alone. Then, early one morning the week before, on the way back from the bathroom, Lucy had seen her mother standing over the cot, and heard her whispering that he was so special, the most special little baby ever born.

Was he special simply because he was a boy? Lucy extended a forefinger, very gently as her mother had shown her, and stroked the fuzzy, funny hair on his head. His dark eyelashes fluttered and his breathing quickened, but he didn't waken.

Her sister, Charlotte, said that she didn't care, that she was six and the eldest and always would be, and it didn't matter to her who the baby was. It was all right for Charlotte: Jeremy hadn't hurt her like he had Lucy. Charlotte didn't feel things. Even the day before, when neither she nor Charlotte had answered their mother, and her face had gone suddenly bright red and she'd seized Charlotte by the arm and shaken her, Charlotte hadn't cried. If she had then maybe her mother wouldn't have slapped her, once, twice, hard, before her hand had flown to her own mouth and she'd run from the room, crying.

Lucy shivered. Then, as if of their own accord, her fingers crept to the top of the baby's quilt and pulled it back. Jeremy was wearing his Teddy Boy Blue pyjamas that her grandmother had bought. She took hold of the cloth, wormed her way deep into his flesh and pinched very hard, the way she had before. Then she turned and ran before his cries brought her mother running.

CHAPTER SEVENTEEN

Four years before, Tony Holland reminded himself, the office in which he now sat had been the domain of the Tenterden chief inspector – his nameplate was still on the door – who'd commanded a team of ten officers, two parish constables and five civilians. The two large rooms along the corridor had housed CID and uniform; the charge-room had been a working office, not a depository for derelict paperwork; and the glass-fronted enquiry desk by the front doorway had been permanently staffed by a desk sergeant or constable.

At least, he thought, the present state of affairs had breathed life back into the place, however briefly. He felt that the building itself, post-war and purpose-built on the edge of town, was grateful, in spite of the carnage that had been wreaked upon it. Floorboards had been ripped up to install extra computer cables; fax and telephone flexes now snaked across floors and ran down corridors; loops of lights that hurt the eyes had been strung up like early Christmas festoons; furniture that had sat quietly accumulating dust had been either pressed into service or dumped unceremoniously in one of the empty cells.

Of course, when the first reports had come in late on Friday night, no one had known what they were looking at. Murder,

quite possibly, abduction of a minor, rape, organised child-abuse
. . . The setting up of a dedicated incident room at Tenterden had
been, quite rightly, a priority, as had the calling in of the police
search adviser from headquarters, the putting on standby of the
dogs and their handlers, the divers, the call to Sussex police for a
loan of their helicopter (Kent didn't have one) and co-ordinators
to organise civilian volunteers in case of a ground-search.

Holland gazed through the window. It was grimy; he saw that no
one had prioritised cleaning. Out in the overflow car-park (the tiny
one at the front now accommodated the mobile communications
unit) was an array of police vehicles, marked and unmarked cars,
Land Rovers, motor bikes, even a mobile kitchen and temporary
lavatory, the facilities of the station having proved insufficient to
cater for the needs of thirty-odd guests. In rooms overhead, once
civilian offices, camp-beds had been erected which the night before
had provided sleeping quarters for any that wanted them. Holland
had gone home.

Mary Kennedy had been seen entering the Henshaws' house the
evening before her disappearance, and leaving it forty minutes
later with two young males. That piece of information had been
supplied the previous evening by the Henshaws' elderly next door
neighbour, not as a result of door-to-door enquiries, but after the
woman (who'd been out when the officers had called) had returned
home and switched on the local evening news. She'd been able to
identify Mary quite clearly, there being a lamppost between the
houses. Neither young man, she reported, had paid the girl much
attention, not even responding to her 'goodbye' as she'd walked off.
The neighbour thought that one of them ought to have offered the
child a lift – they both had cars – on a dark winter's night.

One of the men, Holland now knew, had been Stuart Richley.
He'd met Richley once and hadn't been impressed; a surly lump,
he'd thought him, and had felt sorry for his father, still a serving
officer and a widower. But then he wasn't viewing Richley with the
eyes of a fifteen-year-old girl.

Mary had been spotted again the next afternoon, very soon after
her departure from school. This time she'd been running down the
path of her home towards a waiting car, the Henshaws'. Caroline
had been at the wheel. Mary had been carrying a small overnight
bag, and recognising the witness – a young mother for whom she'd

babysat – she'd giggled and waved before hopping into the car and being driven away. News of that sighting had only come to light that morning, after the witness had read one of the Sunday papers. She'd heard about a missing schoolgirl but hadn't known her name, and her home, at the other end of town, hadn't come within the immediate house-to-house area.

Holland picked up a pencil from the desk and started rolling it under his palm.

Mary Kennedy had gone voluntarily, there could be little doubt about that. She'd collaborated in the deceit of Caroline Henshaw's telephone call to the school. Her motive was still in doubt, although at this juncture credence had to be given to the theory, so hyped by the papers that morning, of sexual involvement with Henshaw or Richley, or both. An extended *ménage à trois*? He'd heard of stranger things. The pencil, a hexagonal one, made clicking sounds as he moved it to and fro. No matter what her parents said, Mary Kennedy was not the little innocent they believed her to be.

Since the beginning of the autumn term, according to a couple of schoolfriends of hers, Mary had seemed a bit different – quieter. Twice she'd ducked out of something at the last minute, and when challenged, hadn't provided much of an excuse. They'd felt that she was keeping something back; they'd accused her of having a boy-friend behind their backs, but infuriatingly she'd neither admitted nor denied it, and so, on principle, they'd stopped asking.

Holland added a second pencil to the one under his hand and began rolling again. Two weeks earlier, Mary had told her parents that she was sleeping over that Thursday night at one of her friends' homes. Her parents hadn't questioned it, but as a matter of routine the police officers did. Mary had lied. She had gone to school that morning, taking her night things and a change of clothes, and at the end of the afternoon she'd walked out of the gates and, apparently, vanished until twenty to nine the following morning, when she'd reappeared punctually and without anyone noticing anything untoward, for assembly.

She hadn't gone to Richley's. He still lived at home with his father, who, upon careful reflection, remembered that night. Stuart had gone to play pool with friends in Rye and hadn't got in until the early hours. Nor did it appear that she had gone to the Henshaws'. The elderly neighbour, a notorious curtain-twitcher, had been adamant that her first and only sighting of Mary had been four days before.

Holland sighed and pushed the pencils to one side.

After watching the local news the previous night, another member of the public had called in. A customer services assistant at Eurostar in Ashford, he remembered selling four tickets to Brussels on Friday evening to a woman answering Caroline's description. And the same news bulletin had jogged the memory of a passport controller inside the terminal. The man had clearly seen fit to ignore the official all ports appeal that had been issued early on Saturday morning, Holland thought sourly. Only when he checked back did he discover that he'd waved through the four missing persons the previous night, in time for the 19.27 to Belgium.

Interpol had been alerted, as well as the Belgian and French police, the train having also stopped at Lille in northern France.

Holland frowned. The missing persons were not sophisticated absconders from justice; they weren't criminals. Indeed, prior to this, none of them had attracted any police attention whatsoever. They'd bolted without a plan, simply leapt on the first train they could, and run.

What had scared them?

A loud crash came from the corridor outside, followed by furious swearing about 'bloody cables' and 'godawful death-trap linoleum'.

'Sir?'

Julie Milton appeared, one of his sergeants, who had the unnerving habit of not knocking on doors before entering.

'Yes?'

'We've just had a call from the police in Lille. Our four hired a car there yesterday morning.'

His adrenalin surged. Back to the real world, he thought, following her out into the corridor and towards the noisy, overcrowded and glaringly-lit incident room.

CHAPTER EIGHTEEN

God bless you Charlie, Sasha thought.

'Sure, bring him on up,' had been his cheerful response when she'd called from the front reception area ten minutes earlier.

She hadn't been able to explain anything – Mike had been standing right beside her, as had the two uniformed security men – but Charlie had been the embodiment of tact. He'd met them at the lift, swiped them through the entry system into an empty reception area, explaining as he led the way along deserted corridors that the floor was still mainly unoccupied, that it was a good thing his organisation didn't rely on drop-in visitors – there'd be no one to let them in. They'd walked through a plain door into two large rooms that was American Global News in London.

Now Charlie was effortlessly engaged in impressing Mike by demonstrating something complicated on the computer. Sasha raised her eyes. All those computers! Mike was in heaven, a different boy entirely to the spooked-out kid, who'd certainly spooked her out with his stories of dead friends and government agents back in Brixton. He looked more normal, too, she thought – less green and a lot less nervous. The awful cough, she realised, had entirely gone.

He was talking to Charlie. 'I want to be a journalist,' he was telling him confidingly.

'Uh huh. TV or print?'

'TV. I mean, there's no future in print, is there?'

Well, she thought, staring at his thin profile, thanks a bunch, kiddo.

Over his head, Charlie gave her the flicker of a smile. 'I wouldn't say no future, Mike,' he responded seriously. 'And whichever field you choose, there's fierce competition for every job.'

'Yeah, well, actually, I think I've got a pretty good story right now,' and Sasha watched disbelievingly as he bent down and pulled out the laptop from his rucksack. 'I'd like to see what you think,' she heard him say as he opened the lid.

She meant to say something but her voice had apparently deserted her. She stared at Mike as he tapped on the mouse a few times and Charlie, after a few moments, said, 'Cute graphic.'

'Yes. It is, isn't it?' She shoved her chair into both of theirs.

'Hi!' Charlie made room for her. 'I've been asked to give a second opinion on your story.'

Mike now glanced round. 'Yeah, just a second opinion. She hadn't a clue about this,' he added to Charlie, and she was filled with the sudden desire to smack his head.

'I might not know what that graphic means,' she started, 'but I've got lots of—'

'I don't have a clue either,' Charlie interrupted.

'What?' Mike flipped round. 'She said you'd be able to get me in!'

'Sorry to disappoint.' He smiled disarmingly. 'And thanks for the build-up, Sash. But . . .' He pointed at the screen and she saw a city skyline in red. 'This looks like someone's personal security route.'

'We know that!'

Huh! It's 'we' again, she observed.

'And I have no idea how it works. Not the foggiest, as you say. This could mean anything. It could be anywhere. Could be a town, or a city, or an imaginary place on Mars. Could be that you have to double-click on this rooftop here to get in . . .' He did so and the machine bleeped warningly. 'Clearly not. I apologise again, Mike, but,' and he turned to him, 'I'd have to get inside the head of . . . what's the name of the guy who owns this?'

'Colin,' Sasha supplied.

'Thanks. Colin's head, to get past it.'

Mike stared, then he blurted, 'There's two other pictures. Look at these.' One was the Robin Hood man she'd already seen; the other was three champagne bottles, their corks flying up into the air.

Charlie shook his head sadly. 'It's the same story, I'm afraid. Someone else's head. There's no point in doing in our own heads trying to figure it out. Mike, you could spend days trying. You could take it somewhere else . . .'

Sasha held her breath.

' . . . but they'd tell you the same thing. The only person that knows the secret to these pictures is the guy who drew them.'

'Oh.' Mike looked utterly crestfallen. Now she wanted to pat him, Sasha thought.

'It's OK, Mike, there's lots of other ways to figure out what's going on at those labs.'

'Yeah?' he didn't sound convinced.

'Yeah.' For a moment her mind went blank. 'We could do a company search for a start. Couldn't we, Charlie?'

'Sure.'

'What good would that do?'

'Well, it would give us a list of the directors and shareholders. If it was a secret government installation . . .' Charlie's eyes lit up, and she felt hugely pleased. '. . . perhaps something odd would show up.'

Mike sighed heavily. 'I think Winston already did that.'

'What? A search? You didn't tell me.' She was unable to keep the indignation out of her voice.

'You never asked.'

'I'm going to go get some coffees,' Charlie said quietly, and eased out of his chair. Sasha hardly heard him. 'So what did Winston find out?' she demanded.

Mike shrugged.

She tried to moderate her tone. 'Did he find out who owned the company?'

'I dunno. He only spoke to me once about it. He said the search wasn't conclusive.'

What had she expected? A secret government site would hardly declare itself as such to Companies House.

Mike yawned. He was exhausted, Sasha reminded herself. She shouldn't push him. But then he spoke up again. 'He thought REDEV was part of something else. I dunno what, and he didn't say. But he thought they were doing some really bad stuff, same as some other bastards he knew about, who'd done these experiments on Beagle pups even when they didn't need to, when the information was already there. Makes you fucking sick.' His brow knotted and his face went red. She could see the activist in him now, she thought.

He went on. 'Gerry's old group had done a raid on this other place near Brighton, and taken about twelve pups. They wanted more. There were loads of them.' An angry tear escaped down his cheek. 'But it was all they could get in the jeep. He said it was one of the worst things he'd ever done, choosing which ones to take. That's why, on our raid, we had the big Bedford.' He sniffed. 'But there weren't any pups.'

'No,' she said gently. 'That was a good thing, wasn't it?'

'Yeah. That's what Gerry said. He kept apologising to everyone, you know, on the way back that night. Said he'd been so sure. It's what all his research had been about.'

'Research?' Notes, she thought at once. Documents, trails.

'Yeah. He was writing a book. After he got out of prison he decided he couldn't do direct action any more.'

'So why . . . ?' she started and stopped.

'I dunno. He said Caroline persuaded him to. She can be a bit, well . . .' He tailed off.

What, she wondered? But it wasn't important. 'D'you think it's possible that those men you saw in Winston's house weren't looking for that,' she indicated the laptop, 'but his research notes?'

Another shrug.

Fair enough, she told herself. 'D'you want to call your friend now?'

'Lucas? Yeah. Can I?'

She pushed the phone at him. As she did so she saw Charlie standing at the other end of the room by the TV wall. He'd got out of her way, she realised gratefully. She hoped he didn't think she'd taken over his desk – which she had, rather, she thought guiltily. He caught her eye and gave her a thumbs-up.

'No reply,' Mike said.

She could hear the number ring out. 'Remember, that doesn't mean anything.'

'No.' But he sounded doubtful and his worried look had returned. 'Can I call my mum now?'

'Course you can. Would you like me to talk to her?'

'What for?'

'Oh, nothing really. Just to tell her you're OK, you know.'

'I can tell her that.'

'Course you can.'

'Uh . . .' He blushed. 'Could I, er, go into that room there?'

He wanted privacy. She was sure that Charlie wouldn't mind. 'Go on. I'll wait here.'

In the car at the bottom of the road the man appeared to be most comfortably asleep. Dressed in a hooded tracksuit, he lay back in his semi-reclined driver's seat, his arms crossed and his eyes shut, clearly no longer listening to his Walkman, although it was still securely in place.

In fact, made drowsy by the car's heater, Bennett had dozed off once or twice during the day. Waking, he'd felt no guilt. He'd been hired as a technician and an expert, he thought resentfully; he'd been promised perks and bonuses, a team working under him – and what had happened? He had ended up as the lowliest of the low: a pair of ears sitting in a Sierra.

He scowled at the dashboard clock. It was already dark. Twelve-hour shifts were ridiculous; no one could concentrate for that long. And what about meal-breaks, rest periods, a person's rights?

They were short-staffed, Control had informed him after he'd installed the bug the day before. So, would Bennett mind . . . ? Bennett felt his blood pressure rise considering exactly how much he minded. He'd been finally relieved at eleven o'clock at night, had only just talked himself into a damp pub bedroom, and then, that morning, when he'd been about to leave for home, Control had called again. Would he do the day-shift for them? There wasn't anyone else.

Bennett glowered out at the night. He knew the score now. Oh yes. The thin veneer of politeness that he'd been treated with at first had entirely gone now. He was the hired hand, the laughing stock, because he never got his hands dirty. He had to do what he was told and shut up.

Bennett had only just started work in the private security field. He couldn't go back to his old job – it paid a fraction of what he was on now, and he'd promised his girlfriend all sorts: a new kitchen, a playroom for their twin baby girls . . .

He was three streets away from Liz Pearce's house, well within the radius of the transmitter. As soon as she picked up her phone, the voice-activated tape recorder (that looked so like a Walkman) on his lap would start to spool, and through the headset he would hear every word.

He yawned. Since ten o'clock that morning she'd received one call, from her work, asking if she could switch shifts that night. She could. She'd made one call to a woman who hadn't been in. It hadn't mattered, she'd said, ringing off, but from her tone it clearly had. Bennett had shared her disappointment; a long, gossipy chat with a friend was exactly what he'd been hoping for, one innocent remark that would get him out of there.

He opened an eye and looked at the time. Four-thirty. He'd been in situ for a couple of hours; he ought to be moving on. In a place like this people tended to be generally more observant, especially with the police crawling all over Tenterden, not two miles away. He brought his seat into the upright position and leant forward to start the ignition.

And at that moment she lifted the phone. An incoming call.

'Mum? It's Mike.'

'Mike? Oh thank God, where are you?'

'Still in London.'

'Where?'

'Docklands, Mum. I'm up this tower. I can see the whole of London, all the lights. I'm on about the fiftieth floor . . .'

Bingo, Bennett thought, his complaints dissolving. He picked up his mobile to call Control.

Sasha replaced the receiver, feeling rather shaken. The police press officer, relieved to be talking of something other than the 'Tenterden Four,' had been very helpful. Now, reviewing the account that he'd given her, it sounded vaguely familiar. She must have read about it in the papers.

'How goes it?' Charlie asked quietly beside her. 'It's OK – he's still on the phone in there.'

'Well . . .' She glanced in Mike's direction. 'It makes me reassess him a bit. He didn't mention, for instance, that he and his chums used a gun on the security guard.'

'They shot him?' Charlie's voice rose.

'No, just threatened him with it. Left him tied up in his car, scared shitless. He hasn't really spoken since, apparently. He's still receiving psychiatric care. Pretty unpleasant, don't you think?'

'Yep.' He followed her eyes. Through the glass partitition they could see Mike's dark head bent over the phone. 'I know what you mean. He doesn't seem like that sort of kid. Doesn't look strong enough, for one thing.'

'I think he's been sleeping rough. He's scared to death and brimming with conspiracy theories.' She gave him a shortened version.

'You're sitting on quite a story, there, hon. You don't mind me calling you that, do you?'

'No.' She smiled. 'In fact, I like it.'

He grinned. 'So, what's your next move?'

'I don't know.' She glanced down at the notes she'd made. 'What *is* odd is that the press officer said nothing had been taken. I asked him twice.'

'No mention of this?' He touched the laptop.

'None.'

'Odd, as you say. Makes you wonder if it's the police covering up or the company.'

'Or the government.'

'Indeed.' He pulled the computer towards him. It was still on. He studied the red skyline graphic on the screen. 'What secrets are you hiding?' he asked it softly, and without pause he casually asked, 'D'you think you're going to be free tonight? Only I thought maybe we could spend it together.'

'Ah.' He'd caught her off-guard and she could feel herself blushing. 'It sort of depends on all this – what I'm going to do with him. I mean, I'd really like to, but I—'

The phone on the desk suddenly cheeped and Charlie snatched it up. 'Page,' he barked, and she was taken aback at the change

in him, the serious mask slipped so quickly over the easy exterior.
'Yeah,' he was saying, moving his chair along the desk to another
computer. 'Hang on.' He hit the return key a few times and stared
at the screen.

'New York?' Sasha mouthed, and he nodded. She thought she'd
better leave him to it, go and hover somewhere else.

Ever since his father had left home, barely a year after David had
departed for London, Mike had felt responsible for his mother.
They'd always shared a special bond anyway. Now, for the first
time that he could remember, he was refusing to do what she asked.
She wanted him to go home.

'Please, pet. If you're in trouble I want you here.'

'Mum, if I come home I'll be in trouble. I'm sorting it out, I
promise.'

'How? You're sixteen years old. They'll have a search-warrant
out for you. They'll be looking for you up there.'

He bit his nail.

'I'm ever so sorry I told them you were in Brixton. I didn't think.
But it's a big place, isn't it?'

'Yeah, don't worry.'

'Look, I'll come up to you. I'll call work—'

'No, don't do that,' he said quickly. 'I'm with these journalists
and they're working on it. I've . . . I've got to be with them all the
time. It's going to be OK.'

'What? They're going to expose what the police are trying to do
to you?'

He hated lying to her. Most times he managed to avoid it. 'Kind
of. Mum, don't come up. You need the money and that bastard
might sack you. I'll be home in a couple of days.'

'Oh, Mikey, I don't feel good about this. You'll get yourself a
solicitor?'

'Uh, I dunno. I'll ask the journalists.'

'And you're looking after yourself? Dave's giving you enough to
eat?'

He caught his breath. 'He hasn't called you, has he?'

'Dave?' She laughed shortly. 'When does your brother ever
call me?'

'I miss you, Mum,' he said.

'I miss you too, love.' She sounded choked, worse when she tried
to sound brighter. 'I know I'm being silly, but I'm feeling a bit
jumpy without you in the house.'

'You've been on your own before.'

'Yeah, I know. But ever since the police came I've felt . . . I don't
know. I can't relax.'

Was she safe on her own? he wondered suddenly. 'Mum, why
not go and stay with Alison?'

'I might. Now listen, I want you to call me tomorrow . . .'

There were miniature Christmas trees lit up on lampposts all along
Piccadilly. As Anna drove she listened to McMahon speaking to
Control.

'You're sure? I see. Yes. OK.'

The call ended and he turned to her. 'It must be Canary Wharf.
He said he's on the fiftieth floor; there's only one building in
Docklands that high.'

'Did he say which journalists he's with?' It had been a bad
moment when she'd heard that. She'd remembered someone telling
her years ago that she was lucky, that the cards natually fell in
her favour – but to bear in mind that luck, in the end, always
ran out.

'No. The tower's full of them.'

She stopped at traffic lights. The traffic was quite heavy, but at
least it was moving. They should be there in half an hour, McMahon
said. Fingers crossed. And glancing over she saw that he had done
exactly that, and realised that he was superstitious too.

Simply by the way Mike was sitting, his shoulders hunched up
around his ears, Sasha could see how tense he was, how faraway
his thoughts. She tried again. 'Mike? How's your mum?'

'The police've been,' he answered tonelessly, not turning round.

'Oh.' A dozen thoughts collided in her head. One was: forget
the cover-up, this was the police doing exactly what you'd expect.
Another: Mike was going to be arrested; that machine was going
back to its rightful owner. Another: she could kiss goodbye to
her story.

'They know that Mary and the others were at the labs as
well.'

'Oh. Perhaps that's why Lucas isn't answering his phone. He's been arrested.'

He turned to look at her.

'Only a suggestion.'

'D'you think Lucas talked?'

'I've no idea. But someone has, haven't they?' She stared at him. 'Look, Mike, I'm going to go down to Tenterden tomorrow.'

'You are?' His face lit up. She was glad he approved; she'd only just decided.

'Yes. D'you want a lift home?'

'What, and get arrested? No thanks!'

She gazed down at the floor: practical dark-blue carpet. If he did what she was about to suggest she really could wave the story goodbye. However . . . 'It might be better to turn yourself in, you know. That raid was a serious business, but you're very young and I'm sure they'll be lenient with you, especially if you co-operate.'

He gave her a scornful look. 'If I talk, you mean.'

She studied him for a moment. 'Whose idea was it to use a gun?'

'Why, you going to tell the police?'

'No, I'm not,' she said quietly. 'I was just curious. From what you've told me I find it difficult to believe that your group was violent.'

'No one got hurt.'

'That's not strictly true. The security guard's in a pretty bad way psychologically. He's only nineteen, just a few years older than you.'

'He shouldn't have been working for a place like that then, should he?'

'A place like *what*? From the evidence of your own eyes, nothing so terrible was going on there, was it?'

He said nothing.

'The guard, by the way, wasn't employed by REDEV. He was from a small local firm, working on contract. In case you're concerned.'

But he was affecting total disinterest, swinging gently in his chair. She was sure she'd never been as irritating as that, but at his age she hadn't been breaking and entering or witnessing people being abducted by mysterious strangers. In comparison, she'd been rather dull.

'Hi.' Charlie appeared in the doorway beside her. 'What's the plan?'

She told him, adding that she'd leave in the morning after hiring a car. Don't do that, he said, she could borrow one of his, he had three.

'You've got three cars?' Mike echoed, coming back to life.

'Yep. Well, they're the company's. They bought them back in the good old days. I keep thinking someone's going to realise that there's only one of me now, but no one has – yet.'

'Cadillacs?' Mike queried eagerly. 'Chevvies?'

'No, sorry.' Charlie shook his head ruefully. ''Fraid not. European vehicles for the European bureau. But they're not bad. BMW seven series convertible, air-conditioning, on-board radar-assisted parking . . .'

'Neat.' Mike's eyes shone.

'. . . computerised information console giving interior and exterior temperatures, traffic information, route maps and a whole lot more. Plus a Range Rover and a jeep. They're at Floral Street,' he added, lightly touching Sasha's arm. 'You can take your pick tonight.'

She swallowed. 'That's fine. Great. Thank you. Um . . .,' She glanced down at Mike, who was watching her curiously. 'The question is, if you're not coming with me . . .'

He shook his head vigorously.

'. . . how do I contact you?'

'I'll call you,' he said quickly, avoiding her eyes.

'Right.'

How to suggest what she wanted, she wondered, without insulting him or giving him the wrong idea? 'But I'd feel much happier if I had a number for you. In case I need to get hold of you fast – check things out, you know.'

He looked at the floor. Suddenly he coughed in that painful way he had in the café.

'That sounds pretty rough,' Charlie said sympathetically. 'I don't want to interfere with any plans you might have for kipping on someone's floor, but I can offer you a bed at my place. I've got three bedrooms.'

Mike glanced up, his relief obvious. About as great as her own, Sasha guessed, mentally worshipping Charlie. Of course, the thought occurred a split-second later that this would put on hold any other plans for that night.

'I'd really appreciate the chance to look at your laptop again,' Charlie was saying. 'I test-drove one over the summer, one like it anyhow. New York was thinking about getting some.'

'Sure,' said Mike generously. 'You got cable at your place?'

'Obligatory throughout. You can't get away from it.' He checked his watch. 'Ah, I hate to say this, but I'm going to have to get on with a story New York want. Maybe you two could . . .'

Sasha nodded. 'My flat's in the same building as Charlie's, Mike.'

'You don't live together?'

She felt herself blush. 'No.'

'Not yet,' Charlie told him seriously. 'Ah.' One of the journalists was waving a phone at him. 'I've got to go. See you later.' He left them.

'In the meantime,' Sasha said to Mike, 'I'll show you my computer. Give you a laugh.'

'Why?' He frowned, but it faded into a grin. 'You're still red, you know. You really fancy him, don't you?'

'Oh, come on, you,' she muttered, going out.

By one of the marble pillars in the lobby, Anna waited. With her, ill at ease, stood the London end of the team. She hadn't met them before, which was how she preferred it; apart from when it was unavoidable, she passed her orders through a go-between – in this case, McMahon – who relayed them to Control. The fewer people who could identify her the better. Additionally (and she wrinkled her nose slightly), these two men looked dishevelled; the larger looked like a thug, the smaller was shifty-eyed and jumpy. They didn't blend in.

She glanced about, taking in the grandeur of her surroundings, and took a small step away from them. They didn't know how to relate to her. When she'd arrived they'd mumbled and nodded their heads in her direction, then with their eyes longingly followed McMahon as he walked over to the reception desk to make enquiries. They thought he should be in charge, not her.

It didn't matter what they thought, but in her current frame of mind it had the power to irritate. She lifted her own eyes in McMahon's direction, taking in the broad outline of his back.

McMahon she could respect; he had some good ideas and he obeyed orders, and in spite of his size — six foot three and muscular — he understood about fitting in. The two security guards he was addressing now in his quiet, low voice, showing them the boy's photograph — she could see it being slid across the counter — would believe that he was a policeman, or the father of the boy, or whichever figure he had decided to impersonate.

Whereas these two . . . The smaller one was shifting from foot to foot; the larger one scowled at a passer-by, a woman carrying shopping bags, who immediately quickened her pace, glancing back at him over her shoulder.

Anna exhaled slowly. On the wall opposite there was a brass plaque listing the building's companies. Her eyes ran down it, counting nine newspapers, sixteen magazines, four news bureaux, five agencies. Some gave their floor numbers, others not. She frowned. There was nothing listed for the fiftieth floor.

McMahon was coming back. When he reached them he said quickly, 'He came in with a girl about half an hour ago.'

'This is the only way in or out?' Anna asked.

He nodded. 'There's four banks of lifts.'

And there were four of them. 'You,' she said to the smaller man, 'take that lift over there. Cover floors one to ten.' McMahon and the bigger man were to split the next twenty between them, and she would take the rest.

The lift doors opened and closed, one after another, behind them all.

The first lift was too crammed to admit anyone else. Sasha stepped back, saying to Mike, 'I hadn't realised this place was so popular.'

'It's the view,' he said. 'You can see all over London from the fiftieth floor. Didn't you know that?'

'No. Well, I might have. Ah, here's another one.'

It was fairly full with Japanese tourists, but there was enough space for two. She stepped in, holding the doors open, but Mike didn't move. 'Come on,' she said.

'I'm not going in there,' he muttered.

'What?'

'I get claustrophobia,' he hissed, his face flaming.

The tourists stared.

'Oh, for goodness sake!' she exclaimed and stepped back out.

The door slid shut. She turned to him. 'I don't understand. You were all right on the way up.'

'It wasn't crowded.'

She took a deep breath. They were on the thirty-first floor. Another lift arrived, this one three-quarters full. Sasha glanced at Mike. He shook his head, and the lift departed.

'So, uh, how many people are you OK with? Ten? Five?'

He gave her a hurt look. 'It's all right for you to mock.'

'I'm not, honestly. But I do want to go home tonight, and I don't see how else—'

'I guess ten would be OK,' he conceded reluctantly.

'Great.' She smiled encouragingly. 'We'll just wait.' She lolled against the wall. 'How long've you had claustrophobia?'

'About four years. That's why I went to those demos. I couldn't stand the thought of those lambs being crammed in like that, hardly able to stand. It made me sick.'

'Me too.'

'Yeah?' He glanced at her. 'I never thought journalists . . . I mean—'

'Had hearts?' She raised her eyebrows. 'But you're the one who wants to be a journalist, aren't you?'

He blushed. 'Yeah, but—'

'You can't categorise people. Some of the ways animals are treated make me want to throw up. Why's that so shocking?'

'It isn't. It's just that the reporters at Shoreham seemed more in with the police. And they twisted people's words, tried to make us out to be anarchists.'

'I didn't.'

'No.' He blushed again. 'I never saw what you wrote.'

'It's in German. I'll show you. Ah! Lift number four . . .'

There were far too many people in the lift, a whole hoard of them, a sightseeing party, chattering away, jabbing into Anna with their video cameras and umbrellas. She held herself in, closing herself off, imagining herself elsewhere: on the private beach beside the villa in Cyprus. She stared above their heads, at the indicator, telling herself that it would only take a moment; she was only travelling one floor.

The lift stopped and she prepared to breathe fresh air. She stepped out on to the blue carpet and glanced to her left, to a view of the city at night spread out below. Then to her right: double doors, obviously locked, and behind them, darkness. She looked left and just caught a flash of red as someone disappeared behind the doors of the lift beside her.

CHAPTER NINETEEN

It was such a relief to be returning to London after the weekend – particularly *that* weekend. Glancing up and seeing another motorway junction slip past, the minister sighed happily and deeply. She would soon be back where she belonged.

Whenever she was asked (and she often was), Philippa Tyler was able to speak movingly and convincingly about quality time with her daughters. The truth was, they bored her. She simply wasn't interested in their concerns, their endless chatter about best friends, teachers and clothes. The latter frankly amazed her: how children their age craved designer labels!

However – she readjusted her skirt to prevent it wrinkling – it was a good thing that they did. It meant that, by the simple expedient of a telephone call to the nanny, she could discover that week's particular craving, despatch her secretary to acquire two of them – Samantha always wanted what Katie did – and know that at least her arrival would be greeted with enthusiasm and, hopefully, good behaviour. Generally the latter was merely desirable, but occasionally (like this weekend) it was essential.

Philippa compressed her lips. Following the tremendous publicity of the previous week – her inauguration as (she smiled briefly, she so loved the title) Queen of the Genes – one of the Sunday papers had

asked to profile her. As part of the package – it was to be a whole
page – they'd requested photographs of Philippa in the bosom of her
family. She'd had to agree; it would have looked too odd to refuse;
she'd just finished gushing to the journalist about so much looking
forward to 'a whole weekend with my little girls. No meetings, no
engagments – what a treat!'

Gianni, her husband, had agreed; he found such occasions
quite amusing. The girls, on the other hand . . . Gone were the
days when they could be dressed up in frocks and told to be nice.
Katie had called her at work half-way through Friday afternoon,
saying she 'understood' (Philippa had done a double-take; the
child was only eight years old) that she and Sam weren't to be
allowed to go riding in the morning, that a photographer was
coming for breakfast.

'Yes, dear?' Philippa had tried to keep the edge out of her voice,
but she'd had a host of paperwork to get through, then a late-night
drive home and an entire weekend with the girls rather than a day
and a half (or, when work allowed, simply Sunday). 'What is it?'

As well as the trainers that she and Sam needed – designer, of
course, Katie had told her they wanted new ski-wear for Verbier
later in the month. Everyone else had it. Katie said she'd told Sam
that they could wait, but Sam was being a baby and said that she
might be upset in the morning if she didn't have it. 'She mightn't
look very happy, Mummy. For the pictures . . .'

Philippa had had no choice. Her secretary had been sent out
again, and the outfits, criminally expensive, purchased and left at
the bottom of their beds.

The girls had played their part, been angelic, nauseatingly so:
skipping through the house hand in hand, smiling winsomely, Sam
actually lisping, making eyes at the photographer. But they'd said
'please' and 'thank you', there'd been no tantrums, and mercifully
the session hadn't lasted long. By midday, anxious to catch his
deadline, the photographer had gone.

'Excellent little actresses, aren't they?' Gianni had commented
as they'd retreated to the conservatory for drinks. Through the
window the girls, adorned in their glistening ski-wear, could be
seen imitating the photographer. 'They take after their mother,
I think.'

Philippa gazed thoughtfully at the back of her driver's head.

Though she'd laughed the comment off at the time, and her husband had had the grace to let her, she now admitted that probably he was right. The thought was more than a little unnerving. She sighed. If only he hadn't been so insistent on having children. But then, he was an Italian; and she was very fond of him, always had been.

During both pregnancies, the first occuring when she was thirty-five, she'd kept up a punishing work schedule, but both babies had been faultless and born easily at full-term. Gianni had been disappointed (but only briefly) at their gender. Now he revelled in them, adored them, lazily accused Philippa of being a dreadful mother, but added that they'd pay her back in the end; children always did.

Philippa raised an eyebrow. Perhaps that weekend's exhibition had marked the start of it. A disturbing development, yes, in a way – but also, she had to admit, quite interesting. Certainly of more interest to her than anything they'd demonstrated thus far.

'Traffic's light this morning, Minister,' the driver called out cheerfully. She blinked. They'd already left the M4 and were entering London.

'It is indeed,' she answered. They'd be at the BBC in about twenty minutes, well within time for her interview, scheduled for just after the seven o'clock news. She was going to be asked about the rumours, circulated in some of the Sunday papers, that she was about to make a leadership challenge. Ridiculous, Philippa told herself, adjusting her engagement ring; an outright challenge was not her style, didn't suit her image – and besides, she wasn't yet ready.

She glanced at the pile of newspapers in her lap. She'd already skimmed through them, but ought to do so again. She opened a middle-market tabloid, saw an interview with the shadow health secretary, talking about closed wards. How handy, she thought, beginning a mental rehearsal. She'd deal quickly and decisively with the leadership question, then move back on to firmer ground, citing the article as proof that the opposition had yet again missed the boat. Had her counterpart not heard of the new government policy on *opening* wards? As in the case of St Peter's and IVF patients . . .

Pause for sigh, not too long or the interviewer might jump in, then: 'My own children are *so* precious to me. I can only imagine the heartache of those who are unable to conceive . . .'

*   *   *

At a little before seven o'clock that morning, Melanie gave up the struggle for sleep and eased herself out from under the duvet, taking care not to wake Patrick.

She went softly downstairs, tiptoeing past Ludo's door and into the kitchen where, very quietly, mindful as always of the thin walls, she switched on the kettle. She felt much better standing up than lying down. While she'd never actually vomited during her pregnancies, she'd often felt, at about this stage, fairly nauseous. It would pass, she told herself, only another few weeks, and until then she would be able to handle it easily.

She glanced over at the draining-board, saw the stack of plates and cups haphazardly balanced there, and smiled. Patrick was trying to be so helpful, not letting her do anything, deaf to her protests that she wasn't made of glass. Even Ludo, not usually very receptive, had noticed, and asked if she was sick. And suddenly, though not as they'd planned, the moment had arrived.

'No', Melanie had said carefully, 'Mummy isn't sick, only . . .'

'What?' Ludo had demanded. He'd been on the floor, playing with his cars. He'd repeated the question more loudly, not used to his questions being ignored.

'Would you like a baby brother?' Patrick had sounded so natural as he'd said it. Beside him on the sofa, Melanie had felt her heart hammering. She'd placed her hand gently on his arm.

Ludo had gazed expressionlessly, first at his father, then at her. Oh God, she'd thought, panic-stricken. He hates us. He thinks we've betrayed him, that we're trying to replace him.

'Darling, don't think that—'

'I wouldn't mind,' he'd said casually, and gone back to his game, seeming at once to become engrossed. Patrick, glancing at her, had crossed his fingers, and at that moment Ludo had raised his head again. He'd been smiling.

He hadn't smiled at her like that, she'd thought, staring, for years. Not since he'd been really small. 'I'd really like it,' he'd said simply, and she'd had to leave the room because she hadn't wanted him to see her cry.

Behind her she'd heard Patrick say in a choking voice, 'Sorry about this, Ludi. Your mum and dad are a right pair of cry-babies, aren't we?'

The kettle switched itself off. She was aware of the sound but didn't respond to it. After she'd gone back into the room, the three of them had sat on the sofa watching Ludo's silly videos, laughing at them although they'd all seen them countless times, much more of a normal family than they'd been for as long as she could remember. Probably pre-diagnosis.

It was as if, Mel thought slowly, someone had placed an enchanted spell on her family, finally, after so much heartache. She smiled, remembering Dr West's high-domed head and nervousness; he didn't look like much of a guardian angel, although perhaps he was exactly the sort she would get. Feeling absurdly happy again, the nausea gone, she spooned coffee into a mug. She'd written a letter last night to the doctor, after Ludo had gone to sleep, thanking the man for what he'd done. He probably got letters like hers all the time; he'd probably chuck it in the bin, although she hoped not. However inadequately she'd expressed it, she'd meant every word.

Checking the time, she saw that it was almost seven-fifteen, time to wake her boys. She switched on the radio.

'. . . We estimate that within three months, St Peter's will be able to offer that precious hope to nearly a hundred couples seeking IVF.'

Oh God, Mel thought automatically. Everywhere you went, even in your own home, there was always someone pushing in – doctors, or in this case politicians – extolling IVF. Her hand reached for the 'off' button, then stopped. It didn't affect her any more. She wasn't going to have to go through that terrible process again: girl babies only, kill the boys.

'Mum,' Ludo muttered, only quietly, but she heard him.

'Coming, darling,' she called back, and she felt light as a feather, enormously lucky, as she left the room and the voice of the health minister behind her.

By seven-twenty Sasha had cleared the remnants of the south-eastern suburbs and was on the short stretch of the M25, heading for the Hastings road. She didn't feel entirely awake yet, six-o'clock wake-ups not being her forté, but she knew it was necessary to avoid the rush hour. She was hoping to get back to London that night, and she'd a lot to pack in.

Of course, she told herself, slipping into the slower lane to avoid the advance of a flashing Porsche, it would have helped if she'd gone to bed before one o'clock, and once there had been able to sleep. But her mind had been buzzing, partly with the gallons of coffee she'd drunk by then, but mainly with the story. Tried though she had to find a logical explanation to it all, it wouldn't fit. Sharp angles kept prodding at her, like broken glass in a sack, jolting her awake when she'd just slipped into a doze. At almost two in the morning she'd actually considered getting up and going down then, but by that time she'd been too tired to move. When she had finally fallen asleep she'd dreamt of animals screaming behind bars, of a woman with a perfect face but whose eyes were evil, dead with what they'd seen and done – Mike's woman, she realised now. She wished his description, or rather the look on his face when he'd talked about her, hadn't been quite so graphic.

'She looked as if . . .' He'd bitten his lip, apparently unable to continue. They'd been on the tube, approaching the Temple, the last stop on their journey. He'd lapsed into a silence so long that she thought he'd fallen asleep. Then he'd raised his head. 'She's really beautiful, you know?' His voice had been barely audible. 'Perfect. But the way her eyes were . . . they were . . . It was as if she'd done so many terrible things that she didn't see properly any more. The way she looked at me, as if I was nothing, as if she might kill me or not, as if it didn't matter . . .'

Once inside her flat, however, his demons had receded. True to expectations he'd jeered at her computer, couldn't believe that it wasn't in a museum, couldn't understand anyone, especially a journalist, working on something so ancient and slow. Could it even take a modem? he'd asked incredulously.

Slightly stung, she'd asked, 'So, what's more important to you, computers or animal rights?'

'Computers are . . .' He'd shrugged. 'They don't need me, not like animals do. Computers don't feel, do they?' Lounging back against her computer desk, Mike had regarded her critically. 'I mean, if you stick a prod in a computer's brain, it's not going to hurt it, is it? It's not going to scream. But animals . . .' His eyes had screwed up. 'You know the kind of things they do to non-human animals in these places? Cut their brains open and take bits out, to see what their drugs have done. Or,' he'd shifted and she'd seen the bench wobble, 'put shampoo in their eyes to see if it's going to hurt humans.'

He had looked so belligerent, actually quite intimidating. A devil of her own had made her say, quite casually, 'So, how far would you go in this defence, Mike? Would you kill someone? Bomb their home?'

'A human abuser? Sure.'

'Even if it meant innocent people getting hurt? Like children? Or a cat or a dog?'

'We'd make sure.'

'How? Suppose something went wrong?'

He'd turned his back, rubbed his finger along the casing of her computer. 'Casualties of war,' he'd mumbled.

She wasn't convinced. A little later, while she'd been cooking spaghetti and cheese, he'd appeared in the kitchen doorway. 'That guard. Is he going to be OK?'

When she'd told him she didn't know, he'd fallen silent again, started plucking at a piece of loose formica on her work-surface. Then he'd muttered something about how no one was meant to have been hurt; they'd only meant to scare the guard into doing what they wanted.

Sasha had gone on stirring the pasta. 'So, how much preparation did your group do for this raid?'

For ten weeks prior to the raid, he'd told her, the unit had mounted a full-scale surveillance operation on REDEV employees. They'd been followed home, sometimes by car (Stuart, Chris, Lucas, Andrew and Caroline), at other times by bicycle (Mary or Mike). Not Winston, because of his record and the risk of someone reporting him. Mike and Mary had quite often teamed up – hanging around outside someone's house had looked OK, he'd said, blushing, 'sort of boyfriend/girlfriend, you know?'

'How did you all communicate?' Sasha had interrupted. 'You said that you didn't have meetings.'

He'd sighed impatiently. Word of mouth, of course. He'd slip into the library to speak to Caroline, or pass on a message to Andrew through Mary. Chris Manyon would drop into the farm-shop where Lucas worked. It was easy. They'd only ever had two full meetings. Caroline had never known that Mike had visited Gerry occasionally.

They'd eaten, and Mike had slid down on to the sofa and

fallen asleep. Watching him, thinking how young he looked, she'd wondered whether she shouldn't phone his mother after all. But that would wreck her relationship with him and ruin all hopes of the story. If he went home he'd be arrested. Then, fortuitously, Charlie had rung the bell. Though Mike had stirred he hadn't woken, and she'd let Charlie in, whispering, 'Ssh.'

'Baby asleep?'

'Dead to the world.'

In her tiny hallway, standing so close together, they'd had no other option than to touch, the back of her hand against his, his arm against hers, then he had pulled her towards him, into himself, his arms coming about her, gentle but insistent. She had tilted her head up, felt the touch of his lips, soft as velvet on her brow, moving down slowly over her face. 'Oh, Sash,' he'd whispered, tightening around her. She'd felt herself melting into him.

'Excuse me.'

Mike's sudden appearance behind her had caused her near heart-failure, closely followed by acute embarrassment. She'd leaped away from Charlie as if he'd electrocuted her.

She grinned, remembering Mike's flaming face, his mumblings about hearing a noise and coming to investigate. It was difficult to say who'd been the most embarrassed.

Charlie had saved the day. At his suggestion they'd adjourned to the basement to look at the cars, and any conversational contribution from Sasha had become extraneous. Charlie and Mike had talked of speed, turning-circles and three-litre engines. Mike had drooled over the jeep before coming to an adoring halt in front of the BMW.

'Isn't she a beauty?' he'd crooned.

'She's cute, yeah.'

Sasha had opened her mouth to comment on the colour, a blue so dark it was almost black, but had realised in time that it was too much of a cliché.

They'd been too interested in the dashboard anyway by then, Charlie explaining the gadgets, Mike eagerly questioning, exclaiming at the way the hood vanished so discreetly into the cavity at the back. (She'd been impressed too, but no one had seemed very interested in that.)

She'd been extremely tired by the time they'd returned to the flat to collect Mike's things, and he'd been asleep on his feet in the lift; but, annoyingly, inside he'd revived and requested more food. So too, when asked, had Charlie. Poor man, she thought now tenderly – he hadn't eaten since noon, he'd been too involved first in looking after them, then in his story, and he'd had nothing in the fridge. So she'd ended up raiding her tins. Mike had abandoned his portion of bean stew but Charlie, though not enthusing, had swallowed every mouthful. Then, mad though it now seemed, they'd sat up until nearly midnight, puzzling over the hunter graphic on the laptop. She'd been well into her second wind by then, could have stayed up all night, and it had been Charlie who'd eventually called a halt, ushered Mike to the door, turned to kiss her: just a peck, because Mike had been there . . .

Tonight, she thought, taking a deep breath, making the promise. Charlie's shift wouldn't finish until the early hours – which was fine, it gave her more time, until midnight if she needed it.

She glanced at the clock, and turned on the radio for the news headlines.

'. . . the health minister denied reports that she was seeking to challenge the party leadership. Mrs Tyler said that her role was to show the caring side of government and to promote the interests of British biotechnology, as in the case of Infutopin, the IVF "cure" . . .'

Sasha grinned and shook her head. For how much longer could Philippa continue to milk the story? Go for it, girl, she urged, and accelerated out into the fast lane again.

CHAPTER TWENTY

It was eight-thirty on Monday morning. The meeting had been in progress for ten minutes, and the mood of the chief executive had never been better. Branium's share prices that morning had risen to an all-time high.

'Imagine what they're going to do when we launch the Infiltrator,' he chuckled.

The legal director closed his eyes, the better to savour the moment. 'It'll be an historic day on the Stock Exchange.'

Together they turned to the third man present. 'John, tell us when that's going to be.'

Sitting in his customary place to the left of the chief executive and opposite the lawyer – all of them grouped round the steel and glass coffee-table – John Stockart looked to them as he always did, well-groomed in an expensive suit, from the sleeves of which peeped silver stirrup cuff-links. But he gave no indication that he'd heard the question.

'John?'

His stomach gnawed, but he was in such a strange state that he could distance himself from the pain.

'I'm sorry.' He blinked, coming back to the present.

The chief executive and the lawyer were watching him with

amusement, actual fondness. Their golden boy. 'Another late night?' The chief executive raised his eyebrows. 'What we wouldn't give, eh?' He turned to the lawyer. 'To be single again?'

Stockart smiled. Play along, he told himself, go through the motions, give yourself time.

The chief executive repeated his question, and Stockart referred him to a date in late March.

'We ought to do something really big to mark it. Something spectacular.'

A silence fell. He *must* tell them, Stockart thought, gazing over at the chief executive, a large man, big-boned and barrel-bellied, but with his confidence able to carry off his size.

'I know!' The man's eyes sparkled. 'Why don't we hire Concorde? Go supersonic!'

'Show us going through the stratosphere?' The lawyer slapped his leg. 'With our logo on it. Brilliant!'

He really meant it; he wasn't toadying. That's what these 'GO' meetings were all about: Gloves Off time, as the chief executive had told Stockart when he'd first invited him to join them. He was to feel entirely free to say or ask anything he liked, and they would do likewise. No having to mind one's 'p's and 'q's, no worry about treading on people's toes; they were all friends, all big boys together, not given to attacks of the vapours. So it had been in there, five years before, that they'd decided to dedicate a team to the discovery of the intelligence genes, no matter what the other directors, executive and non-executive, might have been told. And it had been in there only a month before that they'd celebrated the team's findings: the identification and isolation of a human brain cell gene which produces a protein that increases the speed with which nerve cells transmit their signals. In short, an IQ enhancer. Use the Infiltrator to insert it into fetuses – and they would be really into the multi-billion market. It wasn't a dream, they'd told each other, everyone grinning. They were looking at reality. One of West's back-room team was already working on it.

'When d'you think these people are going to produce the first bright baby, John?'

He turned slowly. The lawyer had asked the question. Was the man reading his mind? He shook himself. This was their favourite topic; they always came back to it.

He cleared his throat. 'Two years?'

The chief executive sighed happily. 'Perfect! The public will've got used to the idea by then. What's after Duchenne's?'

He knew perfectly well but he always liked to hear it. Following the 'test-drive' of Duchenne's, the Infiltrator was to be used to cure Cystic Fibrosis. Two terrible diseases, but with relatively few sufferers. Which of course had financial implications for Branium: all things taken into account, the R and D costs of the Infiltrator ran into millions, and the company had no intention of squandering that money on what was termed 'orphan' conditions. So, after two 'good guy' cures (during which any final adjustments to the technique could safely be made), the Infiltrator was moving out into the real world, where the money was, to take on the major players in the market of life and death.

The chief executive beamed. 'Pinch me, someone, will you?'

The lawyer laughed and Stockart joined in, but his own laughter sounded somehow wrong to him. They were obviously fooled. Still, he'd have to tell them what he knew, and the sooner the better.

It had been in this strangely shaped, artifically lit room that, less than a fortnight before, he'd told them about the break-in. Up to you, John, they'd said. The same way they had over the Albanian report and the SWii Syndrome. The same way they had over West. You look after him, John, give him anything he needs, pamper him, don't bother us with the details.

Go meeting, he thought bitterly. Oh yes, but only on their terms. They set the agenda.

For the first time since his discovery that morning he pictured West's face: the mealy, arrogant mouth, the bulging eyes, the whiny voice. He could kill him; he wanted to. He could feel his hands round the man's throat. The pain surged in his stomach, and he distanced himself again in mind.

Less than forty minutes before, arriving in his office feeling pretty good – well, not too bad – and remembering that one of the boys, Subject Six, was due to be born that day, he'd decided to check on whether he'd arrived yet.

He wasn't a medical man, but he knew how to operate DAMR. He'd keyed in the command and waited for the names to appear. What he'd seen on the screen had made him freeze.

Anyone with the normal amount of intelligence could work

DAMR. That was one of the things that angered him most: that West obviously hadn't credited him with sufficient intelligence to figure out what was going on, what he was trying to cover up.

Of the five babies who'd been born, three were displaying symptoms of Leukaemia. Two were already in hospital. The third, Subject One, the boy who'd promised so much, whose good health had led to his commissioning of that report, had been taken to his GP on Saturday morning. He was suffering from unexplained bruising. Stockart knew what that meant. Soon it would be Subject Three's turn – he was six weeks old, ripe for it – and then Subject Five, the baby so to speak, only nineteen days old. But one mustn't forget the new arrival, Stockart had told himself, the infant due to arrive that day. And then there were the ten still to be born in the coming year. Two of the pregnancies were too far advanced to be aborted. It was Doomsday. Eighteen subjects, eighteen deaths – whether by miscarriage, Leukaemia or medical termination.

Stockart looked over at the chief executive. He was grinning broadly, lots of big teeth, quite coarse features – he could be coarse. Then he looked at the lawyer, almost sixty but looking younger, dark-rimmed glasses, neat, close-cropped grey hair, proud of the fact that he still had to shave twice a day, imperturbable as lawyers should be.

What were they going to say when he told them the news? That the whole programme would have to be cancelled? That the secrecy of the UK trial – probably Albania too – was about to be exploded? That they faced God knows what kind of government enquiries, all research halted, themselves investigated, arrested, put in prison?

They were talking now about photo opportunities. 'How about West with some of the parents and kids?' the lawyer suggested. 'The parents will know by then, won't they? And it'll be West's big moment, his day.'

'God, no!' The chief executive shuddered theatrically. 'The guy's ugly as sin! The kids will scream their little heads off.'

Stockart opened his mouth to speak but the words wouldn't come. His mind seemed to swim out of focus. They'd only tell him, he saw in a flash, to take care of things, the way they always had, the way everyone expected him to.

So *why* tell them? He frowned. Surely it couldn't be that simple.

But the thought, now inside his head, wouldn't be dislodged. They wouldn't want to be bothered with how he sorted it out, only that he did. He could hear them saying it: the chief executive drawling that they'd leave it up to him; the lawyer holding up a halting hand. Let not the right hand know . . . Sort it out, John.

He was on his own now, the way he always had been. The problem was a hard one, but not insurmountable. Nothing ever was. He concentrated hard. In the unborn section: the three youngest fetuses, those under thirteen weeks, could be aborted without much difficulty. He felt a light come on, his mind kicking in again, working properly. A medical excuse would have to be thought of for the parents. The worm in his stomach turned a tighter knotch. West could do that – and why shouldn't the scheming, stupid old bastard get his hands dirty for once? Stockart smiled to himself. West could handle the later pregnancies too. He was the medical genius, wasn't he? He could prescribe something for the mothers to make them miscarry. Why, several of the parents had already booked into the Mistletoe for their sons' births, so West could be on hand to sort them out one by one. Even in this day and age, Stockart told himself, birth was still a dangerous time. Some babies simply didn't survive.

That was the unborn dealt with. Stockart felt quite light-headed with relief. It only proved, he told himself, that problems needed to be looked at logically, broken down into small manageable units – and before one knew it, problem solved.

There remained, however, the other problem. He rubbed his chin thoughtfully. In fishing for subjects, they had tried to throw as wide a net as possible across the country, to ensure that there weren't any clusters. But it hadn't been that easy. Although initially there'd been a good spread of referrals, as luck would have it, most of the 'successful' candidates – those carrying DMD fetuses – had come from around the south and west of England. It had given them two pretty significant clusters, five in the Greater London area and three around Bristol. Of course, those figures were for live births, and he was going to make sure that, after today, there weren't any more of those. But even so . . .

Subject One, Jeremy Gilbert, lived in Clapham, South London. Subject Three lived in Fulham, just over the Thames, and he wasn't sick yet. Stockart chewed his knuckle. And Subject Two: he'd been transferred from the hospital near his home in Frome, Somerset, to Bristol. Subject Five, the youngest, lived in Bristol. When he started displaying symptoms, when the two sets of stricken parents met in the children's ward, started comparing notes: Duchenne's, West, and the Mistletoe . . . Stockart felt himself pale.

It had been all right when everything had been going well. The risk factor had been assessed as small – none of the trial parents shared the same GP or attended the same pre-natal class. But now the disease itself would draw them together, into the same hospitals, to the same doctors. Statistically the chances of that happening were high; he dared to think how high, statistically.

He stopped, his eyes becoming fixed on a minute smear on the coffee-table. He'd always enjoyed statistics, hadn't he? What could be done with them? The truth massaged, black made white. Compared with what he'd done in the past, he thought. All he had to do was whittle down the statistics. Muddy the waters. So if anyone ever came looking, what would they see? No common denominator, but a sad parade of tragedies. One Leukaemia, an accident, a murder. He nodded to himself, acknowledging the source of his inspiration, feeding on it: Hall shrugging at him, suggesting a heart attack, a drunk-driver . . .

He glanced at his watch. Hall would be in his office by now.

'Are we keeping you, John?'

'Sorry.' He smiled expansively. Amazing, he thought, how good he was feeling again. The pain (he made an internal inventory) had vanished. Like magic. Give John a problem, he told himself exuberantly, and watch him solve it. He wondered fleetingly whether he should share his solution with the other two after all: bathe in their admiration again. But no, he had already had enough of that.

He'd go ahead, as planned, on his own.

He turned an attentive face to the chief executive. 'Just wondering whether Subject Six has been born yet.'

'You big softie.' The man chuckled again. 'You ought to have some kids yourself, John boy. That'd cure you of it, I can tell you.'

The baby had been born an hour before.

'Look,' his mother said adoringly. 'He's got the tiniest little fingernails. And his eye-lashes! They're so long! He's just perfect!'

Her husband smiled through his tears. Unlike many in their situation, this was their first child. They hadn't wanted the anguish of producing a daughter with the same inheritance as the mother's, and to have a male child and watch him waste away would, they felt, have been too great a suffering. The decision to be childless had been terrible at first, but they had accustomed themselves to it over the years. When the woman had missed a period they'd assumed it was the first sign of the menopause; she'd been forty-four. Then had come the explosion of joy that had followed the pregnancy test – the turning upside-down of everything they'd taught themselves to want – before the awareness had kicked in; that with the woman's genetic make-up, on top of her age, the chances of the fetus being viable were minimal.

They'd called it 'it', had referred to having it 'taken out' like a bad tooth, and had been mightily relieved to hear of the Mistletoe's 'quickie' test. 'Soon be over,' they'd counselled one another, each being brave for the other, the way they always had because they were all the familly they were ever going to have.

Then, against all the odds, to be told that the fetus was male and healthy . . . It had seemed like God's own miracle.

He hugged his wife tightly as she cradled the baby. He'd been afraid to touch him, but now, as if drawn by another force, he very gently stroked the tiny, soft cheek.

'Oh, my darling,' he said, and broke down utterly, his sobs shaking the bed.

'Don't. Please, don't.'

'Why? After everything?'

Stillborn.

They'd left them alone in a private room with their dead son for as long as they wanted.

She patted her husband mechanically, her eyes never leaving the baby's pale face, her smile of wonderment still intact.

'D'you think it's something we did?' he blurted. 'We were so careful with your rest and everything! D'you think,' his blood-shot eyes widened in shock, 'it's what *they* did? That bloody test! They ruined him!'

'Sssh, Sssh. Of course they didn't ruin him! See how beautiful he is. Artist's fingers, look.'

'But he's dead! He was born dead.'

She turned blank eyes upon him. 'At least we had him. Our son existed. He never had to suffer. No one can take that away.'

A stillbirth always depressed the delivery team, no matter how many times they'd witnessed it before. However, procedures had to be followed, forms completed. Subject Six's entry and exit from the world was duly recorded and entered into DAMR at ten o'clock that morning.

On the way over to Hall's office in a taxi, Anna had felt a spasm of apprehension.

During the brief telephone call, Hall had said that he wanted to see her on her own and at once. He'd sounded as polite as ever, as quietly professional, but she'd never received a summons from him before during an operation, and it had occurred to her as she'd quickly finished dressing and left the hotel room that he might wish to voice his displeasure in person at her failure.

But now she allowed herself a small smile. Seated in Hall's office – rather overstuffed Louis XIV, too pink-and-gilt for her taste, but good for clients, confirmation that, sitting there, they need never dirty their hands – she could see how foolish her fears had been.

Hall hadn't asked her there to reprimand her. In retrospect she realised that he'd looked slightly taken aback when she'd launched into a detailed report on the search of the Canary Wharf tower the previous evening: how most of the offices had been closed, and those that had been open allowed entry by swipe-card only; how she and McMahon had tried a dual approach on the security guards – her, the tearful mother; him, the desperate father of a missing boy – but the guards genuinely hadn't known any more.

She'd kept everyone there until midnight before concluding that the boy must have gone before they had arrived. She'd left one man on duty, but he'd attracted the attention of the day-shift guards, who'd been dubious about his lost-nephew story and suggested that he might like to talk to the police about it. She'd pulled him out, intending to send someone back later in the day, although with so many news organisations in the tower, and without knowing that Pearce would return there . . .

'Quite.' Hall had nodded. 'Potentially a waste of manpower. It's quite probable that Pearce was not even believed last night. Which would explain why his visit was so short: he was thrown out.' He'd flexed his fingers. 'Apparently, whatever's on the laptop he's got is inaccessible. So you can imagine: a young boy like that, turning up with a wild story, producing a computer that no one can get any information out of.' He'd shrugged dismissively. 'We'll soon know if a journalist starts sniffing around. In the meantime, there's another matter that has arisen . . .' And he'd opened a slim folder on his desk and seemingly become absorbed in it.

Her heart pumped with relief; her confidence was restored. The boy would resurface, and this time she would find him.

At last Hall looked up. 'It's a delicate matter . . .' he began.

'Yes?' Whatever it was, she could do it.

Hall outlined the additional assignment succinctly. 'At the moment the client's given instructions in two cases, but he's warned that there could be two, possibly three more – he's uncertain at this stage. If that happens, I think we may need to consider extra help.'

She frowned. Hall knew that she hated to be overstaffed; too many people talking too much about the job and about her. 'But not at moment?' she murmured.

'No. As it happens, I've got a man whom I can call upon in the Bristol area.'

'Excellent.'

'And I was wondering, for the London case, perhaps you could spare one of the men?'

Her men were fully engaged: two in Kent, two in London, with McMahon and herself as back-up. Was Hall testing her? she wondered suddenly.

'It's up to you, of course,' he went on indifferently.

She cleared her throat. 'I believe that, in such cases, a woman often stands a better chance of success than a man.'

'I take your word for it.' He consulted a piece of paper on his desk. 'It must look like an accident.'

'I understand. If I may have the details . . . ?'

CHAPTER TWENTY-ONE

If anything, Sasha thought, turning into the police car park, it appeared more crowded now than it had an hour before, when she'd first visited. Then it had been busy, but only with cars and motor bikes; now there were two sizeable lorries, one of them parked like a great slumbering dog across the entrance to the building, while another waited behind, its engine idling. There was no room for her, she thought, wishing she'd parked outside – but then she saw a space between a Range Rover and a transit van, and slid into it.

Checking her reflection in the mirror, hoping that her paleness might pass for interesting rather than white-tired, she got out and activated the car's self-locking system. Be in, she muttered silently to the man she'd come to see. Give me a break.

Her plan to arrive by eight, thus catching Christopher Manyon at home before he set off for work (according to Mike, he never left before eight-thirty), had been scotched by an overturned milk-lorry outside Lamberhurst. She'd finally got to the address at ten to nine to find his curtains wide open, no car outside and, unsurprisingly, no answer to her ring. She'd tried the upstairs flat – it was a short terrace of maisonettes – but there'd been no reply there either, or at the one next door; so she'd had to leave, unsatisfied.

By then it had also been too late to try Clive Lucas's home, eight miles away at Wittersham. Mike hadn't known which farmshop he worked at, only (unspecifically and irritatingly) that it was 'down about Rye somewhere'.

So she'd have to wait until at least five that evening, she'd supposed, before she could check on her two main leads – infuriating, but there was nothing else for it.

She'd debated her next move. The police, her instincts had told her.

Detective Chief Inspector Holland, the unsmiling desk sergeant had informed her, was expected (he'd lingered tantalisingly over the word) at eleven, but he was a busy man. She could get any details she needed from the press office in Ashford.

Naturally, he'd assumed that she'd been enquiring about the Tenterden Four. Keyed up only to be rebuffed, she'd taken solace in an enormous breakfast at a greasy spoon in the High Street.

Now she re-entered the unimpressive front office. A man, backing out of an inner doorway with a computer in his hands, side-stepped her to avoid acquision. 'Nearly gotcha,' he grinned, and his eyes travelled appreciatively over her legs, shown to advantage beneath the short skirt of her red suit. The door swung open again and two more men emerged, dragging a vending machine between them.

She turned to smile at the desk sergeant. 'Are you moving out?'

'In a manner of speaking.' His sour expression hadn't changed. With a jerk of his head he indicated a hard bench behind her. 'Take a seat. I'll see if Mr Holland's here yet.'

'It's about REDEV,' she called to his departing back. 'REDEV. Not the—'

'I heard you the first time.'

He withdrew from her line of vision. She waited, her eyes on the connecting door, hoping for an immediate summons. It opened, she tensed – but it was only two uniformed officers carrying box files, stacked chin-high. After a while, seeing nothing else to do, she sat down on the bench, as far away as she could from the wide-open outer doors.

An intermittent flow of people issued back and forth, some smiling at her, some not seeing her. Ten minutes passed, then

fifteen. The parade continued: computers, fax machines, chairs
. . . A full-scale evacuation seemed to be in progress.

From her bag she fished out the copy of the local weekly paper
that she'd bought and read over her breakfast. The front-page
photograph of Gerry Winston showed an anxious-looking man
with a deep frown mark between his eyes. One of life's worriers,
she thought, re-reading the story, noting again the existence of
the ex-wife, the unsympathetic tenor of her comments and her
observations on the nuclear power station.

After twenty-five minutes she stood up. Her muscles were
cramped with cold. There was no one that she could see behind
the glass, and it suddenly seemed a long time since anyone had
passed her. In fact the building was eerily quiet beyond the closed
doors. The thought struck her that they'd all gone, slipping out
through back exits, climbing down fire-escapes, clambering over
the roof, doing anything to get away from her, to avoid her
questions. But then the inner door banged back against the wall,
startling her.

'It's what the Dutchman wants,' said a crisp female voice.

'And what the Dutchman wants, he gets,' muttered a male
one darkly.

Sasha turned round. A youngish couple, the man about her age,
the woman a few years older, were already at the outer door.

'Excuse me.'

The man looked her up and down, and smiled. It flashed through
her mind that her outfit, a new one, had been something of an
investment.

'I wanted to see DCI Holland,' she said.

The man raised his eyebrows in mock amazement. 'You *do?*'

She nodded. 'Not about the runaways. About REDEV. There
was a break-in there about ten days ago. I'm a freelance journalist.'
She fished in her bag and produced her press-card. 'D'you think I
could speak to him?'

The woman seemed to be in charge. She took the card and studied
it. 'What's your interest in REDEV?' she asked carefully.

Sasha felt her heart thundering, but she'd come prepared. 'I'm
researching an article on rural crime, and I saw a little bit about
the raid in one of the nationals.' She smiled blandly. 'I was
in the area, so I thought it might be worth finding out some

more.' Not bad, she thought. Plausibly delivered. 'D'you think he'll see me?'

'Should think so.' The man winked. 'We don't get many pretty girls round here.'

The woman directed a withering look upon him. 'Go and let him know that Miss Downey's here,' she ordered.

'Wouldn't you rather I—'

'No. I'll wait with her.'

The man disappeared through the internal door.

Am I being guarded? Sasha wondered, and her heart thumped. She smiled at the woman. 'Thanks very much. I don't know how long I'd have been sitting here waiting for the desk sergeant to come back.'

'That's OK.'

'Does the sergeant not like journalists?'

'He's had a bit of a bellyful these last few days.'

The door swung open and the man's round face reappeared. 'Miss Downey? If you'd like to come through . . . He says he'd very much like to meet you.'

'Oh, great.'

Sasha's stomach was flipping as she ducked under his arm and followed him down the corridor. It seemed very dark after the brightness outside, but her eyes quickly adjusted. She noticed with some surprise the general shabbiness of the interior: the worn linoleum and dirty walls, the gutted rooms where even the doors appeared to be missing.

'Here we are, sir.'

The man stood back to let her through into a large, square room with little furniture beyond a filing cabinet with a dusty plant on top and a desk placed in front of the window. Behind the desk sat a man in his mid-forties. He was wearing a dark jumper over a shirt and tie, with short grey hair and a tanned, fit-looking face.

He stood up as she entered. 'Miss Downey – or is it Ms?'

'Oh, miss is fine.' They shook hands. He had a nice smile.

'Take a seat. Thanks, Jem.'

'You wouldn't like me to hang about for a bit, sir?' Sasha's escort hovered hopefully at the door.

'No, I wouldn't.'

'Right. Only, there's no one on the outside desk.'

'Not our responsibility any more, is it? On your way out, you could always put your head in to the kitchen and mention it.'

'Oh.' He sounded deflated. 'OK, sir.'

The door closed.

'So, a freelance journalist from London is intrigued by a twelve-day-old break-in in the depths of Kent.' Holland spoke pleasantly, but his eyes were bright and watchful.

Sasha nodded seriously and repeated her story, but it didn't sound as convincing the second time around. She brought it quickly to an end. '. . . so, as I was in the area anyway—'

'You decided to pop in.' He nodded in much the way she had. 'Lucrative business, this freelancing,' he commented after a moment.

'Sorry?'

'Nice car. I saw you parking. Which paper's this rural crime article for?'

'I'm not sure yet. One of the news magazines. I specialise in in-depth investigations.'

'Uh huh.' He contemplated a jam-jar full of pencils on his desk and, as he did so, she thought, he wants to talk; he's looking for an excuse to do so.

He switched his gaze back to her, and under the beam she felt like a bug under a microscope. She dropped her eyes. Remember this next time you're tempted to test the water, she admonished herself.

'I'm willing to talk to you, Miss Downey, on the strict understanding that it's for background purposes only,' he said.

'Absolutely.'

'No "Senior police officer involved in the inquiry told me", OK?'

She had to smile. 'OK.'

'Otherwise I'll come after you with all the hounds from hell. So . . .' His hand strayed to the jam-jar but stopped just short of touching it. 'What do you want to know?'

'Anything you care to tell me.'

'You're aware of the basics?'

'I've read the local paper. I, er, don't know much about REDEV itself.'

'Mm.' He pulled a face. 'It's a drugs research place, REDEV

standing for research and development. It's owned,' he took a breath, 'by an offshore company in the Cayman Islands.'

'The Cayman Islands?' she echoed.

'Precisely so. Company there by the name of World Med Inc.'

'Who're they?'

He pulled a sheet of paper towards him and studied it. 'No description supplied on the company search documents, but presumably something to do with medicine. All we know is that the address is a PO Box number on Grand Cayman. Its directors are other companies, most of them also dotted about various other offshore islands. In my opinion,' he looked up, 'World Med's gone to considerable trouble to make sure no one finds out who or what they are. Wouldn't you agree?'

'Yes.'

She felt confused. Was this the company that Winston had found out about? From what Mike had told her she'd assumed it was there in England.

'Of course, there are probably dozens of perfectly good reasons for the parent company being where it is. Tax dodge, for instance.'

'How about REDEV itself? What do they say they do?'

'They don't.' He set the paper down. 'They say, as you'll no doubt discover, that they conduct "highly confidential" drugs research and marketing work. Period.' His hand reached into the jam-jar and withdrew a pencil. Slowly he started to roll it on his desk. 'But just because a company's not very talkative, it doesn't mean there's anything sinister going on, does it?'

'Well, er, no. I s'pose not.'

Another pencil joined the first. They clicked rhythmically together under his hand. 'And if, for whatever reason,' he continued slowly, 'a company that's been the target of a criminal act doesn't wish to have the police poking about into its private affairs, or wish to tell us what may or may not have been stolen . . .'

She compressed her lips.

'. . . that's absolutely that company's prerogative.' He shot her a look from under his eyebrows. 'Wouldn't you say?'

'I . . .'

'Or perhaps investigative journalists such as yourself view these matters in a different light?'

Talk about a shove in the right direction, she thought; he was throwing her at the story. Or was he, pursuant to government orders, merely trying to put her off the track? 'REDEV's nothing to do with the MOD?' she ventured.

He shook his head. 'They bought the land from the MOD about twelve years ago. Tore down the buildings, built their own. It's quite a place, very low-key from the outside, very camouflaged. You've seen it?'

'Not yet.'

'Take a look. It's only about a half-hour drive from here. Not that they'll let you in, but you can walk round the outer fence, get a feel of the place, see the cameras.' He resumed his clicking. 'You can't miss them. Every thirty feet. Our perpetrators,' he cleared his throat, 'rewound the film and trashed it.'

'Oh.' She scribbled industriously in her notebook. 'Do you, er, have any idea who they are?'

He studied her for a moment. 'Initially I considered animal activists.'

She dropped her head and kept scribbling.

'It's an automatic assumption when there's a break-in at a drugs company.'

'But not in this instance?' Her voice sounded unnaturally high to her.

'We don't have many activists in this area. Plenty of cat and dog rescue places, but actual animal-lib types are pretty thin on the ground.'

She frowned down at her notes. He sounded so completely genuine. But the police had visited Mike's mother; they knew about his involvement with the others and the break-in. Could Holland be lying? Don't, she told herself as the next thought occurred. But another part of her was already saying brightly: 'Actually, I was reading about an animal rights man in the local paper. The dead one on the beach.'

'Gerald Winston.'

She glanced up. He was watching her closely.

'But I don't suppose just one man could've done it all.'

'No.' His eyes didn't waver.

She cleared her throat. 'Perhaps an outside group?'

'Perhaps.' He'd stopped moving his pencils. She wished he'd start again.

She looked down once more at her notebook. 'You said initially you thought animal rights, but . . . ?'

There was a pause, then he seemed to shake himself. 'I haven't ruled them out, let's just leave it at that.'

'You haven't issued any warrants?'

'No.'

'You're not looking for anyone specific?'

'No.' His gaze was still direct.

He was telling her the truth, she knew it. So who *had* visited Mrs Pearce? She swallowed. The same people who had abducted Winston? She had to concentrate, or he'd wonder what was going on. 'Are you considering other alternatives then? Industrial espionage?'

He gave a small shrug.

'Maybe an inside job?'

'Maybe.' He started moving the pencils again. 'Both are obvious possibilities. I don't know that much about the industry, but I do know that drugs are very big money indeed. Millions of pounds. Years of research. You can see how someone might be tempted.'

'Any ideas who?'

He smiled. 'No comment.'

Time to push. 'So, you feel that REDEV aren't being open with you, even to the extent of telling you what's gone?'

He rolled the pencils.

'D'you think they're conducting their own inquiries?'

'I'd be surprised if they weren't.'

They looked at each other. Why was he still investigating? she wondered. Why, if nothing had changed? Aloud, she said, 'Have there been any new developments?'

'Why d'you ask?'

'Only that, with the Tenterden Four, you must've been off this case for at least four days.' She paused. 'If not more.'

He was giving nothing away.

'REDEV, from what you say, are still being wholly unhelpful. You don't have any suspects . . .'

The pencils clicked on.

'. . . Witnesses? A new witness?' She ran through Mike's account in her head. 'How's the guard?' she asked. She knew she'd got it, although he didn't raise his head and didn't stop his rolling.

'Is that where your detectives were going? On their way to interview him?'

'No comment. But, Miss Downey . . .' The clicking stopped.

'Yes?'

'Please don't make any attempt to approach the guard.'

'He's talking, then?'

'I've been open with you . . .'

For your own purposes, she thought.

'. . . I've told you as much as I know about REDEV. In return, I'm making a simple request. If you choose to ignore it, you'll find yourself in trouble. OK?'

His eyes had a steely quality about them now. 'OK,' she said.

'Although I've had not entirely pleasant dealings with members of your profession in the past, I think it's foolish to lump everyone into the same category. I know some journalists are trustworthy.'

She felt vaguely uncomfortable. This is madness, she thought; he's got his own agenda. 'So you'd like me to dig about into REDEV?' she asked.

'Seems like a good idea.'

'Shake them up a bit? Write a story asking why they aren't prosecuting?'

'I'd read it.' He grinned, suddenly attractive.

'And if my investigations happen to coincide with a statement from the guard describing who assaulted him . . .'

'You see?' He picked his pencils up, examined their points with a practised air. 'It's not true that journalists and the police can't work together.'

She had to smile. Of course he was using her, but if he'd the vaguest inkling of what she was keeping back . . . She noticed his wedding ring for the first time, the air of dependability he generated, of being fazed by nothing. In a way it would be easy to tell him everything, off-load the burden. If Mike's (and increasingly her own) fears were justified, he could be in serious danger . . .

She caught herself. What was she thinking of? She'd lose the story. Mike was all right; she and Charlie would look after him.

Holland was dropping the pencils back into the jam-jar. They clinked against the glass. 'When have you got to have your story written by?' he asked.

'Wednesday noon.'

'We can be in touch. Here's my card.'

She took it. Beside a printed number, there was another written in pencil.

'You can get me on either number. Ashford will always take a message.'

She stood up. 'Thank you.'

'Not at all. Happy hunting.' He cocked an eyebrow. 'At REDEV.'

Thoughtfully, half-turned in his chair, Holland watched her progress across the car park. Good legs, he registered, and a smart dresser – a smart girl all round. Then it struck him that, if she turned round, she would see him. He swivelled back to his desk. It would never do to be thought of as a Peeping Tom.

He picked another pencil from the jam-jar on the desk and started rolling again. This case was getting to him. Partly it was seeing the catatonic state of young Tim Dacre, the security guard. He might never properly recover, the doctors had said at first. Partly it had been the company's attitude; but mainly, he admitted, it was his own sense of guilt, his suspicion that, because of the burglary, because of his own mishandling of a situation, a man had died.

When the news had come through about Gerry Winston's death, he'd felt sick. He'd been back in Ashford – the REDEV incident had detained him only for that one unsatisfactory day – juggling ten things at once, when he'd heard. A heart-attack in a man of forty-six, an ex-con who'd probably never been very healthy in the first place, but whose physical and spiritual stamina had been sapped by his time inside. Holland had briefly met and liked Winston, and now he had to come to terms with the fact that he'd probably contributed significantly to his death.

After quitting REDEV that morning, alone (he'd been in no mood to be sociable) he'd driven to Tenterden, past the police station in which he now sat, and on to a café in the high street where he'd eaten a late breakfast. By his third mug of coffee he'd been in a better mood. He'd let his mind dwell on the rumpus that would be going on at REDEV: the silver-tongued Stockart, dishevelled, ranting and raving; the laborious internal machinations of tracking down whatever had gone missing without alerting anyone else in the industry. He'd wondered what it was. Documents of some sort, he'd supposed, remembering the way that the man's eyes had become riveted as he'd stared at the space on his desk beside the PC. Not a very large space – but whatever it was, however small, it had been crucial. No one trembled like that over a matter of small consequence. Perhaps the missing item was a report on Beagle puppy experiments, or simply an address list – one single piece of paper – of REDEV's animal laboratories throughout Europe or the world. Why not? Holland had thought, eagerly slapping down a pile of coins on the café table. That would have explained the unit supervisor's panic. Perhaps, he'd thought, this was not a run-of-the-mill animal rights attack at all, but something much more sophisticated – the sort of something that the only animal rights activist in the area might well know about.

Driving to Gerry Winston's place, stuck out on its own half-way up a hillside outside town, Holland had toyed with the notion that the man might have participated in the raid. He'd visited Winston once before, when he'd just been released from prison, and Winston had told him that nothing would ever entice him to go on another 'direct action', that the very idea of prison was enough to cause him a sleepless night or bring on an attack of claustrophobia. That was the reason, he'd claimed, why he'd chosen to live where he did – with open views all round, so that he could see who or what was coming. And Holland had believed him.

Winston hadn't been at home. Holland had banged on the front door and then gone round to the back. Along the kitchen window-sill, on the narrow tiled ledge behind the sink taps, a grey cat had lain like a long streak, watching him. Holland had rapped on the door, then opened it and called, but there'd been no response. The cat had merely sat up, affronted. So he'd gone back out again, and there, way below in the valley, he'd seen the lone figure of Winston, striding off in the direction of the woods. He'd shouted, but the man hadn't turned – probably hadn't, in all fairness, heard him – he'd simply kept going until he'd been lost to sight among the tree-trunks. Holland hadn't had any intention of following him – the distance was too great and, unlike Winston, he didn't know the countryside around there. Nor had the prospect of awaiting his return pleased him; he was tired, and needed to go back to Ashford before going home to sleep.

He'd re-entered the kitchen, and there, under the gaze of the cat, he'd scribbled a note. Just a line on the back of his card: 'In need of your expertise. Call me.' Then, after pausing in front of the cat to admire its pale green eyes, he'd gone out, unsatisfied.

Now he selected two yellow pencils from his jar and added them to the one already under his hand. (His pencil-clicking drove his wife insane; thus he wasn't allowed pencils at home.) He set them in motion, telling himself, not for the first time, that he – his note – hadn't been to blame for Winston's death. None the less, he wished he'd never written it.

Holland was much more of a worrier than most people gave him credit for. He looked so capable and broad-shouldered – the dependable type – that people tended to off-load on to him and assume that he didn't have the need to do likewise. But at home he bit his nails and suffered from toothache, the cause of which, his dentist had told him, was nervous, not physical.

He was afraid that Winston had been involved in (or at least had knowledge of) that raid – and having read the note lying there on his own kitchen table had come to the natural conclusion that Holland was after him. He'd taken off, presumably by train, with no clear idea of where he was going, had by some quirk wound up on that beach in Suffolk where he'd gone for a walk, and in a state of panic and terror, suffered his fatal heart attack.

Holland had heard the news about Winston on Tuesday morning. Later on the same day, he'd heard that the tyre tracks found running along the edge of the woods next to REDEV exactly matched the tread of those belonging to a van, midnight-blue in colour, windows painted black, that had been discovered in rough undergrowth down the hill from Winston's home. The man's fingerprints were on the steering wheel – all over the van, in fact, as had been the prints of at least six other people: the whole gang.

Knowing that Winston had been guilty hadn't made his death any easier to cope with. Nor had the knowledge that a second prison term would probably slowly have killed him anyway, that a massive heart attack might have been the better end. Subconsciously,

Holland felt that he had failed himself (as a policeman) and, more obscurely, Winston.

He'd revisited the cottage, looking for any clue as to the identities of the other members of the group, but had found none. Indeed, there was scarcely any evidence that a man had lived there. In the back room on the ground floor was a single bed, a chest of drawers containing a few clothes, and a trestle-table on which sat an electronic typewriter and, beside it, a half-empty pack of A4 typing paper. The two bedrooms upstairs were empty, as was the front reception room below. Only in the kitchen, with a mug that Holland recognised on the drying rack by the sink, had there been confirmation of Winston's occupation of the place. That one item, and – his eyes had travelled downwards – the two cat-bowls on the floor, one dirty with dried remnants of food. Those had given him brief pause: there was no sign of the animal now; had Winston taken it with him? He couldn't imagine him simply abandoning it, whatever state he'd been in. But he supposed it would hardly have been a priority, worrying about a cat.

He'd searched the kitchen, opening and shutting drawers, not entirely sure of what he was expecting to find. A list of his co-conspirators would have been nice, along with Winston's reasons, clearly set out, as to why he'd reneged on his decision.

He'd walked out of the house with no answers, departing as the Scenes of Crime people had arrived. They'd had no joy either, leaving him in the unenviable position of not even knowing if the rest of the gang was from his patch or from further afield – and, if the former, who they might possibly be.

Sufficiently riled, Holland could be single-minded to the point of intractability, and everything about the REDEV case riled him. Completely frustrated by one side, he'd returned to the other, worrying away until a plan of action had occurred that had pleased him. He'd called in his 'close-team' (the chief constable seriously believed in empire-building) and revealed his plan to them. As it entailed them enduring long periods of boredom, quite possibly for no result, neither had been very enthusiastic.

'But sir, he never leaves the place!' Jem had exclaimed that morning.

'I know.' Holland had kept his pencils rolling. 'I know it's boring. I've done a couple of stints myself.' And he had – very briefly during the weekend on his way to and from home. 'And even if he *does* leave,' he'd added sharply (because Jem could be a bit of a loose cannon, and he had to be told, several times sometimes), 'you're not to follow. I want to wind him up, not send him over the edge.'

'You really think this is going to work?' Julie Milton had questioned.

'I wouldn't be wasting your time if I didn't.'

He hoped that he was right, that his assessment of the fellow was going to prove correct: that, already terrified, cross-examined by his employers, perhaps no longer trusted, living in an isolated cottage where he worked day and night (one of Holland's visits had been at one in the morning), the presence of strangers in the track outside his door – strangers who made no move to hide themselves but whose faces he couldn't quite see – would prove too much for him. Particularly on top of the strange clickings there would have been on his telephone line since the previous Thursday.

Privately, Holland had been hoping for a call by now. He'd left the man his card, but so far Colin Davenport hadn't rung. He could, of course, have run to his boss with his worries, and that person could have called the police – but if he or she had, Holland had made sure, any such enquires would have been routed straight to him. That hadn't happened. Poor Davenport, with his stammer and his gooseberry eyes. He must be in quite a state by now. Holland rolled his hand ruminatively. He considered that the reappearance of Jem and Julie would do the trick. Otherwise, he planned to give him another twenty-four hours before calling on him personally.

He checked the time and dropped the pencils back into his jam-jar, then picked up the screw-top lid and put it on, ready for its transportation back to Ashford. When the Tenterden Four case had first arisen he'd been relieved, in a way, that he was forced to concentrate on that rather than the REDEV business and Gerry Winston. Now he was glad to be back. He had a hunch that things were finally falling into place: Davenport would break; the guard, talking again, would give a decent description of his attackers; and the journalist would do as he'd told her, dig about into REDEV, unsettle them, so that when he announced the decision to prosecute, based on the guard's evidence, the company would be pushed into compliance, would feel that, in the glare of publicity, it had no other option.

CHAPTER TWENTY-TWO

At last, Anna saw the door open and the woman with the baby emerge on to the street. She walked quickly, paying no heed to the small girl who was running to keep up.

'Mummy!' the child's voice wailed. She was an attractive child, with a mop of curly hair, and the doll she was carrying was almost as big as herself. Passers-by looked round but the mother marched on, preoccuppied and frowning, coming quickly into range of Anna's mirrors.

She was a tall woman but she carried her height badly, as if she was ashamed of it, and she wore no make-up even though her face was grey and her lips pale. Her hair, too, seemed ignored, pushed up anyhow behind her ears; and in spite of the miserable morning she wore no coat, nothing to cover the sagging leggings and big jumper.

Anna suppressed a shudder at the sight: everything let go in the cause of child-rearing, the self forgotten. She saw the woman's sudden glance down, noticed the transformation take place, from drab weariness almost to prettiness, as she beheld her infant son.

Mother-love, Anna judged – but of the selective variety. Blind both to the eyes of a stranger and to the older child, and deaf also to her cries.

The girl was coming into view now, the face screwed up and pink, the mouth open and the sound escalating like a siren as the need for attention grew desperate.

'Mummee! Wait for meee!'

She'd been crying when Anna had first seen her that morning. Then, her mother had been stuffing her into the back of a battered Volvo. 'For God's sake, get in! You're not a baby any more, Lucy.'

That sight, as Anna had been driving past on her first visit to the house, envisaging nothing more than a mapping out of the locale, had come as a surprise. More proof, she'd thought, continuing smoothly to the end of the street before reversing, that such cases never run neatly to plan. One always had to be ready – years of experience had taught her that – and she had been: her clothes nondescript, her dark glasses in place, her car untraceable. She'd had only to quickly call McMahon to tell him that, barring emergencies, he was temporarily in charge, and then she'd followed Rose Gilbert to the doctor's surgery.

She jumped. Something had hit her door. Her hand moved instantly to the side-pocket, closing around the weapon there and releasing the safety-catch.

'What d'you think you're doing?' The words rang out sharply in the cold morning air. Anna froze. Rose Gilbert, son in arms, was rushing towards her. Not at her, she realised a moment later, but at her daughter, who'd fallen and was now howling on the pavement.

'Lucy!' Level now, baby over one shoulder, the shoulder nearest Anna, Mrs Gilbert was bending down. 'I'm warning you, young lady . . .'

Move, ordered a voice inside Anna's head. Open the door, snatch and shove; be gone in seconds, too quickly for the mother to do anything, probably even to scream. The chance wouldn't come again.

'As if I don't have enough to worry about!' Rose Gilbert bent down, shifted the baby to the other side.

An elderly couple stopped to watch. Anna's chance had gone.

'I've hurt my arm!'

'You have not! You've hurt this nice lady's car.' Mrs Gilbert's big face, now suffused blotchy red, loomed at Anna's window. 'Not really,' she mouthed, giving a ghastly grin before returning once more to her task.

'Lucy, you've got three seconds . . .'

'Tiggy's hurt too!'

'Right.'

Anna stared straight ahead, but out of the corner of her eye she saw the woman swoop, heard the child's yelp and the scuffle of her shoes upon the pavement.

'I've just about had enough of you! Now come on.'

Anna watched them go, saw the Volvo's doors open, heard the wailing mercifully subside. She slipped the safety-catch back on and replaced the gun in its compartment. Looking up again she saw that Rose Gilbert, three car-lengths away, had moved quickly. The children were already strapped in, the rear-lights on, the car moving off.

Anna waited until they were out of sight before setting off herself, back to her hotel. She'd been seen, and at close range. In order to continue her task she needed to change both her appearance and the car. She knew that she could have handed over the assignment to McMahon, but she wanted it herself.

Next time she knew that she would not fail.

By the time the ambulance arrived, a gaggle of people had gathered at the scene. It was a terrible tragedy, they said, a heinous crime. The police – they glanced sharply at the nervous constable who was supposed to be holding them back – must catch the culprit and make sure he was given life.

The mother and her tiny baby had been hit on the zebra-crossing near Bristol Zoo on the Downs. They'd been half-way across, the baby snugly wrapped in his sling, a bobble hat pulled well down about his head, when the car, a white Audi with a P registration, had mown them down. That much had been seen by one witness, a university student who now waited apart, sitting silent and green on the kerb.

The traffic had been slight at that time in the morning; the driver *must* have seen the mother – she'd been wearing a bright yellow padded duffle coat . . . To have driven off afterwards, screeching round a corner out of sight . . . The only other witness was an elderly lady with thick glasses. 'Just a white blur,' was how she'd described it.

A drug-crazed maniac, the onlookers surmised, too out of it to have known what he'd done, to have seen the mother and baby flung in the air like rag dolls. The baby had remained in his protective pouch, had been crushed by the weight of his mother, the ambulance crew said. One was close to tears as they laid them together on the stretcher. The baby had hardly been born, had had no life.

The doors slammed behind them and the siren carried them screaming away.

'Don't know what they're hurrying for,' muttered one man, his eyes sliding to the stain in the road where the mother had fallen. The mark was already diffusing, becoming part of the whole. 'Never stood a chance,' he said, and the others, suddenly quiet, began moving slowly away.

At home, a serviced flat in Bloomsbury, Will West showered thoroughly. He hadn't realised the state of his appearance until his secretary had come into the lab with his elevenses and nearly dropped the tray. Her reaction had hardly been surprising. The mirror above his sink had shown a face that he scarcely recognised himself: wild, bloodshot eyes, a scraggy half-inch of stubble, grey lips; and his clothes were the same ones that he'd been wearing since Friday, three days and nights before. He'd smelled, he'd realised on quick inspection, abominable. No wonder the girl had backed off fast. The telephone messages she'd been whimpering about couldn't have been that important.

'Tell them I'll call back later,' he'd told her shortly on his way out.

They – whoever they were – would have to wait. He squeezed out more shower gel and applied it vigorously with a scrubbing brush. He had seven months before Melanie Alder's baby was to be born – not long at all if he wanted to have a second go with the Infiltrator. He ought to be in there again in the next six to eight weeks. After twenty, when the growth rate increased, there would be hundreds of thousands of cells, making it much more difficult for the good gene to be successfully incorporated into each. But he ought to have enough time, and data – or would have, once the biopsies of the others had got underway – as long as he was allowed to work without interruption.

He lathered for the second time under his armpits. The physical cleansing process was one which he had to duplicate mentally. Wash his mind clean of all else, all irritations and impurities, so that it could devote itself in its excellent entirety to her.

He sighed deeply and happily. The thought of her, her tremulous lower lip, her trusting blue eyes – or were they brown? No matter. He could check back in her medical records, to her birth if necessary – made him feel renewed. She'd energised him, giving him the stamina to stay awake all night – quite a feat at his age, he told himself proudly. She'd made him brave, elevating him above the reach of Stockart, letting him see the paltriness of that inept, self-seeking little mind. It was she, not Stockart, who was going to be responsible for getting his name up there with the gods.

Now it was just Melanie and himself. His Mel.

He stepped out of the shower and pulled on his towelling robe, started quickly rubbing himself dry. He had to get back to work. He went through to his bedroom, selected underpants from the appropriate drawer, a laundered shirt still in its cellophane wrapping from another. He felt refreshed, at ease, now that his relationship with Mel was clarified. At first, surprised by his new-found emotions, he'd confused them with – he blushed deeply – well, with something else. But now he understood that his feelings for her were strictly in the protective category.

He sat on the bed to pull on his socks. He wanted to protect her, oh so fiercely. Tears suddenly pricked at the mere thought of harm befalling her, of anything he might have done to cause her sadness. All he wanted to do was make her happy, to see her laughing like a child.

He paused, one thin leg inside his trousers. 'I'm coming, little Mel,' he whispered. 'Don't be scared, I'm going to make it bett—'

The telephone was ringing. He frowned. He couldn't think who it would be. Most people knew to call him at work, that it was his custom when at home to take the receiver off the hook.

He hopped, one leg in, one out, into the hall. It would be that foolish girl, his secretary, calling to see if he was all right.

'Oooh, Doctor, you do look ill,' she'd said, backing into some of his test-tubes, knocking them over.

'IQ of a cretin,' he murmured viciously, snatching up the implement.

'Will?'

His senses chilled.

'It's John Stockart here. Remember me?'

He had to protect her. She was his baby. What would this madman do to his baby?

'What was that?'

He couldn't speak.

'Are you trying to tell me something, Will? What is it? Sore throat? Your secretary said you looked ill. And you haven't been answering your e-mail, have you? I've been trying to reach you, you see. Point out something that you seem to have missed on DAMR.'

He mustn't listen. He had to get back.

'You'll find I've already taken matters into my own hands, somewhat, Will.'

'You . . . you . . .'

'Mm? And not before time either. Subject One – you probably remember him, seeing as he was the first. Jeremy James Gilbert – his mum's just taken him back to the GP this morning. More bruising, so it says on DAMR. Poor little mite.' He made a tutting sound.

West wanted desperately to speak, to stop that terrible voice dragging him in.

'It's sweep-clean time, Will. You remember sweep-clean? Though you probably didn't do much actual sweeping yourself, did you? You had a whole team working for you in Albania.'

A tremor shook West's spindly frame. Not all the SWii Syndrome boys had died quickly – three had lingered in intensive care. Then had come news of a inspection by the Albanian authorities – such things couldn't be avoided, they'd only heard it was coming due to a tip-off – and the evidence, the infants, had had to be dealt with. West, already shaken by those parents walking in, had washed his hands of the business, but he remembered the effect on the young medic who'd drawn the short straw. He'd had a breakdown and had to be repatriated. West had heard later that he'd died in some sort of accident.

'But we're not in the Albanian backwoods now, are we? It's just you and me, in London. And we've got to keep it to ourselves. In the family, so to speak.'

His precious Mel, his baby.

'DIY. I'll handle the ones that've been born, you deal with the rest of them. Personally, I think you've got it easy. Just a few abortions. Will?' The man oozed awful sympathy. 'You sound distressed. I can understand.'

'I won't do it.' His voice shook, then steadied. He had to be strong, not for himself but for her, and the baby. He gulped. *Their* baby.

'Oh, you will, Will.' A bark of laughter, then silence. Then, very softly: 'You probably haven't been watching, been keeping that old cranium of yours buried in the sand. I bet you don't know about Subject Six yet, do you?'

He closed his eyes.

'No, you haven't been looking at DAMR. He was born dead this morning, Will. Are you there?'

A stillbirth. West's mouth went dry.

Stockart carried on. He sounded quite cheerful. 'Subject Two's in intensive care now in Bristol. They think he's got a bit of a rash developing. Hardly a surprise to us, is it? And Four, he's being monitored by morons in Northampton. I know you were probably going to get round to telling me about him sometime – and about Master Gilbert who, I sadly predict, is never going to make it to a hosptial. Will, are you still there?'

'Yes,' he whispered. Stockart couldn't seriously . . . He'd be caught, he'd ruin everything, implicate him, stop his work before he'd had a chance to put things right.

He leant back against the cold wall, his lips moving soundlessly.

'Good. It's all about statistics, you see. I've worked it out. It would look a bit odd, wouldn't you say, if they all died of the same thing? It would get people asking questions, checking back. It would ruin everything. But a hit-and-run here, a murder there . . . well, it muddies the waters nicely, doesn't it?'

The man had truly gone insane. West knew that he must stop him, that he ought to phone the police.

But what would happen to his work? To Mel?

'You can induce labour or something in the later pregnancies.

The earlier ones are pretty straightforward, aren't they? Just give them a pill.'

Mel's sweet face, the innocent eyes pleading for her baby. He had to save their baby. He had to be strong. If that meant going along with Stockart, then so be it.

'All right,' he said dully.

'I'll be watching you, Will. Remember that.' All teasing had vanished, the voice now ground glass.

'I'll remember.'

'Good. Because if I catch you trying to double-cross me again, I'll kill you. Got that?'

'Got it.'

'You'd better get back to work then, Will.' He was pleasant again, quite companionable. 'No slacking now, d'you hear?'

CHAPTER TWENTY-THREE

On leaving the police station, walking to the car, Sasha had felt self-conscious. It wasn't simply the knowledge that Holland could see her through his window, that he might be thinking her skirt too short or her legs too skinny, because the feeling had persisted as she drove out of the car park and back into town. It was the eerie sensation that, even out of sight, he knew what she was doing, like a headmaster always one jump ahead of his pupils.

She wondered, uncomfortably, just how far ahead he was, or might be once his detectives had finished interviewing the security guard. If the man had got a good look at Mary's face, if Holland made the link, put out a press release . . . She felt slightly sick.

But he didn't have all the answers. She had Mike, and the laptop – she sighed – for all the good that did. She slowed down, joining the tail-end of a short line of cars that she supposed passed for a traffic-jam in Tenterden. Dotted about the wide pavements were little groups of people, well wrapped up against the cold, greeting each other, gossiping: no one in a hurry, no one else biting their fingernails or involved in a race against time with the police.

She could always forget about *Comment*, do a spoiler story for one of the nationals. But she still hadn't any firm evidence, she reminded herself, agonised. If only she'd got to Manyon's and Lucas's earlier.

Perhaps she could drive down to Rye now, look out for farm-shops
. . . But no, she'd already seen how many of those there were. It
would be a wild goose chase.

Having reached the end of town without a definite plan in mind,
she pulled into the kerb and leaned back against the headrest. The
police knew nothing about Mike, although someone else did.
She saw two young women with pushchairs strolling towards
her, laughing together about something over the heads of their
children. It didn't seem possible that another agenda was being
played out here: one involving police impersonators, abductors,
even killers. But Holland had been telling her the truth, she was
sure of it. He'd kept things back, certainly, but in some ways, even
if it had been for his own benefit, he'd been remarkably upfront. For
instance, with the information about the Cayman Islands. Her brow
furrowed. What on earth was an offshore company in the Caribbean
doing with a little research place in the middle of the Kent?

Of course, she thought, stretching out her legs as far as she
could, she didn't actually know that REDEV was little; she was
simply assuming that it was. For all she knew it could be the size
of ICI. There was only one way to find out. She flicked opened
the local map-book she'd bought. REDEV was off the main road
to Lydd.

She sat forward, ready to start the ignition, and saw that the
clock on the dashboard read 12.20. She'd told Charlie that she
wouldn't call before noon, so that both he and Mike could get a
good night's rest – unlike her, she added. She ought to be going,
she didn't have time to waste, but one quick call wouldn't make a
difference.

She picked up the mobile, and as she did so her mood lifted.
She could imagine Charlie at the other end, hearing it ring, hoping
it would be her, excusing himself to another room so that Mike
couldn't hear.

An exaggerated engaged tone blared in her ear. She jumped, held
the thing away and pressed the 'end' button. If she remembered
correctly, that klaxon noise denoted that the call hadn't been
connected, that the signal wasn't strong enough.

Growling, she turned the key and glanced in her rear-view mirror.
She was facing the wrong way for Lydd; she'd need to do a U-turn.
A space came up and she swung the car in a neat arc. Her wish to

speak to Charlie had now become an urgent need. OK, she told herself, simmer down, there'll be a telephone-box.

It didn't take her long to find one – or at least, what had been a telephone box. It had been hit, pushed over at an angle, like the Tower of Pisa. 'Out of Order' said an unnecessary notice on the front.

'I don't believe it,' she muttered, slowing down, then got hooted from behind and drove on quickly. It must be, she thought, that she and Charlie weren't meant to talk to each other right now. She'd have to be patient.

Ahead, the road divided and she took the right-hand fork, marked for Romney Marsh – the road, she realised at once, that led back to the police station. She was retracing her steps. Holland might see her passing, might rub his hands in glee, seeing her do his bidding. Let him, she told herself, driving past; it wasn't as if she hadn't been intending to go to the site. She saw that the dark car that had been parked on the forecourt when she'd left had now gone. That absence worried her obscurely. But she put it from her mind and drove on.

There were fewer houses now, the last trickle before the country-side took over. It felt colder, and she turned up the heating system, revelling in the blast of warm air. If Mike's version of events and his suppositions were correct, she thought – and it was beginning to look that way – then her race was not simply with the police.

She glanced in her mirror. It's all right, she reassured herself. She wasn't being followed. Bogus police officers were one thing; killers another matter entirely. And Winston's death still may have been natural. She had to keep calm, gather evidence, build the picture.

It started to rain, and she fumbled in a hurried search for the windscreen wipers' button, before a crescent of clear glass appeared before her. It wasn't rain, she realised with a start, but sleet, and moments later, snow. It was falling so thickly that already it was settling on the tarmac and the fields either side.

The road narrowed. She was out in open countryside now, and the snow was falling even faster, covering the hedgerows and the trees. It might be a white Christmas, she thought, dropping her speed to below thirty as she took a bend. She couldn't remember the last one. Perhaps when she'd been twelve or so, and her sister, three years older, had refused to have a snowball fight because it was too childish and would make her mittens wet . . . The car hit something hard and she was jerked forward, feeling the back swing out as the car went into a skid. She steered into it and regained control. She couldn't see what she'd hit – a hole in the road, probably, that had been covered by snow. Driving too fast in bad weather conditions along country lanes she didn't know . . . She could almost hear her father's voice. She switched on her lights, slowed down to barely more than a crawl, and kept her eyes glued ahead.

The countryside had now opened up into large flat fields where sheep huddled, suddenly dirty against their new backdrop. The sky was dark grey and leaden, sucking out the light; it seemed as if the day was already over. She couldn't see a house, or any building. No sign of life. It must be the marsh, she thought. She could see how people got lost in such a landscape without markers; she could understand why smugglers had once used it to their advantage, might do still.

She checked her mirror again. There was nothing behind her except snowflakes falling, already concealing the fact that she'd ever passed that way. She turned on the radio. 'Frosty the Snowman' was playing. She'd always loved the song; but just now she wasn't in the mood. She tried for a news station, and suddenly got '. . . severe weather conditions affecting the south-east, particularly Kent.'

Tell me about it, she thought, switching it off.

She'd never been in one before, but wondered if this constituted a 'white-out'. Or did they only have such things in vast countries like the States, where hurricanes, cyclones and tornadoes seemed regular meteorological fodder? It was becoming difficult to tell where the road ended and the ditches began; her eyes were smarting with the strain. She tried to keep to the middle of the narrow road – in itself not an easy task with the snow drifting and piling. She could feel her eyelids grow heavy, drowsiness nagging at her. She mustn't fall asleep. She pressed the automatic button for her window, a little too far, and was hit full-face by cold spikes of snow. Gasping, but fully awake now, she kept on.

She drove over a level-crossing, then a sign for a village appeared, picturesquely decorated with a little drift, and Sasha had passed it before realising that she recognised the name. This was the village which Mike had said was the nearest to REDEV. She looked at the clock and did a double-take. It was over an hour since she'd left Tenterden. But the snow was stopping now and the conditions were better, the snow already turning to slush. She could hear the wet sound of it hitting her wheelrims.

The village wasn't a big place – a small supermarket, several antique shops and two pubs – but with lights blazing it looked welcoming enough. Through the window of the better-looking pub she could see the flames of a log-fire. The temptation to stop and go in was considerable. She desperately wanted a hot drink, and as if to tempt her further she saw a 'genuine filter coffee' sign as she passed. But she'd lost enough time, she told herself resolutely, driving on.

Three miles outside the village came the group of buildings that Mike had described. Stuck out on their own, incongruously large when there was nothing else around, the old Victorian brewery fronted the road. The main building, a vast, empty edifice of red brick, was several storeys high, its great, Gothic windows reflecting the vista of dazzling snow. Crowded either side and behind were lesser buildings, some apparently rented out to small firms. Although Mike had warned her that the sign was difficult to see, she still almost missed it: a narrow white pointer, stuck into the snowy bank, with neat black lettering. REDEV.

She turned, aware that her pulse was pumping. The small road ran down between the high buildings; she saw cars parked, a man in a suit heading for a doorway, glancing round at her approach. It all looked reassuringly normal. She kept on.

There, at the bottom, as Mike had said, was the security barrier, and to the left of it, the booth. It was manned; she could see the uniform of a guard. Behind it, set back, was REDEV, although all she could see were metal gates, chain-link fencing, and the cameras.

She reached the junction. The guard was looking at her now. She could distinguish no facial features, only the uniform and a pair of dark glasses. Remembering Mike's instructions, she turned right where the road ran briefly along the back of the last brewery building, and abruptly stopped. Anyone could walk there, Mike had said; the surrounding land was open to the public. Part of it contained a nature reserve – that was where she could be going. She got out, telling herself that the guard probably wasn't even looking at her. Then she saw the red eye of the camera on the fence swing in her direction, and in spite of her best intentions a shiver ran through her.

With the toe of his shoe, his hands being already occupied, Charlie gently pushed shut the sitting-room door. From what he'd just observed of Mike – head flung back, mouth open, softly snoring – the boy looked set to sleep for some time yet, a state of affairs that he'd no wish to interrupt.

He sat down on the vast purple sofa, deep enough and long enough to accommodate him easily, and placed his mug of coffee on the polished floorboards at his feet.

He put the computer on his lap and opened it thoughtfully. He'd meant it when he'd told Mike that he wanted to have another look at the laptop. There was something about it that he knew he ought to be remembering, that might help the story – Sasha's story, he corrected himself with a slow grin. He wasn't trying to take over. Stealing other journalists' work wasn't his line – a reasonable one, he'd always considered, until New York had told him otherwise, that his failure to divulge details of a fellow journalist's scoop on the Russian Mafia showed that he lacked the killer instinct, that he'd be better off behind a desk than on the road. He knew what that meant. He loved being out on the road, and they knew it; they'd probably hoped that he would walk without their having to pay him off. But living in London had always appealed, and he hadn't done too bad a job on the desk. Still, he ought to be moving on. He stretched his long legs. Seeing Sasha all fired up with her story had brought it flooding back, in a way that speaking to his own reporters, even face to face, never had. But then, he reminded himself with another grin, he wasn't besotted with his reporters. He glanced at the laptop. He wanted to help her, to share everything he had with her, to make her life happy, to see her eyes light up.

She had violet eyes. They amazed him. He'd heard of people in books having them – Scarlett O'Hara types – but he'd never actually seen them in real life before. Wide, violet eyes, the colour of twilight or peacock's feathers, fringed with black lashes that somehow gave her the look of a startled fawn. The first time he'd seen her – she'd been getting out of a taxi in Floral Street – he'd turned and stared, drinking in that beautiful colour. And she had stared right back, straight through him, her mind clearly elsewhere – probably, he now acknowledged, being better acquainted with that look, on work. Even when he'd asked if he might take her cab, she'd simply mumbled something politely English before heading straight for the lobby, her raincoat belt hanging out of its loop and trailing on the cobbles.

After that encounter, in a series of short takes, he'd kept seeing Sasha. She'd be at the front of the queue in the supermarket when he'd be at the back; on the bus when he'd be driving his car (and just when it seemed as if she might glance down and see him, the bus would move off); in the tube at Leicester Square, standing on the opposite platform (and he'd waved, but it had been another girl entirely who'd caught the movement and waved back). He'd kept missing her. It had driven him crazy, utterly mocking the thing he most prized about himself, his laid-backness – some, his father for instance, called it laziness – exposing it as a sham. But then she'd always had the power to do that to him, from the very first, through to the time he'd helped her with her computer. God! That feeling when he'd touched her. How often, he admitted to himself now, he'd relived that. And the time at the restaurant, when he'd been put through the mangle (again) by Tamarin, when, on the way out, he had kissed her. Although he and Tamarin had split up by then she'd still flayed him alive, but it hadn't mattered a bit. He'd felt on fire inside with Sasha, from his lips down to his toes, not at all relaxed or laid back.

And now they were dancing a dream. Himself and his long-legged English fawn – vulnerable, beautiful, innocent. He knew (because he'd called up her cuttings files on screen) that she was a real pro, but still marvelled at how she'd survived on a national newspaper. Presumably by using whatever powers she possessed that had bewitched and enchanted him.

He leaned back into the sofa, imagined her there with him, her dark head against his, his lips seeking hers, his hands exploring . . . He'd held himself back, not wanting to push her, but he knew he couldn't wait much longer. The night before, when he'd gathered her into his arms, he'd wanted her so much that he'd ached – would have taken her there, because he'd felt her wanting it too, had they not had to break off because of the kid.

Tonight, he swore to himself, after his shift, after Michael was safely asleep . . .

He glanced at his watch, picked up the mobile beside him and dialled.

'It has not been possible to connect your call. Please try again later.'

He pressed 'end' and put it down. She must be in a dead reception area. Perhaps there were a lot of military installations where she was. A coldness crept into his guts, radiated up into chest. She'd be all right, he told himself, but the coldness persisted. She might be a professional – but she'd done those things he'd read about before he knew her, not now, when if anything should happen to her it would be unbearable, the extinguishing of all joy.

He switched on the laptop. He'd been right, he thought as the brand name appeared on screen. The machine had been manufactured by the same people as the one he had tried out the previous summer. 'A powerful laptop for powerful people' – he remembered the pitch from the smooth, ginger-haired salesman who'd obviously been hoping for a big order from AGN. (He'd been disappointed; New York had ruled them too expensive.) The menu appeared. He ignored the first item – 'Colin's Files' – it would only show those crazy graphics again. It was the second item that interested him, the one simply called by the name of the software package, 'CommLink'. He double-clicked on it and computer icons and titles appeared: Information; Utilities; Library; Tools; Fax; Fastlink; Safe & Sound . . .

His eyes stopped on the last one. The back-up. The salesman had been so irritating, so oily, that it had been difficult to listen to him. But it was beginning to come back now: '. . . and it is conceivable, is it not, sir, that a busy man such as your good self, your mind being on higher things, may forget to save the odd document . . . ?'

Charlie clicked on the icon, an old-fashioned safe with a combination lock on the front. The lock changed into a tiny clock, the long hand slowly sweeping round, telling him to wait, that the information was coming. He felt a flicker of excitement. If the software was the same, and it looked it, then everything that the user had written would be in there.

'. . . You see, sir? You need never worry about losing anything. Ever. It's automatically duplicated and stored. Safe and sound – ' he'd smiled widely – 'in Safe and Sound.'

Charlie wetted his lips. The long hand had reached the twelve, the safe door was opening. He felt like a burglar in an empty house, an intruder into places where he had no right to be . . .

The safe stood open. It contained shelves or boxes, the bottom three of which were coloured green, which meant that they had information in them. One each, Charlie thought, conscious that his breathing had quickened, for each of those hidden documents. He was going to do it; he was going to crack the story. Sasha was going to be so proud – he grinned – or mad at him. He clicked on the top box.

''lo, Charlie.' The sitting-room door opened. Mike stood there, yawning and rubbing sleep from his eyes. 'Have you got any cornflakes?'

'Hang on.'

The screen had cleared; he was in. He stared. The screen was empty. 'Oh shit,' he swore loudly. 'Fuck and shit.'

'What?'

But the document had a title: 1-C:\BR\GH.1. Something had been there once. He ran the cursor to the bottom of the page, on to the next, and that was the end of the document. Nothing. Whatever had been there, had gone. He swore again, returned to the safe icon, clicked on the second box.

Mike appeared at his shoulder, lolling against the back of the sofa, resting his chin on his hands. 'What're you doing?'

The second document, similarly titled, was also empty. Charlie felt sick, dumb too: of course it wouldn't have been that easy. No one who protected his information with such intricate password graphics would leave a copy of the lot lying around for the casual enquirer. Cursing, he went back to the icon, clicked for the last time on the third box.

He turned round. 'Hi, Mike. Sorry.' The third document also was blank. 'I was just trying something out.'

'That Safe and Sound icon?' Mike sniffed. 'I already tried it. Nothing there.'

'No.' Charlie tried not to sound short. He pressed 'end', turned his head and said more affably, 'What was it you wanted?'

Mike didn't answer. He was staring, eyes on stalks, at the screen. 'Look at that,' he whispered.

'What?' Charlie glanced back, then he too stared. The screen wasn't empty any more.

'How'd you do that?' Mike was awed. 'It was never there when I looked.'

'I don't know.' Charlie shook his head, then he remembered: 'I pressed "end". I must've got mixed up with the mobile.' He bent forward for a closer look. The page was numbered seven, and under the heading 'Addendum: Graphics', was a series of what appeared to be pink blobs with dark centres. Each one was labelled: twenty-four hours, forty-eight, seventy-two, a week and on. He pressed the down cursor: the blobs grew larger, acquired thin red threads, were more clearly photographs now, and more familiar – although he still couldn't quite identify them. Page eight appeared. The first image on it was marked 'ten weeks' and showed a thin implement, like a needle, stuck into the pink. 'What are they?' he asked out loud.

'Don't you know?' Mike's head came in closer, his hand took over the cursor. The last two photographs appeared.

'Mary, mother of . . .'

'It's embryos,' said Mike. 'Little babies. Look, you can see their fingers.'

After her early-morning radio interview, Philippa Tyler had gone on to do two more at television studios before rushing back to the ministry for a two-hour budgets and planning meeting. It was nearly lunchtime before she had a moment to enquire about her post that day.

'Ah,' Sebastian smiled. 'Funny you should mention that, Minister. I think we might need extra help to cope with it.'

'Really?' She smiled back. It was what she'd hoped for; what, if truth be told, she would have been disappointed not to hear. 'Lots of it?'

'Bags, Minister. I haven't seen so much for a long time.'

'Excellent.'

'Most of it's begging letters. Childless couples pleading to join your Infutopin quota.'

'Ah ha. Well.' She adjusted the ruby ring that Gianni had given her for Katie's birth. 'Select, say, the best ten?'

'Twenty, Minister. Let's maximise our opportunity.'

'Very well then. Twenty, over the next few days. Better make it quite a cross-section, but pleasant-looking people, please, Sebastian. And then I suppose I'll have to press the flesh for the cameras.'

She smiled again; she couldn't help herself. Things were going so very well for her at the moment.

The snow was soft underfoot and Sasha's wellington boots sank into it. She wished her made-for-the-Arctic jacket was a bit longer, or that she'd changed into the jeans that were in her overnight bag, but that would have meant awkward manoeuvring inside the car and she'd had no wish to become a spectacle for the guard or anyone else.

Not that there was anyone else about, she thought, shoving her hands deeper into her pockets and surveying the snow-covered, deserted countryside. Just herself, and – she looked up at the fencing – the cameras watching her. She looked away. Over to her right were the woods that Mike had told her about, the trees which had provided cover for them that night, when they'd come with their high hopes of rescue, the climax to those weeks of meticulous planning.

Now one was dead, two were missing or worse, and the others were on the run. She looked to her left, studying the fence at close quarters, then saw the glint of another camera eye suspended on its perch. It swung her way, seeming to keep pace with her as she moved forward. She looked back over her shoulder and it was still watching.

Creepy, she thought. Very Big Brotherish. Difficult not to feel threatened by them. She stopped, put out a hand and touched the chain-linking, her fingers a clumsy claw in her gloves. On the other side the land rose steeply like a Roman fort, concealing its buildings, what went on there, what products it produced for what end. Purpose-built to conceal its purpose, its very existence. She felt a flash of admiration for Gerry Winston, for breaching this barricade. Had he discovered what went on there? What medicines World Med were manufacturing?

Was this the spot, she wondered, where his group had hacked their way through? Her eyes roamed over the steel, taking in the roll of barbed wire at the top, bald and ugly, untouched by the snow. There was no sign of damage anywhere. Of course not, she thought, staring into the camera. REDEV would have been out there repairing its defences as soon as the police had given the go-ahead.

She walked on, thinking that, given other circumstances, she would have enjoyed the snow. She looked at the time. It was fifteen minutes since she'd set off. She planned to gauge the distance by the time it took her to walk.

She took several steps back; the fence ran on round, uninterrupted, out of view. It was, she admitted, much bigger than she imagined. It was going to take her some time. The wind picked up, throwing little flurries of snow, sending miniature storms racing across the land. She put her head down and trudged on. She thought of that guard at the gate, thought of the other one probably now revealing all to the detective. She wasn't going to call in on REDEV. Not yet. No, she planned to make contact later, when she was fully armed, when she'd figured out her attack. Now she was merely surveying the terrain. She smiled. Doing what Holland had told her.

In the booth the guard watched her make the circuit. Crazy kind of thing to do, he thought, in such weather and in that short skirt. Nice legs, though, he admitted, and a nice car. He looked over at it again and, as instructed, wrote down the registration number of the visitor.

He'd been in the job for a week. He knew Tim Dacre and what had happened, but he didn't have much sympathy for him. He should have pressed the alarm buzzer: rules were rules and there to be obeyed. You didn't leave the booth until your replacement had arrived, and you didn't set foot inside the compound unless accompanied by REDEV's general manager. Too young, that was Tim Dacre's problem. Not enough discipline at home.

He saw that the girl was within range of the fourth camera now, looking straight at it. He zoomed in on her, but she ducked before he could freeze the frame. It didn't matter; he'd already got a close-up of her. Nice face, but difficult to tell what kind of figure under that great jacket she was wearing.

'Bit extreme,' his wife had said when he had told her about the level of security, the way that now all visitors to the site – external as well as internal; every jogger, bird-watcher and stroller – were to be photographed. But he didn't think so, not after a company had been raided like that.

The machine that developed the film whirred, and he went over to it, removing the flimsy photographs. Two of the girl and one of the car. He clipped them to the page with the car's number, slipped them into the envelope provided, sealed it, and placed it with the others in the tray, ready for collection later that afternoon.

CHAPTER TWENTY-FOUR

On Monday mornings Mel worked from nine-fifteen until one o'clock at a firm of accountants in town. Her duties as a receptionist were hardly onerous, comprising of, in the main, 'May I help you?' and 'Putting you through', but it was a friendly office and she'd been grateful to be offered the job. It got her out of the house, gave her the chance to be someone other than Ludo's mother for a few hours, and provided a little extra money that, although Patrick denied it, they needed.

Deciding that she looked 'peaky' over breakfast that morning, he'd urged her to phone in sick, and she'd promised that she would if the nausea didn't lift. It had, as she'd known it would (she'd also known that, after taking a day off sick for the CVS the week before, she'd used up her sick-leave for the month) but she hadn't argued with Patrick because he'd clearly been anxious about her and in need of reassurance that she was taking care of herself. By the time that first he and then Ludo had left the house, she'd been feeling a bit better, and by ten o'clock, installed behind her desk in office clothes, she'd been absolutely fine. In fact, bursting with health and a wild sort of happiness – and when one of the accountants had asked if she had got over her bout of flu, she had been on the verge of laughing and saying it hadn't been flu at all, and there and then announcing her news to the world.

But she hadn't, because the last time she'd been pregnant, with her IVF babies, she'd told everyone at work, and though they'd been very supportive, and then incredibly sweet to her when she'd miscarried, she didn't want any similarities between her current pregnancy and that one. Once she was past twelve weeks, she'd told herself, once the fear of miscarriage had diminished, then she'd tell the 'girls', as they referred to each other, although the youngest was twenty-nine and all of them had children.

Home again, she'd heated herself some soup, stuffed some clothes into the washing machine and told herself that now would be an excellent time to sort out her wardrobe, tidy up Ludo's bedroom or start making a Christmas card list. But she could settle to none of those things. Instead, restlessly she had moved from room to room, picking things up, putting them down again, winding herself up until finally she'd admitted what was wrong, what she had been putting off. She wanted to tell her mother. No, she corrected herself, returning to the kitchen where the clothes were now churning, it was stronger than that: she *needed* to speak to her mother. It was a fundamental urge that she had suppressed all those weeks – first until she'd told Patrick, then until she'd had the CVS. But now, after that morning, when she'd so nearly blurted it out to the girls, it was bubbling up inside her, demanding that she take action.

If Mel miscarried – she sent up a quick prayer – her mother would hide her own heartbreak and be terrifically strong for her, the way she had been before, the way she had been (and still was) with Ludo. But she would never understand Mel not rushing to the phone to share her wonderful news as soon as she'd known. Patrick had told her to put off telling her; he didn't see why she always had to be the first to know, anyway – but then Mel suspected that he was slightly jealous of her mother. Perhaps, she thought now, picking up the phone and taking it out into the hall as far as the flex would reach, she would tell a little lie to her mother, say that she had only got the CVS test result that morning. She couldn't bear for her mother to be hurt any more. Subconsciously she felt that, in giving birth to Ludo, she had already unbearably hurt her.

She shut the kitchen door on the flex and the noise of the washing machine grew muffled. Her mother had always been so good at comforting her that Mel hadn't realised how much she had needed comfort too. Both back then and when she miscarried. She adored children, had always regretted only ever having one – 'not that you're not worth a dozen, darling' – had looked forward to a brood of grandchildren, a whole tribe as she'd put it.

Well, she didn't have to withhold secrets from her own dear mother any more. They were going to have a Christmas like no other, Mel thought. The best one ever. She hit the memory code, heard the ringing tone, imagined her mother hoisting herself up from an armchair, hastening out to the hall and snatching up the phone, saying breathlessly: Hello?

'Mummy?'

'Mel, darling.' As ever, the joyful recognition in her voice.

'Mummy, I've got some wonderful news. I just got the results this morning . . .'

The secretary's desk was immediately outside his door, and by not quite shutting it and pressing his ear right up against the crack, West could hear every word she was saying. She was on to her third call by now and she had the script off-pat.

She hoped everything was going well . . . Oh good, lovely. She was just calling to book in Mrs X for her second trimester check-up. Didn't Nurse tell her? She ought to have done. Mrs X was twenty-three weeks now, wasn't she? She could come in any time within the next five weeks, though with Christmas just around the corner . . . Next Monday morning? She'd just check Doctor's diary . . . That would be fine . . . Yes, if she could come in by ten o'clock . . . ?

Again, West found himself impressed by her acting skills. From his previous contact with her he had judged that she hadn't any, that she was indeed a borderline cretin. He hadn't wanted a secretary at all, but Stockart had insisted, saying that it would look odd otherwise, that there must be someone to deal with appointments, and that he, Stockart, would find someone suitable. And so a nineteen-year-old girl had arrived, despatched from the IVF clinic above, and any fears that West had entertained about the project's security, or someone interfering with his work, had vanished.

She did not possess an enquiring mind; she could scarcely operate a word-processor. Besides, her main interest in life was not work but talking, constantly it seemed, to her friends on the phone – about marriage, boys and babies. But mainly babies.

West hadn't yet clearly worked out how he was going to achieve what Stockart had ordered: the terminations of ten subjects. 'Terminations', he thought. My God, that was a laugh! Three of the pregnancies were in their last trimester, the fetuses at thirty, thirty-one and thirty-three weeks. My God, he thought again, Subject Seven was due to be born in the delivery suite in less than a month! What a fool Stockart was in all medical matters; what an ignorant, crazy fool. How did he expect him to carry out such a 'termination'?

He'd asked his secretary to call them back in, telling her that in the light of that morning's stillbirth he simply wanted to check up on them all, make sure that each one was progressing satisfactorily. But – he'd cleared his throat – he didn't want any of the women to panic, to start imagining that anything was wrong, go rushing off to their own GPs. That thought had certainly alarmed him; he needed to make sure they came to him personally. He'd stood over her until she'd completed the first two calls, and then had retreated behind his door. Yes, he thought now, hearing her start on her fourth, she was doing surprisingly well. No doubt because she believed herself to be engaged on an important medical mission, part of the team. And because she believed in the rightness of what she was doing, her sincerity came through and there'd been no questioning from the subjects.

That dealt with all bar the last of the subjects. The last, he would never have entrusted to her. He moved away from the door over to his desk.

The last was Melanie. The superior feeling all at once left him. She wasn't going to be treated like any of the others. He wasn't going to terminate her baby; no one was going to harm their baby. Her perfect son – and *his* child too, his one perfect boy . . . or it soon would be, once he had corrected whatever tiny error he had made with the Infiltrator.

The trouble was the time factor. Stockart was breathing down his neck, would expect results, would – and he shuddered – take matters into his own hands if West failed. The thought of Stockart doing anything to Mel . . .

He licked his lips, gazed down at the index-card on which he'd jotted her telephone number. If he didn't bring her in like the others,

Stockart would find out. How, West wasn't sure, he only knew that he would. So he had to bring her in to protect her, and though there wasn't much time, there was some – enough to examine the DNA of the stillborn baby, to see what had gone wrong and correct it in Melanie's baby.

His heart was thumping. If he could arrange for Mel to be there the next morning – he felt suddenly light-headed at the prospect – that would spur him on. He blinked rapidly. He knew he could do it. And once he'd done it, once he'd corrected his mistake, safeguarding her future, their future, he would be able to do those other things, the terminations, because the rest of the trial infants wouldn't be necessary any more. He'd have the one that he needed, the proof that the Infiltrator worked, and the rest could be disposed of. If they were born it would only be to die, so better not to be born at all, better not to live.

His hand reached out for the telephone, and he lifted the handset and dialled, feeling his new firmness return. He didn't know what he was going to say, but that didn't matter; she would understand, he knew she would, by intuition.

Her line was engaged, But that was all right, he told himself dreamily; she knew that he would be calling; she wouldn't be long. And then she would be on her way, coming to him, and they would all be safe together.

Worriedly watching her baby sleep, Rose Gilbert pondered what the GP had told her less than two hours before, when she'd told him she wanted a second opinion.

After he'd recovered from his surprise he'd been civil enough to her, saying that if she truly felt further investigations were necessary, then she should take Jeremy to the Accident and Emergency department of the local hospital. They were always extremely thorough with tiny babies; they would conduct every test.

That had given her pause. She didn't want Jeremy to be pricked with needles, connected up to drips, taken away from her. The very thought was sufficient now to bring a lump to her throat.

She looked down at him sleeping so peacefully, one tiny fist clenched beside his rattle, the other flung back, open, above his head – like a little prince, she thought with the ghost of a smile. Terribly softly, she touched his forehead with two fingers, tried to gauge if it was warmer than it had been five minutes before. She thought not, but she couldn't be sure. And was she imagining it, or did he seem paler than normal? She swallowed awkwardly, felt tears swell. Was she simply being neurotic, which was what the GP had implied, or was she crazy to delay taking Jeremy straight to hospital? Could he even now be being treated? And would she find out later – too late – that early treatment could have saved him?

She took a deep breath and stood up. She'd check him in ten minutes – she would hear anything untoward on the baby-monitor – but in the meantime, she ought to go downstairs to see what Lucy was doing. She'd been so naughty at the surgery, suddenly bursting into tears for no reason, then having another tantrum in the street when Rose was already so worried about Jeremy. No doubt picking up on the 'atmosphere', she thought, rolling her eyes.

'Little madam,' Rose muttered now, descending the stairs. The sooner January arrived, and with it Lucy's place at the nursery, the better. Then Rose could relax and give Jeremy her full attention.

'Lucy?' She wasn't in the playroom at the back of the house where she should be. Brow knitting, Rose headed for the sitting-room, heard the sound of the television – forbidden to the girls unless she or Edward were in attendance – the weatherman talking about heavy snowfalls.

She switched off the set. 'Lucy, what're you doing in here?'

Lucy was standing on the sofa with her back to her. She didn't turn round, nor did she answer. She was staring at a woman passer-by in the street outside, a passer-by who had stopped and was returning Lucy's stare.

Rose started. There was something familiar about the woman's face, but she couldn't quite place it. A pretty woman with bobbed, fair hair under a headscarf, very well-groomed. What was she doing out there, staring in so intently at her daughter? Who *was* she?

'Lucy! Get down at once!'

Lucy took no notice. Instead, raising her hand, she gave the woman a tiny wave, and the woman, suddenly seemed to collect herself and stepped back hurriedly to move on. But not before she'd met Rose's own puzzled gaze, and given her such a strange look. Hatred, Rose thought, stunned. Then she shook herself: she was over-anxious at the moment, a bit too imaginative.

'Did you hear me?'

Lucy turned slowly. She had chocolate around her mouth and on her fingers which, Rose saw, had now been transferred on to the back of the sofa. 'Get into the back now!' she roared. 'And what have I always told you about strangers?' she demanded as her daughter edged past her and ran, whimpering, for the playroom.

Once returned to the sanctuary of her car, a roomy five-year-old Fiat, perfect camouflage for the area, Anna's breathing slowed. The mother hadn't recognised her. If she had, she would have called out or given chase. But perhaps she'd telephoned the police? Anna glanced quickly up the road, then back over her shoulder. It appeared perfectly quiet.

She had been a fool, she acknowledged that. She ought never to have left the car. She knew that when one was on surveillance one never unnecessarily exposed oneself. But arriving half an hour before, driving past the house, she'd seen the girl in the window, and something had drawn her over like a sleepwalker in a trance.

In the mirror, Anna straightened the blonde wig that she was wearing. She doubted that the mother had recognised her. But obviously seeing a strange woman staring in at her daughter the woman would have been suspicious. Anna's mouth tightened.

She guessed that the girl was three or four years old – she wasn't very good at guessing children's ages. Close-up, she was very pretty, but it hadn't been her prettiness that had attracted Anna, riveting her to that spot, allowing herself to be seen by the mother for the second time in just a few hours. Anna's frown deepened. She didn't know why she had done it, what quality the child possessed.

There was much of her own early childhood that she couldn't remember – she'd no photographs to prompt her – but there was one scene that was clear: herself standing against a window, late at night, watching her own reflection, waiting desperately for her mother to return. Anna shivered. The memory, as ever, brought with it fear and confusion. She blotted it out, gave her attention instead to her mirrors, saw again that the road was quiet, that no one was looking for her. She must concentrate, rather than yield to uncharacteristic bouts of weakness and self-doubt. The Bristol man, she reminded herself, had already completed his task successfully. She straightened her shoulders.

The boy, it was true, remained at large, but that state of affairs could not endure much longer. Either he would reappear at his or his brother's home – in which case he would be taken immediately – or he would attempt direct contact again. Or – and Hall thought this the most likely scenario – they would receive news of his whereabouts through a newspaper or some other media organisation.

Anna felt her mind quieten. She had left McMahon in temporary charge, and she had no doubts about his abilities. From experience she knew that no target could remain hidden indefinitely. The boy had simply, thus far, been very fortunate. But even now, she thought, he could be approaching the site on foot, the laptop tucked under his arm, fondly believing that he could do a deal, barter it for his life.

A movement caught her attention. She looked carefully in her wing mirror and became still. Side by side, advancing towards her, walked two uniformed police officers, a man and a woman. Anna found herself unable to move, incapable of thought when she knew that she had to think, had to find an alibi, quickly now, to explain her presence there in the car, and earlier outside the Gilberts' window. She could only stare. They were inches away from her now; she could hear their shoes on the pavement, see the black gloved hands of the woman, the big red fingers of the man. She had her gun, she could use that, or she could drive off. But her body failed to respond.

They were level. Anna saw the policewoman pause. She bent down and looked in. Anna wondered wildly how far Hall would go to save her, if he would. She turned to face the woman, saw that she was not looking at her but at the passenger seat. Then, catching Anna's eye, the policewoman smiled before standing up and walking on.

The shock had been so great that for a full minute Anna sat, doing nothing. Then she glanced sideways. She'd forgotten that she'd already prepared her alibi. Who would suspect a mother, sitting in her car with her baby, of anything? Who would think that the tiny figure, secure in its baby-seat, its head and face hidden by a pink blanket, could be a life-sized doll?

Anna fancied that she heard laughter, full-bodied childish glee. She did not suppress it. The mother hadn't called the police; they were merely on their beat. She smiled and pulled the blanket higher, then settled back in her seat to watch the house.

CHAPTER TWENTY-FIVE

It was Colin Davenport's first day back at REDEV since the break-in. He would never have imagined that he would have wanted to go back there, to those unseen eyes and ears in the walls, but that had been before the telephone calls and the clickings on the line, and the watchers in the car outside his gate.

Was Stockart trying to drive him mad? Phoning up at all hours with those horror stories? Davenport shuddered as he reminded himself that they weren't stories, made-up nightmares to frighten children with, but true, unsparing accounts of what had really happened to those poor bastards who'd broken in that night.

The last call had come that morning at one-thirty. Stockart had sounded wide-awake and cheerful.

'Did I tell you exactly how they found out who's got your laptop?'

'Y-yes. You d-did, John.' Please God, not again, he'd prayed, trembling in his pyjamas on the cold kitchen floor.

'Well, I'm going to tell you again . . .'

'J-J-John?' Desperation had suddenly overcome his dread.

'What is it, Colin? Feeling queasy?'

'I . . . I . . .'

'Spit it out, there's a good boy.'

'I-I think I'll have to go to the s-site in the morning. I know you said I was to work from home, but,' he'd been panting with effort, 'y-you see, I've still got to get quite a bit from the database, and . . . and . . .'

'Deep breaths, Colin. Take it easy.'

He'd sounded kind but Davenport hadn't been fooled. 'Using a laptop here is so much s-slower than the PC at the s-site. To get the data I need, I mean. There's so many h-h-homeworkers trying to ac-ac-access at the same time.'

Nothing from the other end.

Sweat had trickled into his eyes. What he'd said was half-true – the network got jammed; the laptops, being less powerful, were slower – but he'd already pulled down most of what he needed. He didn't need to go to REDEV; he needed to get out of that house.

'I know how important it is th-that I get the report finished qu-quickly. I can get everything I need in probably one day at the site.' One day would do it. A brief respite.

'Fine, Colin. You can go in today. I trust you implic – What's that?'

Bastard, Davenport had thought. He could imagine him, lying back on a sofa in a comfortable London apartment, a Martini in one hand, the other operating the clicking device that had suddenly interrupted the call.

The clicking had abruptly stopped.

'Wh-wh-what?'

'A noise.' Stockart had sounded briefly suspicious. 'Didn't you hear it?'

'A-a-a . . . ?'

'Oh, never mind. It's gone now. You'd better get back to bed. Get in that beauty sleep.'

He hadn't slept until dawn, then hadn't woken until after midday, half-way through his one precious day of freedom. Quickly dressing, he'd snatched up the car-keys, dashed for the stairs, then seen, out of the landing window, the car parked at the top of the track by his back field. His heart had lurched in his chest. The same car, the one that had first appeared the previous Wednesday night. The man and the woman and, sometimes Davenport had thought, there'd been another man, on his own watching the house, watching him. That's why he'd stopped going out. He never knew when they would be there, daytime or night-time; whether, after slowing down as they passed the cottage, they'd simply glide on by down the lane, or turn in and stay for hours. He'd seen them, quite clearly, several times. They seemed to make no effort to hide themselves, rather the opposite. They often had the map-light on; one or other of them would get out, stand and stretch, stare boldly at the house, seeming to know that he was there, flattened back against the wall by the window.

Even when he didn't see them he suspected that they were there, hiding in the woods, perhaps, or behind the old barn. Visible or invisible, they were pawns in Stockart's game, part of his plan to drive him insane.

But not today, he'd vowed. He was going to go to work; he'd got permission. With his chin determinedly high, he'd walked out of the front door, a mere four metres from where they sat, and on, perfectly steadily, towards his car. Reversing, he'd wondered if they'd follow him, and when they hadn't, when he'd seen them diminish and vanish behind him, his spirits had risen like the sun.

Freedom and a bit of human contact was all he needed, he'd told himself, swishing along the slushy lanes, revelling in the snowy scene, the bare trees, the other houses and cars, the sight of people. He'd bash on with the report, perhaps ring Stockart, flannel him, get permission to stay all night. Never have to go back to that cottage again.

Before being allowed entry to the site he'd been given the fifth degree by an officious new guard at the barrier. At first, fearfully gazing at the man's dark glasses, he'd wondered if this was one of Hall's 'professionals', those torturers that Stockart had bragged about. But there had been a stupidity in the man's demeanour, a slowness in the way he did things – his finger following each word as he read out the questions from his clipboard – that had argued otherwise: that he was in fact just a little man in a uniform.

At reception there'd been a further grilling – his date of birth, his bank details – before he'd finally been given a temporary identity card and allowed to proceed to his building.

As he'd entered the unit, Sophie's music had been blaring out, making his ears ache. He'd paused in the doorway. She and Mark had been engrossed; she in a magazine; Mark in taking apart a small radio. He'd had to cough several times.

Sophie had finally looked up. 'God, you look awful! You sure it's only the flu you've had?'

'We thought you were swinging the lead, mate,' Mark had said comfortably. He'd been sitting, legs up on her desk, and made no effort to move. There had been a cosiness about the pair, an absence of the old sexual tension that would have indicated the new status of their relationship had Davenport been the type to notice.

'Could you turn the sound down, please? I need to do some work.'

Reluctantly, and not by much, they'd done so. He'd lingered, and Sophie, a kind girl, had said after a moment, 'You seen the new list of security procedures? ID cards to be worn at all times, swipe cards to be left at reception when leaving the premises. Doors and windows to be locked at the end of each working day, or "disciplinary action" may ensue! God, what're they going to do? Fine us?'

'Isn't that new?' Mark had pointed to the laptop he carried.

'Yes, I upgraded.'

Eventually he'd left them, approached his own door, locked for the first time that he could remember. He'd used the key that reception had supplied him with, and which he had to return when leaving. Stepping inside, looking round, he had noticed the dust first, lying thick across his desk in the hard winter sunlight. Everything else looked the same. There was no sign that there had ever been an intruder.

Switching on the PC, waiting to go on-line – demonstrating, if Stockart was watching, that he was doing what he said he would – he'd wondered where the cameras and the microphones were, how they were concealed. Behind him? So that they could see what he wrote or looked at? But behind him was the window, the Venetian blind now tightly shut against the glare. Impossible to put one in there. His eyes had wandered on, sweeping the walls, running along the skirting boards, up and over the door-mantel, across to the harsh central light. Not a sign. And so, quickly, he'd stopped looking or even thinking about them. The knowledge that they were there was easier to deal with, to accept and dismiss, than the multitude of suspicions at home.

He glanced at his watch and sighed. He'd been there nearly two hours now, and all he'd done was fiddle around with the report, tinkering with a sentence or two.

He stared at a space half-way along the wall. It had been there, by the radiator under which his damp shoes stood, that Stockart had lounged that morning, alternately taunting and threatening him. It had been in the very chair where he now sat that Hall had brooded, a silent, terrifying presence – and how much more terrifying in retrospect! – watching him stumble, evaluating his every look and word, weighing up his truthfulness or otherwise, deciding what should be done with him.

He shuddered. No, it wasn't the fear of being spied upon that was slowing him down. It was the associations that the room now held for him. It would never again be a haven, a quiet place where words came easily, where the odd snatch of conversation, even burst of music from Sophie's room, could be a pleasant, controllable interlude.

He stared straight ahead at the closed door, remembering the policeman's concern for him that morning. In his mind over the last eleven days he'd replayed the scene, making the inspector older, kinder, a father-figure. 'If you should ever want to talk,' Mr Holland had said, handing over his card, smiling, patting his shoulder. Stockart might have confiscated it, but Davenport had already memorised the name. It would be child's play, he told himself, to drive to Ashford and ask to see the man. Tell him everything, shop Stockart and his security people.

Davenport blinked rapidly. How many people had died, horribly, because of his carelessness? And it was within his power to do something about it; it was his responsibility.

On the desk in front of him the telephone was cheeping. He picked it up. The dialling tone. He stared. Had they somehow known what he was thinking? With great self-control, without visible shaking, he replaced the receiver.

He should call the police, he told himself, ask to speak to Holland directly. Not from here, clearly, or home – but he could drive to a box, or use the one in the pub in the village. His mouth went dry. He could see himself doing it, hear his voice as he asked for the policeman to meet him at the pub, stay there beside the blazing fire, shielded by the regulars, until Mr Holland came.

He dropped his eyes to the keyboard. He was deceiving himself. He would never make it to the pub; they would be on his tail as soon as he drove out of the main gates. He would be intercepted, smoothly, neatly. The only reason that those two hadn't followed him from the cottage was that they'd known where he was going and that there would be someone else already there at REDEV, watching every move he made. Where would the watcher be? In the car-park? Or at reception? Perhaps, and he swung round, on the other side of the window, beyond the blind, lurking there, a dark shadow in the snow.

He swallowed noisily and the sound seemed to fill the room, panicking him. The microphones would have picked it up, be even now relaying it . . . He took a deep breath. He must hold himself together, finish the report, and then be gone. Never again would he work for Stockart, no matter what the man promised him, how much money he offered. He didn't need any more money, the vital things had already been paid for.

He squared his shoulders at the screen. He must forget Stockart, shut himself off from what had happened, block out what might yet happen, refuse to allow himself to be distracted.

'I said, d'you fancy going for a drink?'

Mark stood in the doorway.

He blinked. 'It's only three o'clock,' he said.

'Yeah, but the heating's broken down, old son. Didn't you get a call about it?'

'I . . . No, I don't think so.' He frowned, then suddenly noticed the cold and shivered violently. 'But I've got work to do.'

'You can't work in these temperatures, mate. No one can. They're closing the site.' He was beginning to look exasperated. 'Any road, if you don't want to come . . .'

Davenport felt an unaccustomed lump in his throat. 'You'd like me to come with you?'

'What? Yeah, I don't mind.'

Sophie appeared by Mark's shoulder, her jacket already on, hood up. 'It was my idea. I thought with you just getting over your flu and being stuck out there where you live all on your own . . .'

'That was very kind of you, Sophie.' She was so young. She didn't frighten him.

'Let's go then.' Mark looked resigned. 'I'll give you a lift and drop you back later.'

Davenport stared. Was this his means of escape, in the back of Mark's car? He scraped his chair back and got up. 'I'm ready,' he said eagerly.

Neither of them moved; they were both grinning down at his feet. Sophie said with a giggle, 'Don't you think you'd better put your shoes on first, Colin?'

It had taken Sasha forty-five minutes to complete her circuit of REDEV. That made it roughly three miles in circumference, she estimated. While she had no way of knowing how many buildings were concealed behind that mound, the site itself was sizeable: no ICI, but not the little place she'd imagined either. Certainly the reality, the whole hidden nature of the place, made the mysterious offshore company involvement more likely. And it would provide excellent copy, she congratulated herself, especially as she'd seen it: the harsh steel fencing, the rolls of cruel barbed wire, the gleaming red lights of the cameras, suitably stark and sinister against the virgin snow. She was glad, she told Holland silently, that she'd decided to come when she had, her timing couldn't have been better.

Back at the car, stamping her wellingtons to rid them of their wedges of snow, she saw one of the cameras, high up on the fence, swing in upon her. She turned away. She was blasé about them now, and they must, she told herself, have got dozens of close-ups of her – if that was what they wanted.

She opened the car's boot to divest herself of her jacket – she was hot now – and to retrieve her boots. It was a little after three. She was going to make a serious effort to call Charlie again, then drive back to Manyon's house to be there waiting for him when he got in from work. She hoped. The next few hours would tell.

She divested herself of one wellington, and was standing stork-like as she zipped her leg into the thin black suede, when a movement caught her eye and she turned her head. She stared. The guard was out of his booth, and beside him, on the REDEV side of the barrier, a car was waiting. The green and white pole rose and the car slid under it, out on to the road, passing within fifteen metres of where she stood. She saw that a young woman was driving, a perfectly pleasant-looking person with glasses shoved up into messy hair and wearing a dark blue fisherman's jumper. Not sinister at all, she thought, her eyes following the car's tail-lights as they retreated cautiously up the narrow road. Her first sighting of a REDEV employee. What had she expected? she asked herself, still staring: horns and a hazard-warning label on the forehead?

She opened her door, glanced back over her shoulder for one last look, and stopped. Another car was waiting at the barrier, a low, dark-coloured saloon with its side-lights on and its sun-visors lowered. Much more sinister, she thought, feeling her heart pump faster as she moved clear of her own car in time to see the guard give a half-salute – someone important? – and retreat to his booth to operate the barrier. It rose as before and the car emerged, but this time, though she bent as it passed, she couldn't make out anything about the driver, except that he or she was huddled in dark clothing. The car shot up the lane, swerved and vanished in a spray of wet snow. Only then did she properly come to. What was she thinking of? Why had she stood there like a dummy, allowing the cars to pass in front of her nose? Maybe it wasn't too late, she thought frantically, jumping into her car and starting the engine, cursing the automatic gearstick until she found reverse and then shooting backwards in a wide loop.

The guard was openly staring now, and if she wasn't mistaken he'd picked up a phone and was talking into it. Let him, she thought, turning into the lane; there might still be time for her to catch that last car. There wasn't. The small road was clear right to the top; the car had gone. Softly she applied the brake, pulled into the side and closed her eyes, communicating further oaths.

Remembering the guard, she told herself that this was not a clever place to sit; he'd probably summoned security on that phone – if she'd been him she would have. She glanced in the mirror ready to set off, and her eyes widened. The barrier was rising again. What was this? she thought weakly, going-home-early day at REDEV? Or did they only ever work until three? The car was coming towards her, and out of instinct she snatched up the map-book from the passenger seat, stuck it in front of her on the wheel and ducked her head. Sliding her eyes sideways as the car came level, she saw a poppy-red MGB roadster, crammed with people, all legs and heads, or so it seemed. With difficulty, she kept her head lowered as it passed, counted ten, twelve, then looked up. The little car was travelling fast – it was already nearing the junction with the main road – and Sasha pulled forward after it. It would look so obvious, she told herself, chewing her lip, but she didn't have time to hesitate.

The car was indicating left, back in the direction of where she'd come. She followed suit.

Davenport had long legs. Like a spider playing dead, he sat miserably scrunched in the back of the roadster.

He shouldn't have come, he told himself as the car bounced painfully along the road leading to the village. Almost as soon as they'd left the site, as the barrier had descended after them, he'd known he was making a mistake. He was wasting precious time and jeopardising his position with Stockart even further. If Stockart had been watching, listening, he'd have heard Mark's offer, would have seen, possibly – God knew where those bloody cameras were – the look of delight, even hope, cross his face at the chance of escape. His grandmother had always told him that he had a face that was as easy to read as a book. Now that thought was making him feel sick – either that, or it was the way the car kept bucking and grinding, as if it were constantly hitting ruts in the road.

He tried to turn in his seat, but he was so cramped and it was nearly impossible to see out of the rear window anyway, it being plastic and, on top of that, very dirty. A tank could have been bearing down on them and he wouldn't have seen it until the tread obliterated him. He sighed dolorously.

'You're still breathing, are you, back there?' Sophie called out, and he mumbled yes, but she didn't hear him – not surprisingly, considering the noise the car was making.

Davenport regarded the landscape. The road here was higher than the reclaimed land, the flat marshes stretching away almost out of sight. From where he sat everything looked pure white with little black lumps here and there, tree-trunks, telegraph poles. He imagined himself down there and running, his pursuers fanning out and closing in behind him, catching him, carrying him away to be tortured, never to be seen again.

'Almost there!'

'Yeah! Get a few rum punches inside you!'

They entered the village, and fractionally his spirits rose at the prospect of leaving the pit that was the back of the car (one couldn't really call it a seat). The tires crunched on to gravel. He peered up at the sign, saw it was The Oak and Ivy, and his mood plummeted once more. He'd been there once before and hadn't liked it. It tried too hard. He thought Mark had mentioned the other pub. Then he remembered sharply, as if his mind had taken a photograph, exactly where the pub's telephone was: in the nook under the stairs, by the men's toilets.

He felt suddenly icy cold, his hands clammy.

'Mulled wine for me,' Sophie sang out, heaving herself out of the bucket seat and holding the door open for him.

'Can I take that?' she offered sweetly, pointing at his laptop.

'No!' He snatched it to himself, disentangling his legs from the car, and caught the heavenwards look she exchanged with Mark. He'd offended her. But he didn't have time to worry about that.

He wrapped his arms more protectively around the computer, glancing furtively about. Apart from the pub's van, there was only one other car in the car-park, a few parked in the high street, and virtually no traffic on the road. No one had followed him – yet. He set off quickly towards the pub.

'Hey, hang on, wait for us!' Mark called out. 'Bloody charming!'

But the complaints faded behind him. He entered the pub's tiny vestibule, saw the plastic snowman on the door marked 'Lounge', and turned sharp left towards the stairs. The phone was there.

His stomach was lurching. Very carefully he set the laptop down on the small shelf by the phone. What he'd imagined was about to happen. He'd wait there for Mr Holland to fetch him, to take him away from it all, then he'd unload his burden on to those broad shoulders. He didn't know if he'd broken the law in doing his work, massaging the facts, being economical with the truth, but he was sure that, in return for telling the inspector everything he knew – the Albanian cover-up, all about Stockart, Hall's terrible deeds – something could be worked out, a deal struck.

The telephone directory was lying on the table. He didn't need to look up the number – it was one of those deliberately easy ones, a couple of figures followed by a lot of zeros, and he knew the code for Ashford – but still he picked up the book, leafed through the tissue-thin pages for the entry, giving himself time. Once he had made the call there would be no going back. He could kiss goodbye to the work he did so well, and for which he'd just begun to be so handsomely, deservedly rewarded. No company or organisation would ever trust him again. But perhaps the government, or the police themselves . . . He was sure that the police could occasionally use his services. Mr Holland would sort something out.

He lifted the receiver. It was slippery in his hand. He inserted the coins, stabbed in the number, and huddled himself further back into the shadow of the stairwell.

Pushing open the door, Sasha saw that the pub looked much better from the outside and from the speed and distance of a passing car. The interior had already been lavishly decorated for Christmas. Tinsel strewed the old beamed ceiling, there was a large blue tree in one corner, and inflatable Santas on the bar. The only good thing about it was the real log-fire, blazing away in the vast brick fireplace.

Beside it, at a small table, sat the young girl in a mini-skirt whom Sasha had seen get out of the roadster. Her boyfriend or colleague was at the bar. Sasha glanced quickly about. Apart from an old man nursing a pint in a dark corner there were no other customers. So where was the second man, the tall one with the flapping raincoat who'd run into the pub ahead of the other two? She hadn't got much of a look at him – not wanting to make herself too obvious she'd pulled into the kerb on the other side of the road to watch – but she'd seen him cradling something in his arms as he charged for the door. From the expressions on his colleagues' faces, he seemed to be an oddball.

She went to the bar. The man who'd been the driver was ordering two pints and a shandy. The barman glanced over at the girl and said to him, 'Thirsty, eh?'

'Someone else is joining us. We hope.' But his tone indicated otherwise. He paid, balanced the glasses carefully and headed off.

Sasha ordered a coffee, and realising that she was hungry, a packet of crisps. Then she took both items to the table on the other side of the fireplace, close to the other two.

They were both young, the man only about twenty-five, and judging by their clothes, the environment inside REDEV was informal. She could hear snatches of their conversation: they were discussing Christmas; the man wanted the girl to stay with him, the girl was protesting that her mother wouldn't like it.

'You're twenty, Sophie. You're not a baby.'

Judging the right moment was essential, Sasha knew – butting into something too personal could be disastrous. She ate another crisp. Sophie wanted Mark to meet her mother. For the first time, Sasha wondered how her own mother would react to Charlie. Stiffly, she thought gloomily, remembering how she'd been with her sister's husband. Nervously offering little bowls of nuts, a glass of dry sherry, or something stronger, and looking alarmed if the answer was yes. But she was doing Charlie a disservice, she told herself, sipping her coffee. Charlie would put her mother at ease, talk about serious issues in depth with her father, be charming to her sister and fun with the children. Or was she being fanciful? Were her feelings clouding her judgement? Nope, she thought, taking a crisp, she was not. He was lovely. He'd reduce the hardest heart to jelly.

'Where's he got to?' the young woman asked, glancing round.

'Who cares?'

'Don't you think you should go in and see if he's all right?'

'Give it a rest, will you, Soph?'

Now, Sasha thought.

'Excuse me . . .' She smiled brightly across at them. She never knew how to begin so she plunged right in. 'D'you by any chance work at REDEV?'

They both turned round to look at her.

'Yeah,' Mark said cautiously, setting down his pint. Sophie was sizing up the red suit and boots.

'Oh great, that's just great!' Sasha beamed. 'I wonder if you could help me? You see, I'm a journalist . . .'

'Oh yeah?' Mark's rather dull face was illuminated. 'With the telly?'

'No, freelance. With a magazine, *Comment.*'

'Never heard of it,' said Sophie rudely.

'Hardly anyone has. The thing is . . .' She leaned in closer, confidentially, but she was still too far away. 'Can I join you?' She got up and did so. Mark made room for her. 'I'm researching an article about crime in the countryside.'

'Oh yeah?'

'And I wanted to write about your raid.'

'Right.' Mark looked gratified. It wasn't an uncommon reaction: people liked to be in the news.

'But the trouble is getting any sort of half-decent comment about what *really* happened. Your spokesman,' she raised her eye brows – she was taking a risk, she knew, but neither of them looked like management – 'is very tight-lipped.'

'Yeah, they're really up their own—'

'Mark!'

'Well they are, aren't they?'

'The thing is, it makes it really difficult for me to do the story if no one will talk to me.'

'Gotcha.' Mark frowned at his glass. He could see his moment of glory slipping away. 'What sort of thing did you want to know?'

'I'm not sure we should be speaking to the press,' Sophie said primly.

Mark shot her a withering look.

'No, I mean it.' She tossed her head back. 'You know what personnel said about our work being confidential.'

'Don't be a pain, Soph.' He turned back to Sasha. 'You're not going to use our names, are you?'

Sasha shook her head. 'I only want to get a bit of colour. I know the facts.' She produced her notebook. 'What I want to know is how it's affected people who work there, whether you feel more nervous, that sort of thing. What do you do, by the way?'

'Mark . . .'

'Not a lot,' Mark grinned. 'I'm a sort of handyman, and Soph's a secretary. When she feels like it.'

Sophie looked thunderous and Sasha began to feel sorry for her. She knew what it was like to have your boyfriend put you down in public. The girl couldn't stalk out; there was only one car.

She smiled at her. 'What sort of secretarial work do you do? Reports? Medical stuff?'

She gave a non-committal shrug.

'Who is this?'

They all jumped. It was the tall, gaunt man from the car-park. He was holding something by his side; Sasha couldn't see what it was. His face was drained of all colour and there were beads of sweat on his brow. 'Who are you?' he demanded harshly of Sasha.

She found her voice. 'I'm a journalist. Sasha Downey.'

'It's all right, mate.' Mark was trying to sound cool. 'She was just asking us a few questions. Sit down, I got you a pint.'

The man stared at Sasha. She saw how his eyes bulged, how he sweated and swallowed. He looked on the verge of passing out.

'Mark.' The Adam's apple bobbed. 'Take me back to the office.'

'What?'

'You heard me.'

'Don't you order me about, old son.'

'We haven't finished our drinks yet,' Sophie chimed in.

'Now!' the man suddenly screamed, and the pub went silent, deathly still. 'Right now!'

'All right, all right.' Mark stood up. 'Keep your sodding hair on,' he muttered.

'Please,' Sasha made a last appeal, 'I only want to ask you—'

'No questions! No questions! I've got nothing to say!' And he turned and rushed for the door. Now Sasha saw what he was holding: a laptop, very similar to Mike's.

'What did you say his name was?' she asked Mark.

'What?' Mark was looking shocked. He shook his head. 'Come on, Soph. He's fucking flipped.'

'Are you coming back?' Sasha called as they headed for the door.

But neither of them answered. The door banged shut after them. She ran to it herself, saw the man dancing by the car, waving his arms in the air like a madman, one of those arms extended at its end by the rectangular laptop. Should she run out after them, chase them back to the site, lay in wait for them to come out again? No, she decided, she'd push him over the edge and get herself picked up, hauled in by REDEV security – he'd be bound to report her – if not worse.

The roadster's doors slammed and the car took off at speed.

'Well,' said the landlord, 'I could use you at closing time. If you ever need a job, just let me know.'

She smiled dazedly. Whatever she'd been expecting, she thought, what had just occurred hadn't been it. 'Have you got a phone?' she asked.

'Just round under the stairs. Towards the toilets.'

She picked up the phone. It felt damp. She wiped it on her sleeve, then inserted some money and dialled Charlie's home number. She heard the ringing tone and felt the tightening knot in her stomach, loved it and wished that it would never leave her, however long she and Charlie lasted . . . He was taking a long time to answer. She frowned. The penthouse couldn't be that big – and Mike was there too. Just then the phone was answered.

'Charlie, it's me.'

'. . . of Charles Page. If you'd like to leave a message . . .'

His answerphone. She blinked. She hadn't envisaged him going out, but of course there was no reason why he shouldn't. Perhaps, with Mike, the apartment had seemed claustrophobic. She left a brief message and, turning to go, saw that someone had been phoning the police – the display advertisement was open at the page. If Holland could only see her now, she thought despondently, opening the outer door and letting it bang shut behind her as she returned once more to the car.

CHAPTER TWENTY-SIX

In the laboratory, the radio was playing an old Boy George song. Charlie, dressed in ill-fitting hospital blues, tried very hard to listen to the words rather than the cries coming from the operating theatre on the other side of the hatch-door.

There came a particularly mournful wail.

It was barbaric, he thought, gripping the cold metal rim of the sink behind him. Operations without general anaesthetic on the eve of the twenty-first century. If the doctor hadn't told him about it, hadn't invited him to stay and watch the procedure – egg-retrieval, the first surgical step in the IVF process – he would never have believed it.

His eyes slid over to Mike, also in borrowed blues, seated at a lab-bench a few feet away. He was such a pale kid that it was difficult to tell what effect the whole visit was having on him. Then he saw him gulp hard.

'You OK?' he asked quietly.

'Yeah.'

One of the embryologists looked round from her microscope. She was very young, quite pretty, and very disdainful. 'You gonna chuck?' she demanded.

Mike glared back. 'No.' He stuck his hands under his armpits.

'Cause if you are—'

'I said I'm not.'

'. . . Don't do it down my back.'

'Not much longer,' Charlie said under his breath, and he hoped that he was right, that the whole traumatic affair – and surely watching childbirth couldn't be much worse – wasn't going to prove to have been a waste of time. It was already four-thirty, and they were supposed to have had their meeting with the senior embryologist half an hour before. She went home at five-fifteen.

It occurred to him for the first time that perhaps Mike had been right, that they could have found an expert to explain the laptop's embryo graphics on the Internet. But he'd vetoed that route on the grounds of jeopardising security. They had to assume that the material was highly sensitive.

After realising what the graphics depicted, Charlie had racked his brains and consulted his contacts files about who he knew in the British medical world. No embryologists – that, he told himself with a downwards twist of the mouth, would have been too easy. As it was, he'd used one of the few good contacts he'd made in the UK: an immunologist from Leeds who'd been hired by British and American soldiers claiming compensation for Gulf War Syndrome. That man, after much deliberation, had given him the name of a woman in London. She hadn't had time to see them, but she'd suggested four others – of whom the second, the head of the IVF unit at a large teaching hospital in North London, had said she could 'squeeze them in' that afternoon.

But she'd been rather peremptory when they'd arrived. She was extremely busy, she'd told them, eyeing Mike a little distastefully, and they'd have to wait. The problem was, she'd gone on with a light trill (and in retrospect Charlie wondered whether there'd been a calculating glint in her eye), there wasn't really anywhere *for* them to wait. The staff room had long gone, eaten up by Hospital Supplies; even the waiting room had vanished under the decree of reallocation of resources. So she'd suggested a brief tour of the Egg Lab. This turned out to be a bright, busy room with a lot of efficient young women in uniform seated in front of microscopes and peering at things in Petri dishes. The radio had been an extra welcoming touch and, due to a short break in the operation schedule, there'd been no gruesome sounds coming from the adjoining theatre.

They'd been handed two piles of laundered uniform – God knew why, but it seemed it was a hospital rule that all lab visitors wore it – and were told to change in the men's lavatories. On their return the doctor had shown them the operating room: hot bright lights, gleaming tiles and boxes – there seemed to be cardboard boxes everywhere in that hospital – and, on the side, trays of ugly metal implements and sealed, sterile packages of foot-long, hair-thin needles.

Those were the needles, the doctor had explained, that were used in the procedure. Guided by ultrasound, one would be inserted through the top of the vagina into the ovary, where the eggs (hopefully several of them – the IVF patients had already been on a course of drugs to hyperstimulate their ovaries) were sucked from the follicles into a test-tube, which was then immediately passed to an embryologist to examine.

'They're awake?' Mike had blurted, and Charlie had realised what he'd meant: that the doctor hadn't mentioned an anaesthetic. Mike had been rocking back and forth on his heels, fighting to keep control. He should never have brought him, Charlie had thought, but what other option had he had?

The doctor was a pleasant black woman with dark circles under her eyes. She'd nodded. 'Yes. But they're given tranquillisers and an IV of Pethidine – that's a painkiller – and—'

'But doesn't it hurt them?'

Please Mike, don't lose it, Charlie had begged him silently. We've got to be here. Try to think of something else.

The doctor had sighed. 'Some of them don't feel it too much – but others, yes, one has to say that it does hurt them.'

'But,' Mike had gnawed at his lip, 'why can't you just knock them out?' Two bright pink spots the size of pennies had appeared on his white cheeks.

'Oh, my dear,' the doctor had lain a hand on his arm, 'we're not animals . . .'

Charlie had seen him flinch.

'. . . and, yes, it would perhaps be better to give them a general anaesthetic. They usually do in private clinics, but we're NHS here and a general anaesthetic is very costly. Besides, these women . . .' The door had opened, revealing the blue-uniformed back of a hospital porter wheeling in a patient. The doctor had lowered her voice. '. . . are desperate. They're prepared to put up with quite a lot.'

She'd smiled a welcome at the newcomer and Charlie and Mike had retreated quickly to the laboratory, where a junior embryologist was now collecting a test-tube that a member of the surgical team had just deposited on the hatch-ledge. It contained a reddish liquid, blood from the most recent patient, and, Charlie fervently hoped, an egg or two. The previous poor patient had had none.

'Now, let's see what we've got in here,' the embryologist said, her voice becoming absorbed. She was working only a metre away from Charlie, and he watched as she poured the contents of the tube into a Petri dish. She glanced up. 'You want me to show you what I'm doing?' she asked, looking also at Mike, but he only gave a non-committal shrug.

'Please,' said Charlie, smiling down at her.

'OK. I'm passing it through a flushing medium, that gets rid of the blood. Then we have a look . . .' She bent her head. 'See?' she said with satisfaction. 'There's an egg.'

'You can see it with the naked eye?' Charlie was genuinely surprised. He stared hard, but all he could see were tiny pieces of matter that could have been anything.

Mike's head appeared on the other side. 'I can't see anything,' he said, peering.

'Well I can,' she countered with a touch of pride. 'I'll put it under the microscope and you'll be able to see it on the screen up there.' They looked where she pointed. Perched on top of a cube-shaped incubator, itself balanced on another, was a small monitor. A moment later they saw the dark circle of the egg's nucleus appear.

'Wow,' they both said.

The embryologist grinned. 'Yeah, it's OK. If you don't mind . . . ?' She reclaimed her microscope. 'I'm using a pipette to suck up the prepared sperm. Then . . .' She squeezed out the contents into a Petri dish of pink liquid beside her. 'I'm putting it in this little well where our egg is waiting.'

'Petri dish baby,' Charlie said.

'Yeah,' Mike frowned. 'Why do they call it "test-tube" then?'

'Sounds better,' said their guide. She repeated the procedure for each egg – the patient had produced four – then placed the Petri dishes in an incubator. In the morning, she explained, each egg would be checked to see if fertilisation had occurred, and if it had, the embryos would be graded.

'Graded?' Charlie queried.

She nodded. 'Only the Grade Ones – that's embryos whose cells have divided perfectly – are replaced inside the woman's womb. Grade Twos, or any spare Grade Ones—'

'Spare?'

'Yeah, spares,' she said. 'We're only allowed to put three embryos back in the womb. It's the law in Britain. So, if there are any spare Grade Ones or Twos, they're used for research.'

The trigger word. Charlie glanced quickly at Mike, but there was no visible reaction; he was clearly fascinated by the whole subject. Perhaps human experimentation, Charlie thought, wasn't an issue for him. He turned back to the girl.

'Into all sorts of stuff,' she was saying. 'A lot to do with investigating infertility.' She glanced at the digital display on one of the incubators. 'In our unit upstairs they're trying to find ways to make embryos live longer outside the womb.'

Charlie's skin prickled. 'What for?' he asked as lightly as he could.

But she was frowning at the incubator reading and didn't immediately respond. There'd been a fractional drop in temperature, she murmured; it was crucial to keep the embryos at exactly the right heat, and in exactly the right mix of carbon dioxide, otherwise they would die. She pushed the door, and the temperature jumped up again. She turned back to Charlie, and he repeated his question.

'Oh, just so they can be monitored for a bit longer before being put back into the womb. At the moment, the longest they survive outside is six to seven days, not that we keep the Grade Ones out that long. We don't want to risk it. They go back in within forty-eight hours. But if we could get them to survive longer, then we'd be able to detect more abnormalities that might cause miscarriage. See? Lower our IVF failure rate.'

'But I thought Infutopin had taken care of that.'

She shot him an old-fashioned look. 'D'you know how much Infutopin costs?' she demanded, no longer looking quite so sweet.

He nodded. He felt that Infutopin was one subject he knew fairly well. 'I know it's very expensive, but I thought the government—'

'Our government's engaged in a PR exercise,' the girl snapped. 'Take it from me: Infutopin's for the private sector. That's the way Branium wants it, and they're calling the shots.' She gave a brittle smile. 'Infutopin's their baby, isn't it? They can charge what they like, and us down here at the bottom of the pile . . . What do they care if we can't afford it? If our patients don't get it? They've got half the world willing to pay for it.' She shrugged. 'Sure, Branium's made it so you really can have a baby – but only if you've got the money, or if you're one of Phoney Philippa's chosen few.'

'Phoney . . . ?'

She pulled a face. 'It's what we call Tyler. She doesn't care, she's just doing it to look good.'

Sasha would like that, Charlie thought. 'I'm sorry,' he said inadequately; the girl looked suddenly so despondent.

'That's OK.' She sighed, then gave an apologetic smile. 'It's not your fault. It just makes me sick sometimes, you know? You slave your guts out here, doing your best, knowing that the cure's already out there, only not for the likes of us. We're still stuck in the stone-age. Anyway,' she resumed, pulling out another tray of Petri dishes. She seemed completely recovered. 'Back to where we were. You see, you can't detect very much when you're only putting back six or eight cells. You don't know what they might be hatching.' She pushed the tray back in and took out another. 'This lot are no-hopers,' she said matter-of-factly. 'Grade Threes and Fours. No good even for research.'

Charlie nodded sagely, but inside something lurched.

'No-hopers?' Mike said, and he didn't sound happy at all. 'What happens to them?' He ended on a croak.

'We put them over here.' She placed one of the round dishes by the sink. 'And leave them for a bit.'

The three of them grew quiet. Charlie broke the silence. 'Why d'you do that?' he asked her gently. 'Are you giving them some kind of last chance?'

'No.' Her eyes lingered on the draining board. 'Oh no, they've had it. I dunno why we leave them here.' Her gaze hovered for another instant. 'Out of respect, I s'pose. I dunno, something like that.' She turned away. 'We leave them till the pink turns red. That takes about an hour.'

'And the red means what?'

'That's it. Then we dispose of them.'

Presumably by flushing them away down the sink. Charlie looked at the rubber hose that was attached to the cold tap. Water from it flowed constantly down into the drain, taking with it any unwanted debris of laboratory life. It was only cells, he told himself – and wonky cells at that. But he didn't like it.

He dragged his eyes away, met Mike's, also looking troubled, and tried to smile reassuringly.

The door opened. It was the senior embryologist. She looked pleasanter than she had the first time. 'Survived then, have you?' she asked, and held the door open for them as they filed out of the lab.

The office that she took them to was windowless and tiny. There was a desk, spilling over with paperwork, piles of books and letters on the floor and crammed on to shelves. There were only two chairs; she took one herself, swept some magazines off the other and indicated that Charlie should sit. Mike she ignored. He slid half-way down the wall and rested on his haunches.

'Now then . . .' She smiled, and lines appeared round her eyes, making her look friendly for the first time. She wasn't unattractive, Charlie thought, if only she'd ease up a little on the schoolmarm image. 'I take it that you've found the tour . . . beneficial?'

'Absolutely.'

'Yes, I find it's the best way to handle media visitors: throw them in at the deep end.' She gave a short laugh, then frowned at the wall clock and pulled a notepad towards her. 'Now, let's get on. If you can give me some idea of what you want . . . ?'

He already had, twice. He'd suspected on each occasion that she hadn't really been listening: she'd heard the word 'television' and switched off, convincing herself that they wanted to make some kind of fly-on-the-wall documentary about the hospital.

Charlie turned towards Mike, who looked back blankly. 'We're not absolutely certain at the moment. There's some material that one of our researchers has come across, and we really need the advice of an expert.' He held out his hand to Mike for the laptop. It was not immediately forthcoming. 'It's a series of photographs showing the human embryo in the first few days and weeks of life . . .' He leaned down and tugged the machine from Mike's hands. 'The thing is, there's a needle or something in some of them.' He switched on and waited for it to boot up. 'We can't fathom out what it means,' he said disarmingly, starting to click his way through until he found the icons. 'Perhaps you'll be able to tell us.'

'I certainly hope so.' The woman gave her trilling laugh again. 'From what you say, it sounds pretty straightforward.'

'It does?' He felt an adrenalin surge. The photographs came up on the screen and he turned the machine round to face her.

'Yes.' She inched forward to see better. 'It sounds to me like scans of amniocentesis or CVS.' She frowned at the screen. 'Where's this needle?'

Charlie hit the down cursor, and the relevant one appeared.

She took a brief look.

'Yes. Amniocentesis. You know what that means, I presume?' She threw him a coquettish glance, but his mind was elsewhere, thinking numbly, oh no, all that for something so obvious. Why hadn't he thought of it himself? How would he ever tell Sasha? Perhaps he wouldn't.

'But . . . excuse me. I can't really see,' a note of perplexity had entered the bossy voice, 'why you needed an expert to tell you that this is simply . . .' Her voice trailed off as her eyes studied the screen. Her brow wrinkled. 'What the . . . ?' She snatched the laptop quite roughly from Charlie's hands, held it up to within a few inches of her own eyes. 'But this is utterly extraordinary,' she murmured.

'What is?' demanded Charlie and Mike together.

'These are photographs.' It was a statement, but she sounded doubtful. She seemed to have forgotten they were there. 'But the endometrium's all wrong . . . the density, there's no irregularity . . . It's perfect.' She looked up at Charlie. Her eyes were round and shocked-looking. 'Where did you say you got this?' she said in a breathy, excited tone.

What on earth? he wondered. 'Oh. It's, er, just some notes, er . . .' He stalled, then remembered the half-baked cover story. 'One of our researchers came across this material. It hasn't been published yet. It's very confidential.'

Beside him, at knee-level, Mike grunted. Say anything and I'll kill you, Charlie swore silently.

The woman's eyebrows rose. 'I'm sure it is,' she said. Her complexion had gone lumpy, red and white, and her throat worked like a turkey's. 'This material is,' she licked her lips, 'quite extraordinary. If I hadn't seen it with my own eyes I wouldn't have believed it. I'm still not sure I do.' She picked up the machine again, blinked at the screen, shook her head, then continued in that spacey voice: 'But there's no blood vessels, nothing. It's—'

'You mean something's missing?' Charlie demanded sharply.

She blinked slowly, then looked over at him. 'Oh, yes,' she said heavily, 'you could say that. A whole lot's "missing".'

Mike moved impatiently at Charlie's feet. He placed a calming hand on the boy's shoulder, smiling at the woman. 'Please could you explain what's there? I mean – what's missing?'

She studied him inscrutably. Then she said quite calmly, 'Only the womb.'

'The . . . ?'

'What?' said Mike, but the rest of the room – indeed, the entire noisy, clanging hospital – seemed to go absolutely quiet. 'The womb?' Charlie repeated, feeling his head spin.

'Yes. In a normal scan one would see the irregular lining of the womb. Here,' she swung the laptop to face him, 'what do you see?'

He stared. Simply what he'd seen before.

'You see?' She ran a shaky finger round the circle. 'A perfectly smooth surface, no differentiation of layers. No layers at all. No blood vessels.' She looked up, as if expecting some spark of recognition. 'This is man-made. Like glass. What we have here is an artificial womb. A glass womb.'

Charlie could hear his heart thumping; he expected that she could too.

'Look at this.' She ran the cursor down herself. 'Twelve weeks. Twelve weeks,' she repeated, and seemed about to drift off again.

Charlie coughed. 'I'm sorry, I've never heard of a glass womb.'

'Don't apologise.' She took a deep breath. 'It's not supposed to be possible. Not yet. They've tried . . .' She nodded her head, then shook it. She seemed confused. 'I think we've even tried it upstairs, but it's never worked. The embryos don't survive outside the womb—'

'. . . for longer than six or seven days,' he finished for her. 'Your girl just told us.'

'That's right. They can only sustain them for so long.' Her eyes returned to the screen. 'The medium's got to be exactly right – the nutrients, the hormones, the whole environment.

Horrendously difficult.' She blinked. 'But they've done it. Look, there's the placenta. However have they done that?'

'This . . . glass womb.' Charlie could see that he was in a battle for her attention. He tapped the screen. 'What is it? A Petri dish, like the ones in the lab?'

'What?' she frowned at the petty interruption. 'Well . . . yes, probably, at the beginning.' She scrolled up. 'They'd start them off in something small like that, then transfer them to the larger container when they got bigger. This last one would be about nine centimetres long.' She looked up suddenly. 'Is this all there is?'

'I'm sorry?'

'There's no more of these graphics?'

'No, that's it I'm afraid.'

'I wonder if that means . . .' She seemed to wander off again.

'Excuse me?'

'I was just thinking, perhaps they couldn't get them beyond this stage.' She focused on him. 'Can't you ask them?'

'Ah, well, that's not easy.' He coughed and, from the floor, Mike echoed him. 'So,' he fingered his collar, 'these people are using the glass womb to ensure that the embryos are completely healthy before putting them back in the mother?'

She gave a quick snort. 'I don't think we're talking about IVF here. At least,' she raised an eyebrow, 'not in its conventional sense.'

'I'm sorry?'

'Think about it. A twelve-week-old fetus can hardly be put back into the mother's womb,' she said scornfully. 'It would be too big, it wouldn't implant; there wouldn't be any placenta for it – unless they were thinking of grafting the artificial one . . . No, that really is too much.' She pushed her hair back. 'Although, with what they've done already . . .' Then she shook her head decisively. 'I think what we're looking at here is the first stage of something much more . . . well, *outrageous* than prolonging test-tube life. Or amazing, I suppose, depending on your viewpoint.' She blinked rapidly a few times.

Charlie waited.

'Think what it would mean . . .' She was away again, talking to herself. 'If you could bring a baby to full-term *outside* the body.'

'Full-term?' The words hit him in the stomach. 'D'you mean . . . ?' Giant babies in glass cages, rows of them ranged according to size. Parents' viewing days, through the eye of a microscope, then

clearly, without the need of optical aids. Their baby at three months'
development, at six. Then coming in on the appointed date to break
open the baby's glass.

'D'you think that's what they're up to?' he gasped.

'Possibly.' She eyed him calmly. 'Probably. I can't think what
other purpose they'd ultimately have for it. It would be an astounding breakthrough. It would revolutionise life, quite literally, as we
know it!' Her eyes widened and her voice became lower. 'Women
would no longer be child-bearers, unless they wanted to – and I can't
imagine why anyone would, not if they were guaranteed a healthy
baby in vitro. No pregnancy problems, no childbirth.' She snorted.
'No stretch-marks, no health risks for older mothers . . . and you
could forget all about the surrogacy debate, couldn't you?'

Charlie watched her numbly; he was having difficulty taking it
in. Mike had become completely still.

The woman looked straight ahead. 'Why risk paying someone
else to have your baby when you can have a nice new one –
your own or, if you don't like the kind of embryo you and your
partner might produce, someone's else's – monitored every step of
the way in a sterile, perfectly controlled environment? All the tests
can be done on it; we've already seen they can do amnio.' A gleam
entered her eyes. She looked round at Charlie. 'The commercial
potential for whoever's developed this is absolutely enormous, you
realise that?'

He was just beginning to, and to appreciate that a company might
go to enormous lengths to protect such a development. He glanced
at Mike's bent head; his story didn't seem so far-fetched any more.
Indeed, it fitted. And Sasha was down there on her own, asking
questions, digging away, not knowing what she was up against. He
tried to banish the notion that she was in danger while he sat back
in safety.

'People could select what they wanted, and the embryo could be
defrosted and matured for them.' The woman's nostrils flared. 'Yes,
quite a development.' She turned to him. 'Can't you give me any
idea who's behind this?'

'Sorry.' The response was automatic.

'I see.' She was piqued, but not to the point of huffiness; she
wanted what they had too much. He could see her figuring out her
next move. It was her misfortune that she had that sort of face. 'I

take it,' she said slowly, 'that you're not in contact with whoever is responsible for these pictures?'

'How d'you know that?' Mike blurted.

'Mike . . .'

'Because, young man, you wouldn't be talking to me if you were, would you?' Her eyes narrowed. 'Which means you've been given this information on the quiet, I'd say.' She looked from one face to the other.

Charlie cleared his throat. 'The data comes from a most unusual source.' He looked her straight in the eye. 'I'd ask you not to make any guesses. My organisation . . .' He stopped himself, as if he'd said too much. 'I am, at this stage, unable to confirm or deny anything.'

A little of the self-assurance left her. He could see her wondering exactly who he was. Her eyes flicked to Mike and back again, and she frowned uneasily.

'However, in the course of the next two weeks, we're expecting more data to arrive which will either serve to authenticate this data or not.'

'You mean,' the frown deepened, the eyes returned to the screen, 'this might not be true?'

'We have every reason to believe that it is. However, until we have further confirmation, we're taking it no further. We have our reputation to consider.'

She ruffled a bit. 'And I mine.'

'Precisely.' He gave her another, full-volt look. 'For that reason, we'd ask you to say nothing about this to anyone.'

'Don't worry.' He saw that she was beginning to feel she'd been made a fool of, that she'd wasted her time, or had it wasted.

'Until we contact you again.' He smiled. 'We need an expert, and you've been terrific.' Mike squirmed against his chair. 'I'd really like it if you'd agree to be on the programme. For reasons I can't go into now, we need a British embryologist.'

'Well, I . . .' The suspicious look had vanished. She crossed her legs and fluffed up her hair at the sides.

'If necessary, if you're worried about security, we could do you in silhouette, disguise your voice.' He wasn't sure why he'd said that, except that it added to the air of vague conspiracy. It left her looking slightly dazed.

'Well, thank you again,' he said, leaning over to reclaim the laptop.

She nodded at him. 'Of course. It has to be American,' she said thoughtfully. 'I should have realised that at once.'

Mike had already stood up, and Charlie wanted to be gone now too.

'American or some other country. Certainly it couldn't have been ours. Stupid of me,' she muttered under her breath. She was obviously as hard on herself as she was on others. It made her marginally more bearable.

'Why d'you said that?' Charlie asked, smiling at her.

'Because it's so elementary. In Britain, embryos can only be used for scientific research up to the age of fourteen days. Then they must be disposed of.'

Charlie's smile stayed in place, but his flesh was crawling. So REDEV's monumental breakthrough had been arrived at illegally. No wonder the company was so desperate; they weren't just worried about protecting a commercial secret.

'It's the law in this country. I don't know what the limit is in the States.' She looked up expectantly but he gave no answer. 'Perhaps there isn't one. Perhaps they just let your researchers get on with what they're good at.' She shook her head. 'No wonder we always get left behind in this country. Too many stupid rules and regulations. You'll let me know, then?'

'I beg your pardon?'

'About the programme – I think I'd be willing to appear,' she said graciously.

'Sure.' He stood up. 'I'll give you a call just as soon as I know. Come on, Mike.'

Driving away from the pub, Sasha saw a sign for the village where Mike lived. Not knowing what else to do (it would be an hour or more, she guessed, before either Manyon or Lucas would return from work), she decided that she might as well have a look at his house from the outside.

The road in which he lived was just beyond the village, in a council-house development close to the railway station. Driving slowly past the house, she noticed the general state of disrepair: the front gate hanging on one hinge; the overgrown, scrappy front garden. Both sets of front curtains were closed; a full milk-bottle stood on the doorstep. She wondered if Mike's mother had also been infected with his fears, to the extent of fleeing her home. Then she remembered that the woman worked nights; she would be sleeping. The thought made her yawn suddenly. Taking the next road, and finding at the bottom a cul-de-sac with a view over open land and rolling hills, she decided to catch up on some of her lost sleep. As her eyes started to close, she noticed the car parked on the other side of the road, its driver apparently asleep, listening to music on his headphones. Lulled by the sight, she fell asleep herself.

CHAPTER TWENTY-SEVEN

When the telephone rang, Mel had just staggered into the house with the last of the bags of shopping. Ludo was already in the kitchen, having announced, uniquely in recent memory, that he wanted to help put things away.

'I'll get it,' she heard him call out eagerly, and she smiled, remembering him at two years old – always so desperate to answer the phone but then saying nothing, simply pressing it against his ear and breathing hard into the mouthpiece.

'Ludo,' she heard him say, and she frowned slightly, wondering who it was. Probably only one of her friends – but then, why would they ask who he was?

She hurried into the kitchen. Ludo was twisting the flex in his fingers. He looked up at her. 'It's a man, mummy,' he said blithely, holding the phone out to her. 'He wants to speak to you.'

'Hello?'

The man cleared his throat. 'It's Will,' he said.

She knew no one called Will. And the man sounded peculiar, sort of strangled.

She glanced down at Ludo. He was on the floor, stacking tins into a cupboard. 'I'm sorry,' she said briskly, 'I don't know any—'

'West. Dr West.'

A hundred thoughts ran into her head. There was something wrong with the baby, of course there was. That's why the doctor was using his Christian name, trying to sound comforting. The baby, who she'd thought of naming after him, the doctor who'd allowed him to be, was now never going to be born. She sank into the chair. Why had she ever rung her mother that morning? Why hadn't she waited? Her mother was sixty-two now, getting on; how much more could she take? Mel's eyes filled. And Ludo. Poor little boy. He wanted his brother so much now . . .

'Just a minute,' she croaked into the phone, and covered the mouthpiece with her hand. 'Ludi . . .' She had to spare him as much as possible. She tried to make her voice sound normal. 'Will you go and watch some television while Mummy's on the phone?'

'But I'm doing the cans! You said I could.'

'Please, darling.'

'But . . .' For a moment the brows knitted and the old mutinous look returned. Then he shrugged, raised himself awkwardly by holding on to the side of the cooker, and went out. He didn't slam the door in his usual way.

Tears trickled down her cheeks. 'What's wrong?' she said dully into the handset, and she looked down to where she imagined that tiny baby waiting too. She didn't know if she could bear it. They'd make her abort him – West and Patrick – they'd force her to, drag her in, strap her down. She felt dizzy. She closed her eyes and saw herself back in the hospital, in that hot, bright operating room. Suddenly she had a very strong sense, as she had before, that it was her and the baby against the world. No one could *make* her do anything; no one could force her against her will. If Patrick left her, so be it. She was going to have this baby.

'Dr West?' she said more composedly. 'It's all right, you can tell me.'

He hesitated, undoubtedly trying to frame the words. It must be an awful job, she thought, and felt a spasm of sympathy for him – which she was aware was extraordinary, in the circumstances. She felt her strength grow. 'Please, Doctor,' she urged.

When he told her, at first she didn't actually believe him. She asked him to him repeat it before the truth of what he was saying started to seep into her brain.

'So you'll come in tomorrow, then?' he asked for a second time.

She stared at the packet of corn flakes. She stared at the window beyond, at the garden and the swing that Patrick had erected. Then she closed her eyes, opened them again, and saw that she wasn't dreaming. 'Yes,' she whispered. 'Of course. What time?'

'As early as you can make it.'

'Just me, or . . . ?'

'Just you,' the doctor cut in quickly. 'At this stage.'

After she'd hung up, quietly replacing the handset in its cradle, she looked slowly around the room. Everything was as normal: the clutter on the breakfast bar, the dent in the side of the toaster where Patrick had dropped it on moving-in day. Something, she felt, ought to have changed. There must be a sign when the world changes on its axis.

She let out a loud whoop of joy.

'Mummy?' At once Ludo's voice pierced the wall. He sounded alarmed. She jumped up, brushed away the tears, and took a step for the hallway, ready to run in and pick him up, to hold him tightly to herself and tell him.

She stopped. With a great effort, she made herself stand still and consider. What if she rushed in now and told him, and then something went wrong? Oh, but the yearning to tell! And nothing would go wrong; Dr West wouldn't let that happen. She moaned softly. Her heart wanted to go to Ludo, but her feet were glued down, holding her back, making her be sensible. 'It's all right, angel,' she called. 'Mummy nearly slipped, that's all.'

'Oh.' Immediately he was reassured; she heard him turn the sound up on his programme, blessed him, then silently shut the door. She glanced at the time. It was five-twenty-five; she might just catch Patrick at the office. Taking the phone to the other side of the room, telling herself to keep her voice down, she pressed the memory key for Patrick's office.

He answered at once, saying as soon as he heard her voice, 'There's nothing wrong, is there?'

Why did he always think there should be something wrong? Then she smiled mistily. Look's talking, she thought.

'No, Pat. Nothing's wrong. Everything's right. Oh God.' She couldn't help it, the hot tears were flowing again.

'Mellie? Is it the baby? Oh God. It is, isn't it? I'm coming home, just hold on, darling—'

'Pat, no. It's not the baby. It's . . .' She took a deep breath. 'The doctor's just called. Dr West. In tandem with his pre-natal work on DMD . . .' That was what he'd said, she thought, amazed. Word for word. 'He's also been conducting a gene therapy trial for,' she struggled over the next word, got it out, 'boys with the condition. One set of parents backed out this morning, some weird religious reason.' She gave a sudden laugh. 'Can you imagine? And,' her tears were thickening her words, 'Dr West was wondering if Ludo would like to take that boy's place. He's been trying me all afternoon, he said. After I picked Ludi up I went shopping. Just think, if he'd given up, he'd have gone to someone else!'

There was absolute silence at the other end of the line.

'Patrick?' Perhaps he'd fainted. Perhaps – and everything faltered – he was going to say no. Oh God, no. Was she going to have to fight him on this?

There was a choking sound, then Patrick whispered, 'What are the chances?'

'Of it being a cure?' She wiped her hand across her face, remembered now that she'd asked Dr West the same question, although until this moment she'd had no such recollection. 'Between eighty-five and ninety per cent.'

'Side-effects?'

She'd asked that one too. 'None.' She remembered the exact phrase again. 'Nothing significant.'

'Oh my God.'

She cradled the phone like a baby. 'We'll say yes, then?' she asked tremulously. 'Patrick?'

'Of course we will. Oh, Melly . . .'

'I know.' She nodded, carried on rocking. 'But it is true, my darling. It's true. He wants to see me first thing in the morning, then the therapy can start next week. Oh, Patrick . . .' He was sobbing like a broken child. 'Come home, darling. Everything's going to be all right.'

Sitting in the armchair that he'd occupied for most of the afternoon – and it was now early evening, he saw by the mantelpiece clock – Tony Holland had to admit that the E-fit officer was doing a superb job with young Tim Dacre.

'Think of yourself as a camera, Tim. You're only watching; there's no need to be afraid. OK. There's a security guard sitting in his booth late at night; he hears a noise, sees a movement, looks up. What can you, the camera, see? What can you show us?'

'A girl . . . woman.' Dacre's throat worked. 'She's at the front of the car. She's swinging her arm back. She's holding a spray can. Her arm's going up and down. Her hair's glinting. It's lit up by the lights.' His eyes were half-shut. He was no longer sitting on the sofa in his parents' home; he was back there on the tarmac, reliving it. 'It's very blonde, white-blonde hair, and it moves all . . . sort of funny, sort of all in one piece.'

'A pony-tail, Tim?'

'No.' He frowned. 'That's not it, but . . .'

'Take your time, Tim.'

'Thanks.' Dacre nodded seriously.

Of course, Holland reminded himself, the E-fit constable had been specially trained for this; he knew how to handle the most reluctant of victims. When Holland had first called him two hours before, asking him to bring his kit to Dacre's, the officer had tried to argue for Holland bringing him to the E-fit house at headquarters. Victims did well there. It was a building designed specifically for them: a kitchenette, where the officer could make tea or coffee before taking them through to the 'living room', furnished to look as much as possible like a real one, decorated in soothing greens. There the officer would conduct the 'cognitive interview' – which meant that he'd talk about anything and everything *except* the incident, until he judged that the person was sufficiently relaxed to begin relating what had happened. Once he was 'locked on and focused', the officer would suggest going through to another room to make an E-fit, a picture of the attacker, using the Electronic Facial Identification Technique on a computer.

Dacre had refused point-blank to budge so the E-fit man had come to him, with his easy line in chat, his laptop that now lay between them on the sofa, uniting them, pushing Holland out of the picture. That was fine by him, he thought, deliberately not looking at them, letting his eyes wander round the room – the brown and yellow carpet, the tiled fireplace, the curtains with the hummingbirds on them – so long as they let him stay to eavesdrop.

'She was wearing a wig,' Dacre said slowly and clearly. His eyes opened. He turned to the officer. 'I've only just remembered,' he said excitedly.

'That's fantastic, Tim. Well done!'

'It fell off when she put the hood on. I saw it on the road. The man with the gun picked it up.'

The first mention of the gunman since the raid, since Dacre had lapsed into total shock. Holland kept very still.

'Did you see what he looked like, Tim?'

'No. Sorry. He had a hood on all the time.'

'Did you see the woman's real hair colour?'

'No. No, I'm sorry.'

'That's OK, that's fine. Let's go back to her, shall we? Let's focus on her jaw-line. Does she have a round face? Like this?'

Dacre shook his head.

'Oval?' The man hit another key.

'Sort of oval. Yeah, that's it.'

'You're doing really well.'

The man sounded as if he meant it, Holland thought, as if he really liked Tim Dacre. It couldn't just be his training; it must also be his personality: kind, unthreatening, sympathetic. Holland decided never to tell him how he himself had finally got through to Dacre; how after nearly an hour of doing his best, coping with rudeness and a lack of response, a plan had suggested itself to him.

He'd known that it was risky, but he'd gone ahead and acted upon it anyway, and been horrified at the effect, afraid that he'd pushed the boy into permanent madness, wrecking his own career in the process. The hospital psychiatrist had forbidden Dacre to see his car until he was stronger. Holland, despite this, had thought that it might spark off some recollection in the lad, unlock some hidden memory that would bring Holland closer to the perpetrators. He'd been sitting with Dacre in the kitchen, alone, and had punctured a long silence by clearing his throat, causing Dacre to look up at him.

'I hope our forensic people didn't make too much of a mess of your car,' he'd said.'

'What?' The pinkish eyes had met his own for the first time.

'Only they can, sometimes. They don't mean to, of course. But scraping off samples, especially paint, can be tricky. The original paintwork tends to get scratched.'

Dacre had continued to stare.

'I could take a look for you if you like.' Holland had offered. 'Do a quick check.' He knew how much that car meant to the boy; it had been almost his sole topic of conversation when he'd first come round. 'Is the garage locked?'

It hadn't been. He'd raised the metal door and switched on the light. The car was sitting low inside. Most of the offensive word had been splattered across the bonnet, but the last letter had made it on to the passenger door. The paint had run and smudged. It was pitiful. It looked like a class of toddlers had been at it.

Dacre's scream had frozen him. He hadn't heard his approach. He'd deliberately not looked back to see if the lad had followed. The noise had ricocheted round that small bleak garage.

Dacre's face had been bright red, his mouth wide open. He'd staggered forward and embraced his car, as much as he was able, spreading his arms wide across the bonnet. 'Oh my baby, my poor, poor baby!' And pressing his face against the metal he'd blubbered like a child, before raising his head and howling, 'That fucking whore! That fucking little *whore!* What's she done to you?'

Which was how Holland had been made aware of the sex of the graffitist. At the time his mind had been busy with other matters, like running for help, trying to explain to the doctors and his superintendent how he'd let such a thing happen. But then, quite suddenly, Dacre's rage had been over. He'd swayed to his feet, wiped his eyes on the back of his sleeve, and pronounced himself, astonishingly, 'feeling better now'. And yes, he'd nodded after Holland had got him back inside, he did think he'd be able to give a picture of the woman.

Then he'd lapsed into silence until the E-fit man had arrived.

'Sir?'

Holland blinked. The officer and Dacre were both looking at him, the officer holding out a sheet of paper.

'Would you like to have a look? This is Tim's first effort.' The man smiled proudly. 'And a pretty good one.'

Holland took the printout. It showed a woman with a hard, sexy mouth, and large eyes that were strangely childlike in that face. He looked closer. It was familiar. Take away the blonde hair, plump out the lips, and it was almost like . . . He nearly blurted it out. That Thursday night, when Mary Kennedy was supposed to have been at a sleep-over . . .

He asked, with commendable casualness, 'What sort of age did you say she was, Tim?'

'Not sure. Twenties.'

'Not younger? A teenager, say?'

'No.' Dacre shook his head emphatically. 'She wasn't no kid. No way.'

Of course, there was no way Dacre's ego was going to allow her to be, Holland judged shrewdly. No way he was going to admit that he'd been duped and his precious car trashed by a schoolgirl.

'Let's think about her height now, Tim. What she was wearing? Close your eyes, focus on what the camera's seeing . . .'

Holland stared again at the picture. Slim down the cheeks, bring the eyes a fraction closer together, and it was Mary Kennedy. He was sure of it. He'd studied her face often enough in the previous three days – seen her grow up from babyhood, for God's sake, through the family album. What the hell was she doing mixed up in the REDEV business? Playing decoy for Winston's gang?

His mind slowed. Her fellow runaways, of course. The missing link between them had to be REDEV. Which one of the two men had brandished the gun that night? The scared schoolteacher or the policeman's son? He could see Richley enjoying himself in the role. But – and his brow furrowed – none of the checks into their backgrounds had thrown up any animal rights involvement. Unless they'd never been arrested or cautioned, never in any way aroused the interest of the ARNI collators. And around there, as he'd discovered since his arrival, intelligence-gathering was patchy. There simply wasn't the daily manpower available.

Still, he'd order a re-check. He glanced at his watch. He'd see if there wasn't a file on one of them somewhere. And he'd find out if any of the fibres found on the torn hole in the fencing belonged to Mary or Richley or the Henshaws. A piece of black denim, a bit of black wool, a piece of rubber from a shoe: none of them had made a match with any of Winston's belongings. But then, Holland reminded himself, Winston had been the professional in the gang; the others hadn't known how important it was to be careful. Forensics had judged by the skid-marks running downhill to the hole that there might have been a bit of a scramble to get out. The shoe-prints had been difficult to determine, owing to the heavy rain that had fallen both prior to and after the raid, but the way that the ground had been churned up indicated that the perpetrators had been in a hurry to leave.

Why had they run? Holland gazed into Mary's eyes, compelling them to provide him an answer. He could understand the stampede from the labs – someone had heard something, someone had got spooked – but why had they gone on to leave the country? Was it simply the fear of being caught? And why had they waited over a week? Why hadn't they scarpered at once?

Holland sighed, looked again at the face that he held. The woman's eyes weren't Mary's. Similar, yes, as was the shape of the face – but the suspicion grew that he was seeing the child in the woman's cruel face simply because he wanted to; he needed a solution and his imagination, fuelled by elements from both inquiries, had suggested one.

The woman's mouth seemed to harden, mocking him. He looked up.

'Brown eyes, would you say, Tim? Blue? Very pale. Excellent.'

Mary Kennedy had very pale blue eyes. Noticeably so. Not only her parents had mentioned it, but also her friends, her teachers, lots of people. And of course, he'd seen photographs.

His glance fell on the coffee-table, where he'd previously noted the presence of a pencil beside a puzzle-book. If he dashed back to Ashford now, alerted them about his suspicions, what good would it do? How would it change the nature of the hunt? Perhaps only for the worse: if the European police were told that the runaways might be criminals they'd lose interest, plaster their pictures about the place, causing them to go to ground, even do something desperate. Holland decided against it; he wasn't willing for that to happen, not on the basis of what might simply be the product of his imagination.

He'd wait until the morning, when some of those checks could be done; when he'd pay another visit to the Kennedy parents, if he had the time, or get Jem and Julie to do so.

He looked up and caught Dacre's eyes upon him. 'You're doing so well, Tim,' he said, and smiled as if he meant it.

CHAPTER TWENTY-EIGHT

It was pitch-dark, fuggy, and Sasha's neck ached. She experienced a moment of panic before realising that she was safe, that she had merely fallen asleep in the car.

She read the clock on the dashboard and came fully awake. She'd slept for almost an hour; it was now six o'clock. According to Mike, Chris Manyon would have been home for at least thirty minutes.

She drove quickly to the flat that she'd already visited that morning. It looked in darkness, she saw as she parked. That didn't necessarily mean it was empty, she told herself. Manyon might live predominantly at the back of the house.

She picked up the mobile from its charger, got out of the car and started down the pathway to the simple two-storey building. Before allowing herself to doze off she'd tried Charlie's number again, with no success, but she'd left another message on his answering-machine. It hadn't been a very successful day at all, she concluded; at the end of it, she still was in possession of very few facts.

She'd scared off the REDEV man, was no more knowledgeable about what the company did, beyond what Holland had told her – and of course there was Holland himself to worry about. His officers must have finished with the security guard by now, must have reported back to their boss. Was Holland at that very minute preparing a press statement for the rest of the pack while she trudged wearily and in ignorance down an unlit path? And then there were the others, the unknown factor. How much more did Gerry's abductors – Mike's woman and the bogus police officers – know by now?

She negotiated an icy-looking patch, took a deep breath, and rang the doorbell. It buzzed, uncompromisingly loud, and she knew instantly that he wasn't there. Noise in empty places always sounded like that: unmuffled, long and lonely. She tried again, leaned forward and pressed her ear to the door: no radio or TV, no movement, and no chink of light coming through the ill-fitting letterbox. Either he'd been delayed, or . . .

She jumped. A door had opened somewhere. She could hear heavy footsteps.

'Hello?'

The voice didn't come from within the flat, but from the side of the building; the footsteps from the wooden staircase that led to the first-floor flat.

'Oh, hello.' Sasha took a step back and saw, half-way down the steps and lit by a lamp on the wall, a large young woman with a toddler on her hip.

'Can I help you?' The woman heaved the child a bit higher. They both regarded her, Sasha thought, as if she were a curiosity. The woman looked oddly excited.

Sasha smiled at her. 'I was looking for Chris Manyon. I understand he lives here?'

The woman glanced at the BMW and back again. 'You a friend of his, then?' Now she sounded excited too.

'A friend of a friend,' Sasha said briefly. 'He's obviously not in. I'll call back later.'

The woman sucked in her breath, and the child – a boy of three or so – stuck his thumb in his mouth and sucked too. His mother snorted suddenly. 'Not much point in doing that,' she said and smirked.

Oh no, Sasha thought, knowing what was coming but not wanting to, wanting to turn and run so that she wouldn't have to hear it.

'He killed himself drink-driving last Friday, didn't he?'

'D–did he?'

'Mm.' The woman worked her tongue round the inside of her mouth. 'Stupid fool. Not the first time he was drunk out his skull behind the wheel, I can tell you.'

Mike had been right all along. She'd been stupid ever to doubt him. He was in real danger, maybe Charlie too . . . My God, she thought, was that why they hadn't answered her calls?

'Not that I'm not sorry for him, and his poor mum. Gone out of her head so I've heard, poor cow. But what did he expect? Six times over the legal limit, the policeman said.' She paused, clearly enjoying the effect of her words. 'Yeah. It's a shock, isn't it, anyone young going like that? But at least he only topped himself.'

Sasha stared, no longer seeing the woman. Her hand slid into her bag, wrapped itself around the mobile. She had to get away from this awful place and call again.

She started walking back to the car. 'I mean,' the fat woman's voice called behind her, 'he could've killed a kiddy, couldn't he? Or anyone.'

She stepped into the car, slammed the door, saw that the hand holding the key was shaking and tried to calm herself. Deep down she'd always known that what she'd just heard was possible, even likely. In one horrible way, she admitted, turning the key in the ignition, she'd been hoping for such news, confirming the story as it did. But no. She slipped off the handbrake and prepared to move out, remembering at the last moment to put on the headlights. She'd never do that, surely. No one had to die for the sake of a stupid story.

She moved off. Getting away from the place soothed her; she could feel her heart-rate slowing. Nothing she'd done or wished for had influenced Manyon's death one way or the other. She mustn't give into panic or fear; she must simply find somewhere to park, call Charlie, make sure he and Mike were all right . . . She turned a corner and pulled in.

'This is the answerphone . . .'

She nearly screamed. She switched on the map-light, rummaged in her bag and found her wallet. If she had genuine cause to fear for Charlie's and Mike's safety – and she had – she really had only one option to call the police. Specifically, the policeman who would be most easily convinced and who would subsequently act the quickest. She pulled out Holland's card, and with it came Charlie's. AGN

Bureau Chief, London, and the company's logo, the American flag flying over the globe. Under his name were his work number, his home number (which he'd scribbled in for her) and two mobile numbers. She stared. One of those belonged to the handset she was holding, but the other . . . the other was entirely unfamiliar. She swallowed, cancelled her current call, started putting in the new number. Of course. An organisation that gave its bureau chief a penthouse and three cars would give him more than one mobile. She pressed 'send' and waited. If it was that woman's voice, saying it had not been possible to connect her call, she *would* scream.

It was ringing. It was poor reception, the tone was fading in and out, but she could hear it. She bit her tongue. Why didn't he answer?

'Hello?' Charlie's voice coming through a storm.

'Oh, Charlie, thank God! Are you OK?'

There was a burst of static in her ear. She held the phone away, brought it back, heard Charlie say, '. . . sha?' then another crackle, then, 'you OK?'

'I'm fine! What about you, and Mike?'

'Yes, we're . . . on the laptop . . .'

It was torture. But he was OK, they both were, that was all that mattered.

'. . . glass . . . gist said that it . . . legal . . .'

'Charlie, this is mad, I can't hear you!'

' . . . really . . . D'you think you should . . .'

She remembered something. 'Are you on your way to work?' she yelled.

Nothing, then a painful crackle. He'd told her that his weekday night-shifts started at eight. It was now six-twenty. 'I'll call you at work,' she yelled through the static, 'or at home. Are you going home now?'

'. . . hear you . . . you later . . . after eight.'

The line went dead. She pressed 'end'. It sounded as if he'd been saying the same thing: that they'd speak later, when he'd got to work. It wasn't so long to wait.

She felt her shoulders relax into a more natural position. They hadn't been kidnapped or killed. In fact Charlie had sounded really cheerful. They'd found something on the laptop, she thought he'd said. Perhaps they'd managed to fathom what those pictures were about. The yawning hunter and the city skyline. What had he said about glass? And about something being legal?

But her initial elation at hearing Charlie's voice soon faded as the reality of her own situation crept back in. Chris Manyon was dead. That made two out of the eight raiders, too high a ratio to be a coincidence, however plausible it might appear on the surface – an unhealthy man suffering a heart attack, a stupid young drunken driver. She was cold. She switched on the car's heating system, saw that it had started snowing again, that already a thick covering lay across her windscreen.

That awful woman – Sasha thought she'd never forget the relish on her face – told her that Chris Manyon died last Friday. Had that, she wondered suddenly, been the reason the Tenterden Four had taken off? She was sure it was. Then it struck her that Mike didn't know about his friend, and her heart sank. She would have to tell him – and if she'd been freaked out by the news, what would he do?

She sighed. A small tension headache was beginning to take root in the middle of her forehead. She rubbed her eyes, trying to think clearly, to examine things objectively. She was sure that Winston and Manyon had been killed, but could she prove it? Presumably the police had found nothing suspicious about either death, otherwise they would be investigating them. The local paper reported that Winston's death was from natural causes. Of course, in Manyon's case, having died only last Friday, it might be early days regarding the publication of an inquest's results. The story wouldn't be in the local paper until the next week's edition, due out on Thursday. She would phone the police as soon as she could find a decent phone and ask.

That ratio. Two out of eight dead. But extraordinary coincidences happen, she told herself. Was she willing to stake her reputation on what she felt to be the truth – what must surely be the truth – rather than hard facts? She took a deep breath. No newspaper or magazine would run a story based on her hunches; they'd need more. Just as *she* needed more, she told herself. She needed to find out about Clive Lucas.

It was six-thirty now. She could either drive, find a phone and keep calling Charlie's mobile, or she could go to Lucas's address. He lived at Rolvenden, another four miles distant, and would be home by now – or not. She had to find out, she realised suddenly. She couldn't wait. Besides, Charlie definitely had said eight, so he might not even be contactable until then.

She switched on the windscreen wipers and watched them shove the snow off, revealing a scene, she thought, that could have been straight out of a Frank Capra movie: a small group of children in bright-coloured bobble-hats and flying scarves having a snowball fight. Two of them, a boy and a girl, were on a sledge and the others were bombarding them, scooping up the soft snow, hurling it through the dark air. They were all laughing and shrieking with excitement, oblivious to anything else. Sasha found herself smiling, but also feeling slightly sad without knowing quite why.

She turned up the wipers to a faster speed – the snow was really falling thickly again – and reversed into a driveway. The children, she saw in her mirror as she drove off, hadn't paused in their game; they had merely appropriated the space she had vacated.

She left them and their village behind her, retraced her route to the main road, where she saw a sign for Rolvenden. The snow was as bad as it had been earlier, quite mesmerising to watch against a night-sky – millions of tiny flakes spinning and dancing and hitting the glass – too easy, she judged, blinking, to be hypnotised by it, drawn into its vortex, to find oneself smashing into the car in front, flung through the windscreen, dead.

Clive Lucas, Mike had told her, lived in a rented house next to a windmill. 'Even you couldn't miss it,' he'd said with a smirk, 'it's a big white thing with sails.' But there were lots of big white things now, she thought worriedly – houses and trees and barns – and it was dark. How was she meant to identify windmill sails? Then she saw it. It stood on a slight mound off to her right, and the size of it, its vast sails, took her by surprise. She approached gingerly. The snow on the road, lit up by her lights, looked as if it was already hardening into ice; indeed, the whole scene seemed to have changed in a few minutes from a plaything for children to something much more serious. Now the snow thudded on to her roof, flung itself against her windows. She slowed still further, saw the house, and pulled up thankfully beside it.

She got out, zipping up her jacket, pulling her hood tightly round her face. The wind whistled and the snow bombarded her and she gasped, taken aback by the strength of it. She heard a terrible creaking, and feared suddenly that a tree was about to come crashing down on top of her, but when she looked up she saw that it was only the windmill, its huge sails straining against the onslaught. It was like an old ship, she thought, beguiled for a second, before putting her head down and making for the door.

There was no bell so she lifted the letterbox handle and let it fall several times. The wind howled harder and the storm seemed suddenly cruel, intent on doing her harm. Please be in, she prayed, forgetting about Lucas, wanting only shelter. Squinting, she saw that there were three cars to the side of the cottage. That was good, she told herself. Mike had said Lucas shared with two other men, so they had a car each. Although, if Lucas had been abducted . . .

Her teeth were chattering. She grabbed the letterbox again and rattled it hard and the wind dropped. The door was yanked open and a large man stood before her, dressed in overalls.

'Hi!' He was thirtyish, curly-haired and exuded warmth. He grinned. 'You a carol-singer?'

'Uh, no. I—'

'Didn't think so. They usually come in groups, you know. And generally speaking they sing. You can always tell.'

He was Australian, but even without his accent she would have guessed.

Snow was falling on her eyelashes. She put up a hand to shield them and smiled at him.

'I wonder, is Clive in? Clive Lucas?'

'Another one!' He had forget-me-not blue eyes which he rolled exaggeratedly. 'How many girls has that guy got?'

'I'm sorry?' It wasn't what she'd been expecting to hear. The wind caught her and she staggered suddenly.

'Say . . .' The man was immediate concern. He put a hand on her arm. 'Come on in. It's a hell of a night to be outdoors.'

She stepped inside gratefully. The heat hit her first, from a massive log-fire in the old inglenook, then the smell of oil, which she guessed came from bits of what looked like a car's engine, dissected and spread out on newspaper in front of the TV. Also in front of the TV, sprawled out on a sofa, was another man, considerably younger than the first, thin and dark.

Clive, she wondered?

'Hi, there'. He sat up and raised his eyebrows appreciatively. 'I'm Pete.'

'Too late, mate,' said the Australian. 'She's here about Clive.'

'*Another* one?'

'That's what I said!'

What was this? Sasha wondered, gazing at their grinning faces. 'Is he in?' she asked carefully.

They looked at each other, then back at her. 'Damn,' said the first man, 'I thought you were going to clear it up.'

Her hopes wavered. 'What? Is there some mystery about Clive?'

'Well, I dunno if you'd call it a mystery. He seems to have gone AWOL, that's all. Hey, you OK?'

She'd swayed suddenly. Three out of eight: the figures hit her like a blow.

'Sit down,' the Australian ordered, sweeping some debris off an armchair and on to the floor.

The younger man had sat up and switched off the television. 'Aren't you one of Clive's girlfriends, then?' he asked.

'That's not very tactful, Pete. You feeling better now?' the first man enquired kindly of Sasha. 'My name's Chris, by the way.'

She recollected herself slightly. 'Mine's Sasha.' She cleared her throat. 'How long's he been missing?'

Chris rubbed his hands. He looked embarrassed. 'We dunno if he's missing, love. He might just have – well, you know . . .'

'Gone off with someone else?'

'Well, it's possible. Don't get upset about it, though.'

'It's all right.' She smiled weakly; she had to rally and ask questions. 'I'm not a girlfriend. I don't even know him.'

'You don't?'

She shook her head. She didn't want to tell them too much; she was sure they were innocent, nice boys, but one never knew. On the other hand, she needed their co-operation. She told them that she was a freelance journalist investigating a story about a number of people who may, or may not – she emphasised the phrase for all their benefit, even though she didn't believe it herself – have gone missing.

'The Tenterden Four?'

They'd chorused it.

'Um, not really,' she mumbled. 'D'you think you could you tell me,' she went on quickly, 'when you last saw Clive?'

'Friday morning,' Chris said promptly. 'He was on the phone. I was going to work.'

'How did he sound? Nervous at all?'

The man shook his head. 'No, more sarcastic. He said something like, "I've made it through the night." Something like that. If it helps.'

It didn't, but she thanked him anyway. 'And you haven't seen him since?' She looked over at Pete. 'Either of you?'

Pete shook his head. 'His work rang this evening . . .' Her heart sank further. '. . . said he hadn't been in. They also said he'd done it before . . .' She see-sawed. '. . . and to tell him to be in tomorrow or else. But we can't, can we? I mean, we dunno where he is. We thought he'd just gone off, like we said, with a girlfriend.'

'Having himself a lost weekend, you know?' Chris put in. 'A long, lost weekend.'

It was, Sasha told herself, just possible. Highly unlikely, but . . . 'He's got lots of girlfriends?' she asked.

'Seems to. He's, you know, secretive. He hasn't lived here long, only a couple of months, but he keeps himself to himself. One time, only a week or so back, he didn't come home all night. I asked him if it was a girl,' Chris shrugged, 'and he said, "Not just one, mate." He could be a bit of a wanker sometimes, you know?'

'You thought he was just boasting?'

'He wasn't much to look at . . . but he did have one girl. What was her name, Pete?'

Pete was frowning. He had sobered suddenly. 'She phoned last night, asked for Clive, seemed sniffy when I said we hadn't seem him. That's why we thought . . .' He trailed off. 'D'you think he's in trouble?' he asked.

'I don't know. Maybe, but—'

'D'you think we should phone the police?'

She felt an awful compulsion to tell them everything. But she didn't know for sure that Clive was in danger. Or dead. Not for definite. 'It's difficult. There's a chance that he could, as you say, just have gone off.'

'And he is twenty-four,' Chris added. 'I don't think the police are going to start a manhunt for him. Besides,' he looked awkward, 'it might be a bit of a problem if they came round here asking questions. I've overstayed a bit.'

'I shouldn't think that would . . .' She stopped herself. Sometimes she really did feel despicable. 'Well . . . I see,' she murmured. 'Why not leave it another couple of days, see if he turns up?' she said more brightly.

'You reckon?'

'I do.' She got out a business card and scribbled the mobile's number on it. She asked for theirs. 'Just in case I hear anything,' she added, getting up. 'I'll call you.'

Chris got up too. 'And we can call you?'

'Sure.'

'You don't want to stay for a coffee?' Pete called.

'Do,' said Chris. 'Or you could stay the night if you like. We've got loads of rooms.'

He – they – were really very sweet, she thought. But she needed to get away, to be by herself, figure out what else she had to do before heading for home. And – she sneaked a glance at her watch – she had to find a phone so she could be sure to get through to Charlie by eight o'clock.

'You're really very kind, but . . .' She gasped as he opened the door and a flurry of snow rushed in.

'If you're sure . . .'

'I'm sure.' She turned her back to the weather and smiled at him. 'Thank you so much. And . . . er, don't worry too much about Clive.'

'If you say so.' Chris smiled back. 'You're got a lovely face, Sasha, you know that? I don't only mean pretty, either. You're a good person, honest. It shows. It's good of you to care.'

She ducked her head and ran for the sanctuary of her car. Snow, no longer swirling flakes but hard, sharp spikes, hit her face; the wind screamed and buffeted around her. By the time she had reached the car, flung open the door and leaped inside, she was breathless. It must be a blizzard, she thought. She'd never been in one before, didn't think she'd ever seen the weather so angry. She started the engine, thanked God that she was in a luxury car, pushed the heating up to full power, and was rewarded by a blast of cold air in her face. In the short space of time that she had been away the windscreen had again been covered in a sheet of snow, and for a moment, switching on the wipers, it looked as if they had been frozen. They tried to move, but couldn't. Then they jolted back into life.

Three out of eight, she thought.

But she knew she mustn't let herself dwell on it now, she had to concentrate on driving. She set her jaw, bent forward over the steering-wheel and crept out gingerly into the lane.

To sleep with one's eyes open, to relax the body and mind while the senses remain fully alert, was a skill that Anna had acquired many years before.

She had been a soldier once, although not for the cause for which she had longed throughout her childhood to fight. That had been denied her. Those people among whom she had been reared, and for whom she would willingly have given her life, had driven her from their midst, sent her to a foreign land which was, according to the papers she carried, her land too.

Her father had been a soldier in the British army. With this in mind, and hoping among those people to find acceptance, Anna had joined the army herself. The recruiting officer had believed her story for she had told it well, remembering to adhere to the facts which could be checked: that her father had been stationed near Dusseldorf; that there he had met and married her mother, a Turkish 'guest-worker', who had given birth to Anna and three years later to a son, who had tragically died as a small baby; that her parents had separated, her father had left the army, drifted and died a few years later, and her mother had taken Anna home to Turkey.

The story was true in all particulars save for the last. Her mother had returned alone to Turkey; it was her father who had taken the three-year-old girl with him into his new life. It was a period Anna remembered only in snatches: strange people, strange houses, terrible loneliness, never being allowed out; then being snatched from bed, and a long, drowsy sleep. Until one morning she'd woken and there'd been stillness and peace. She'd been in a little bed, in a room with other children, and warm light had been streaming in through the window. Later, a breakfast of yoghurt and hot sweet tea, and songs in the nursery. The message in those songs she could still recall with clarity: with their blood and with their bones, they the children would crush the enemy . . . With their fingers and their nails they would tear out the eyes and hearts of the occupiers . . . and the land itself would sing as they returned, the children leading their parents by the hand, coming home after twenty long years in exile.

Life for Anna had really started then: with the learning of her new language through those songs; the adoption of the other children as her brothers and sisters, the orphanage 'mother' and 'father' as her parents, while her own father had become an increasingly infrequent visitor, his language, even his face, slipping away from her as the years passed. And so, when one day the orphanage father, a doctor, had led her into his office and told her gravely that her father had been killed fighting the enemy, she had felt little grief. She had relegated him to the small place in her memory, to her life 'before', about which by then she could remember so little: a glimpse of her mother, dark-haired and beautiful, wearing a pretty blue dress; herself warm in a bed with teddies on the wallpaper; and then the terrifying night when she had stood, cold, pressed hard against a window, staring out at her own reflection, crying for her mother to come back.

Anna's mother had died of an overdose shortly after returning to the Turkish village where she'd been born. She'd made no attempts to trace Anna, left no photographs or letters, no explanation as to why she had abandoned her small daughter. She had systemically, it seemed, erased all records of herself and her family before taking her own life.

Anna had stayed at the Syrian orphanage until she was sixteen, when late one night she'd been woken by the doctor and his wife. The woman had been crying. The man also had had tears in his eyes as he told her she had to leave at once because she was in danger. The Western powers had carried out an air-strike on one of the commando bases. Many had been killed, and some of the more extremist elements were demanding vengeance: blood for blood. Several Westerners who worked in the city had already been seized.

In the back of the doctor's car, lying under rugs, Anna had wept for the last time that she could remember. Across the border in Turkey, delivered to an English teacher and his wife, the doctor had taken Anna's head in his hands, blessed her, and bade her farewell.

The British embassy in Ankara had examined her birth certificate and issued her passport. In London she'd been unable to trace her grandparents. Knowing no one else, she'd got temporary work where she could, gradually regaining the use of her father's language, until eventually joining the army.

She hadn't stayed long. She'd expected to learn how to fight, how to use a gun, and they'd taught her instead how to march in a skirt, to arrange flowers in the officers' mess, to stand to attention on the parade ground. Women, she was told, were never sent into combat.

If there was a war, their place would be behind a desk doing useful office work, keeping up the spirits of army wives – at the most, driving truck supplies.

Anna had left and gone to one of the local pubs, where she'd heard about a man offering work in the security industry – bodyguards, close-target work, weaponry – to ex-squaddies. But he'd laughed outright, told her bluntly that he wasn't looking for little girls. She'd persisted, however, and he'd ended up giving her an 'assignment' – spying on an erring husband – and her success on that first job had led to other offers.

She'd lived frugally, saved her wages, learned from those around her and set about training herself properly. She'd bought tuition from the experts and had become a markswoman. A cause no longer mattered to her, nor a sense of belonging. Her own survival was all, and she would do most things provided she was paid. Money was essential to her – not that she lived ostentatiously – but she needed to know it was there, hers whenever she wanted it, in the way that other people had a family or a home.

Anna started. On the other side of the street the door of the Gilbert house had opened. She sat up. The small girl appeared on the doorstep, and behind her the mother, propelling her forward with one hand while the other was occupied with the infant. The front door slammed and shoes came slip-slapping along the slushy pavement.

Anna lowered her head and waited for the figures to pass. She heard the shoes stop, car doors being opened, then very quickly afterwards the engine kicking into life. She forced herself not to look up as the Volvo went by, but when she did, she saw that it was going at some speed, that it had already reached the end of the road.

She sped after it and saw with relief that the traffic on the South Circular wasn't allowing it in. Anna applied her brakes and came to a stop behind it. In the back window was a sticker saying 'Baby on Board'; in the back also, leaning on her arms, her round eyes staring out, was the girl, Lucy. Anna felt her pulse quicken. Would the child recognise her and call out? But Lucy simply continued to stare.

Minutes ticked by. Weren't children of that age, Anna wondered, supposed to be strapped into safety-seats? Why hadn't the mother done that? Why did she care so little for her daughter while smothering the baby with love? She came to. Mrs Gilbert was nosing her way out into the traffic, hooting her horn as she did so, yelling something out of the window, although Anna couldn't hear the words. She pushed in after her, cut across two lines of traffic, allowing another car to come between them. Mrs Gilbert was driving wildly, swapping lanes, apparently impervious to the blaring horns and flashing lights. She swung off sharply to the right, and Anna saw a hospital entrance marked 'Accident and Emergency'. She followed. Had the baby had an accident? Or had the husband, as yet unseen, been taken ill? This could be the perfect opportunity, Anna thought, seeing the Volvo catapult over a speed ramp. The mother would have to park, then make a dash in the sleet.

Anna stopped, turning off her headlights but keeping the engine running, the revs up high. She stared. The mother hadn't driven into the car-park at all. Instead she'd screeched to a halt right outside the casualty department where, under the full glare of the hospital's lights, she was out of the car, running with the baby in her arms. She disappeared inside.

Anna got out, tucking the blonde hair of her wig under her scarf. She had to find out what was happening. She walked swiftly towards the Volvo with its yawning door, heard the sound of Lucy crying, and stopped.

'Mummy!'

The girl's face was pressed to the back window, tear-stained and frightened. Anna stared. She put her head inside the Volvo and said stiffly, 'I'm going to get her now.'

Then she shut the door quietly and headed into the hospital.

The snow was so thick that Sasha could hardly see the edges of the road. She was afraid of driving the car into a ditch, getting injured, being stuck inside. She skidded. This, she told herself, was no fun at all; this was a nightmare. She kept on, trying as much as possible to steer into the middle of the lane, praying that no other car would suddenly come round a bend, straight into her. She took a deep breath. Any moment now, she told herself, feeling the car start to skid again, but remembering this time to swing into it, she'd reach the village high street, which was sure to have been treated. Then she'd zip back up the A21, pausing somewhere closer to home to phone Charlie, maybe eat something, then on to the motorway and home. If she needed to come back in the morning – fine – it wouldn't take long. But for now she wanted Covent Garden, a long, hot, soak in the bathtub, a couple of hours' sleep, and then Charlie. At the prospect of seeing him she felt a glow begin inside her.

She peered hard through the hurling snow. There were lights up ahead: street-lights, she saw, her heart lifting. The main road. Now she could see the backs of houses. She crawled towards them. Civilisation soon, she promised herself, lovely snow-ploughs and salted roads, the beastly snow fended back to where it should be: decoratively adorning trees and settled nicely on the ground for winter walks and children's snowball fights.

She came to the road and slowly applied the brakes. 'I don't believe it,' she muttered. The snow lay virgin: not a sign, anywhere, of removal in progress. Though there couldn't be that much, she told herself – three or four inches, maybe – she could see that the surface was ice. It occurred to her to whimper, but that seemed a stupid waste of time and energy. She edged the car out on to the road, pointed it towards London, and went into a spin.

She'd heard that in car accidents time slows right down, and this happened to her. She watched, as if from above, the nose of the car swing out to the centre of the road and round further, towards the row of houses on the other side. She saw herself sitting open-mouthed and helpless at the wheel, watching the slow-motion film. She wondered when it would end, whether she would be hurt, and she marvelled that she felt no fear. Then the front of the car hit the opposite kerb, she bounced up and forward, and everything stopped.

She raised her head. She wasn't hurt, only a little dazed and in need, she realised, of sitting quietly for a few minutes, maybe with a hot drink. She opened the door and was hit full-face again, but managed to confirm what she thought she'd seen: a pub-sign, lit up by white fairy lights.

She walked towards it, keeping as far from the edge of the kerb as she could – she didn't want to be hit by any other drivers. But there weren't any about, she noticed as she battled along the pavement. She could easily have been the only traveller there; everyone else, seeing the blizzard, seemed to be safely locked up for the night.

She reached the pub door and, feeling like a lost explorer, flung it open. This was where everyone was, she saw – not at home knitting and stoking up the fires at all. The pub was completely packed: men, women, children, dogs, even (by the sound of it) a few babies. No one seemed much interested in her as she fought her way to the bar.

A beefy-looking man, pint glass in hand, let her in. 'Awful night,' he commented.

She nodded. She was really exhausted, she realised. She tried to remember how long she'd been awake. But a coffee was all she needed, she decided, then she'd be on her way. It was almost eight o'clock. In a minute or two she could call Charlie, from a payphone here if there was one, and if she could be heard above the noise . . . The big man was speaking again.

'I'm sorry?' she said.

'I said, at least it brings everyone together. Never seen this place so packed out.' He smiled at her. 'Never seen you in here before, for instance.'

She smiled vaguely back, wished her coffee would hurry up.

'Not from round here, are you?'

She shook her head.

'Where you from? London?'

'Yes.' She tucked a lock of hair behind her ear. She supposed that he was only being friendly, but she wished that he'd leave her alone.

'You'll be staying around here, then?'

'No. I'm going back tonight,' she said shortly.

'Ha!' A great grin spread across his face. 'That's what you think.'

'I beg your pardon?'

'A21's blocked from Flimwell. Snow drifts. Can't get the ploughs through,' he chortled. 'We're cut off. Didn't you know? Haven't you been listening to the weather warnings?'

'No.' She could hardly speak, she felt so sick at heart. The prospect of imminent escape, she realised, had been buoying her up, a respite not only from the harsh weather but from the can of worms that the story was turning out to be.

'Not to worry, though.' The man's expression became more sympathetic. 'There's bound to be a bed going spare here.'

Oh God no, she thought. To have to shack up in the home of a villager – this one's, maybe – to make polite chit-chat, sleep in a damp, lumpy bed . . . And how on earth was she going to have a proper conversation with Charlie? She felt her eyes fill with tears. She was so tired, it wasn't fair, she wanted to go home.

The man had looked away to speak to someone else. Now he turned back. 'There you are, you see. Dead easy.'

'I'm sorry?'

'This is a hotel, love. Well,' he lowered his voice, 'a pub with some bedrooms upstairs. And you thought I was trying to get you back to my place!'

'Oh no, I—'

'I'd have been so lucky.' He smiled. 'Ah, here's mein host now.'

The landlord confirmed that he did indeed have rooms, and she gratefully accepted his offer to be shown one at once. She followed him up the staircase, realising that the noise followed them too, and sighed, expecting the worst. But the room itself really wasn't bad, she told herself moments later as she gazed round. En suite, she noticed, pleasantly surprised; tea and coffee-making facilities . . . and then her eyes lit upon the phone by the bed.

'I'll take it,' she said at once. 'It's perfect.'

As soon as the man had gone, she jumped on to the bed, grabbed the phone and dialled Charlie's work number. It rang twice only.

'Charlie?' Her pulse was racing.

'Sasha?'

She gulped. 'Are you OK? Both of you?'

'We're fine. Mike's here with me. How about you?'

'Oh . . .' She didn't know where to start. 'I'm great.'

Then they both started to speak at once and at speed, and she couldn't make any sense of it.

'Hang on,' he said, laughing.

She laughed too. Not that any of what she'd been telling him was funny in the least, but it was so good to hear his voice. 'You first,' she said, hugging herself, then grew still as he spoke. She could hardly believe it.

'A glass womb?' she repeated, her voice a whisper. 'How . . . I mean, is that *possible*?'

'That's what the embryologist said, and she's supposed to be an expert.'

'REDEV's growing babies?' She had a sudden flash of that camou-flaged fortress, saw behind the fencing, labs where children were being created, eggs and sperm manipulated into life by scientists.

'I don't know if it's going on at REDEV,' Charlie said.

'You've asked Mike if he saw anything?'

'Yeah. He said he sure didn't see any babies about.'

She almost didn't hear him. What were they growing them for? she wondered, and her flesh crawled again. How long had it been going on? Had full-term babies been produced? Were the first batch toddlers now?

'Sash? You OK?'

'I'm sorry. My head's reeling.' She closed her eyes. 'Has Mike said whether he saw anything – anything at all – that might have been these glass wombs?'

'He doesn't know. He said there were some Petri dishes. The embryologist said they'd probably start them in that kind of container.'

'So it's possible they're in there?'

'I don't know.' Charlie sounded doubtful. 'I suppose so.'

She tried to make sense of it. Perhaps REDEV only dealt with the first stage of the process. Perhaps World Med Inc had different 'growing centres' in satellite labs all over the country – or the world, she thought, swallowing. Those babies could be anywhere. There could be thousands of them.

'It's explains why they're so desperate, don't you think?' Charlie's voice had become quieter. 'Mike's gone into the other room,' he said. 'What were you saying about Manyon and the other man?'

She told him, trying to give as objective an account as possible. 'Of course, if Manyon regularly drank and drove, and Lucas *is* always disappearing after a girl . . .'

Charlie was silent. After a moment he said, 'I don't think so, do you?'

'No,' she said huskily, 'I don't.'

'I think you should come home. Or I'll come down to you. I promise not to interfere.'

She told him why that was impossible, heard his sharp intake of breath. 'The weather's that bad? Hang on, let me see.' She heard him tap computer keys. 'Shit,' he muttered. 'Yeah, it's all here. Freak blizzards on the Kent–Sussex border expected till dawn, roads closed, emergency helicopter called out to a mother in labour . . . Shit, hon, I don't like the thought of you down there with all this stuff going on.'

'I'll be fine.' Indeed, she felt much calmer. Partly because she had to be, but mainly it was through talking to him. She told him where she was staying but nothing about the skid in the road.

'OK. But no heroics tonight.'

'No.'

'No breaking into REDEV.'

'Couldn't get out there.' They both laughed a bit too hard. She told him about Holland, and the Cayman Islands, and her fear that all her trouble would be for naught once the police issued a press release about the interview with the security guard.

'Hang on,' Charlie said again. He was scanning the news services. There was nothing from the Kent police except for weather warnings. He promised to check on World Med Inc, see if any of the services AGN was linked up to could come up with anything more on them, 'us being an American corporation and all'.

She smiled at the drawl. He sounded much more American on the phone than he did in the flesh.

She glanced at the time. They'd been speaking for nearly thirty minutes but she didn't want to let him go. She told him about her earlier encounter in the pub with the REDEV man.

'Not keen on talking to the press, huh?'

'You could say that.'

Charlie's voice dropped to a whisper. 'Sash?'

'Yeah?' She snuggled down into the duvet; she was beginning to feel sleepy.

'Should I tell Mike about Manyon and Lucas?'

'No.' Her response was immediate. The morning would be early enough to tell Mike that his worst fears were realised.

She frowned. Rather than feeling frightened by the deaths, she was beginning to feel angry. How dare a company kill people, little animal rights people who only wanted to save animals, just to protect its secret? Wasn't it bad enough that they were tampering with human life in the first place? It wasn't her job to be scared of them; she had to expose them, write the story for the world to read about. 'I'll tell Mike, but not tonight,' she said.

'OK. You warm and safe where you are?'

Very, she told him. She realised that he didn't want to say goodbye either, that they would both willingly stay talking all night.

'Sash? I'd better go now. I've got to chase someone up. You

take care. Call me in the morning. That mobile doesn't work, you know.'

'I know. Bad reception area.'

'I love you, Sasha.'

'Me too. You, I mean.'

'Please look after yourself.'

'You too.'

'Night, angel.'

'Night.'

They hung up together.

In spite of everything she felt protected and comforted. She knew that she was hungry and thirsty, that she wanted a bath, and that she ought to bring her stuff in from the car – she couldn't even remember if she'd locked it. But not now, she told herself, getting further in under the duvet. She'd do all those things later, after she'd had a little rest.

Her eyes closed and she surrendered herself utterly to sleep.

For a full minute after Sasha had gone, Charlie sat staring into space. He hated everything: that she was trapped in a snowstorm; that he couldn't get to her, that no sensible person, certainly no investigative journalist, could any longer give credence to a 'mere coincidence' theory. People were dying and disappearing at a rate of knots down there, and Sasha was stuck in the middle of it.

He scowled over at the side-office, through the window of which he could see Mike, lolling back in a chair, feet up on a desk. If it wasn't for that bloody boy, he thought savagely, Sasha would be in London; he'd be with her tonight, making love for the first time, waking up tomorrow in each other's arms. Instead . . .

He got up. It wasn't Mike's fault, poor kid, any more than it was Sasha's that she was the kind of journalist she was. He might as well blame the weather. He passed by the door, which Mike had left ajar.

'Charlie, is it OK if I phone my mum now?'

The bitterness returned in a wave. 'Sure,' he said curtly, and kept walking. Bloody Mike, he swore silently and, turning his head, saw snowflakes battering themselves to oblivion against the windows. Bloody awful English weather too.

*   *   *

As regards professionalism, Bennett knew that his position was deplorable. He'd stationed himself in the boy's road, on the opposite side of the street to the house but really only yards away. If anyone noticed him – the mother, for instance, or a neighbour – he was a sitting target.

But his mood was truculent. He knew that the blizzard he'd been stuck in for most of the day – his *third* day, he reminded himself bitterly – might be affecting the transmitter's reception. And however much he'd come to hate the job, Bennett was determined not to muff it. He wouldn't give Control that satisfaction. Let his replacement, due in ninety minutes, move elsewhere if he wanted to; let *him* miss the vital call.

As soon as the man arrived, Bennett promised himself, he would be gone – off to the little pub marked on the street-map. He'd phoned them earlier, and they were expecting him. He'd an en suite room booked, a late meal, and breakfast in the morning.

He was starving, actually. Since a couple of pork pies at lunchtime – all that the corner-shop had afforded – he'd only had a packet of throat-sweets to keep him going. He felt he was coming down with something, which didn't surprise him. The other man, he remembered, had sneezed that morning before leaving, and in this stuffy car germs would have a field day.

He jumped. Pearce's telephone was ringing. Bennett pushed the headset properly to his ears, feeling himself grow sweaty when he heard the voice.

He could hardly wait for it to finish before calling Control. 'The kid's just called. The name of the journalist he's working with is Charlie.' He said it all in a rush, feeling very pleased with himself. 'They've discovered some real interesting stuff today. Uh . . .' He tried to remember what else; there hadn't been much.

'So where is he?' Control asked. He sounded sour, not in the least bit impressed.

Bennett blinked. 'I don't know! He didn't say. She didn't ask him. Someone's on their way round; she had to finish the hoovering.'

'Pity,' said Control.

'Well, aren't you interested?'

'Fascinated.'

They hated each other silently.

Bennett had a brainwave. 'Say,' he tried for the matey approach, 'the kid won't be coming home in this snow. It's two foot deep here.' It wasn't, but Control wouldn't know that. And he was so hungry, the vision of a hot meal and a soft pillow almost hurt. He wanted them now, not in another couple of hours. 'There's no point in me staying any longer tonight, is there?'

Control chuckled softly. 'Whatever gave you that idea? You're staying there, chum, until your relief arrives.' They never used names over the radio. 'But if the weather's as bad down there as you say . . .' He snorted, enjoying himself.

'What?' Bennett bleated.

'Your relief might be a bit late getting to you. Thought of that?'

Bennett thought. He couldn't bear it; it wasn't fair.

'Think of the money,' Control said, then laughed again. Bennett had learned that his wages were far less than anyone else's on the team.

'Call me if there's anything else,' Control said sweetly.

Miserably, Bennett ended the call. He saw something in his mirror and glanced wearily over his shoulder. A woman was coming down the road, bundled up in a coat and hat and wellingtons, moving cautiously through the snow. She turned on to the Pearce pathway. Bennett stared after her. He didn't care who she was, didn't have the least interest.

He sniffed, then sneezed violently.

CHAPTER TWENTY-NINE

The breaks were coming thick and fast now, Stockart told himself gleefully. He rose and crossed his sitting-room to the bar to mix himself another weak whisky and water. He was rationing himself carefully, had been ever since he'd got the call at ten o'clock the night before – when he'd realised that, as ever, there could never seriously be a time at which he could consider himself off duty. There would always be someone, somewhere, needing him to sort things out for them.

Now it was approaching five o'clock in the morning. He took out his pills and swallowed three of them down in one big gulp. He'd been awake most of the night, not that it felt like that; he felt more alive, invigorated, than he had done in days – the effect, he appreciated, of so much good news arriving at once.

The first indicator that things were finally going his way had come at lunchtime on Monday, when he'd heard that Subject Five, the Bristol baby, could be factored out of the equation. And any minute now, Bernard Hall would be calling him again with perhaps the best news of all – and half of Stockart's problems would be wiped out in one stroke.

He gazed out happily at the night and the swirling snow. He never drew his curtains, could see from his apartment window the rooftops of surrounding houses and the lights of the bridges strung out down the river. How pretty, he thought, quite magical.

That first call had concerned the woman, Hall's head of operations. Stockart swilled the liquid in his tumbler, allowing himself a minute's fantasy about her appearance. Tall, blonde, he imagined, striking features, cold eyes which he knew that he could ignite. He had a way with strong women; he could make them melt. Hall had promised him on Sunday that he could meet her if she hadn't caught the boy within forty-eight hours. Her time was nearly up, and though it was looking as if her people would indeed have Pearce very shortly now, Stockart knew that he could persuade Hall to affect an introduction with the – he smirked – *femme fatale*. Hall owed him.

In that call, Stockart ruminated, smiling, Hall had sounded somewhat less than his customary cool, unruffled self. His operative had followed the Gilbert mother and son to her local general hospital, to the casualty department, but the baby had been released two hours later. Hall's woman had followed the car again, expecting it to return to the Gilberts' home. Instead the mother had driven to another hospital where, owing to the very well-lit nature of the car-park, it had been impossible for the woman to act. She'd gone in after Mrs Gilbert and the baby, ascertained that the child was being examined, but had been unable to make any further moves without arousing suspicion.

Stockart had felt himself grow cold. The infant must have been referred to that second hospital, the mother opting to take him rather than hand him over to the impersonal care of an ambulance crew. It would be a specialist hospital, he'd thought, similar to the Bristol one where Subject Two had been installed for twenty-four hours. No doubt those two centres of excellence would be in communication with each other and the extraordinary co-incidence of Leukaemia in two very young babies quickly noted. After that, the sharing of a few other salient points – the DMD, the 'quickie' pre-natal test . . . It was all over, he'd thought, frantically glancing round the flat, wondering what to take, whether simply to run, when suddenly he'd remembered something. Babies got stolen from hospitals, didn't they?

'Which place is he in?' he'd asked hoarsely.

Now, savouring that moment again, Stockart allowed himself a beatific smile. It had been perfect, orgasmic. Master Jeremy Gilbert was in the Mistletoe Hospital on the Thames Embankment, less than half a mile from Stockart's own flat. Bits of it were even visible from his window. Clearly, Mrs Gilbert, dissatisfied with the NHS hospital, had rushed her precious son to the place where he'd been born, the hospital which held such good memories for her, which, ahead of its time with the CVS, would undoubtedly be able to offer her baby the best treatment for his disease.

Hall had asked if this latest development in any way altered Stockart's wishes concerning the infant?

'Give me five minutes,' Stockart had barked, crashing down the phone with one hand while the other stretched out to switch on his computer and activate DAMR.

'Come to Daddy,' he'd whispered, keying in Jeremy's name, running through the record, past that morning's GP visit (which he already knew about), arriving at the first hospital . . . The doctor there had concurred with the GP's opinion that the bruises appeared to be tiny pinch-marks. The mother had insisted on a blood-test but had suddenly changed her mind, telling staff that she wasn't happy with their standards and she was going elsewhere.

Quite right, Stockart had murmured, forgetting himself for a moment, actually feeling quite indignant on her behalf. No wonder the NHS was falling apart. She wouldn't receive such shoddy treatment at the Mistletoe. He had scrolled down and smiled. Indeed she had not. Jeremy had been admitted for observation overnight. The mother had obviously felt more confident; she'd given permission for a blood-test to be taken.

He'd wondered if the results had come through by then. That thought had galvanised him. He'd immediately called West, finding him (as he'd expected) still at work and rather dazed-sounding when given his new instructions. But he'd called back soon enough: the blood test had only just been taken; the baby, his mother and an older child were in a 'family' room; the father was due to arrive soon. Apparently the mother had asked to see West, but had been told that it was impossible, the doctor didn't work nights; they hadn't known, West had continued, that he was still there . . .

'But I really don't see what you expect me to do tonight, John,' he'd continued in a quavery voice that Stockart would normally have found so irritating. 'The parents are there, and—'

'It's all right, Will,' he'd responded soothingly. 'It'll wait until morning.'

Which it would, easily, he thought. Much better, in fact, to give the little family time to settle in, relax in that excellent medical environment – so that when, the next day, the baby was taken away for a test and the inevitable happened, they would be less likely to reproach themselves – or anyone else – having 'bonded' with the hospital by then.

He'd called Hall and told him to send his woman home; that he had his own man inside the hospital who would be dealing with the matter from now on. Hall had sounded surprised, as well he might, which had pleased Stockart, as much as it had pleased him to able to rely on West.

West's sudden obedience, indeed, had come as something of a shock to him. For a moment it had looked like the old man might refuse to obey orders, but all it had needed was a little push from himself. After that, as his monitoring of the doctor's computerised diary had revealed, West had been most diligent. Each of the other mothers-to-be – or not – had been contacted, and appointments already made in four cases.

One, in fact, the last subject on the list, a Mrs Melanie Alder, would be seeing West in the morning. Once he'd dealt with her, Stockart considered, it wouldn't be so difficult for him to slip down to the second floor and handle the Gilbert baby. He'd be into the swing of it by then, so to speak; and there was no need for the kid to suffer. A quick jab of something, and lights out.

He'd let his eyes close at that point, had dozed dreamlessly until the telephone had shrilled at three o'clock. Hall had wanted to let him know at once (into that, Stockart had read a desire on the other man's part to regain the upper hand) that it looked as if they had tracked down the name of the news organisation to which Pearce had gone.

Stockart had been bolt upright in his chair at once.

American Global News, a news bureau with its European office based in the tower at Canary Wharf. One of their company cars had been spotted outside REDEV earlier in the day, its registration number noted and passed on to Hall's police contact, who had just come through with the information.

'Bit late, isn't it?' Stockart had growled, but his blood had been racing. He'd cut off Hall's unhurried explanation that the officer worked nights and had to be careful. 'So . . .' His mouth had gone dry. He'd raised the tumbler to his lips, seen that it was empty, set it down. 'You've got people at the tower now, have you?'

'On their way. However, we know that no one's there at AGN now.'

'How d'you know?'

'I called them myself. There's a recorded message. They've gone home for the night.'

'They could be faking. They could still be there.'

'I don't think so.'

'But you'll check, will you?'

'Of course. I'll call you.'

That promise, Stockart realised now, turning from his window and the snowy night, had been made almost two hours ago. Was Hall messing him about? Deliberately keeping him in the dark? He'd had enough of that already with West. He wasn't paying Hall to get temperamental.

He reached for the phone beside him on the floor, and as he did, it rang.

'Sorry it's taken me so long to get back to you.' Hall's voice was its old self, confidence restored. 'I'd hoped to be able to tell you completely good news.'

'Oh?' Stockart's mouth tightened. 'Another hitch?'

'Indeed, but only a small one. One of my operatives managed to gain entry to the AGN offices. They were empty. However, most helpfully, there was a staff-list placed under glass on the main desk. The name, address and telephone number of Charles Page, Bureau Chief, was clearly displayed.'

'So?' Stockart frowned. 'How d'you know it's him you want?'

'Because earlier the boy called his mother and said that he was working with a journalist called Charlie. Besides . . .'

Stockart gave an impatient grunt.

'. . . some money changed hands with the security staff. They remembered Mr Page coming out of the lifts and heading for the car park at three o'clock this morning.'

'Pity your police contact wasn't a bit quicker off the mark, isn't it?'

Hall ignored him. 'He was with a young boy. When showed

Pearce's photograph they thought it was him. He was carrying a laptop.'

The words sank in, and Stockart felt the rocks roll off his shoulders. Nevertheless, he said sharply, 'So why isn't it *completely* good news? Haven't you got the kid yet?'

'No. But I've got a hunch . . .'

Heavens above, Stockart silently swore, his mother's favourite phrase popping up inadequately from nowhere: a hunch.

'. . . that Pearce is with the journalist at his flat – at Floral Street in Covent Garden. The reason I think that,' Hall continued softly, 'is that the night-porter told my operative that Page got home at three twenty-five and he wasn't having him disturbed.' He cleared his throat. 'If he'd left the tower at three, he wouldn't have had time to drive the boy elsewhere. Certainly not back to Brixton.'

'Pearce hasn't turned up there then?'

'No.'

'Journalists don't normally take their informants home, do they?'

Hall made a non-committal sound.

'I suppose Pearce is only a kid. So, why can't your "operatives" go in and get him?'

'The concierge appears to take his duties very seriously.'

'Surely your professionals,' Stockart let the sibilance hiss, 'can deal with one man?'

'He won't allow uninvited entry to the vestibule. There's not much that my people can do about that – tonight. In the morning they won't have a problem.' Hall spoke confidently.

'Let's hope not.' But it sounded good, Stockart had to admit: boy and journalist dealt with together; computer retrieved.

Another shadow appeared. 'What about the other journalist, the one sniffing round at the site?'

'A young woman,' Hall said smoothly. 'She made no attempt to approach the guard; if she had, we'd have had news of her earlier. She simply walked round the perimeter.'

Stockart chewed his lip. Now he thought about it, he didn't like the sound of that, not one bit. If the news bureau was sending people down to check things out, they were taking things seriously. What had that little runt Pearce told them? Had Davenport lied to him? Was his laptop not in fact one hundred per cent secure?

'We'll be able to identify her tomorrow, once we've got the boy and Page. Mr Stockart, you do appreciate that the matter may not entirely die with them? Their colleagues may know something about it.'

'You'll be able to find out, won't you?'

'Yes, but there's a limit to how many journalists one can deal with.'

'I don't see why.' Stockart glared at the silent handset. 'So what're you telling me?'

'Only that it might be beneficial at this juncture to introduce an alternative line of inquiry. Put anyone else off the scent.'

'A red herring?'

'Precisely.' Hall explained in detail. Stockart smiled: he liked it, it would work. He felt a rare sense of camaraderie with Hall, which produced a pleasant feeling that lasted after he'd replaced the receiver but evaporated as he dialled Davenport's number.

The anonymous telephone call to Dungeness Nuclear Power Station came through at 07.21. The caller's voice was male, the accent neutral. On the shingle bank on the far side of the power station, close to the coastguard's look-out on the track from Denge Marsh Lane, was the body of a man. He had not died by natural causes.

The duty operator had received crank calls before, but this man didn't sound like a crank. When, in response to her polite enquiry as to his name, she got the dialling tone, she immediately notified the police.

Weather conditions along that stretch of the coast were better than they were inland – there'd been some snow, but it hadn't settled – and within an hour a police Land Rover was following the caller's instructions and bumping along the rough track off Denge Marsh Lane. The vehicle's lights were on – although it was past eight the heavy, leaden sky provided little light – and it was the driver who spotted it first, over to the left, within the sweep of the beam, lying heaped like a pile of old clothes. On foot and closer to, the twisted angle of the shoes, obviously still attached, became apparent. Then the bloody mess of the hands, and the face, black with bruising, beyond recognition as human . . . A sick mind had been responsible for this, the sort of mind that took pleasure in notifying the authorities of its victims' whereabouts, in deliberately leaving identifying documents – clues, even – on the body. In one trouser pocket was a wallet, containing, apart from some cash, a National Insurance card; in the other, a handbill protesting against nuclear power, across the bottom of which was scrawled in black capitals: 'ACTION NOW! KENT STRIKES BACK!'

'What the hell are we dealing with?' the chief superintendent demanded first of himself, then the DCI to whom he had assigned the case. The DCI, who was speaking by telephone from the power station, said wisely that he didn't know, but that the superintendent ought to be aware that the forensic pathologist had already made a startling discovery: it appeared that the body had been frozen.

'I should think it was! It was bloody cold out last night.'

'No, sir. He thinks it was *deliberately* frozen, then reheated not very long ago – and, incidentally, not very well. With a hair dryer, probably, which left lots of it, well . . . It's a bit like a half-defrosted turkey, he says.'

The superintendent closed his eyes. The Tenterden Four had still not been caught; Mary Kennedy's parents were due to be on local radio that day with a list of complaints about the way the police investigation had been handled from the start (which was the main reason why Holland, his most able DCI, wasn't at Dungeness). And now it looked as if there was a loon with a roomy deep-freeze about. Why couldn't he have dumped the body somewhere else? Sussex was only over the border. What had the county of Kent ever done to him?

The next piece of information that his DCI divulged succeeded in making him feel quite unwell. Was he aware, the man asked, clearing his throat, that this was the second local man to be found dead near a nuclear power station within a week? That even though the first one had suffered a heart attack and wasn't being treated as a homicide, one could imagine the sort of song and dance the media would make of it . . .

The superintendent recalled that he had never liked this particular DCI very much; that he far preferred the older and generally more cautious Tony Holland. Then he pictured a few front-page headlines, remembered what a circus the Tenterden Four had brought to town, and imagined what the papers would do with a sicko serial killer on his patch. He suppressed a shudder. It was going to be a very long day.

Although in one way it was disappointing to have been called off
the Gilbert assignment, in another Anna acknowledged that it was
a relief. With the net closing in on Pearce, it was essential she be
accessible and unencumbered.

'Ma'am?'

McMahon always called her that, betraying his military background. They were in her hotel room, facing each other over the
small oval table in the window. She became aware that she hadn't
been giving him her full attention.

'Yes?'

McMahon replaced the receiver of the telephone in front of him.
'It seems that the day porter's as bad as the night one.'

Their second man at Covent Garden was due to have attempted
entry to the journalist's flat twenty minutes before.

'I see.'

'He won't allow any unauthorised access beyond the vestibule.
Not even for a charity collector. He could leave his envelopes in
the pigeon-holes, he said.' McMahon sighed. 'There's no way Page
is ever going to authorise our entry.'

'No.'

'Or the boy. Although I suppose if we got him on the intercom
we might be in with a chance.'

She suddenly felt very tired. She'd scarcely slept, having returned
to the hotel at eleven only to be alerted by Hall with the host of new
developments shortly afterwards. Two hours' sleep at most . . .

McMahon was watching her with a crease in his brow which
immediately vanished when she looked at him. He cleared his throat.
'I was thinking that I might go over to the flats myself – see if I have
any more luck with the day porter. Apparently he's just come on
duty. There might be a loophole the others haven't seen.'

She inclined her head. 'An excellent idea,' she said.

With McMahon there it wouldn't take long. As far as possible,
everything else was covered: the listener was still in position outside
Pearce's home; the other man in Kent, the floater who'd so
ably carried out her instructions regarding placing the body that
morning, was now, weather permitting, on his way back to London.
Briefly she'd considered leaving him down there to search for the
other journalist, the girl. But not knowing her itinerary or having

the means to discover it, the task would have been extremely difficult and very time-consuming. Much better, Anna had decided, to have him as a back-up to the Covent Garden team. This was where all the action was going to be. Besides, once they'd taken Page they'd be able to lure the girl in.

She nodded at McMahon. 'I'll monitor the news. If nothing's appeared by noon I'll let you know.' She couldn't be the one to phone the Press Association; on tape her faint accent sounded more pronounced. It might lead to identification.

McMahon stood up to go.

'Don't start anything until I get there.'

'Very good, ma'am.'

As the door closed behind him, Anna felt herself relax. She was perfectly in control once more.

CHAPTER THIRTY

For several seconds Sasha couldn't trace the source of the sound – an electronic jingle she'd never heard before – although she'd realised at once that it was coming from within her room. Then she grabbed the mobile phone and pressed the button to receive the call.

It would be Charlie, she thought warmly. What a wonderful man to set his alarm, depriving himself of much needed sleep – it was nine o'clock; he could only have had about five hours – so that he could be sure to catch her before she set off.

'Is that Sasha Downey?'

It was a male voice with an accent, but not American. 'Yes?' she said hesitantly.

'It's Chris . . . Bailey. You came round last night.'

Of course, the Australian. But why was he calling, and why did he sound so strained?

'The police are coming.' She heard the break in his voice. 'There's been a body found at Dungeness.'

'Clive?' she croaked, although she scarcely needed the confirmation.

'Yeah. They're pretty sure. His wallet was on him. But they're going to need someone to identify his clothes.'

'His clothes?'

'Yeah, his face is too . . .'

Oh God, no. Her hand tightened around the phone.

'I'm sorry to have called you. Pete had already left for work when they rang and all my family's in Perth, and I didn't know who else to . . .'

He broke down. The sound of it, the thought of that big, kind man sobbing so brokenly, brought tears to her eyes too. She'd suspected such news, but to hear it . . . 'It's OK,' she whispered, comforting herself as much as him.

'That's them now.' He gave a shuddering sigh. 'I'd better go.' And the line went dead.

She went quickly into the bathroom, cleaned up her face and recombed her hair, glad that she'd already done the necessary things: a lengthy bath; breakfast; bill paid. Going down earlier to fetch her overnight bag, she'd checked the car and thankfully found it undamaged. She'd discovered from the radio that many of the local roads were clear or would be shortly, but that the A21 to London was still partly blocked with snow and further hampered by abandoned vehicles.

Very well, she thought resolutely – she was ready for work and would simply continue her investigations there in Kent.

She sat down on the bed, found the number she wanted in the telephone directory, and dialled it.

'Superlative Security,' said a voice drearily.

She identified herself and asked if she could speak to someone in authority. While she was waiting to be put through she had a mental picture of Holland glowering at her. But he'd only told her not to approach the guard; he'd said nothing about the company he worked for. Surely they would know something – if only rumours – about what went on at REDEV. And maybe someone had heard what Dacre had told Holland the day before, if anything.

'Is it about the REDEV business?' said the same voice, sounding quite lively now.

'Er, yes.'

'I'm sorry, but I'm afraid we can't help you.'

'But—'

'The police have asked us not to speak to the press.'

Well, she thought, ruefully replacing the receiver – one up to Mr Holland. She wondered whether he was involved in the latest murder inquiry; perhaps even now he was guiding the big Australian gently through a statement. How long would it be, she thought, staring, before he mentioned her visit the night before? She tried to remember if she'd said anything that would tell Holland what she knew, then she stopped, realising the futility of such speculation. Her mere presence at the house was incriminating enough.

Her cover was blown – if he'd ever believed it. He would now know that she must have information he needed – urgently, now, in the wake of two 'nuclear' deaths. He'd be after her.

She stuffed her notebook into her bag, slung her holdall over her shoulder, left the room and went straight to the car. If she was being chased, she preferred to be running rather than standing still. She glanced at the mobile phone lying on the passenger seat, working perfectly well today. Suppose Holland tried to reach her on it, demanding that she meet up with him? If she refused, she could envisage real trouble. On the other hand Charlie might try reaching her too, but that was unlikely, given the phone's performance the day before. She switched it off and set off gingerly along the road in the direction of Cranbrook, a village which lay about seven miles west.

The sky had brightened to a peerless blue and the snow, glisteningly fresh, steeped on cottage roofs in fat wedges and running along field fences, was very pretty – but Sasha didn't have eyes for it. Frightened of another skid, she kept her gaze fixed on the road surface and her speed hovering around twenty. Several other cars were similarly crawling along in front of her, and she saw some evidence that gritters had already been at work.

How long, she wondered, was it going to be before the news of Lucas's death leaked to the media? And how long after that before Winston's death struck a chord? For the local journalists, moments, she thought gloomily. And they'd tip off the nationals. It was a good story: the twin bogies of Dungeness and Sizewell, death, mystery . . . The nuclear angle should detain most of them, she reckoned, but she could imagine some of her colleagues from the Sunday papers coming down for a closer look. Which meant, she thought, biting her lip, that her time was running out. She debated whether to call Hornby at *Comment*, alert him to what she had. But she still had no solid evidence. She couldn't prove that Winston or Manyon had been murdered; she couldn't accuse REDEV of anything, the lawyers wouldn't allow it. They'd bin the lot, including Mike's testimony. There was no point in whetting Hornby's appetite only to let him down.

She lowered the sun-visor against the glare of the snow and concentrated again on the road. Ideally, she told herself, slowing down as she reached a junction, she would be gathering evidence, building pictures of people, picking up clues by visiting each of the Tenterden Four's homes, plus Manyon's and Lucas's relatives. But she suspected that the former would have been told not to say anything to the press, and the latter would be too upset to talk. Not that she'd any desire to approach more bereaved people that day.

The next part of the road was busier and much clearer, and she found herself quite suddenly in Cranbrook, passing along the long L-shaped high street, looking out for the road she wanted. It was a little distance outside the village, the first street on a modern estate on its own.

She pulled in, feeling the crunch of untouched snow beneath her wheels, and came tenderly to a halt beside the kerb. She got out, scanning the rows of small, neat houses, saw an elderly man fumbling at his door and approached him. She had to repeat the name twice, but once he'd heard it he knew the person she sought all right, although judging from his expression, not as a friend.

Number thirty-eight had curtains at the windows and milk bottles by the door, but no one answered Sasha's ring. Her mood, which had been determinedly optimistic, plummeted. She didn't know what else she was going to do. Sit about biting her nails, she supposed miserably, knowing that she was wasting precious time, that her headstart on the rest of the media could well be ebbing away. She looked at her watch. It wasn't yet ten – too early to phone Charlie.

She turned to walk away, and as she did so, she saw a white Fiat Uno come creeping into the avenue from the main road. She couldn't be certain at such a distance, and the winter sun was shining right in her eyes, but it looked like the shape of a woman at the wheel. She waited hopefully, stamping her feet in the snow.

Not by a muscle did McMahon's face betray his true emotions. He gazed down at the day porter, who hadn't allowed him entry to the building unless he removed his crash helmet. He held it loosely

by his side now. 'But I was told to see that Mr Page got this . . .' He
held out the package marked 'URGENT: NEWS DATA'. 'Personally.'

'As I've just told you, you can either leave it here with me, as is
customary, or you can come back after midday and call up to Mr
Page on my phone.'

Thus exposing McMahon to awkward questioning from the
journalist or simply being told to leave it at the front desk for Page
to collect later.

'You're not from the usual place, are you?' Alexander said
challengingly.

One short blow to the carotid artery would do it, McMahon
thought. But it would be the second and a half before that, as he
lunged, that would present the danger. Old as he was, the porter's
eyes were button-bright behind the glasses, and he was already
suspicious, McMahon could see that. He could also see the red
panic button on the desk. This place, he thought, eyes flicking
up briefly to see the small video camera on the ceiling pointing
straight at him, was extremely security-conscious. 'No,' he agreed.
'We're new.'

'Funny. Mr Page never mentioned that to me.'

McMahon shrugged. It was time, he saw, to depart. He hefted
the package under one arm. 'I'll come back,' he said, stuck the
helmet back on his head, and left.

He walked the length of the next building – an empty block –
before turning sharply into an alleyway.

One of the two men was waiting there for him. 'No luck?'

McMahon shook his head briefly. All three of them had tried a
direct assault now; there could be no more such attempts. He gave
his package and helmet to the other man to hold for him, unzipped
his leather jacket and ran his fingers through his hair, reasserting its
normal side-parting. Then he went forth again into Floral Street, but
on the other side of the road, and keeping far enough away from
the apartment block so that if the porter looked out he wouldn't
see him.

The trouble was, he thought, strolling past a coffee shop and
seeing his second man (who was supposed to be on patrol at the
other end of the street) enjoying a plate of steaming food, that
covert surveillance in such an area was extremely difficult. One
could not loiter effectively, even if the weather – raw cold – had

been more conducive to such activity. There were too many police about looking for pickpockets – he was passing two of them now – and as for sitting in a car . . . He looked up and down the cobbled street. Impossible. Double yellow lines on either side as far as the eye could see. All in all, McMahon conceded, a difficult task. He reached the end of the road and crossed to the other side, heading back for the alleyway. Not insurmountable, of course.

He saw his own reflection in a shop window, went in and selected several garments. Five minutes later he emerged, looking, as the shop assistant had cooingly observed, a 'new man'. He wore a full-length overcoat that fell to mid-calf; brogue shoes had replaced his trainers; there was a muffler round his neck and he'd found a hat with ear-flaps. He was thoroughly concealed. Even so, as he passed the entrance of the flats he lowered his face.

He went on to the top of the street, where the real tourist traffic began and carols were being sung by a group dressed in Victorian clothing, then doubled back on himself.

A place where he could hide and watch in safety . . . He passed a bookshop, several women's clothing shops, a gym . . . then a building set back slightly from the street, its entrance (between two pillars and two ceramic planters) very discreet. Some sort of club, he thought, or part of the gym. Then he saw the smoky glass door open, and a concierge emerge carrying suitcases.

McMahon paused. He saw 'The Heathman' engraved on a modest brass plaque on the wall. He looked up, saw that the hotel was slightly higher than the block of flats directly opposite and smiled softly to himself.

He went inside. The sweet-faced girl at the reception desk said that she did have a room on the top floor – three, in fact.

One would do, McMahon said, returning her lovely smile. It was only for himself – although a couple of his friends might be dropping in during the day, if that was all right . . .

'Certainly, sir,' she replied, and he understood at once that it was the sort of hotel where questions weren't asked.

How perfect, he thought then, and again several minutes later, after the porter had shown him into the 'deluxe front' and departed. Quite perfect. The room had double windows looking on to the street and also down into the highest flat opposite – which, if the scribbled insertion alongside the address in the journalist's office was correct, was 'Page's Penthouse'.

With his naked eye, McMahon could see into the sitting-room. With his pocket binoculars he could see more: a large purple sofa, the back of a television set and over to the right, bookshelves, a desk and a chair . . . and someone sitting in it, drinking from a mug and staring at the screen of a laptop computer.

McMahon's lips curved in a smile. He knew that face well. He slipped back from the window, pressed a number on his mobile, and told the woman that he could confirm Mike Pearce's presence in the flat. There was no sign yet of the journalist – he assumed that he was still sleeping – but from his new vantage point, he assured her, and with two men outside, he was confident of being able to monitor and pick up the targets whenever they left the building. They had a car and a motor bike. It was simply a matter of waiting.

That call concluded, he made two more: first to the man in the coffee shop, telling him curtly to get back outside and do his job (and adding that, from now on, he could see him); then he called the second man, who reported up to the room, changed quickly into the biker's gear, and reappeared a few minutes later astride the Honda in the street below.

By that time the boy had shifted position to the sofa and was, by the look of things, watching morning television, lolling back against a fat cushion. McMahon studied him through the optic glass, saw him suddenly grin, and thought that he should take as much pleasure as he could now, for the rest of his day would hold little.

CHAPTER THIRTY-ONE

According to the local paper Penny Winston was forty-one years old, but she possessed the figure, Sasha observed when the woman had finally positioned the car to her satisfaction on the driveway, of a considerably younger person. She was wearing tight blue jeans and a brown suede jacket over which her blonde curly hair fell attractively.

She stepped towards Sasha, smiled and rolled her eyes. 'I only just made it, didn't I? You people, honestly!' She stuck her head back inside the car, withdrew finally with a carrier-bag, and slammed the door. 'You say you're coming in the morning and expect us to sit about twiddling our thumbs. I knew if I went out you'd come, but I had to get some basics in case we get snowed in.' She gave Sasha a quizzical look. 'Shouldn't you have a clipboard or something?'

It was the first pause that she'd let fall. 'I'm sorry?' Sasha said, feeling breathless.

'You are the from the developers, aren't you? About what's wrong with the central heating and the kitchen?'

'I'm a journalist.'

'Oh.' The bouncy good humour vanished. She sighed. 'It'll be about Gerry, I s'pose?'

'Yes.'

'You're a bit late, aren't you? The other paper was here last week.'

'I'm a freelance.' Sasha was about to explain further, but Penny didn't seem interested. She'd already started up the path and Sasha hastened after her.

'I don't know what else I can say. Poor old Ger, dying like, miles from anywhere. God knows why he went to Sizewell.' She shook her head in genuine puzzlement. 'I mean, I should know if anyone should.'

Sasha shot her a quick glance. The woman was looking genuinely troubled, not at all like the disinterested former wife that she'd appeared to be in the newspaper article. She said cautiously, 'You were still quite close to him, then?'

Now Penny looked sharply at her. 'Why'd you say that?'

'Well . . .' Sasha felt herself blush. 'It was just that in the paper it said you hadn't seen him for several years.'

They'd reached the front door. Penny had the key in the lock. She opened the door and stepped inside before turning to answer. From her step she looked down at Sasha shrewdly. 'It's what I told that reporter.' She shrugged. 'You people think you can barge in asking any questions you like, don't you? You never stop to think of the damage you could do.'

'I'm sorry. I suppose not, sometimes.' Sasha wasn't at all sure what was going on or who she was apologising for – but Penny, she realised suddenly, was on the verge of shutting the door in her face. 'Please,' she said quickly, letting some of her desperation show, 'I'm only trying to find out more about why Gerry died. I need to speak to you.'

Penny hesitated, her hand on the doorknob.

'I'm not going to quote you. I'm just trying to get to the truth.'

'Are you, indeed?' She studied her for a long moment. 'Who'd you say you work for?' she demanded.

Sasha gave a brief explanation. Instantly she perceived that it had made a difference. Penny's brow cleared. 'Ted – that's my fiancé – he not going to read something like that, is he? And I wouldn't mind people knowing the truth.' She looked suddenly bitter. 'Come on in.'

The house was very hot inside. The thermostat was faulty, Penny said, pushing open a door on the right, telling Sasha to take a seat while she put away the shopping.

It was a small sitting-room, slightly overcrowded with furniture. Sasha sat down in an armchair. A very large grey cat, curled up tightly on the sofa, opened its eyes and watched her unwinkingly as she looked about her. On the mantelpiece was a framed photograph of Penny and a muscular-looking man.

'That's Ted. He's a fireman.' The woman had come in without Sasha hearing. She sat on the sofa, picked up the cat and started stroking it. 'He's a good man, and he thinks the world of me, but he's a jealous bugger.' She took a deep breath. 'He was here the day that kid from the local paper came. That's why I said I hadn't seen Gerry for years.'

'But you had?'

She nodded. 'About the first thing Gerry did when he got out was come looking for me. On the off-chance I was "between boyfriends", as he put it.' She smiled a little mistily. 'We were married eighteen years, and we were happy. I thought he was cracked to do the direct action stuff – I never would, even though I love animals.' She bent to kiss the cat's head. 'But he said he had to, so that was fine by me. Then he went inside, and prison killed us stone dead.'

This was so sad, Sasha thought. They'd truly loved each other.

'I was lonely, and . . .' Penny swallowed. 'Those bloody visits, kids screaming, and there were some real nasty types he was in with. I mean, Ger wasn't a violent man. He shouldn't ever have been in that place. I know he put the fire bombs in that shop, but it was at night and they were never going to harm anyone, only the bloody fur coats. But the judge said he was like the IRA come to Tunbridge Wells and he had to be punished . . . Well, they punished him all right. And me.

'After that first year, Ger told me I wasn't to visit any more. He could see what it was doing to me. He said I wasn't to wait for him, I was to find someone else, 'cause he didn't know if he was going to make it till the end of his sentence.'

She'd met Ted two years before. They'd got engaged the previous spring, just before Gerry had been released early for good behaviour. She hadn't known until he'd rung the doorbell. He'd accepted the news of her engagement, had promised her that there'd be no problem over a divorce, and that he'd leave her in peace. But when he'd got up to go . . .

'I just couldn't bear it. I . . .' She broke off, shaking her head, and Sasha saw a tear trace its way down her face. Feeling helpless, she made a small, sympathetic noise.

'I couldn't face not seeing him again. I told him so – which wasn't fair, not to anyone – but . . . Those last six months,' she took a deep breath, 'I saw him about five or six times. We never had sex – that part was over – but we talked, held hands like we were brother and sister. He told me everything. Which is how,' she looked up and her pretty face became hard, 'I know what really happened. The truth. Want to hear it?'

Sasha gave a quick nod.

'You've heard about the Tenterden Four?'

Her mouth went dry.

'Don't believe what they're saying in the papers.' Penny's eyes narrowed. 'That woman, Caroline Henshaw. Looks like Mrs Butter Wouldn't Melt, doesn't she? Well, I'm telling you . . .' she sat forward, engulfing the cat, which didn't seem to mind, '*She's* the reason Ger died.'

'Oh?' Sasha croaked.

'Yeah. Bloody bitch, using him like that. He got so worked up about her stupid "mission", he gave himself a heart attack.' She took another deep breath. 'He went to the library to do some research and she was waiting for him, like a bloody spider sitting in her web.'

'I'm sorry?'

'Scheming little . . .' she broke off, calming herself. 'You see, Ger had this idea in prison about writing an animal rights book. *A Treatise for Animals*, he called it.' She looked suddenly proud. 'Setting down all the arguments against animal experiments and the fur trade and fox-hunting. Everything. He said, if he could write it well enough, he'd convince people.' She made a face. 'Maybe, maybe not. Anyway, first few months after he got out he was happy enough, doing odd jobs, thinking about writing it.' She smiled sadly. 'I don't know if he ever actually got round to writing anything much.

'Then last August,' she sighed and pulled at a loose thread on the sofa, 'he was driving through Appledore and who should he see but this chap, a scientist. A real bad bastard that he'd known about for years. Used to work down near Brighton, did horrible things to Beagles.' She frowned. 'I think it was Beagles. Anyway, he was a sort of legend in the animal rights world. Well, of course, that was that. Ger was off.'

Sasha resisted the temptation to take notes. She didn't want to break the spell by producing her shorthand book.

'He followed him to where he worked. It was a place called REDEV. There was a raid there a couple of weeks back.'

Sasha nodded.

'Yeah, I suppose you being a journalist, you'd know that. Anyway, he tried phoning, asking to be put through to this man, but the switchboard was really cagey and wouldn't do it. So he went to the library, to the reference section, to find out how he could investigate the place, and like I said, she waiting for him.'

Penny rearranged her features into a tortuous grimace. '"May I ask what your interest might be, sir?"; "Ooh, how very fascinating"; "And you're going to do a book about it? How exciting! If there's anything I can do to help . . ." She wouldn't be fobbed off, Ger said, so he told her a little bit, and after that she wouldn't leave him alone. Thought it was "wonderful" that he'd been in prison. "An example to us all."' Penny's nostrils swelled. 'Stupid cow,' she muttered.

'They used to meet at the leisure centre for coffee. I felt funny when he told me that – jealous, I suppose – but there I was with Ted, so . . .' She drifted off again, stroking the cat's broad head. It pushed itself up against her hand, purring in ecstasy.

Sasha remembered that the developers might be arriving at any moment. 'Gerry told her about himself?' she prompted.

'Yeah. He was grateful to her, you see. She was the one who told him to go to London to do a search on REDEV.'

'He did that?'

'Yeah. Said he'd been flattered by her interest. Stands to reason, doesn't it? She never wore a wedding ring, and he was lonely, and I'd gone off . . .' She pressed her lips into a thin white line. 'I hadn't see him in over two months. Then he came here a week ago last Thursday lunchtime. "I've got something to confess, Pen," he said. Then it all came out. He knew if he'd told me earlier what he was getting into, I'd have hit the roof. I'd have tried to stop him. Of course, by the time he did tell me it was too late.'

'Oh?'

She nodded down at the carpet. 'He was going off that night to do a raid on REDEV. He sat where you're sitting now, white as a sheet. Said he'd got himself too far in to get out and he'd have to go through with it.' She gave a long sigh. 'He said he'd been a fool to tell her anything, that he could see now that all she'd been doing was spinning him along, letting him do her work for her and letting him think she was interested in him.' A corner of her mouth went down. 'Which she was, of course, in a way. He was just the man she'd been waiting for, she told him.'

'What did she mean by that?' Sasha asked cautiously.

Penny exhaled loudly. 'She had her own group. Not like one of Ger's, but some daft underground movement that she'd "hand-selected" over a year. Her husband, that creepy Ethics teacher, he was one of them. Have you seen his picture in the paper?" She rolled her eyes. 'Shows you what her taste is really like. And there were some local lads she'd picked up by going to meetings.'

Caroline Henshaw was quite amazing, Sasha thought.

'There's a notice-board at the library, see? So she'd just go along to anything that took her fancy, didn't have to be about animal welfare. Anyone who was a bit rowdy she'd slime up to. Went through dozens, she said, before she got the right ones. Then there was the last one. Richley.' Penny's face hardened. 'He'd gone into the library asking for a book on covert warfare and insurgency. He wanted to be one of these Rambo-types. He was right up her street.'

Sasha frowned. 'What do you mean?'

Penny snorted. 'Ger thought she didn't even like animals particularly. He asked her outright in the end, and she got all flustered and spouted this garbage about the rights of one species being as important as another, one group leading the other – but all she wanted was a little war. Any cause would've done for her. She'd done some course, political science, and got hooked on it. The idea of "striking back" against the state. Ger said it was amazing, the stuff she came out with. How "the people" had to form into secret cells to do one action, then split up, re-group and spread. The "scatter-gun approach", she called it.' She rolled her eyes again. 'Can you believe it?'

Oh yes, Sasha thought, but she only raised her eyebrows.

'She got those two kids involved too. After she met Ger she went on a school-trip to London with that creepy bloke of hers. It was to a demo on cruelty-free farming.' She frowned. 'Loads of kids from all over the country went to it, at Trafalgar Square. She got the boy first – Ger liked him, said he was a good kid – then his little girlfriend, the kiddy they've hauled off to France with them.'

Sasha kept her face impassive. Penny seemed to know everything.

'A right bitch, picking on kids like that. I mean, they're impressionable at that age, aren't they? If he'd had his way Ger wouldn't have had them. He never let anyone under eighteen in his groups. Anyway, after he found out what he did about REDEV, she must've thought Christmas had come early.'

Sasha felt her skin tingle. 'What did he find out?' she asked.

'About the company that was behind REDEV.' Penny spoke casually. 'One of the big drug companies, he said.'

Sasha caught her breath. Did she mean World Med Inc, or someone else? 'Did he say which one?'

'No.' Penny shook her head firmly. 'He wouldn't tell me, and he wouldn't tell *her* either, though she badgered him for it something rotten. She wrote down a list of the companies world-wide and read it out to him. She said he only had to nod or lift his finger when she said the right one. But he wasn't having any of it. He'd sweated to find it out, and he was keeping it for his book, he told her. He told me there was another reason as well.' She gave a half-smile. 'He thought it might be dangerous for me to know. Poor old Ger. Prison had made him a bit paranoid, I think. He thought the company had gone to such trouble to hide their tracks, the fewer people who knew who they were the better. "Specially you, Pen," he said.' She smiled sadly again. 'Not that I was that bothered, to tell you the truth – though I'd never have told him that. It would've hurt his feelings.'

Sasha leaned forward. 'Did he, er, say how he'd found out about the company?'

She gave a little shrug. 'No, only that it had taken him a lot of running about. And he was damned if that bloody woman was going to stop him writing his book about it. He'd take them on their dumb raid, he told me, seeing as he had no option.' Her voice grew cold. 'Then he was taking himself off somewhere to write. He wanted to know if he could leave his cat here with me – he didn't want the poor thing being traipsed round the countryside.' Her hand moved over the fur of the cat on her lap, and the purring increased. 'His was called Smokey, like this one. Both from the same sanctuary. Anyway, I said of course he could. I waited in for him, but he never came. He never came back at all.' She gulped and two tears ran down her cheeks. Sasha watched them fall on to her shirt collar, the moisture spreading out, darkening the cotton. She wanted to say something but could think of nothing that wouldn't sound trite.

'That was the last time I ever saw him. Next thing I heard, he was dead.'

Sasha heard the sound of a car approaching. Please God, she prayed, let it pass by. She heard it do so. 'You said he didn't have an option but to do the raid?' She asked gently.

Penny brushed her cheeks with one hand. 'That's right. Even though she didn't know the name of the big drugs company, it was enough that it was big. She said that by attacking it, her group would be making a "direct strike at the capitalist heart". "And rescuing animals?" Ger said. "Oh yes, sure," she said, but as if that didn't matter.' She shook her head. 'Well, after that Ger told her straight: she could do all the striking she liked, but he wasn't having any of it. That's when things got nasty.'

'Oh?'

'Yeah. He said she switched like that.' Penny snapped her fingers. The cat flinched but didn't shift its position. 'From batting her eyelids at him into a right dirty little blackmailer. Said that one of her "strike-force" – Richley –' Penny glowered at the name – 'had connections with the police, and unless Ger did exactly what she wanted she'd get him to tip them off about one of his old raids, one he'd told her about that he'd got away with.'

Penny chewed angrily at her lip. 'Richley had already got into the police computer and done a print-out of the details. She showed it to Ger. He never knew he was only a copper's kid; *I* only knew when I read it in the paper. Anyway, Ger gave in. He couldn't face going back inside.' She stared down again at the carpet and seemed to drift away in her own thoughts.

Sasha became acutely aware of time passing. 'There was nothing else he could do?'

'Like what?' Penny's chin came up. 'He tried telling her that they'd be better off doing it on their own, that his nerves weren't good, but she wasn't having it. They needed someone to show them the ropes.'

'Couldn't he have gone to the . . . ?' Sasha started and wished she hadn't.

'The police?' Penny gave her a filthy look. 'No matter what he thought of her, there's no way Gerry would ever squeal on anyone.'

The cat extended a paw and began washing itself slowly. 'Now he's gone, and hardly anyone to remember him except me. If only he'd done his book. He was going to dedicate it to me – not my real name, but his pet name for me . . .' She seemed about to divulge that too, but stopped herself in time. She made a half-hearted attempt at a smile. 'Now all I've got to remember him by is his notebook and a few papers. He left them with me that Thursday. Said he wouldn't put it past that Henshaw woman to go sneaking into his place to get them.' She sniffed. 'One brown envelope. Not much to leave after a lifetime, is it?'

'Er, no.' Sasha felt the blood pounding in her ears. She tried to sound casual. 'Do you think that I could have a look at it?'

A suspicious look crossed Penny's face. 'What for?'

'If I'm going to write a full account, I need as many facts as I can. His research might be very helpful.'

Penny considered the request carefully, then gave a quick nod. 'It might as well get published somewhere, mightn't it?' She got up, dislodging the cat as she did so.

At the door she paused. 'Could you say that it was *his* research?'

'Sure.' Sasha smiled.

'He'd have liked that, seeing his name in print. Mind you, I don't know how useful it's going to be to you.'

'You haven't looked?'

She shook her head vigorously. 'I stuck it under the mattress after he left that day, and later on, when I heard about the raid on the news, and then Ger . . .' She frowned. 'I just didn't want to touch it. Silly, I know. Superstitious. But I couldn't help remembering what he'd said about it being dangerous. I thought maybe what he'd found out had killed him.' She swallowed. 'I'd have thrown it out, but it was his.'

She blinked down at Sasha. 'I'll be glad to get it out of the house, to tell you the truth. I'll go and get it for you now.'

CHAPTER THIRTY-TWO

After Colin Davenport had typed the final word of the report, he sat for some time staring at the screen. He couldn't believe that it was over: the days and nights of slogging work; the isolation; the terror. But mostly the terror: he was free of it now, or soon would be. He could forget about Stockart, the telephone calls, being spied upon, all the awful business about the break-in and its consequences.

His eyes wandered back to the last sentence on the screen.

'To know one's destiny is the first step to altering it; and if one considers that each of us carries within ourselves a single copy of a lethal gene, one can start to understand the immense significance of the Infiltrator Technique to us all.'

'THE END', he typed on a new line, and smiled. He was pleased with his work. He considered it was clear, as simple as it could be, and readable. Whether or not it was as good as the original was debatable. But as it was highly unlikely that anyone would ever be in a position to compare the two, that hardly mattered.

Of course, Davenport had to admit, it had helped considerably that his brief had been so generous, that he'd been asked to change West's notes, turning the awful results of the first two Albanian trials into something more palatable. Miscarriages rather than fatal infant cancers. In fact, he'd invented so much of it that he almost felt he was the one who'd discovered the Infiltrator. That, as ghostwriter, he should share authorship of the finished product.

He summoned up the last of the original material and deleted it, in case the unthinkable should happen and this laptop should also fall into enemy hands. Some of his pleasure seeped away as he remembered Stockart's last telephone call to him earlier that morning. Davenport hadn't been aware of the time – he'd been working all night – and it was only afterwards that he'd realised it wasn't even six o'clock. Had Stockart set his alarm, he wondered bitterly, so that he'd be sure to wake him up?

And the questions . . . Was Davenport certain that his lock-out system was secure? That the kid who'd stolen the first laptop couldn't have penetrated it?

Of course he was sure! He'd wanted to sound outraged, but instead he'd stammered. Part of the reaction had been simply a result of hearing Stockart's voice, but the other factor had been his guilty conscience, the knowledge of what he'd hidden from Stockart, the presence of the girl journalist in the pub the day before.

A shiver ran down his back. If Stockart should ever find out about that . . . He knew that the first thing he ought to have done when he'd got back to REDEV was call Stockart and tell him. But the very notion of speaking to the man when he'd been so thoroughly frightened, first by his aborted attempt to call the police, then encountering the journalist sitting there, blatantly pumping the other two . . . Davenport had been trembling so much that it had only been with difficulty that he had driven back to the cottage.

Once there, calmed by a stiff whisky, he'd realised what he must do: finish the report, deliver it, then get out. He'd worked like something possessed, only stopping for necessities, and once, when his mind was reeling, a longer break to eat something and scan a newspaper.

He got up and stretched, all his muscles were aching. He went to the window, looked out at the snow-covered fields, and suddenly felt elated with relief. It was beautiful here, he realised. He ought to go for a walk, perhaps up to the pub for a beer and a pasty; the lane had been gritted now, and he could take care to avoid icy patches. He opened the window, took a lungful of cold air, smiled with the sensation of being free, heard, distantly, the sound of a car approaching, saw, though he stepped back into the room at once, that it was a dark car, slowing down as it came round the bend before his cottage.

Damn Stockart, he swore, seeing the car's aerial move majestically past his hedge. He'd done a brilliant job for the man, and this was how he treated him! Like a lab rat to be tortured. He glanced down at his hands, saw that they'd formed two tight fists, and realised that, for once, thinking of Stockart, he wasn't afraid, only angry. If only he'd gone through with his phone call to the police. If only he'd shopped him.

He crept forward from behind the curtain and closed the window. There was no sign of the car now, but he wouldn't expect there to be; it would be where it always was, lurking up the track. Right, he thought resolutely, crossing once more to his desk, he would call Stockart now and see how he wanted the report to be delivered. By hand, probably, which was fine, Davenport told himself. If necessary he would drive up to Stockart's office himself, hand the laptop over, then disappear.

The line was engaged. Scowling, he hung up, waited and tried again. It was still busy. It was as if Stockart was deliberately finding new ways to torment him. Then, in front of him on the screen, the cursor's flashing light caught his eye. He would simply send an e-mail message. He exited his own files, ran through the procedure to get into Branium's database, and double-clicked on the postbox logo.

Conscious of security, he sent one line only: 'Report finished, awaiting your instructions.'

Davenport waited, drumming his fingers, for the message to be acknowledged.

'Come on, you bastard,' he muttered at the screen. He tried the telephone once more, again heard the engaged tone. He ground his teeth. To be kept waiting at a time like this; to be left hanging about, kicking his heels, clock-watching like a civil servant . . .

He grinned. Now *there's* an idea, he thought – something he hadn't done for ages, but which had always in the past proved highly entertaining.

Somehow, he told himself, grinning more at some of the memories, people assumed that what they wrote in internal memos and sent via the company computer network was sacrosanct, invisible to other eyes. Of course, the theory had a lot to do with those people innocently believing their passwords were known only to themselves. Which was how it should be. And was, Davenport thought – except for the few people like himself who viewed the discovery of 'secret' passwords as a game, a bit like solving a crossword clue. Something to do when one had a little time on one's hands, or wished to check up on one's new employer.

During his first few days on Stockart's payroll, Davenport had, as a matter of course, accessed the network manager, discovered the route into the 'highly secure' directors' directory, and there learned Stockart's password. He tapped it in now. MIDAS. Doubtless, he told himself with a sniff, Stockart had considered that name somehow significant. Davenport knew of at least three other corporate men with the same password.

Now he glanced down the list of Stockart's files, accessed one marked 'Sneeze' which proved to be a survey of hayfever sufferers and very dull. Nothing looked terribly interesting. He pulled a face, pressed the down cursor, saw at the bottom a series entitled 'WW': one to four. They were all messages written that morning, Davenport noticed, the first being sent at eight-thirty, then at half-hourly intervals, the last barely twenty minutes before.

What was so occupying the torturer? Davenport wondered slyly. He hit the 'enter' key on WW1.

'Will,

'Don't forget about our little Subject, will you? He's waiting for you downstairs.'

Davenport frowned. It meant nothing to him. He pressed WW2.

'Are you there, Will? I think you are. Why aren't you answering your phone? I promise you, once you've done one it'll be easier. So, see to it, will you? There's a good chap.'

Stockart picking on someone as usual, but it sounded dull, an internal squabble, very boring. Davenport yawned. Realising that he was thirsty, he left the information on the screen and went downstairs to get himself a celebratory bottle of beer.

He couldn't go on sitting there for ever, ignoring the ringing of his telephone, the e-mail messages flooding in from Stockart. Sooner or later someone was going to realise that he was locked inside his own office. Not at home, not battling through traffic. Not down on the second floor dealing with the Gilbert baby.

He shivered; he was cold. Again, he'd passed the night there, at work. He didn't know if he'd slept, but he thought not. After Stockart's call about the Gilbert baby, after he'd done the man's bidding by phoning down to the ward to check up on the infant, he'd returned to what he'd been doing before: staring in disbelief at the results of the DNA tests that he'd just completed on another baby, the one born dead the previous day.

They showed that the good Dystrophin gene was present and viable, and in the right place. The Infiltrator had worked. The cause of death could not be attributed to his handiwork. At first, for a few seconds, West had experienced a great surge of triumph – he was exonerated! – before he'd realised the implications of the results. He'd needed that dead baby's DNA map to show him his mistake. Without the map, he couldn't correct the error in Mel's unborn child.

And hard upon the heels of that realisation had come another: that the results, the print-out he was staring at, didn't exonerate him at all. Far from it. All it showed was that the mistake wasn't evident at birth; it must only become so later, at the same time as (or just before) the onset of Leukaemia.

Then, of course, he'd remembered about the Gilbert baby. He'd gone haring off down to the basement, to the haematology labs. The lab-tech on duty, a dozy young man watching television, hadn't been at all bothered by West's appearance or his removal of a patient's blood sample 'for re-checking in my own labs'. There, in the room next door, he'd extracted the DNA from the blood and, with shaking hands, had looked for the small amount of RNA levels which would show the faulty gene. The baby was the oldest in the study; there were obviously some health problems already showing; the mistake would be clear on his map.

He'd scanned the print-out before his hands had crumpled the paper, then at once straightened it out again, lain it flat on the workbench. 'It can't be,' he'd moaned, glanced over at the sequencer machine, wondering if it could have malfunctioned, knowing that it hadn't.

As with the stillborn's results, so now with the Gilbert baby. The complete Dystrophin gene was there, in the right place and functioning. West had emitted a little scream, then stuffed his hand in his mouth. He didn't have time to get hysterical; Mel would be there soon.

His eyes had fallen for the first time on the lab-tech's diagnosis of the blood sample:

The white cell count was normal.

The lymphocytes: normal.

The haemoglobin count: within the normal range.

West had swallowed so hard that he'd almost choked. The Gilbert boy didn't have Leukaemia. God only knew what he *had* got, but it wasn't Leukaemia. He'd counted to ten out loud to make sure that his voice was all right, then called down to the ward where the baby had been admitted, got the night sister (earlier he'd been able only to speak to a nurse) and asked in as calm a voice as he could muster what was wrong with the baby.

'One moment, doctor.'

That moment had been an eternity.

Then: 'Are you calling from home?'

'Yes.'

'Well, I shouldn't rush in. According to the doctor who admitted him, Jeremy appears to be quite well.'

'Then why—'

'The parents, doctor. Very worried indeed. Demanding to see you.'

'I know, I know.'

'I'd say leave it till morning.'

It had taken him some time to appreciate the truth: that either the Gilbert boy, uniquely, wasn't going to develop Leukaemia, or that he was going to be a later-onset case. Either way, the baby wasn't going to help West, which meant that, in turn, he couldn't help Mel or the unborn child. *His* child. His one golden boy. The thought flickered that he could always switch allegiance, lay claim to the Gilbert boy instead, but that thought quickly died. He'd develop Leukaemia sooner or later; the Infiltrator would see to that.

Besides, he couldn't do that to Mel, not to his darling.

Time had passed. The phones had started ringing, Stockart's memos appearing. West knew that he could have switched off the PC, pulled out the cables from their sockets, but somehow he'd lost the energy to do so. The heating had gone off and he'd been cold, but there'd been no point in going home, no point in anything.

He'd heard the secretary arrive, her tinny little voice on the telephone, and then a timid knock at the door. 'You're not in there are you, Doctor?' And a moment later, to herself; 'I didn't think so.'

Then Mel had come. Like a magnet he'd been drawn to the door, had heard her lovely voice responding to the secretary's chatter.

He gulped now. How was he ever going to tell her that there was nothing he could do to remedy his error? He got up, crept to the door again, pressed his ear against it. 'Oh, angel,' he whispered in agony into the paintwork.

'Is this your first?' he heard the secretary ask.

'No.' Mel sounded hesitant. West leaned harder into the door.

'Boy or girl?'

'A little boy. He's six.'

'Lovely. I bet he's looking forward to his little brother being born then, isn't he? Someone to play football with . . . Oh, Mrs Alder!' The girl's voice shot up sharply and West's pulse quickened. 'Whatever's the matter?'

There was a muffled sound, then a gasp, then Mel was crying. Terrible, heart-rending sobs. West whimpered in utter misery.

He heard Mel say, 'I'm sorry. So silly of me.'

'Not at all.' By the sound of the secretary's voice she'd moved position. Next to Mel?

'He's got Duchenne's, you see.'

'Ohmigod, I'm so sorry. I had no idea.'

The girl knew nothing about genetics, the one-in-two risk for any son of a DMD carrier. West had deliberately kept her in ignorance. She'd never even seen the patients' notes.

'That's all right,' Mel's voice sounded better, though still slightly muffled. West stopped panting. 'He's why I'm here, actually.'

'Oh?' The secretary sounded surprised, and West had a horrible moment of realisation. He'd tricked Mel into coming but he'd forgotten how, what he'd said to her. Whatever it was, he'd known that she wouldn't mind really, not once he explained that it had been necessary, and that he'd corrected the fault in her new child. Only now, of course, that wasn't going to happen.

His flesh began to crawl.

'What d'you mean?' the secretary was asking curiously.

'I wasn't going to tell anyone.' Mel gave a little half-laugh. 'I was afraid of blubbing. And anyway, it's been this awful waiting about . . .'

'I know. I hope he hasn't had an accident.'

'Oh, you don't think so, do you?' The fear in Mel's sweet voice! A tear rolled down his cheek.

'No, I'm sure he hasn't. Don't worry about that.'

'He's got to be here, he's got to come.'

'It's all right, Mrs Alder. He'll come. He's just been caught up somewhere.'

'He's going to cure my Ludi.'

West rocked back on his heels. Beyond the door, the conversation ran on. 'Gene therapy,' he heard Mel say, and like a wave coming ashore it hit him, how he'd tricked her. He remembered the care he'd taken to sound convincing.

'He's such a brilliant man,' he heard her say now, and the secretary's reply: 'He is, isn't he? Well, if he's told you he can do it, he can.'

He staggered away from the door and into the middle of the room. He looked up at the ceiling and opened his mouth in a silent howl. He was a creature in torment. He wasn't God; he couldn't reset the boy's programme. Not now, not yet. Give him five years, he begged her, three – he'd work day and night, he'd do it! Only don't give up on him now.

'Don't hate me, my love. You mustn't hate your—'

The phone rang again. Stockart, West thought, his mind refocusing blearily, trying to sharpen. If he didn't do what he wanted, Stockart would come and get him, and he'd find Mel too. He'd hurt her. But if Stockart was pleased with him, if he knew he was obeying his instructions in one respect, then he might assume that West had done what he'd been ordered to do in others – specifically Mel.

West blinked rapidly. That was it. That was what he had to do to save her; he saw that now. And he mustn't put it off a moment longer. He crossed quickly to the other side of the room, to the door that led directly into the corridor. No one was there, not even the workmen who should have been installing new lighting. No one saw him slipping down the staircase. Two flights, he told himself, and he'd be there. He didn't need to talk to anybody or look anyone in the eye. Just get in there, get the kid, and go. It wouldn't take long. And it wouldn't hurt, he promised. And anyway, Mel was worth it.

The phone line was still engaged and the e-mail message hadn't been acknowledged. Cursing, Davenport set down his bottle of beer. For days Stockart had been hounding him for the damn report, and now, when he'd finished it, suddenly the man couldn't be reached.

'Bastard,' he said out loud, and glared at his laptop where Stockart's dull little memo was still on screen. Trust him not to leave anything incriminating or vaguely interesting lying about. Davenport clicked back to the index, and was about to exit Stockart's files altogether when he saw a new one appear: WW5. It had just been sent. Without much curiosity he clicked on to it, thinking it would probably be as elliptical and therefore tedious as the others.

He raised an eyebrow. The tone of it, at least, was completely different.

'Subject Four's rash is bright red now. Check on DAMR. We don't have any more time to fucking waste. This is SWii, believe it.'

Davenport stared. SW. The Same World Hospital. Then lower-case Roman numerals standing for the second trial. He knew exactly what it meant, but why was Stockart talking about it now? Davenport felt his thought processes slur, felt the whole of him yearn suddenly for sleep. SWii had happened ages ago. 'Bright red,' he whispered, and his stomach gave a lurch as if he'd missed a step on the escalator.

Was it possible that SW referred to something else? Had he missed something? Moving as fast as he could (which wasn't very; his fingers didn't seem to want to obey his command) he called up the first memo again.

'Will . . .'

Will West. In the context of SWii, that had to be who 'Will' was, the doctor who'd run the trials, who'd messed up the first two, got it right on the third. But – and Davenport's mind grappled frantically, but it was like wading through treacle – West's work,

his clinical trials, were over, erased now a thing of the past. In
their place was the report on to which Davenport had just typed
'THE END'.

Sweat glistened across his skin. He remembered, distantly like
a warning voice, that he mustn't spend too long in MIDAS in
case a security system was activated. He'd already been there
longer than he should. He exited back to Stockart's file-list, to
the WW memos, and his finger moved up to the 'escape' key.
Then he paused. His eyes had seen something. Alongside each of
the Will West memos, under the destination column on the right
hand of the screen was the letter M. Davenport's brow knitted.
He couldn't quite remember what this meant, but it would be
listed. He went back to Branium's general directory and clicked on
'Glossary (Internal)', biting his tongue as he waited for the letters
to run down the screen. B. Branium Head Office; L: Leicester
depot; M . . .

The Mistletoe. Branium's own hospital. Davenport's eyes remained
fixed. In a trance, he clicked on the 'query' logo.

'Person required?' the computer asked.

He typed in West's name, requested his current position and
job title. The network was busy: 'Please wait,' appeared on screen.
Davenport emitted a soft groan, saw the telephone beside him,
wished fervently that he could use it.

'Clinical Geneticist. Currently engaged in UK research.'

Davenport's ears rang. He heard Stockart's voice as it had been
just a few weeks before, when it had been 'Colin' and friendliness
and 'we'. 'We need the report as soon as possible, Colin, to present
to the Board for their approval. Once we've got that, we can set
about getting the government's go ahead. So, as soon as you can
– without comprising quality, of course.'

Funny, Davenport thought, that at times of great stress he
didn't shake; he couldn't afford the wasted energy. Slowly he
stood up and descended the stairs, not pausing to check on the
car outside. For whatever reason, Stockart and Will West had
decided to go ahead with the next stage of the Infiltrator trials
without waiting for permission – either from the main board or,
more importantly, the government. What West was doing at the
Mistletoe was illegal.

Davenport shuddered. He entered the kitchen, saw the eggy plate, the remains of his night-time meal, pushed it away and sat down at the table, putting his head in his hands. It looked as though the results of the UK trial were the same as those experienced in Albania.

He belched. For a moment he thought he was going to be sick, but he controlled the impulse. It hadn't been too hard to distance himself from what had happened to the Albanian babies, because by the time he knew about it it had already happened. That was what he'd told himself when, on first reading West's notes, he'd felt a bit squeamish. But now, these British babies were going to die of Leukaemia. And he couldn't massage those facts away, make them nicer. He bit his lip. Should he call the police? But if he did that he would be implicated. Besides, nothing was going to stop these infants dying. They'd been born pre-programmed for an early, awful death. He wondered dully how long it was going to take for the truth to come out. Then the whole edifice would come tumbling down, and under the rubble would be Stockart, West, and himself, poor little Colin Davenport, whose only crime, he told himself pitifully, had been to rewrite a few facts.

He sniffed loudly. He had to do something to protect himself. Perhaps the police, the fatherly Mr Holland, would offer him a deal? But an instant later he remembered Stockart's brag about the superb quality of Hall's police contacts. He trembled. He was completely alone; he couldn't even risk telephoning his grandmother. He whimpered out loud, just once, then admonished himself. He had to think. He had to find a way.

His eye fell on the newspaper that he'd left on the table, folded to reveal the article he'd read during his long-ago meal-break. Normally he'd have skipped over such a feature – the home life of politicians held little interest for him – but the main photograph had caught his attention.

She stood in the country kitchen of her home, an Aga cooker in the background, pots and pans on the walls, a table with a checked cloth; and in the foreground beside her, two small girls with pigtails were seated, elbows on the table, chins in their hands, smiling up at their mother as she fried their break-fast eggs.

'Sunny-side up for Katie. As it comes for my Sammy!'

Davenport had studied the scene, then, bringing the paper closer to his eyes, the woman's face in particular. He'd decided that there was only one word for her: motherly. Eager by then for more, he'd read the entire article, had been slightly surprised by the fervour she showed towards one of her professional interests, but much more surprised at her age: only forty-three. He'd judged her ten years older at least. The combined effect, he'd realised, of her tweedy clothes – he liked women in tweeds – her grey coiffure, and the lines about her eyes. What a perfect mother, he'd thought, leaving the article with reluctance to resume his work upstairs. No wonder those small girls looked so radiantly content, knowing that whenever they had a problem they could climb up on their mother's knee and she would listen to them, soothe their fears, solve their problems.

Davenport blinked. Of course, he thought, and felt himself blush. He ought to have thought of it at once.

His hand strayed automatically to the telephone, then moved quickly away again. Slowly he pulled the paper towards him and turned it over to see the smaller photograph he now remembered: the woman sitting alone in her study in front of a computer.

He scanned the paragraphs frantically to find the one he wanted. She was going to write a book about butterflies, her 'lifelong passion'. It had made him smile before; it had seemed so ladylike. She was particularly excited by the recent discovery of three species of butterfly in woods near Godalming in Surrey. She hoped that other lepidopterists would help her by pooling their knowledge, sending their ideas to her at the House of Commons.

'Where's the other bit?' he moaned, turning the paper again. There it was, as clearly as if she were speaking out loud to him. She also was 'quite an Internet groupie'. 'It's so fascinating, so much knowledge at one's fingertips. And not difficult at all once you get the hang of it. I have a little surf every day, if I can!'

Snatching the paper, he ran back upstairs to the bedroom and sat down in front of the laptop, double-clicking on the Web icon. All he had to do was ensure that she, and only she, picked up the message.

He paused. How could he hook her? His eyes flitted about the room, searching out possibilities. A bluebottle buzzed distractingly against the window pane. He frowned at it, then stared, then grabbed the paper again and laughed out loud. It was all there in black and white. He started typing furiously, humming to himself like an overexcited child.

CHAPTER THIRTY-THREE

The brown envelope seemed to be burning a hole on the passenger seat. In spite of the worsening driving conditions – more snow had started to fall – Sasha kept glancing over to reassure herself that it was still there. It was ten minutes since she'd left Penny Winston's house, and the need to discover what was inside was eating away at her like fire.

'I'm not being rude,' Penny had said, handing it over, 'but would you mind going now? In case one of the neighbours says something to Ted.' Then, clearly not caring whether Sasha thought her rude or not, she'd raised her eyebrows until Sasha had hastily risen from her seat, walked behind her down the narrow hallway, and stood on the threshold, legs apart, arms crossed until Sasha had driven away out of sight.

Sasha had intended to pull in as soon as she saw a lay-by. But she didn't know the area, and with the snow there was none that she could see. Besides, there was a car behind her now, its foglights, dirty yellow moons, bearing down hard upon her. She re-entered the village, saw a sign for a car-park, and thankfully turned in down a steepish incline.

She pulled into the first available space. The packet, she thought, weighing it again, wasn't very heavy. She noticed that her hands were trembling as she held it. 'I'm not bloody surprised,' she muttered to herself. How anyone could have kept such a thing under a mattress was beyond her.

She took a deep breath and tore it open. Into her lap slithered three photocopied sheets of a form, stapled neatly together at the top, and a thin wedge of typewritten sheets protected by a plastic cover.

She took the form first. It was, as she'd half-expected, the company search on REDEV. In a box on the right-hand side it was described as a 'Private Company Limited by Shares'; underneath, on the left, its registered office was given as an address in Hounslow, Middlesex; its principal trading address was Hop Farm Industrial Estate, near Appledore, Kent; its business activities were described as 'Pharmaceutical Research and Development'.

Sasha flicked over the page and found what she'd been looking for: the holding company was World Med Inc. There were also two other companies listed: MedInv and PharmCare; all three had PO Box addresses in the Cayman Islands. Everything was exactly as Holland had told her.

Her eyes ran down the page to where the UK directors were listed. There were only three, all men: the managing director had a Tenterden address; the finance director was from Rye; and the third, the company secretary, lived in a village called Etchingham – a sign for which Sasha remembered having seen.

She turned to the last page. The annual accounts had been properly completed and illegibly signed by the company secretary. It all looked quite above board. She felt profoundly let down.

Without enthusiasm, she pulled out the typed sheets. They were clearly Winston's notes, apparently written with an old manual machine that needed its ribbon changed. Much of it appeared in diary form, with dates and days scattered through the text. Gerry hadn't believed in double-spacing or much punctuation, or even capital letters; everything was crammed and hard to read. Sasha spirits dropped another notch.

He had started off trying to research the three holding companies on the Cayman Islands. There was a list of the books – business directories that Sasha had never heard of – he'd consulted; he'd tried International Directory Enquiries; he'd even, Sasha saw, eyes starting, written letters to the Cayman companies – to which, he had noted in ink, he'd received no replies 'yet'.

Next he'd turned his attention back to REDEV, to the registered address in Hounslow. He'd actually gone there in person. Sasha groaned on his behalf: registered addresses were sometimes no more than a name on the wall. She scooted down to the bottom of the page. As she'd expected REDEV's had proved to be just that. In other circumstances, she thought, it might be funny, but in this instance, bearing in mind what had subsequently happened to the man, it had been a tragic waste of his time. Gerry had obviously been enthusiastic but he was a complete amateur, an unproductive loose cannon.

Sighing, she picked up the next page. Undeterred by his failure he'd moved onto an examination of REDEV's directors. The managing director was forty-nine; his home – her eyebrows rose as she realised that Gerry must have visited it – was a large cottage on the edge of town. Gerry wrote that he'd considered knocking on the man's front door to warn him about the 'sort of evil bastard' he was employing, but had decided against it, as 'he probably knew and was a bastard too'.

Good point, Sasha murmured to herself.

Gerry had failed to find any mention of the MD or the other directors in either *Who's Who* or the *Distinguished People of Today*, or a host of other books which, no doubt, Caroline Henshaw had supplied him with. She could see the librarian at his shoulder, urging him on with helpful suggestions. She sighed and read on.

The finance director was sixty years old, and lived in a 'surprisingly little' house on the main road. Probably a part-time book-keeper, Sasha thought gloomily; he looked like a 'bookish' man who wouldn't know very much, Gerry had decided after spying on the man leaving for work one morning.

She turned the page. The typing here had deteriorated: there were mistakes everywhere, extra notes scribbled in between the lines, balloons with words in them in the margins. She muttered an oath, held the sheet of paper closer to her eyes, and saw with relief that at least there wasn't much more to go, only another half page after this one.

The morning seemed to have got colder; she turned up the heating and read on quickly. As with the other directors, Gerry had positioned himself outside the home of the company secretary at seven o'clock in the morning. The man lived close to the . . . The next word had been overtyped and Sasha screwed her eyes up, trying to read it . . . railway station, she finally deciphered. She sighed heavily at his inclusion of pointless detail. He'd clearly had no idea about how getting to the heart of a story. She dreaded to think what the book would have been like, then felt immediately guilty. The man was dead, after all.

A movement caught her eye, and she looked up as a car drove in beside her and parked. Two very elderly people, a man and wife by the look of them, fully kitted out in hats, scarves and coats, looked over at her and smiled. How nice people were in the country, she thought, smiling back. How nice that they had time to sit and talk to each other before facing the cold world outside.

She resumed her task. The company secretary had left his home at quarter past seven, got into his car (a seven-year-old grey Peugeot) and driven off. Gerry hadn't been able to see him properly and had decided to follow him 'for a bit'. He'd been damned lucky, Sasha thought, that none of the directors had spotted him lurking about outside their homes, but then she supposed that he'd had years of practice in the art. She remembered Mike's description of how the group, presumably under Gerry's instructions, had 'staked out' REDEV employees. But surely, she thought, someone would have noticed if they were being followed, especially at that time in the morning?

She went back to the script, and her question was answered almost at once. The company secretary had driven only as far as the railway station. Sasha frowned, wondering why. Clearly Gerry had also been intrigued, because he'd left his car in the car-park and followed the man over the bridge on to the London platform.

'London?' Sasha said out loud, mystified.

The train was fairly full with commuters. Nevertheless, Gerry had been able to travel in the same carriage as the secretary and, by craning his neck, study him. Sasha skipped over the description. At Charing Cross, Gerry had followed the man out of the station, across the concourse, and into the street.

Sasha picked up the last page. Now she'd ceased to find Gerry's detective work irritating and wanted more, she wished there were more than half a page to go. Her eyes strained to see what he'd written next; there were lots of crossings-out. The secretary had walked quickly, but Gerry had managed to keep up with him.

They'd turned into Whitehall, passed Horseguard's Parade, Gerry still able to remain out of sight because of the throng of pedestrians at that hour. They passed Downing Street and the Ministry buildings, crossed Parliament Square together, Gerry 'not twelve feet' behind his quarry, walked past the Houses of Parliament into Millbank, over a pedestrian crossing, and on into the smaller streets.

Next came two crossed-out lines with writing over the top and to one side in a balloon. Sasha held the paper up to her eyes. Gerry had nearly lost the man, he'd turned a corner so sharply, but there was only one business building in the street, and other people were going into it so Gerry guessed the secretary had gone in there too. He followed – and sure enough, the man was standing in a group, waiting for a lift.

'Where *are* you?' Sasha moaned.

Her eyes flitted to the side of the page, where he'd scribbled in a circle: 'A commissionaire (very smart) saw me and asked me if he could help, so I went outside again and . . .' There was an arrow leading back to the text. 'I thought I'd better write down the address, but I couldn't see the number of the building anywhere. It was quite modern, lots of chrome and glass . . .' For God's sake, Sasha thought, scanning for a pointer, a full-stop, a capital letter – anything to tell her where he was. '. . . and then I realised I didn't need the street number, because the company's name was right there on top of the doors.'

Yes, she thought. Yes!

A balloon led off beneath the final line: 'I hadn't noticed it before because I thought it was a sculpture, very strange with sticks and circles, then I saw there were letters sort of interwoven into it . . .'

She went back to the main body of the text, saw a name in squashed capitals squeezed between two lines. She blinked and read it again. It couldn't be, she whispered, feeling her mouth go dry. And for the first time in her life she realised that she felt quite sorry for a politician.

Generally speaking, Philippa Tyler tried to find a few minutes each day to herself. She found the time essential – an oasis of the soul, as she privately referred to it – in which she could unwind and indulge herself. She might spend the moments planning a future conversation with a colleague, considering house-guests for the coming weekend, or – her favourite – imagining herself in five years' time, when, her current goals achieved, she would be engaged in the fulfilment of her next ones.

She glanced at the time and saw that she had fifteen minutes before her next meeting – with the nursing representatives. They were bound to be worthy but dull. She owed herself a tiny breather, she considered, from the wearisome business of sorting through the latest batch of IVF begging-letters which Sebastian had deposited on her desk that morning. He'd already weeded out the obvious no-hopers – the illiterate, the mad, the over-forties – and now she had to make a start, he'd told her firmly; there were sackfuls coming in, and they needed a dozen to be going on with, as soon as possible. Otherwise, the media might start to lose interest.

She turned slightly in her chair and smiled. She knew exactly what she wanted to do with these precious moments. Leaning forward, she switched on her PC. It was really most amusing, she told herself, waiting to go online. When the Sunday paper journalist had asked her what her hobbies were, inspiration had struck: 'Butterflies, my absolute passion.' And it was true. She did love the creatures, beautiful fragile things, always had; she read anything she could about them. The next words had been out of her mouth before she'd been properly aware of having spoken them. 'Yes, in fact I'm rather hoping to write a book on the subject. A medley. Butterfly folklore. Extinct species and rare sightings . . .' She'd got quite carried away, had been particularly pleased with her suggestion that people send her their ideas – although so far, she thought, frowning, none had. People could be so dog-in-the-mangerish sometimes. However, she didn't have to worry about that.

The article had made her proposed book sound good, a properly formed idea. Really, she told herself, a smile playing again round her mouth, it was no surprise that three publishers had contacted her office the previous afternoon. By the evening, before she'd left for home, Sebastian had found her an agent, who had left a message at nine that morning saying that an auction was taking place during the day between four publishers vying for her book. She wasn't to worry about having time for research or writing; he'd make sure they supplied good people. He would keep her informed of all developments by e-mail, and only in emergency (being aware of how busy she was) would he contact her directly.

She checked her e-mail first, starting slightly when she saw the amount those publishers were prepared to pay. Then she reminded herself of her agent's words: that her name was hot at the moment; that she was the hottest woman politician for years and publishers would be desperate to be her friend now, in the hope of securing her memoirs later. She left the negotiations with the New York publishers upping the offer by another generous ten per cent. Goodness, she thought, waiting to go into the Butterfly web-site, they must be keen. It was barely dawn over there.

The logo for the message-board was, appropriately, a butterfly. Someone was talking about the effects of pesticides, someone else about cabbage-whites. Very unexciting, she thought.

Then she saw the next line.

'Do you want to know the whereabouts of the Pearl-Bordered Fritillary?'

Of course she did! That species was supposed to be extinct; there'd been no sighting of it in fifty years. How splendid, she thought, eagerly clicking on. It was all very well having researchers, but what a fillip for her agent – and for herself – if *she* could produce something truly sensational.

'Answer the following three questions.'

A warning-bell sounded. She wondered if the sender was going to turn out to be a company, foxing clever to sell its wares. But the first question, the only one on screen, showed proper knowledge.

'Where was the Woodwhite recently discovered?'

That was easy: in woods near Godalming, Surrey. She tapped it in.

The next question appeared on screen.

'How many staircases are there in the Palace of Westminster?'

She stopped short. She'd referred to this recently in an interview; she couldn't remember which one. Someone was trying to reach her. Or was she being paranoid, as only a politician can be? But it was with caution that she wrote: 'One hundred.'

The screen cleared and third question came up.

'Who is the mother of eight-year-old Katie and six-year-old Samantha?'

She thought hard. Lots of people wanted her – wrote letters, made telephone calls, sent e-mail – although they were always vetted by one of her assistants. This person, she realised, wanted her alone;

and he or she had gone to some lengths to ensure it happened. Why? Whoever it was, it intrigued her. And it wasn't as if she *had* to meet them; she could always end the conversation, break the connection, then get them investigated if they turned out to be unpleasant or a lunatic.

She tapped in her own name and pressed 'send'.

The screen cleared, there was a minute's pause, and then text appeared:

'Minister, forgive my unorthodox approach but I feel it my duty to tell you . . .'

She uttered a cry at the contents. Then, although she'd absorbed most of the information at first reading, she read it through again. Her mind needed to accept it. She felt numb.

She looked up from the screen. It was as bad as it could be. This could ruin her. She closed her eyes. She could see the headlines, hear the newscasters and the presenters. All her precious, perfect publicity, all her hard work – overturned, gone for nought, herself slithering down into the abyss. She could kiss goodbye to her present job, to the leadership challenge, to her whole political future.

Her hand reached out for her private telephone, then paused.

With a great effort she stood up, feeling suddenly like an old, old woman. She moved stiffly to the door, not recognising herself – that haggard, grey face – as she passed the mirror above the mantelpiece.

In the outer office, Sebastian looked up.

'I'm going out for a short while,' she told him.

'The nurses are already downstairs, Minister.'

'I shan't be very long,' she said, putting on her coat and walking out.

The Gilbert parents were arguing. From half-way down the corridor West could hear the angry voices cutting through the ward's hum, providing interest for the two nurses on duty at the desk who, seeing his approach, quickly busied themselves with other things.

He paused in front of them. 'Dr West.' He addressed the older woman distantly, not meeting her eyes.

'Oh, thank goodness! I mean, they've been waiting for you, Doctor. They'll be pleased to see you. They're in Room Ten at the end, next to the fire-escape.'

He walked on. The quarrelling became louder. 'For God's sake, Rose!' he heard. 'She's six years old. Your mother says she's crying her eyes out. She wants her mummy, God help her!'

West rounded the corner into the room. It struck him as quite amazing that, throughout the verbal barrage, the baby in the cot by the wall had slept. West's eyes travelled over him, noting the pale skin, the pile of pillows stacked on the shelf above his head; noticing too that he was being watched by a small girl in a blue gingham dress and red cardigan. She was squatting on the floor between the cot and a bed, her hands covering her ears. She turned her eyes on West as if she was expecting him to help her.

'Oh!' The parents both said it at once and jumped apart, the mother taking a step towards the crib and the father coming forwards.

'Doctor.' The man cleared his throat. He looked relieved, and West also saw recognition in his eyes – recognition which he failed to share for either of them. He took the proferred hand and shook it.

'My wife . . . We really . . . we've been a bit, well, very worried about Jeremy. We were just wondering if you could have a look at him.'

'Certainly.' West had been worried that it would be difficult, but he saw in a flash that it wouldn't, that the parents wanted him to take the baby, carry him off for tests.

They'd be disappointed if he didn't. He was the doctor they'd been waiting for.

An injection of air into a vein. Death would come very quickly; the child might not even cry out. Even if he did, who'd hear that tiny sound? West already knew where he was going to do it: in the small treatment room at the end of the ward. Afterwards he'd slip out, find a phone, let Stockart know that he'd performed the task, and tell him – West swallowed at the mere thought – that he'd also 'dealt with' Mel.

'Doctor?'

He blinked. The mother was crying now, standing there with head lowered, her hand touching the baby's, her tears dropping on his face. The father was holding the baby out to him, a bundle for transference, his eyes begging West's for help.

'The intern said there wasn't anything wrong, but could you just . . . ?'

West didn't hear him, didn't see him. He heard instead the unfathomable language of that Albanian peasant, saw not the lightly tanned, fresh face of Mr Gilbert, but the wrinkled, desperate visage of that other father.

'Please, Doctor.'

If he didn't take the bundle now, the man would drop it. If he took it, the baby would die in his arms. West trembled at the awfulness of it all.

Now the baby was waking, one small fist flailing in the air. A spasm, precursor of death. West's mouth dropped open. He took a step back, away.

'Doctor?' The man was coming at him with it, expecting him to save it.

West's eyes flickered. He had to get away. 'It's not my field,' he blurted.

'No, we know. But, well, my wife . . . we really trust you. And you're a doctor, aren't you?'

'I'll get you a specialist,' he croaked and backed out of the door, shutting it, looking once towards the top of the ward at the empty nurses' station, to the doors beyond and the main staircase, his rooms above. Mel . . .

He opened the door to the fire-escape and ran.

The blood was pounding in Davenport's head.

When the first two questions had been answered correctly, and then there'd been that awful pause, he'd had to close his eyes and count very slowly. At ninety-nine he'd opened them and she'd been there, her name and personal e-mail address in front of him.

Now he wasn't quite sure what to do with himself.

On one level he felt completely exhausted. There was nothing more for him to do, he realised. Mrs Tyler had all the relevant facts; it was in the hands of the government now. But on another he was far too keyed up to be able to sit still.

He got up and walked around the room, wondering what the minister's first step would be. Obviously she would need to check the information, ensure that it was not a stupid prank – although she'd have been able to see instantly that her informer knew what he was talking about.

He would be called to give evidence, of course. But it was

something, he'd decided, crossing his hands behind his back, that he would be prepared to do. He'd been lied to by Stockart. He'd been used. He looked down at Philippa's photograph in the newspaper. She would understand; she would applaud his courage.

He was like – and he stood still, the better to imagine the scene – the lone voice in the wilderness. The wolves might be circling at his door, but he simply had to keep calm and wait.

He scowled. He wished he hadn't thought about wolves. It reminded him about those two in the car outside. His pleasant daydreams fled. What if Stockart managed to get word to them before he was arrested? He tried to block out the horrid thought, but it had taken hold. He went quickly to his landing look-out at the top of the stairs. He couldn't be certain – the day was dark and it was snowing again – but, yes, he was sure the car was there, lurking among the trees.

He didn't want to be on his own any more.

Well, there was no reason that he should.

He nipped back into the bedroom, picked up the laptop and ran down into the kitchen. He stopped only to grab his hooded jacket and check that his car-keys were in the pocket. He would go into work, he told himself, slamming the door behind him. Maybe even call Stockart with a phoney progress report! He snickered at the brilliance of the idea. It would never do to start acting out of character, to give Stockart a moment's suspicion at such a stage.

He reached his car. He was sorely tempted to look over his shoulder to where he was sure the other car was half-hidden, but instead he opened his door with dignity, got in and started the ignition.

'You wait,' he mouthed at his unseen watchers. 'Just you wait. You're going to be so sorry. You and Stockart and West, all of you.'

It was, Sasha thought, like the aftermath of an earthquake. The shock kept seizing her in waves.

Branium, the industry's gods, the government's darling (God! They were going to crucify Philippa), to the company that was going to make Britain great again, Europe's prize, the world leader.

Branium, the unspeakable monster, breaking the law to create its own brand of life, killing to protect itself.

She shuddered, made herself concentrate on the road, or rather the back of the milk-lorry that was throwing up muddy slush on to her windscreen. This was her biggest story ever. In fact, just about the biggest she'd heard of. People talked sci-fi about genetics companies, what really went on in their laboratories – she remembered the fuss there'd been over genetically engineered tomatoes, cloned sheep, pigs and mice being genetically bred to produce human organs – but imagine the uproar, she thought, when she revealed that Branium was manufacturing its own brand of life!

Somehow she must find out where Bramium's baby labs were – if not at REDEV, then wherever. She needed to get inside, to see for herself, to – and her stomach tightened with excitement – get a photographer in too. This story was absolutely sensational. It was going to make her.

And it was Gerry, she acknowledged, sobering, whom she had to thank. Without him she'd still be pootling around in circles going nowhere. Gerry, she told the dead man silently, I owe you one. And that one, she promised herself, was going to be the exposure of his murderers.

Impossible, she thought, seeing her speedo drop to ten miles an hour as the traffic condensed, to imagine an outfit like Branium endorsing murder. She'd have to prove it, which wasn't going to be easy. Where, she wondered, had it all gone wrong for them? What had happened to tip the company over the edge? To make them go to such extraordinary lengths to safeguard their secrets? She was freshly stunned at the scale of the thing. She supposed that, for Branium, it had simply been one step at a time down a slippery slope.

In front, the lorry's brake-lights went on. Another standstill, she thought. She wasn't going to be in a position to write the story that week, she realised. There was too much to do, too much to prove to the lawyers before publication, too much simply to find out. For example, how it was possible to maintain life artificially? She tried again to imagine what a glass womb looked like. She could only think it was akin to an incubator for premature babies. If Branium had already done that, she wondered, what else had they done?

In her *Comment* piece on Philippa Tyler they'd used a picture of the company's headquarters, a vast modern building with plenty of chrome, very anonymous and discreet, unimpeachable in the heart of London. To accuse it of heinous crime . . . Sasha swallowed again, hard. Or the equally modern Mistletoe hospital, pale yellow stone and tinted windows, built to blend in on the Embankment, with nice views of the river and not-so-nice views of poor NHS St Peter's on the south bank.

'Bridge the gap.' Tyler's words suddenly rang clearly in her ear. Poor woman, Sasha thought again. Although it wasn't fair, once the story was out, she was going to be in for a rough ride from her critics. It was the way she'd so publicly sang Branium's praises, jumped in with both feet, waving their flag, pushing them in everyone's faces . . . Yes, poor Tyler. But what another gold nugget for Sasha!

No smugness now, she warned herself. She'd still a long way to go. On her left she saw a signpost for Appledore, just four miles away. She shivered again, but not from the cold. She was going to have to be very careful indeed. It's OK, she told herself, you're a journalist, they're not going to harm you. She buried the little voice that came echoing back out of her subconscious. Accidents, and other things – she nodded to give herself credence – happened to other people. To amateurs, not to professionals such as herself.

She braked gently, picked up the mobile and put it in front of her on the wheel. She wanted to speak to Charlie – not to be deterred from what she was going to do, she assured herself, but to hear his affirmation, his belief that she would be all right. As she switched it on she heard the warning bleep which meant the signal was too weak to allow a call. 'Shit,' she said aloud.

She replaced the phone and switched on the radio as a distraction.

'A local man has been found dead close to Dungeness Nuclear power station. Clive Lucas, 24, is the second person from the West Kent area to have been found dead in a similar location within the past two weeks.'

Oh great, she thought. The connection had been made. The nationals would pick it up, and the area would soon be jumping with other journalists. She edged round a bend in the road and saw an ambulance and a police car ahead, verification of the cause of the hold-up. A policeman in a yellow cape was walking slowly along the line of traffic, talking to the drivers, presumably telling them what was going on. He was coming in her direction. She felt ridiculously guilty and forced herself to keep her eyes on the road, telling herself that she hadn't actually done anything wrong – but she was none the less immeasurably glad when the man went by and she could continue, creeping forward, to her journey's end.

The sleet stung Philippa's face, making her eyes water. She'd forgotten her gloves, and now her hands were red-raw, ugly and old-looking. It hurt her to see them like that; she had always been vain about her hands, never wanted them to age. She tried to put them in her pockets but they were sewn up tightly, so, as she walked, she wrenched at the threads until they were loose enough to squeeze her fingers inside. She pursed her lips. She must be in quite a state, she told herself, to have left her gloves behind.

'There is nothing that is done that cannot be undone.' In times of shock or trouble she would find herself repeating homely phrases, being comforted by them. It was no wonder, she thought, shuddering, that she was saying them now.

A passing businessman stared and she dropped her head. It would not do to be identified. She pulled the headscarf lower and kept her eyes on the pavement, on the quickly melting whiteness. It was far too bitter a day to be out walking, but she'd had no option.

Once out of her office, unnoticed under the headscarf (even by the doorman, who always drew himself up, muttering 'Minister' in reverent tones), she'd taken a series of small roads, moving furtively away from Westminster and those who knew her, towards Leicester Square. Anyone following her would have been mystified by her progress – not that anyone *was* following her, she reassured herself quickly. The morning's events had made her understandably nervous.

She rounded a corner. A gust of wind caught her, nearly sending her off-balance, but she had seen her goal, and congratulated herself on remembering its whereabouts. There were two booths, one of which was empty. She flung open the door and stepped inside. For a moment she savoured the sheer pleasure of shelter; then coldness from the gap near the ground caught at her ankles and whipped up her legs, and she smelled the stench of old urine.

She picked up the telephone, prepared to dial the number, and saw with disbelief that the equipment was out of order. She stared at the man in the next box, willing him to hurry, to appreciate that her call was of supreme urgency.

CHAPTER THIRTY-FOUR

Normally, when he was on night-shifts, Charlie had no difficulty in sleeping for a full eight hours. On this occasion, however, his sleep had been fitful and punctured by foul dreams. At eleven o'clock, coming suddenly awake from one, he was glad to get up. On his way to the bathroom, still half-asleep, he was momentarily startled by the sound of the TV. Then he remembered about Mike. He nipped quietly down the corridor before he could be spotted.

Under the shower's burst of hot water he came properly awake, and wondered what Sasha was doing, whether she was OK. He realised that he had to speak to her immediately to find out, and that he could do so from there, on the bathroom phone. Hopping out, snatching at a towel, he lifted the receiver, concentrated briefly on the number of her mobile, and dialled it.

'It has not been possible to connect your call . . .'

'Shit,' he said loudly and crashed it back on the cradle.

He slipped back to his room, calling out 'Hi' in Mike's general direction, and dressed quickly. Re-emerging, he heard the familiar jingle of one of the cable news programmes, and remembered that he hated TV in the morning. Then he reminded himself of his duties as a host – and of Mike's age, vulnerability and temporary status there –

and entered the sitting-room, asking as cheerfully as he could whether Mike had slept well.

'No.' Mike sniffed. 'I had bad dreams.'

'Me too. Coffee?'

There was no answer. Charlie went through to the kitchen, took down the coffee beans, ground some and found a saucepan to make scrambled eggs. This, he told himself, cracking the eggs expertly with one hand, was what he ought to have been doing for Sasha. He made mean scrambled eggs – and with smoked salmon – perfect.

He looked up suddenly; he thought he'd heard a cry.

'Mike?'

The sound of the TV continued indistinctly. It must have been that that he'd heard, he thought, and resumed his task, opening the fridge for the milk, searching in the drawer for a fork.

'Charlie?'

The voice made him jump. Mike's face, the dark-circled eyes staring in shock, the colourless lips trembling, made him drop what he was doing. The fork clattered to the floor. 'What's happened?' he demanded, seizing the boy's arm.

Mike made a gagging sound. Charlie got him to a chair and squatted down to his level. 'What's wrong?' he asked again, more urgently, but just then he caught the newscaster's voice.

'. . . whether there was any connection between the two dead men. Gerald Winston, whose body was . . .'

Charlie started.

'It's Lucas,' Mike muttered dully.

'He's dead?'

'. . . The body of the second man, found at dawn today, was positively identified a few minutes ago by his brother, Simon Lucas. Clive Lucas, 24, had been missing for—'

Charlie stood up, reached for the remote control and turned off the set. He glanced down at Mike, saw that he was trembling badly, and tried to remember what one was supposed to do with shock victims.

Then Mike began to cry in great heaving sobs.

'Oh, Mike.' Charlie bent down and put a clumsy arm around the boy's shoulders. 'I'm so sorry, kid.'

'They said it's murder. They killed him too.'

'Yeah.' Mike's tears were making his shirt wet. 'They did.'

Mike raised his blotchy face. 'You knew?'

Charlie took a deep breath. 'Sasha found out last night that he was missing.'

'Why didn't she tell me?'

'She didn't want to worry you.'

Mike stared, and the tears continued to flow. 'What about Chris?'

Oh brother, Charlie thought, trying to find the words.

'He's dead too, isn't he?'

'I'm, er . . .' He swallowed, gave a quick nod. 'I'm afraid so, Mike. Yes.'

'How?' Mike's voice was toneless. Charlie supplied brief details, then started to say what Sasha had said, that it was possible Manyon's death had been caused by drink-driving, but when he saw Mike's expression he stopped.

'Is there anything else?' Mike asked.

'That we haven't told you? No. And it was only because, well . . .'

'I'm a kid.' Mike gave a long, quivering sigh and turned his head away. 'It's my fault,' he whispered finally. 'I killed them.'

'You did not. Mike, look at me.'

Slowly, Mike did what he'd asked. He looked terrible, Charlie thought. He said, 'You did *not* kill them, Mike. There are some evil bastards out there responsible for that. You and I and Sasha know that. And once we find out who they are, we're going to get them.'

Mike stared glassily. 'D'you think the others are OK? I mean, really?'

Charlie had to think for a moment. 'Mary and the others, you mean?' The last thing they'd done before leaving AGN was check on the Tenterden Four. There'd been nothing new about them. He nodded firmly. 'Really, I do.'

Mike fell silent for a few minutes. Charlie hoped that the worst was over, that he'd done and said the right things, and that Mike wasn't going to be emotionally traumatised for life.

'When's Sasha going to write the story?' Mike croaked suddenly.

'As soon as she can.'

'Is she on her way back now?'

Charlie got to his feet. 'I hope so.'

'Are you worried about her?' Mike studied his face.

'Yeah. I am rather.'

'Me too,' Mike said quietly, and he looked away again.

Anna heard the first mention of the body's discovery on the radio news at eleven o'clock.

At 11.25 McMahon called her to say that the journalist was now up and about, and that the boy had suddenly become very upset about something.

Anna was channel-hopping with the sound off. She paused on one of the cable stations and increased the volume so that she could hear the commentary. 'Perhaps he's just seen the news,' she suggested.

'Ah. Yes, that makes sense.'

'What's he doing now?' She found that she genuinely felt quite curious.

'Just sitting. The journalist's in the kitchen.'

'Keep me informed.'

At long last the milk-lorry turned off the road. Sasha watched with loathing as it lumbered away up a farm-track. It had delayed her progress considerably, had given her too much time to think about what lay ahead, what she was going to say, precisely – whether she was being entirely wise.

She saw the sign for Appledore and nudged her speed up. It was too late for turning back now, she told herself. Besides, she knew that once she was actually out of the car and walking up to the security booth, the right words, the appropriate body-language, everything, would come to her. She opened the window a crack, got a blast of freezing air, and shut it again quickly.

Appledore, she saw, entering the village, was preparing itself for Christmas. In spite of the snow – although admittedly there was less of it now – two men in overalls were up ladders, stringing coloured lights above the high street. Christmas, she thought. Her mother picking fault with Sasha's two small nieces and her sister getting tearful over the turkey. Of course, it didn't have to be like that, she told herself, watching one of the workmen attempting to fix a reindeer to a lamppost. She didn't *have* to go home. No, this Christmas could be different: herself and Charlie snuggled up under her duvet, making love, watching TV, eating when they felt like it . . . Bliss.

She'd think of an excuse to give her mother.

She left the village behind her, her destination now minutes away, and realised that she wasn't afraid any longer. She was looking forward to the confrontation.

On his desk, the telephone rang again. Stockart glared, felt the worm in his stomach writhe, before picking up the reciever.

'Yes?' he said quickly.

'Is that John?'

Stockart knew the voice instantly, though he seldom heard it over the phone. 'Yes,' he said, feeling very strange.

'You haven't been telling me everything, have you, John?'

'Everything?' he repeated stupidly.

'Everything hasn't been quote "going great" unquote, has it?'

'I'm sorry, I . . .' Not many people possessed the power to faze him, but she always had – from the first time he'd seen her, speaking at a university debate, when he'd fancied himself in love with her.

'Let's not play games, John. There's too much at stake. Discounting your career – which I do – there's mine to consider. Or hadn't you thought of that?' There was a hard edge of anger to her voice now. 'You told me that any minor problems – those were your exact words, John – had been ironed out. That I needn't have any worries. You told me that the name of Branium was going to be greater than that of Louis Pasteur. You told me it would be a move of political brilliance to link my name with theirs.'

But it hadn't been love he'd felt for Philippa Tyler, although as an eighteen-year-old undergraduate he'd confused her bewildering effect on him – his almost painful desire to be with her, to study her moves, hang on to her every word – for that. It had been her power that he'd craved, he'd come to realise later, her astonishing belief in herself, the certainty that she would attain whatever she desired, even back then. Those things had attracted him like a moth to a flame, and he'd followed her around slavishly. She was two years his senior, and she'd been flattered, amused by his adulation – but not sufficiently to be persuaded into sleeping with him.

After she'd graduated, he'd concentrated his efforts on his study and slowly her effect on him had faded. Then, during his final year, on the employers' 'milk-round', she'd been sitting there behind a desk, smiling at him. She was working for the nuclear power industry, in its PR department. Why didn't he apply? she'd urged him. The industry was new and growing; besides, it was the government's darling. The job would be an excellent first step for him. She'd some influence, she'd murmured; she'd put his name forward.

On Stockart's first day she'd lightly shrugged off his thanks – 'We're friends, John' – she was hissing at him like a snake. 'You didn't tell me, did you, John, that your bouncing baby boys have all got Leukaemia?'

'For God's sake!' His eyes cut round the room. 'How did you . . .' He gulped. 'I mean—'

'How did I find out? Well, John, apart from your other glaring inadequacies, it appears you're incapable of maintaining a tight ship. I had a message via the Internet about an hour ago.'

'On the Inter—' He was starting to hyperventilate. He could feel the serpent twisting and turning, sucking out his air.

'Oh, don't worry. It was for My Eyes Only. Sorry, has that shocked you?'

He could only gasp.

'My commiserations. But imagine my shock, John, to realise that one's been hoodwinked by an old and trusted friend.'

They'd never been friends; they'd helped each other out – very occasionally, and to their mutual benefit – over the years. A word here, a name there.

'I . . .' he stuttered.

'Tell me,' her voice was quicksand, 'did you get some kind of kick out of lying to me?'

He closed his eyes, sucked back the air, forcing the worm down. She was strong. She'd always been strong, but she'd always been on his side before. Now he had to fight her.

'I swear to you . . .' The words came out in a croak. 'One moment.' He counted to ten, mustered all his strength, spoke again: 'I've only just found out about the problems myself.' That was much better. He sounded calmer and his mind was clearing, its own master again, marshalling its defences, its thoughts racing ahead of him as he continued: 'It's only been confirmed in the last couple of days. I was, of course, going to let you know.'

'Of course. So considerate of you. Unfortunately, someone in my position cannot afford to be quite so magnanimous. I'm afraid I'm about to embark on a damage-limitation exercise.'

'No, Philippa.' He spoke with some authority now. He knew precisely what he was going to do. It was perfectly obvious. He'd always known, he acknowledged in that moment, that one day he'd have to play this card.

'Yes, John. I'm about to inform my PR people that I've had a change of heart, that I'm divorcing Branium. Oh, they'll gripe, but they'll think of something, a good reason why. If they don't I could always give them an inkling of the truth . . .'

'No, Philippa,' he said again.

'I'm afraid so. At least I'm giving you notice – which is more than you gave me. Although actually, to be truthful, I wanted to hear you squirm.'

She hadn't realised yet that the power-base had shifted. Poor Philippa, Stockart thought: she would hate to lose control. In that way they were very similar. 'You're not going to do that,' he told her softly.

She laughed. 'Watch me. I'm a professional, John. I thought you were too – it's how we've always worked. But you've just dropped the ball.'

He leaned back in his chair. 'You're not going to issue any statement. Nothing's going to change.'

'Have you gone stark staring mad?' She gave an incredulous, tinkling laugh. 'How can you possibly imagine that you have any influence over anything I do?'

He spun a whole circle in his chair. It was supple black leather, made for him, designed to fit every contour of his body. On the wall opposite was a Lowry painting, stick-people hurrying home from a factory in the north. He'd put it up there to remind himself of his roots, and the silent promise he'd made that once he'd severed them he would never return.

'Those readings, Philippa . . .' he murmured.

'What on earth are you talking about?' She sounded quite ill-humoured now, really rather nasty. 'You really have lost it, haven't you, John? You'd better pop along to your company quack and get a few tranquillisers. You're going to need them.'

'The ones that went off the scale.'

'The *what?*' But she knew what he was talking about; he could hear it in her voice.

He smiled. 'You remember, Philippa,' he went on in the same velvety tone. 'Think back. September the twenty-ninth, 1978.'

Now it was her turn to make gagging noises. 'What about it?' she said hoarsely after a few moments.

'I think it's time to tell the story.'

'You can't mean that.' She tried another trill of laughter.

'Oh, but I do.' He turned a half-circle towards the picture window. Through it, on the other side of the street, was the back of another building, office workers going about their business, little people doing as they were told. 'Call it a guilty conscience or what you will.' He toyed with the band of his Rolex. 'But I've got to get it off my chest, Philippa. Tell it as it really was. Surely you can understand that?'

In the PR department of Nuclear Industries, Stockart and Philippa had made an excellent team: he being the more imaginative; she the steadying, maturer influence. In only a few months they'd made considerable headway in their two main tasks – to quieten public fears about nuclear power, and to discredit nuclear protesters. When the head of their tiny department had retired, Philippa was appointed in his place and Stockart became her deputy. She had toured the country's schools, and he'd become increasingly involved in (and found he had a liking for) the covert dirty warfare being conducted against CND.

Their work had continued uneventfully until one morning in late September, 1978. There'd been a radioactive spill from the power plant at Ayrton on the westernmost tip of Scotland. Neighbouring homes and premises had been evacuated, the beach closed, the whole area sealed off as a precaution. No one knew exactly how bad the leak was, but from a PR point of view it was already disastrous. Philippa and Stockart had been despatched in panic.

But the news that had greeted their arrival was terrific. The leak had been minuscule. Readings taken from within a mile radius of the site indicated that the radiation levels were only slightly higher than usual, and still well within the normal range – even on the beach, by the waste-pipe where it was thought the leak that had originated. There'd been no need to evacuate anyone.

Philippa and Stockart had looked at each other and whooped.

Then they'd hit the phones, notifying head office, the local police and the news agencies. In time for the early evening news, Ayrton's nuclear disaster had been downgraded to a scare, and people were filmed returning to their homes and places of work.

To be absolutely on the safe side, the press release that he and Philippa devised had added that the beach bordering the site would remain closed for three more days to enable further tests to be carried out. Nuclear Industries was aware that this would rule out the annual shinty match and beach-party due in two days' time, and to make amends – and also to thank everyone for evacuating so promptly and calmly (the latter being in many instances untrue) – Nuclear Industries would host a beach party extravaganza at the weekend.

'Pending on the levels?' one journalist had quickly asked.

'Well, of course,' Stockart had responded airily.

The levels had remained roughly the same all week. Then, on Friday morning, as Philippa had been putting the final touches to the party plans and Stockart had been packing his briefcase ready for departure, there'd been a knock at the door. The health physics monitor, a young man Stockart's age (and, as Stockart had been, half in love with Philippa), had entered. At first he'd been unable to speak, and when he had, he'd scarcely been coherent, but finally he'd gathered his wits sufficiently and it had come out in a rush, a torrent pouring over them, drowning them in its wake.

When the leak occurred, he'd told them, he'd used new instruments to take the readings – instruments that had just arrived from America, boasting a far greater degree of accuracy than anything else on the market, including the old British counters. 'I *assumed* – stupidly . . . God! I can't believe how stupid I've been . . .'

Stockart and Philippa had waited in mute terror. They'd liked the guy; he was the only person they'd dealt with at the station near their age.

'I'm afraid I assumed that the base-levels on the American monitoring devices – the starting points – were the same as the British ones. But they're not. They start higher, a whole ten points higher. Which means . . . which means . . .' His mouth had worked uselessly.

'What?' Neither Stockart nor Philippa had been able to bear it.

The readings were utterly wrong. They were wildly out. The beach was hot, burning with radiation. The readings he'd just taken using his old counter – by mistake he'd picked it up rather than the American one that morning – were off the scale.

The next few minutes had passed in a blur, the monitor's voice becoming a drone, saying that of course he'd tender his resignation at once; the site itself wasn't too bad, nor the village – much of the radioactivity had dispersed by now, probably gone out over the sea – but the beach . . . Naturally it would have to be closed again and sealed, and probably the entire area evacuated.

'No.'

Both Stockart and the other man had stared at Philippa.

'We're not closing the beach,' she'd said, and there'd been in her that steely determination that Stockart knew so well even then. Physically, he'd wanted to cling to her for safety.

'But . . .' the monitor had started.

She'd ignored him, turning to Stockart. 'It'll ruin us.' She'd sounded quite calm; only by her rapid blinking had he been able to gauge the depth of her fear. 'We'd be a laughing stock. They'd never believe us again. We'd be finished.'

She'd turned slowly to the other man and Stockart had followed her gaze. 'Where are these readings?' she'd demanded.

He'd handed them over, both sets. 'You . . . you see, Philippa, John . . . the differences? That graph's the American, and this one's the . . .'

She'd picked up the British readings, glanced over at Stockart. He'd known what she intended to do, and had nodded briefly in support. She'd given them to him, and he'd torn them neatly in half and dropped them in the waste-paper bucket.

'We'll go by the American readings,' Philippa had said, quite calmly, in the same voice she'd used minutes before to select the choice of sandwiches for the party.

'We can't do that! They're wrong, I'm telling you! The levels down there are dangerous!'

'Safety levels are always changing. Aren't they, John?'

'All the time,' he'd said.

'But it'd be criminal!'

Stockart and Philippa had allowed the word to die on the man's lips. He was a married man with a one-year-old son and a new baby on the way. 'Criminal negligence,' Stockart had murmured into the silent air, and Philippa had followed up with, 'We'd do what we could for you, of course – but it *was* your mistake, after all.'

He'd been terrified, in awe of them, had agreed to do anything they said. With Stockart looking on, he'd destroyed the British monitoring equipment, and later in the day had put his name to the official report of the 'Great Non-Leak' as it was called, verifying the readings as accurate. The beach had been duly opened and the party proceeded, although without Stockart or Philippa in attendance – both of them having been suddenly recalled to London, they'd said with much regret.

They hadn't discussed it on that journey home or since; they'd each put as much distance between themselves and the incident as they could. Philippa had left first, two months after the incident, taking a job in local government, and he'd quit a week after that, going into a cosmetics firm, telling himself that as time passed the chances of discovery diminished, although he knew that it would always be there, haunting him.

And then came the godsend: an explosion at Ayrton of the most dramatic kind, caused by irradiated reactor fuel being blasted out from a disposal site near the beach. There was a rerun of the evacuation, the sealing, and the inspection, and only when the radiation levels had returned to normal – and in fact, although the fire had been spectacular, there hadn't been very much escaping radiocative gas – was the site reopened. Two years later, when the first cancers started appearing in the children and the older people, it was the explosion that was blamed, even though the experts said it couldn't have been the cause. Everyone had forgotten about the non-leak, the disaster that had never been.

Stockart had privately thanked his good fortune – the same good fortune that, unknown at that time to either him or Philippa, had removed the only other threat to their successful futures: the health monitor. Although he'd continued to work at Ayrton, after a neighbour's child developed brain cancer the man had become increasingly moody, had turned to drink, and eventually, tragically, drowned one night after crazily going for a swim off the very beach that he'd once so carefully checked for danger.

Thus the secret had remained theirs alone, unspoken between them, but binding them together at the core, each one vouchsafing the other's safety. Indeed, so secure did Stockart feel nowadays that when Hall's people had dumped the first body at Sizewell, the location had registered no more than a subconscious 'click' on his inner-warning scale. Hall's choice of Dungeness for the third corpse had struck Stockart as faintly coincidental, that was all.

He wondered now what Philippa's reaction would be if he told her of his own connection with those matters. But on second thoughts she sounded freaky enough. His mission at the moment was to bring her safely back within his control.

'But John . . .' Another hysterical trill. 'I-if . . .' He heard her try to calm herself again. 'If you did that it'd bring you down too.'

He toyed with his watch's metal wristband. 'I'm not so sure that it would, actually, Philippa.'

'What d'you mean?'

'You were my boss, remember?'

'John.' She gurgled again.

In the background he heard a rush of noise, a man saying 'How much longer . . .' before the sound was muffled. Waiting, Stockart wondered for the first time where she was.

'You've no proof,' she blurted.

'No?' He pulled the wristband away and let it fall back, pinching his skin, saw through the window that some of the secretaries opposite were putting up tinsel and red paper bells. It was, or would soon be, the time for office Christmas parties. 'Did you ever wonder what became of those readings, Philippa? The British ones, or should I say the *accurate* ones?'

'You tore them up.' But she couldn't keep the question out of her voice, or the dread.

'But what did I do with the pieces?'

There was silence at the other end.

A frisson ran through him. 'Imagine the public outrage,' he crooned.

She was panting. 'I don't see what good you think it'll do you,' she rasped.

'Oh, I'm not talking about good, Philippa. You misunderstand me. What I'm saying is, there's no way I'm going down without taking you with me. Is that clear enough?'

'You—'

'Mmm. I know.' He did know, too.

He let her ponder her options, started a mental stopwatch, timing her.

'What d'you want me to do?' she whispered after less than a minute.

The moment was a beautiful one. He lingered over it. 'Nothing,' he said softly, picking up a paper-clip from his desk. 'I'll handle it. Leave it to me.'

After she'd gone, he replaced the reciever carefully and turned slowly to the PC on his desk. He hit a few keys, found what he was looking for, and grew very still. Then, still slowly, not looking at what he was doing, he unbent the paper-clip in his hand until it formed one wavy metal line. Someone watching might have assumed that he was deep in thought – important thoughts, for his eyes were distant and his face was drained of colour. Then he snapped back the metal, breaking it, and bent forward over his desk, his eyes gleaming now, a thin smile playing upon his lips.

CHAPTER THIRTY-FIVE

There was a limit, Davenport told himself, to how long he could continue this charade. He'd already typed the same final sentence of his report over twenty times. He suppressed a giggle. It was not a time for laughing, but he was excited. Besides, he kept seeing the look on Stockart's face when the police burst in.

He lowered his head and sniggered again. By now, he thought, inquiries would definitely be underway. Possibly a team of inspectors was already at the Mistletoe demanding to see the medical records, firing questions at Dr West. Davenport could imagine the uproar, the disbelief among the staff. But he wasn't terribly concerned about that. He cracked his knuckles. It was the next bit, when the police stormed into the foyer at Branium, ran up the stairs, fanned out down the corridors and smashed down Stockart's door, dragging him out in chains . . .

He looked up, remembering the hidden cameras in his office, and with an effort pulled his face into serious lines and switched on the PC. He was, after all, supposed to be there using it because it was so much quicker, with its direct line into the company's database, than the laptop. He hit some keys and bent forward to stare at the screen as if he'd truly summoned up some data. Then he nodded to himself – he was becoming quite delighted with his acting skills – and, drawing the laptop towards him, started to type a little.

How long would Stockart get? he wondered dreamily. Ten years? Or would it be longer? He only hoped that they wouldn't put him in one of those open prisons where they were allowed out and got to do gardening. Twenty-three hours a day locked up, that's what Stockart deserved, a hard bed in a cell with other psychopaths.

Davenport stopped typing. He'd just realised something. It was only a little mistake, but . . . He'd sent an e-mail message to Stockart that morning, telling him the report was finished, and here he was three hours later, still typing. Stockart was probably too busy to check on his messages – even if he did see Davenport's waiting for him, he probably wouldn't read it – but even so . . . Davenport licked his lips. At such a crucial stage, discrepancies mustn't happen. Nothing must happen to set Stockart wondering.

Davenport could withdraw the message very easily. It wouldn't take a minute. He turned back to the PC, genuinely now called up Branium's database, and stared at the screen.

'ACCESS DENIED', it said.

He frowned. This could not be. The PC, like his laptop, had a hard-coded password. The user had automatic access to the network; the PC was his passport.

He hit the key again. The message remained the same. He blinked rapidly. There had to be a mistake; the machine must be malfunctioning. He swivelled back to the laptop, saw in disbelief the same message.

He started to shake like a tree in a storm. If access was being denied on both machines, it could only mean one thing.

He snatched up the laptop, forgetting to switch it off, and slammed down its lid. He had one wild moment, seeing the phone, thinking to call Stockart, thinking of something . . . But he didn't have the time. He fled, nearly falling over a flex, reached the door, and flung it open.

'Who's that?' Mark called out as he ran past. 'Colin?'

He stopped at the outer door because he had to. The bloody swipe-card. He fumbled in his pocket. 'What if, what if . . . ?' he whimpered – and the worst *was* happening, the thing wasn't accepting him, the red light wasn't coming on.

The door swung into him and Sophie entered, cardboard boxes

stacked perilously under her chin. 'Ooh, you made me jump! I didn't see you there. Hey!'

He shoved past her, heard the boxes crash behind him, her mewling, the loud voice of Mark saying, 'Bloody maniac! Off his fuckin' trolley, I tell you.'

He gulped in air and ran.

Ahead, Sasha saw the brewery buildings and the turn-off for REDEV. She indicated right and reduced her speed, becoming aware as she did so of a terrible dryness in her mouth. One step at a time, she told herself. It was daylight in England. A simple request to speak to the press officer, then she'd take it from there. She waited in the middle of the road to allow a sudden stream of cars to pass and felt suddenly exposed, stranded there, felt that she was being watched. She peered up at the buildings and told herself that this was an ordinary little business park with innocent people at their desks, clock-watching, gossiping, wondering where to go for lunch that day, whether to risk the drive to Appledore and the pub or to stick with sandwiches from the vending machine . . .

In times of terror, the mundane was her survival kit.

The last car, an old one, seemed to be taking an age to pass. There must have been a slight incline that she hadn't noticed. 'Oh, come on,' she muttered under her breath. Her courage wouldn't last for ever. In fact, she decided on the spur of the moment, she'd just nip in before it . . .

She slammed on her brakes. A brown Citroën had shot out from the turn-off without regard to anything else on the road. She heard the screech of the oncoming car's brakes, heard herself scream as the Citroën slewed across in front of her, saw its back swing out, almost touching her – before it stalled.

For a moment Sasha caught sight of the driver's face, panic-stricken, mad-eyed, before he took off again. It had only been a glimpse, but it was enough.

'I know you,' she said softly, and shot off after him.

On the journey back from the telephone-box Philippa's head-scarf had slipped off, exposing her careful hair to the elements. She'd been vaguely aware of startled glances from passers-by, the doorman, Sebastian even, but all that she'd wanted – desperately

– to do was regain the sanctuary of her own room and close the door.

John Stockart had always been a determined man. She knew that, had admired it, praised him for it. What she had not recognised, she realised, was that he might be even more determined than she.

She ran her fingers through her hair. She'd done what Stockart had told her to do: wiped the memo from her computer. She stood up. The nurses were waiting. She felt a little peculiar still, rather wobbly around the knees, but she had to carry on. She had to believe that Stockart would do what he had promised and handle everything.

What did that mean, exactly? she wondered for the first time. How could he 'sort out' all those babies with Leukaemia? How could he ensure that there were to be no more leaks, that everything was sealed?

In her imagination, an awful chasm yawned. She mustn't, she thought in panic, look in; she must run from its edge. Just hold fast to that simple phrase: that he would handle it. Her brow puckered. What other option did she have?

She walked slowly to the fireplace and lifted her eyes to the mirror. She gave a little cry. Her hair, battered by the rain, had fallen down and now hung in dark rats' tails about her face. And her face! Her hand flew to her mouth. No wonder the commissionaire had not saluted her. Her mascara had run and smudged, her eyes looked wild and too heavily lined; her whole face seemed to have dropped. She looked old, terribly old.

'Oh my dear,' she burst out, stepping back. She had to rescue herself. She felt a spurt of her old energy return and moved swiftly to the small cupboard in the corner by the window. Inside were her 'emergency supplies': make-up, brushes and hair spray, even a small hair-dryer.

Plugging it in beside her desk, she buzzed Sebastian on the intercom. 'You can show the nurses in in five minutes.'

She blinked. She had sounded much as she usually did. Why, she thought, experiencing a little thrill of revelation, all she had to do was act calmly and everything would be normal!

'Yes, Minister. Um . . .'

'Yes, Sebastian?'

'I hope you don't mind me asking, but is everything all right?'

'Oh quite, thank you. I was foolish to get caught in the rain, that's all. You should have told me what a sight I looked,' she added reproachfully.

'Um, yes, Minister. I'm sorry. Should I bring you in some tea?'

'There's not time. I can't keep those nurses waiting any longer. Afterwards will do.'

Extraordinary. She switched on the hair-dryer and started work. Her mother had always said that the best cure for shock was hard work. And if things couldn't be mended they'd best be endured. Life could be as simple or as complicated as one made it.

She looked back into the room. Everything was ready for her visitors. The four of them would be seated facing her in upright chairs, as befitted a formal meeting with those she deemed to be bringing their begging bowls. On her desk were the photographs of the children and their father, and her small collection of gold and blue china butterflies. They were her talisman. She extended a finger to touch one, but stopped. Suddenly she wasn't sure she wanted them there at all. No, they cluttered up her desk.

She put the hair-dryer down, opened her desk drawer and swept them all inside. That was better, she told herself. She finished her hair and took her make-up bag over to the mirror. It was funny, she thought, glancing at the beautiful gold butterfly on the mantelpiece, she wasn't sure whether or not she was beginning to tire of butterflies. Just the thought of them were making her feel . . . not quite in command.

She might get Sebastian to rid the room of them.

CHAPTER THIRTY-SIX

It was clear to Tony Holland that the woman was already regretting her decision to call the police. Liz Pearce had sounded eager, even desperate, he'd been told, on the telephone – but since his and Julie Myers's arrival she'd been off-hand, inviting them into her home with a show of reluctance. Now, leaning back against her washing-machine, she was eyeing them suspiciously and occasionally glancing over at her sister for support.

'Mrs Pearce,' Julie smiled patiently. 'You said when you spoke to me on the phone that Michael knows Mary Kennedy.'

'Yeah.' Her hand reached for a packet of cigarettes on the side. The air, Holland noticed, was already choked with smoke. 'She's been here a couple of times. What of it?'

'You said that Michael's been missing for five days?'

'No.' Liz Pearce lit her cigarette slowly, inhaled deeply.

'I'm sorry, that's what I thought you'd said.'

'I said,' she spoke with emphasis, 'that he's been gone since Thursday night. He was staying with his brother.' She paused and Holland saw that the hand holding the cigarette started to tremble.

'But he's not any more?' Julie prompted.

'He's, er . . .' she faltered.

'Don't upset yourself, love,' said her sister.

Liz sniffed. 'Dave – that's my older boy – he phoned this morning.' She studied the floor. 'He said Mike had left some things. He said,' she gulped, 'Mikey left on Saturday afternoon.'

'But he's phoned you since then,' reminded the sister.

'Yeah, but . . .'

'It's not knowing where he is,' Julie suggested gently.

'That's it.' Liz looked grateful. She stubbed out her cigarette, lit another.

'On top of the visit you had last week,' Julie went on, 'from the two uniformed officers you told me about . . .'

Holland's pulse quickened. This was the turning point; he'd known it as soon as Julie had relayed the conversation. He'd ceased to brood on the fact that a rival had got the Dungeness murder that morning, grabbed his coat and left with Julie. Jem had driven, had wanted to come in too, and was waiting resignedly outside now.

Liz Pearce gave a quick nod. 'You found out any more about them?'

Holland cleared his throat. 'They do appear to have been bogus, Mrs Pearce.'

She stared at him; they all did, as if the news was a total shock, even though the sisters must have suspected, even though it had been Julie who'd done the checks.

'This village was not within the search area,' he continued quietly. 'In addition, there were no male and female officers out together making enquiries into the missing persons that morning.'

Liz bit her lip so hard that it went white. 'So who were they then?' she croaked. 'How come they knew Mike's name?

Holland caught Julie's eye. 'That's what we're here to find out,' he said soothingly. He nodded at a chair. 'D'you mind if we . . . ?'

'Yeah, all right. Sit down.'

Julie tried eking out a description but Liz Pearce, in common with most members of the public, saw police uniforms and stopped looking. They'd have to get the E-fit man in, Holland thought as she stumbled over ages, heights, hair colour.

'I'm sorry,' he said suddenly. 'What did you say?'

Liz blinked over at him. 'They said there'd been a burglary.'

REDEV, he thought instantly. He stared back at her. She hadn't mentioned anything about a burglary on the phone. 'You're sure of that?' he demanded.

The sister snorted. 'You heard her, didn't you?'

'It's all right.' Liz eyed him. 'They said Mikey and the four that's run off had all been involved in a burglary. My Mikey! I ask you.'

REDEV, he wondered again. Was it possible? He saw in his mind's eye the carefully concealed, purpose-built buildings, the high steel fencing, and the cut hole gaping. 'Does Michael know any of the other missing people?'

'What, apart from Mary?' She gave a shrug. 'He used to go to that school, so he must've known the teacher. He never said, though.'

Holland nodded at Julie, and she produced file pictures of Caroline Henshaw and Richley, which she passed over to Liz. It had to be REDEV, Holland thought. Nothing else he could think of fitted. Something crucial had been taken that night – so crucial that REDEV were willing to sanction the impersonation of police officers, knowing that they risked challenge or discovery, especially with so much genuine police activity about. Although, he acknowledged, that had probably been a calculated risk; many people would have assumed that they were part of the inquiry. But how – and he frowned at Liz's bent head – had they known who they were looking for and where to come?

There was a sudden clatter by the back door. 'Cat-flap,' Liz murmured without turning round. Then she pushed the pictures away. 'No, sorry,' she said. 'I don't know them.'

'Did they say anything else about the burglary?' Holland asked.

She sighed heavily. 'I can't remember.'

'Did they say what he was meant to have stolen?'

She shook her head. 'No, they never said, I'm sure. I've gone over and over it in my mind.' Her sister patted her arm. 'They said it was serious, that's all – that Mike was in trouble.' She looked up sharply. 'Is he?'

'Not with me.' Yet, Holland added silently.

She looked suddenly panicky. 'D'you think he's in danger?' D'you think maybe he's got caught up in something, and—'

'He called you last night, Lizzie.'

'Yeah,' Liz swung on her sister, 'but why's he been lying to me? Saying he's with Dave when he isn't? How do I know he's even with this journalist?'

'Journalist?' Julie inquired lightly.

Holland thought grimly of Sasha Downey. He'd suspected her all along.

'Charlie,' said Liz Pearce. 'That's what Mike said his name was.'

No surname, no clue as to where the man worked. Downey was freelance, Holland reminded himself; it was quite possible that she was doing the leg-work while Charlie, the main journalist, concerned himself with the source.

'Where was Mike . . .' That sounded too bald. 'Can you remember where Mike was a couple of Thursdays back? Late at night. Was he at home?'

'Why?'

'There was a burglary that night.'

'Mike wouldn't . . .' She trailed off, tipping another cigarette out of the packet and lighting it. 'A Thursday night?' she said dully. 'I'd have been working. Where was this burglary, then?'

Holland told her. From the blank look she gave him, it didn't seem to register. Then a shadow crossed her face.

'A drugs company? You're not telling me Mikey's got mixed up in drugs!' Her hand flew to her mouth. 'Oh my God, no!'

'It's all right, Lizzie.' The sister squeezed her tightly but she too looked scared.

'We don't think it's drugs, Mrs Pearce,' he said quickly. 'REDEV's a research site. As far as we can tell, drugs aren't manufactured there.'

'Oh, thank God.' Liz slumped with relief.

'But the burglary was serious. A gun was used.'

'A gun! Mike'd never use a gun!'

The sister shifted uneasily. 'Maybe you ought to call a solicitor, Lizzie.'

'What for?' She glared at her. 'You don't know him. None of you do.' Her voice fell to a whisper. 'Mike'd never hurt anyone. He's as soft as butter. Can't bear the thought of anything suffering.' She smiled mistily. 'You ought to see him with those guinea-pigs out there, or that stupid rabbit.' She swallowed. 'That's why he went on those demos.'

'Which demos, Liz?' Julie asked.

'Live animal exports. Sheep, calves, you know.' She blew out a cloud smoke. 'He went to a memorial one down at Shoreham, then the school took them all up to London for a youth rally. Your lot beat him up at Shoreham.' She gave Holland a dirty look. 'You're not setting him up, are you?'

'No,' he said, startled. On the floor, the cat meowed and butted his leg.

'That's what I thought their game was. Those phoney ones,' she added.

'I'm not setting anyone up, Mrs Pearce.' He took a pencil out of his pocket and thoughtfully placed it on the table. 'Does Mike belong to any animal welfare group?' he asked cautiously.

'No. Not that I know of.'

'He's never taken part in disrupting fox-hunts, for instance?'

She shook her head. At his knee the cat meowed again, and distractedly he stroked its fur. Michael Pearce was one of his missing raiders, he was sure of it. But what connected them all? And why hadn't he run with the others? Why had he gone to a journalist – or two – and what had he said to whet their appetites? The pencil rolled back and forth; under the table, he felt the cat's paws land lightly on his knee.

'He's on his own too much.' Liz Pearce gave a long shuddering sigh. 'I've got to work, see?' She wouldn't meet Holland's gaze. 'He's not a bad lad, whatever he's done.'

'I'm sure he's not.' Julie spoke sincerely.

Holland felt he was stumbling when he shouldn't be. 'Is there anything else that you want to tell us?' he asked hopefully.

'Well . . .'

The cat meowed loudly and she shushed it.

'Go on,' urged the sister.

Liz rubbed at the back of her neck. 'I've been a bit anxious about something. Probably just nerves, but . . . If those two could be so good as coppers, they could do other things, couldn't they?'

'Like what?' Holland asked.

Her eyes strayed to the wall. 'Bug telephones?' she blurted.

'Er, technically, it's—'

'Only, after they'd been I had this feeling someone had been in here – you know, tampering with it.' She gnawed at her lip, then said in a rush, 'And I told those two that Mike was up in Brixton with Dave, you see. And now I'm thinking . . .' She broke off.

It was possible. 'We'll get it checked,' Holland promised.

'Thank you.' She smiled hesitantly. 'It's probably just my imagination, but—'

The cat let out a yowl, making them all jump.

'For God's sake, Smokey.' Liz got up. 'I'd better feed him.'

Julie leaned across and asked Holland in a low voice whether he wanted her to call headquarters for a telephone engineer. He didn't reply. He was staring instead at the cat that had emerged from beneath the table, a long, thin, grey cat that was snaking around Liz Pearce's legs.

'Is that yours?' he asked, but he already knew the answer.

'Is now.'

'Mike brought him home?'

'That's right. Monday morning, when I got in from work, it was here. Mike said the owner had gone off and left it, wasn't coming back. "Mum'll let you stay," he says to it.' She raised her eyes briefly. 'Good old mum.'

'Sir?' whispered Julie, thinking he hadn't heard her.

'Yes,' he answered her quietly. 'And I think a WPC too. But you'd better use your mobile just in case.'

He turned back to the room at large and gave a sigh of contentment. Finally, he had a connection.

For the first couple of miles Sasha had been too intent on keeping up with the Citroën to worry about whether the driver realised he was being followed. He'd driven like a madman, throwing his car around bends, going at a speed on those snowy country lanes that would have frightened her if she'd had time to think. Now they were in Tenterden, she was stuck right behind him in a slow-moving line of traffic caused by works to a burst water-main.

She drew breath. He must know that she'd chased him from the site, she thought, and as if to confirm it, she saw him glance in his rear-view mirror. What, she wondered, would she do if he ran?

Run after him, of course. Now that she was so close, she wasn't going to lose him. Not a second time. He knew things, and he was literally running scared. Whatever happened next, he was going to tell her what those things were.

She froze. He'd turned round to look at her, a second's glance over the shoulder – she'd caught another glimpse of that gaunt, white face – then back again. She prepared to release her safety belt and jump out. Then his brake lights went off and he crept forward. What was he doing? He must have recognised her, although . . . She swung round herself, saw only a man's shape at the wheel of the car behind, and acknowledged that the last time he had seen her he'd hardly been in the most observant frame of mind.

The car behind gave a little toot, and she moved on. He had looked so terrified. She could understand now the expression of being 'scared witless'. What was going on in that place to have done that to someone? And where was he running to now? His home, she hoped. It was always easier to get people talking at their homes – they felt more relaxed.

Of course, she could get out now and tap on his window. But then he really might run – and while she was prepared for that if necessary, she didn't want to provoke it. She wanted him to co-operate in as full a manner as possible.

He was looking in his mirror again. She smiled, just in case he could see. Then the temporary traffic lights turned green and she followed him out of town.

Slowly, Bennett manoeuvred his way along the pavement. He could have moved more quickly – most of the snow had been shovelled up under the hedges by now – but there were still icy-looking patches and he didn't want to risk dropping anything.

In both hands he carried a flimsy cardboard tray, the lid of a box, in which were lodged two large polystyrene cups, one of coffee, one of tomato soup, a long, sealed aluminium box of lasagna and, in a paper bag, bread and butter and a custard tart.

He hadn't eaten anything since breakfast but, oh – and his mouth watered at the memory – what a feast that had been! Fried eggs and sausages, baked beans and thick white bread, all washed down with steaming mugs of hot, sweet tea. After the night he'd had, he'd deserved it.

His relief man had never arrived. All night long Bennett had sat in the car, alternately burning up with fever and shivering with cold. He'd eaten the last of his throat-sweets in the early hours, having foolishly (he realised now) believed Control's story that the other man was 'on his way', that the roads had been reopened.

Finally, at five-thirty in the morning, Control had called.

'You'd better stay there.'

'What?' The word had been a painful yelp.

'Your relief is otherwise engaged.'

'You can't be serious! You—'

'Stow it. We're busy. You stay there. Oh, and by the way, if you see the following car . . .'

He was expected to play bloody I-Spy into the bargain! No word of apology or of when, if ever, he might expect to be relieved. He'd shivered and sneezed until seven o'clock when, unable to face a slippery drive, he'd dragged himself to the corner-shop for milk. The man there had directed him to the café, where he'd eaten breakfast. It had been beautiful: not so much the taste – he couldn't taste very much with his cold – but more the simple pleasure of eating lots and lots. He hadn't given a damn in that dazed, delirious state, about missing a vital telephone call. Indeed, a bit of him actually hoped the Pearce kid would call in his absence, or walk through the front door of that scrubby little house. That would teach Control to treat someone of Bennett's calibre like dirt.

Made drowsy by the hot, plentiful food, he'd slept in the car, not caring what passers-by might think, not caring any more about any of it.

He'd woken half an hour before, hungry again, and gone for his lunch. He'd considered sitting again in the warm café to eat it, but his nerve had slightly failed him. Better to be in situ when his relief did finally arrive. It gave him the moral high ground.

He reached his car – which was a good thing because he was feeling suddenly dizzy and hot. It must be the flu, he thought, and no wonder – he should be tucked up in bed. He sneezed. He had some aspirin in his pocket. As soon as he got inside, he promised himself, he'd dose himself up, eat his food while it was hot, then sleep.

Carefully he placed his tray on the car roof, then fumbled for his keys. He glanced blearily down the road. It seemed to him that there was a new car parked outside the Pearces' house, and – he squinted – someone in it? But it was probably just a shadow, or his poor, fevered eyes playing tricks on him; it was probably only the head-rest he saw.

'Who cares, anyway?' he asked himself wearily.

He got the door open at last, took the tray in with him and removed the lid of the soup. The heat and the smell made his eyes stream. He'd just have a mouthful before he had his aspirin.

Reverently, he started to drink.

Having nothing better to do, and precious little to look at, Jem had watched Bennett's progress with idle interest. To him it seemed an odd thing to be doing, tiptoeing down the street with a takeaway, but no doubt there was a logical explanation. Something dull, like the cooker breaking down or the pipes bursting in the freeze, and the husband – he looked the downtrodden type – despatched to get lunch from the local café.

One would think he'd drive though, Jem thought, then, not wanting to be caught staring, looked away.

The Pearce house was not an inspiring sight. The front door badly needed painting, the dustbin beside it was lidless, and there was a cracked window on the first floor that had been inexpertly patched up with black tape. Typical one-parent household, Jem judged, but he could award himself no points for his deduction skills: Julie had already said that there was no Mr Pearce around.

He wondered what was going on inside – how Julie was doing, solo, with the Dutchman. He knew it made sense to wait in the car – no one wanted to overawe the woman with too many (male) police officers, and depending on what she said he might be needed as back-up – but it was difficult not to feel slightly resentful. Though he was younger than Julie and junior to her in rank, Jem was very ambitious. And to his way of thinking there'd recently been far too much of his time (subconsciously he discounted Julie's) spent sitting about in cars watching houses.

A movement caught his eye. On the other side of the street, the fellow with the takeaway had stopped by a car and put his tray on the roof. What was he doing – resting? Jem wondered. Then he saw the man open the door and lever himself and the food inside.

The other car was facing him. Jem watched the bloke drink and start to eat, and raised an eyebrow; he was obviously a very hungry chap, and thirsty too. His first assumption had clearly been wrong – there'd be nothing left for the wife. The man had to be . . . a rep, Jem decided, or . . . He couldn't really think what else. But why bring food back to the car, letting it get cold on the way? Why not eat it in the café? Jem knew the place, it was the only one around, and it was cheerful and warm.

He sighed. He was so bored that he was boring himself. He'd tried calling his girlfriend at work but she'd been too busy to talk to him. At least when he'd been on surveillance at the cottage there'd been Julie to talk to, even if she was a bit up herself sometimes.

The man put a headset on. Jem wished that he'd brought a Walkman as well. He could just imagine Julie's face – the Dutchman probably wouldn't notice – if she caught him listening to music.

Now the man was talking into a little handset. Jem could see him holding it. He studied him for a bit, then, for no good reason other than that he was bored, he called headquarters with the car's registration.

It was a company car belonging to BH Associates in Paddington, London.

'Thanks,' Jem said, chewing on a piece of gum. He knew there had to be a good reason for the car's presence, but for the life of him he couldn't think what it could be.

'Where did you say it was now?' the checker asked.

'What d'you mean "now"?'

'We had a call about it yesterday afternoon. It was in Rushton Lane.' Jem stopped chewing. That was two streets away. 'An old lady called in saying the driver was asleep outside her house.'

'Any follow-up done on the company?'

'Nope. Didn't sound very suspicious, did it? But if he's still in the area, d'you want me to—'

'It's all right, I'll do it. Can you give me the address again?'

Davenport turned right on to the London road, saw that the car behind did the same. He had expected it to. It had been following him since the roadworks in Tenterden, and probably, he told himself, for some time before (he hadn't been in a fit state to notice very much when he'd first left the site).

It was a dark BMW, very much the same shape and colour as the car Stockart had sent to torment him at the cottage. It was also a female driver. Quite often there'd been a woman at the wheel of that other car.

He accelerated along the road, still slushy with the newest snow. In a sense he wondered why he was bothering. They were going to get him; it was simply a matter of when, of whether it would be there, on a quiet stretch of the road – they could overtake, nudge him into a ditch – or whether they would wait until he stopped. He couldn't drive for ever; they knew that.

Already he was starting to tire. He could feel the adrenalin, that had saved him up until now, beginning to ebb. He'd been so terrified back at the office when he'd first realised Stockart had found out. How? he wondered now, frowning. Had someone hacked into his files – impossible – or the minister's? But why would they have done that? Then he realised. He remembered thinking about it at the time. He'd stayed too long in the secret files. One of the alarms must have been activated and Stockart had been alerted. He'd have operated Trackbac, the software package that he'd once boasted to Davenport about – 'It's like a blood-hound' – and found out who'd been snooping. So, when the police or the minister's office had called, Stockart would have known at once who'd betrayed him.

Davenport's flesh crawled. He prepared for the next stage, the sensation of having missed his step on the elevator, but it didn't happen. He guessed he was becoming acclimatised to terror, like a soldier. He knew that certain things would happen and others wouldn't: the car behind would continue to follow; he wouldn't escape.

She was maintaining a safe distance. He speeded up slightly; she did the same. There was a symmetry to the proceedings now. They were locked in a dance in which, until the end, he was the leader. He could let it go on for as long or as short a time as he wished. He didn't feel afraid any more; he felt brave, strangely happy.

Just then he saw the sign for the roadside café. He smiled and indicated his intention to pull in.

Having finished its meal, and failing to gain access to the table-top, Winston's cat had established itself on a kitchen counter, from where it seemed to Holland whenever he looked up to stare straight at him.

As if it knew, he thought, dropping his eyes.

Under his hand, he rolled a pencil. No one else apart from the cat was watching him. Julie was doing a good job – better than he could have done, he acknowledged fairly – in getting information from Liz Pearce.

Michael had been nervous, not sleeping terribly well 'for quite a bit' and off his food, before he'd suddenly taken off for London. In retrospect, and especially to an outsider, Holland knew how those signs must appear as red flashing lights and blaring sirens that something potentially major was amiss with the boy. But as the father of a teenager himself, he knew that wasn't fair.

'I mean,' Liz was saying defensively, 'Mikey's never been a big eater.'

Holland glanced up sympathetically, but it was wasted: again only the cat's green eyes were fixed on him. This time, he stared back.

'But was he quite well in himself?' Julie asked.

'Yeah,' Liz sighed. 'He was fine.'

Holland resumed his rolling, saw that the cat was watching his hand move, completely fascinated. Michael had run first, and then the others. Michael had got scared that someone was after him, and he'd been right. So what – his hand slowed – had forewarned him? He stopped rolling and the cat, with a swish of its tail, transferred its gaze back to his face.

He studied it. According to Liz Pearce, Michael had brought the animal home last Monday or Sunday night. Gerry's body had been found last Monday morning, but not identified until the following day. So how had Michael known before anyone else that the cat's owner wouldn't be coming home again?

News of Gerry Winston's death had first appeared in the local paper last Thursday morning. It had been that evening that Michael had gone to London. But why would a heart attack terrify a boy? It might upset him, certainly. But to make him take off to London, contact the press . . . Unless, of course, Michael had already been suspicious or fearful that his friend was in trouble.

Holland stared at the cat. It looked unblinkingly back.

Heart-attacks could be precipitated, of course.

Had confirmation of his friend's death, the worst happening after days of dread, made Michael run? Had he been terrified of it happening to him, of ending up dead on a beach?

Holland felt his heart skip a beat. The murder victim that morning at Dungeness. He tried to remember what he'd heard. The victim was a young man who'd lived locally. He'd been badly beaten, then stabbed, probably been killed sometime over the weekend, and his frozen body dumped. Papers found on him suggested he'd been an anti-nuclear campaigner – very neat, Holland thought. Perhaps a bit too neat. He recalled the way the local paper had tried putting a nuclear spin on last week's story about Winston. If 'they' had posed as police officers, Liz Pearce had said, 'they' could do other things as well, couldn't they?

He glanced over at her telephone. Like murder, the thought whispered in his head.

He rolled the pencil hard, saw out of the corner of his eye the cat slithering from the counter to the floor. It made its way purposefully towards the table. According to forensics, there'd been at least seven, maybe eight people involved in the REDEV raid. If he was right, two of them were now dead and the others were scattered, in fear of their lives. The Tenterden Four hadn't been seen since the day before, and that sighting – at a supermarket outside Brussels – had yet to be confirmed.

'Have you got a recent photo of Michael, Liz?' Julie asked brightly.

Liz hesitated. 'What d'you need it for?'

'Just so we can see who we're looking for.' She kept the lightness in her voice.

'You're not going to stick him up on a poster, are you?'

'I shouldn't think that's going to be necessary.'

Once they'd discovered who the journalist was, they'd find Michael – and according to Liz the boy was due to phone this afternoon. Holland would arrange for a trained counsellor to be listening in – on a potentially bugged telephone, he reminded himself. But if it was, it wouldn't be much longer: an engineer was on his way. Michael, he thought, was relatively safe – or would be shortly. It was the others he was more concerned about.

'He hates having his picture taken, but I've got a really good one of him. Took it two months ago.'

'Perfect.' Julie smiled.

Liz stood up. At once the cat jumped on to her chair and from there on to the table. It crossed to Holland and batted the pencil out from under his hand.

'It's in this one.' Liz pulled a blue photo-album from a shelf above their heads. She opened it on the table, flicked quickly through.

'Oh my God!'

Holland's head jerked up. The cat fled.

'What's wrong,' Julie and the sister demanded. 'Liz?'

She raised a stricken face. 'It's not here. It's gone! They've got my baby, they've . . .'

Holland saw the empty space on the page, realised that Liz had been right. They'd been in, taken the photograph, bugged the phone.

Liz screamed, and the sound froze them all. Then her hand flew to her mouth, as if she was sorry, and she broke into noisy tears. The sister hugged her, Julie made soothing noises, but the woman was incoherent.

Holland got up. The extra female officer Julie had requested would be on her way, but he considered that some medical attention, certainly a counsellor, was now also required. 'I'm just going to . . .' he mouthed at Julie, making the sign for a telephone, and she nodded.

He went outside. The cold air, the shutting-off of the woman's cries, was a great relief. He strode towards the car, noticing that Jem was using the phone – no doubt to call his girlfriend.

Holland got in. Not unexpectedly, Jem finished quickly. 'Yeah, call me. Bye.'

'May I?' said Holland.

'What?' Jem looked a bit distracted. He was staring at a car on the other side of the road. 'Sorry. Yes, sir.' He handed over the handset. Holland pressed the code for Ashford.

'Sir, that Sierra over there . . .'

'What about it?'

'There's something wrong. I called the registered owner in Paddington, and they say it's one of their rep's cars – he'll be on a break. But it's been hanging around here for a couple of days.'

'It's been what?' Ashford answered but Holland ignored it. He stared across at the car. He could see that the driver was talking urgently into a mobile.

'They said it was an optical glass company, but they didn't know – or wouldn't tell me – who he was visiting. I've asked one of the collators to find out what they can.'

Now the driver was looking straight at them. Holland saw the handset drop from one hand, the other come down on the steering-wheel.

'Come on!' he yelled, leaping out.

'Sir?' Jem's door opened behind him. 'He's going to get away!' And he ran in front of the car.

CHAPTER THIRTY-SEVEN

The wet gravel of the car-park scrunched beneath Sasha's heels. What, she wondered, was the man doing? When she'd followed him into the Happy Eater and parked a few bays away her heart had been racing. This was it, she'd told herself: the showdown. He was going to get out, bang on her window and demand to know what the hell she was doing. But he'd simply sat there with his head in his hands. Every so often he'd peek through his fingers at her – she was quite close, she saw him clearly – and then cover his eyes again, like a child playing hide-and-seek. For ten minutes she'd watched him. Now she decided that enough was enough; she didn't have time to waste.

It was starting to rain. She pulled her hood up and delved into her bag to get her press-card. As she did, she saw the man flinch away from the window and curl awkwardly into a ball. Please God, she prayed, don't let him just be a nutter.

It wasn't death he was afraid of, Davenport assured himself. It was the matter of how they – *she* (she seemed to be on her own) – was going to do it. Stab him or shoot him? Was it a knife or a gun that she was about to produce from her bag?

He was shaking terribly. Would she do it there – shoot him in the head through the glass – or would she force him to drive to some secluded spot where others would be waiting? Would they do it quickly or – and he felt his mouth go dry – would Stockart have given special instructions? Davenport felt sure he had. They were going to do some of those terrible things to him, and then . . . Was his grave already dug?

He moaned aloud. He wanted to behave with dignity, but . . . He uncurled a little, lifted his head and peered through his fingers. Why didn't she hurry up? Was this part of the torture – first making him wait as she watched him from her car, then taking for ever to get to him?

But she was very close now. She seemed young. He wouldn't have thought that murderers wore short skirts. But of course – it would be for camouflage. His eyes travelled fearfully higher. She'd got her hood up – naturally, she'd have a hood. He made himself look at her face to show he wasn't afraid, then frowned slightly. There was something about her that reminded him of someone.

She was level now. He couldn't see what her hands were doing. He wanted to look away but he couldn't move.

She tapped at his window.

He couldn't breathe. Out of the corner of his eye he saw her face was there, her lips moving, presumably telling him to open up. Wasn't it too much that she expected him to co-operate in his own death?

She was smiling, he saw in horror. 'I only want to talk to you,' she called loudly.

Oh yes, he thought, quivering, sure she did.

'Please!'

He bit his cheek. She shouldn't be polite, that wasn't fair.

'Look!' She slapped something against the window.

He flung himself across the car; he couldn't help it. He heard her walking round. She was coming to get him on the passenger side. He clapped his hands over his ears and hummed loudly.

She shouted something but he couldn't distinguish the words. Then she started roaring and he couldn't help but hear it. 'I know about the babies! I know what Branium's been doing!'

He frowned. Why would a hit-woman know about the Infiltrator? She'd fallen silent. Very slowly he took his hands away and looked up at her. She looked exhausted. It wasn't a gun's nuzzle she held against the window but an identity card. 'PRESS' he saw in black capitals, and her photograph. He blinked. This was the woman from the pub the day before.

She held his gaze. 'Can I talk to you?' she called.

He gulped like a man dying of thirst. He didn't want to be on his own any more. He sat up and released the lock. She didn't get in until he'd clumsily moved back to his own seat.

'Do you remember me now?'

He nodded; he seemed to have lost his voice.

'I think people have died because of that break-in.'

He stared at her. His heart, which had started to slow down, speeded up again.

'Because of the laptop that was stolen.'

She was watching him very carefully.

'W-w-what d'you know about m-m-my laptop?' he croaked.

'*Your* laptop?'

With a *whump*, Holland landed in the passenger seat. A second later Jem got in the back. The driver lay groaning against the headrest, eyes closed. He hadn't been wearing his seat-belt, and his head had hit the windscreen with a mighty crack when he'd slammed on the brakes to avoid hitting Holland. A sizeable lump was already forming on his forehead.

Holland caught his breath. 'What have we here?' He picked up a tape-recorder from his seat, removed the earphones from the driver's head and placed them on his own. He rewound the tape and pressed 'play'.

'Mikey, are you in trouble?' Liz Pearce said urgently in his ear.

'Been listening in, have we?' Holland asked pleasantly.

The driver opened his eyes. He looked as if his worst nightmare had come true.

'Police,' Holland continued in the same unruffled tone. He produced his ID, held it up in front of the man's face. 'You're breaking the law, my friend, d'you know that?'

The man's bloodshot eyes blinked rapidly as if to wish him away.

'Who're you working for?'

The eyes bulged. The man shook his head violently, then clutched it in both hands and moaned.

'Nasty bump. Concussion, maybe. You ought to see a doctor. Jem?'

'Sir?'

'What was the name of that company?'

'BH Associates of Paddington.'

'Thank you.' Holland turned back to the man. 'Care to tell us who they are exactly?'

The man quivered.

'Not in optical glass are you? To tell you the truth, you don't look like a rep. They wear suits and they tend to keep their cars tidier.' He surveyed the wreckage of several meals on the floor. 'Though I dare say you use plenty of lenses – binoculars and telescopic sights, that sort of thing.'

The lips went white.

'The strong, silent type, are you?' Holland removed a box of tissues that was jabbing into his back. 'Well, I tell you, you've got two choices. One; you can remain silent. You'll be arrested, charged under the Interception of Communications Act, and a few other things as well . . .'

'Stalking,' Jem put in. 'Kidnap. Breaking and entering. Wound—'

'Thank you, Jem.'

The man squeaked, 'But I never . . .' His eyes darted wildly between them. 'I only . . .'

'You only *what*?' said Holland swiftly. 'Eavesdropped?'

He nodded. 'I'll tell you everything,' he blurted. 'Just don't send me to prison. I've got babies, see? I never hurt anyone. I'm not like the others, I . . .' He sneezed loudly.

'The others hurt people?'

He nodded again.

'Killed them?'

The man wiped his nose noisily.

'How many have they killed?'

The driver opened his mouth but no sound emerged.

'Two? The one down at Dungeness and the other up at Sizewell? Don't go silent on me again,' Holland warned. 'You co-operate, we'll see what we can do. You clam up and—'

'Three,' whispered the man.

Holland reeled briefly. 'Who's the third?' he demanded.

'Dunno his name. Dunno any of them. He was a rep, I think.' He ran his tongue round his lips. 'They made him talk, then they filled him full of vodka, set his car on fire and rolled it off a hill.'

'Where? When?'

'Dunno.' He closed his eyes, spoke with an effort. 'Before the weekend. Before I got here. Hastings.'

'You got that, Jem?'

'Sir.'

'Find out about it – and get a counsellor for Mrs Pearce over here.'

The driver was pleading. 'I've only worked for them this once. I'll never do it again, I'll—'

'Who's "them"?'

'Zodiac. Corporate security. Mr Hall's the boss. There's a woman in charge of this op – I think she's from Cyprus – and McMahon. He's her number two.'

'They're working for REDEV?'

He nodded.

'Why're you bugging the boy's phone?'

'He nicked a laptop from REDEV. They want it back.'

A laptop, Holland thought. He remembered Davenport's eyes, madly searching his desk. But there'd already been a full-sized computer on it; it had never occurred to Holland that the missing item might be another. 'Why kill the others?'

'They didn't know who had it. They kept going till they found out.'

'D'you know what's on it?'

The man shook his head.

'How many of you are there round here?'

'Just me.' The man sniffed. 'The others are all back up in London. Something big's breaking. Dunno what,' he added, pre-empting the next question.

From beneath the dashboard came a buzzing sound.

'It's my radio,' the man whispered. 'Control told me to clear off 'cause the cops were sniffing around.'

Holland stared at the source of the sound. He needed longer to make sure of the man. Ideally, he'd have liked to speak to his superintendent.

The radio buzzed again.

'I'll have to answer it.'

'Go on then,' Holland commanded. 'But be careful.'

The man picked up the handset.

'What happened to you?' snapped a voice.

'I . . .' The man's eyes sought out Holland's approval. 'I had a bit of bother.' He swallowed. 'Skidded.'

'You were meant to call in, remember?'

'Yeah. Sorry.'

'No cops about?'

The man bit his thumb. 'Nah.'

'Must've been a nosy neighbour. Doesn't matter. I was going to call you off anyway. Want you to check out an address down there for us. Got a pen?'

Holland handed him one, and an open notebook lying by the gearstick. He read the name and address as it was scrawled in a shaking hand, raising an eyebrow as another piece connected.

'He's probably not there, but go and ring his doorbell in case. If he is there, you're to detain him. Understand?'

'Yeah.'

'What's up with you?' The voice turned curious.

Holland froze. Had the man been trying to warn off his colleague? He glared over at him.

'I mean, why aren't you whining?' said the voice.

'Tired,' croaked the man.

'You can get all the kip you need once the job's over. Call me when you get there. Don't forget this time.'

The man was trembling when he finished the call.

Holland took the notebook from him and passed it back to Jem. 'Recognise this?' he asked.

'Oh yes, sir,' Jem said meaningfully.

Holland saw a police car coming down the road. He recognised two of the occupants, a motherly WPC and a counsellor. Julie had used her initiative. He guessed that the man in the back was the telephone engineer.

'Wait here with our friend, will you, until I make the introductions, then we'll be off.'

'To where, sir?' queried Jem.

'Where d'you think? And seeing how you've been there so often, you'd better do the driving.' He put his hand on the door. 'I don't think chummy's up to it. Don't let him get away.'

It had come as a relief to Sasha that the man wanted to switch cars.

She felt more comfortable in her own – and she was not, she thought grimly, referring to the BMW's upholstery. Colin Davenport seemed too unstable to drive. She knew his name now, and quite a lot else: that he was working on a contract for Branium; that his stolen laptop contained a highly confidential report; and that he knew people had been killed.

She felt better now that they were moving. He wanted to go to Surbiton – to his flat, he'd told her. He seemed under the impression that she'd do anything he wanted – and in that, she admitted privately, he wasn't far wrong. When he'd told her that he was the owner of Mike's laptop, and that 'of course' he knew how to access the information on it, she could have kissed him.

But she hadn't. She didn't yet know which side he was on. And besides, his manner – extreme nervousness mixed with arrogance – was very off-putting. She'd dodged his questions. 'I know your laptop was stolen,' was all she'd said. No more, she'd decided, until he'd shown his true colours.

London, she saw, was thirty-three miles ahead. The road was clear, washed clean by the rain. She'd plenty of time, she told herself, to win him round.

'So, you've been writing a report for REDEV?'

'Mm.' He gazed out of the window.

'About . . . ?'

'You wouldn't understand.' His terrible stammering had vanished after the first few minutes.

'I think I do a bit. It's to do with the glass womb that Branium's invented, isn't it?'

'The *what*?' he said in surprise.

'Oh, um . . .' She tried to remember the scientific name Charlie had used. 'Ectogenesis. When they grow the embryos outside the womb.'

'Oh that.' He sniffed. 'That's not what I've been writing about.'

'Oh.' Why then, she wanted to know, was it on his laptop? Was he smarter than he looked? Was he trying to put her off the scent? She became aware that he was staring at her.

'How d'you know about that?' he asked curiously. 'It was in the Class A security archive. I thought only the top three people had access to that.'

She shrugged. 'Sources, you know . . . It's amazing that Branium have kept it quiet, isn't it?'

He shrugged too. 'Makes commercial sense.'

'Does it? I'd have thought a breakthrough like that, being able to grow babies in labs, being able to do amniocentesis on them, would have earned Branium a lot of money.'

He was staring at her again, and she hoped she hadn't overplayed it. After a moment he said gruffly, 'I didn't know they were doing amnio on them. I thought they'd just grown them to get that growth factor.'

'Growth factor?' She didn't like the sound of that. Growing babies like flowers in glass cages. 'What's a growth factor?'

He shot her a funny look. 'A protein that promotes growth, of course. Ten weeks of life is when whichever one it is – I can't remember – is being most actively produced. That's when they had to harvest it. You know, stick a needle in, whip it out.'

Her hands grasped the steering-wheel. 'What for?' she asked in a small voice.

'For Infutopin, of course,' he said impatiently.

The name echoed in her head. She squashed the sick feeling down. 'They harvested embryos to get Infutopin?'

'Course. How else d'you think they found that gene?'

The Octopus gene, she remembered dazedly, the basis for Infutopin. She'd never thought about how Branium had found it. Why should she; why should anyone?

'They . . .' Her voice deserted her. Terrible pictures jostled in her head of baby-factories, tiny human beings hooked up for milking. 'They're not still doing it?'

'No point, is there?' His fingers drummed on the dashboard. In her peripheral vision she saw him crane his neck, checking her wing mirror. 'They've got their blueprint, they can work from that.'

'So they only did it once?' Once was bad enough, but . . .

'Hardly.' He turned round to stare out of the back-window. 'It took them a year.'

She couldn't take it in; she didn't want to. Branium had broken the law to get Infutopin – but that wasn't the worst of it. All those poor people, she thought, those desperate would-be parents, believing in the wonder cure, ignorant of how it had been achieved.

How much did a fetus feel at ten weeks? Did it have hands and eyes? Could it hear?

She gulped. 'Where did they get the embryos from?'

'Who knows?' He sounded suddenly bored. 'IVF clinics, probably. A job-lot of frozen ones.'

She shuddered. She remembered the furore there'd been when IVF clinics had started to dispose of 'unclaimed' human embryos. Some people had said it was murder.

'What's wrong with that? They'd have been melted anyway.'

'The ones that Branium used . . .' She hesitated again.

'What about them?'

'They, er, they didn't survive those experiments?'

He gave a short, derisive snort. 'Not likely, is it? You're not a science journalist then?'

'No.'

'Didn't think so.'

She needed him, she had to remind herself, her personal feelings didn't count. 'You've obviously got a scientific background,' she said.

'I've picked up what I need to know. I'm an excellent absorber of facts.' His head bobbed perilously close to hers as he looked in the rear-view mirror.

'I'd know if someone was following us,' she said mildly.

He grunted. 'That's what you think. These people are bloody good. They could be in front of us now. One in front, one behind, then they close in. You wouldn't know a thing about it.'

'OK.' She glanced over at him. He was starting to look wild again. 'Why're they after you?' she queried gently.

'Because I've found out what's really going on.'

Her heart thumped. 'At REDEV?'

'What?' He snorted again. 'Nothing goes on at REDEV. Much,' he added. 'I'm talking about Branium and their Golden Goose or Egg or whatever you call it.'

He wanted to boast, she realised; he was desperate for an audience. She prayed for the right words to prompt him with, and found herself saying inadequately, 'Oh?'

'Billions and billions, that's what they think it's going to make them.' He snickered suddenly. 'But not any more. Not after what I've done.'

She waited, watching the needle, keeping it under seventy.

'Bet your "source" never mentioned anything about the Infiltrator.'

'No,' she admitted.

'Didn't think so. Can't be that high up, then.' He started humming to himself. 'He's never mentioned the name of Will West to you?'

Just a little bit more, she begged him, another millimetre. 'Doesn't ring a bell,' she said levelly.

'It was one of his teams that perfected the glass womb.'

'One of his teams?' she repeated.

'Sure.' He shifted in his seat. 'You've got to understand. This Infiltrator thing of his is enormous. The biggest thing that's ever happened to Branium. Or anyone. So, whatever West needed, he got. And in the early stages he needed human embryos kept alive in vitro at ten weeks and beyond. Ten weeks is also the best time to put in the Infiltrator.'

He cleared his throat. 'Branium had already been researching the glass womb stuff, on and off, without much luck. But when West said he had to have it, the project got the best brains, unlimited resources, the works. And they got the thing up and running. Gave West all the embryos he needed – in vitro, before he moved on to the in utero ones.'

A brief silence fell. Then he added, 'That's how they discovered Infutopin. When they weren't even looking for it.'

She waited.

'The glass womb team had noticed a particular growth factor surge in the embryos at around nine weeks old. They explored further, extracted the protein, worked back, and found the gene.'

'The Octopus gene?'

'I believe it was commonly referred to as such, yes.' He sounded frosty.

'Sorry, I didn't mean to interrupt.'

After that she let him flow, and he was like a river in full spate. She could hardly believe some of what he said, but even as she doubted, she knew that it was true. It had an awful authenticity to it, a logic, that put everything into context and even made the glass womb experiments sound comparatively innocuous. Branium operated a secret medical research centre in Albania, where people with particular genetic traits had been illegally experimented upon by a British doctor and his team. It sounded like what the Nazis had done, she thought, horrified. Even if Branium's goal had been to eradicate a terrible disease – she'd only vaguely heard of Duchenne's Muscular Dystrophy, hadn't realised it was fatal – they'd manipulated and lied to their patients when everything had gone wrong.

'The first batch was duff. Miscarriages all round,' Davenport said.

Duff, she thought, suppressing a shudder. What a word to use. She tried to concentrate on the wipers, the soothing, innocent sweeping away of the rain, but Davenport's voice drew her back. The second batch, born to die one by one, were all dead within twelve weeks. What must it be like to lose a child, a tiny infant? She remembered her nieces at birth, the utter perfection of them, their newness, the exhausted joy in her sister's face.

She tried to close her ears but Davenport's voice was penetrating.

'The third batch . . .' he was telling her now.

She held her breath, not wanting to listen.

'Third time, old West got lucky.'

'They're OK?' It was the first time she'd spoken in a long while.

Davenport turned to look at her. 'Fine and dandy.'

So the cure had finally worked. Sasha swallowed. But did the health of the later patients justify what had happened to the others? Were all great medical breakthroughs achieved by suffering, animal or human? Was it part of the deal? But Branium's ultimate goal was to make money, she reminded herself – billions of pounds, as Davenport had said – and with the gene-therapy he'd just described they were going to put a price on perfect health. It would be survival not of the fittest but the richest.

'That's what my report's about,' he finished. 'The Infiltrator Technique.'

She glanced at the laptop on his knee. She saw clearly now why Branium would have killed to get the other one back: just in case Mike or Gerry Winston or Clive Lucas or Manyon managed to crack the code and see what it held.

'But they've come unstuck now,' Davenport was saying smugly.

'Branium has? How d'you mean?'

He looked out the window. 'They've been running secret trials here.'

'What?'

'Watch it!' The car had veered dangerously towards the outside lane.

Her heart thundered. 'Secret trials?'

'Yeah, Dr West's been at it again, only in the Mistletoe. Heard of it?'

She nodded dumbly.

'They wanted to buck the system. Launch it as a *fait accompli*, so one else could nick it.' He sniffed. 'But it's all gone wrong, hasn't it? Egg-foo-yong on the face time.'

'I'm sorry, I'm not following—'

'They've all got Leukaemia, dear, same as the second Albanian batch. SWii Syndrome – clear as day. They're dying,' he added as an afterthought.

'Dying?' Not a cure then. And not illegal experiments carried out on unwitting patients in a remote corner of the world, but here, now.

'Or dead by now.' He sounded almost too blasé. She glanced over at him but he looked away. She thought that perhaps he wasn't as cold as he tried to appear, that there was still some hope for him as a human being. 'Isn't there something,' she swallowed, 'anything, that anyone can do?'

'Medically, you mean? Forget it. They're being born with it, pre-programmed. But I've done something. I told you.'

'What?' she asked weakly.

'I've sent the true facts to someone in authority.'

Oh no, she thought, the police. For the first time she acknowledged what another part of her had been thinking: what a bloody amazing story, Pulitzer quality. She'd never read, seen or heard anything like it. And what was happening to the British babies right now – horrible as it was, unstoppable as it was – gave it an immediate hook on top of the ones she already had. She had the lot: the sources, the laptop, the real reason why the Tenterden Four had run away, why three amateur burglars were dead. Branium had stopped at nothing.

It was almost one o'clock on Tuesday afternoon; if she worked flat-out she would have time, just, to get the story together for *Comment*. Derek Hornby would hold the space for her; he'd hold the front page.

And now, to be told that Davenport had already talked . . .

'You've told the police about it?' she said as brightly as she could.

'No.' He looked over at her again. 'A politician.'

Almost as bad, she thought. 'Anyone I'd know?' she asked.

'I shouldn't think so.' He darted her another look, like a squirrel with a nut, she thought, then announced proudly, 'I've told Philippa Tyler, the health minister.'

She gripped the steering-wheel until it hurt. When she trusted herself to speak she said, 'Because of her Infutopin connection?'

'What? Hardly! I wasn't thinking about Infutopin, dear.'

But Tyler will, Sasha thought. That would be the first thing she would think of, and the second would be how to save herself. She'd go public with whatever Davenport had told her, as soon as she could.

'I've asked her to mount an inquiry.'

No need to do that, Sasha thought gloomily. Goodbye, story – or a big chunk of it. She tried to remember the *sub judice* rules surrounding government inquiries, whether she'd be banned from writing anything.

She switched on the radio for the news headlines. There was no mention of it. Perhaps, she thought, hope resurging, nothing would be publicly announced until Tyler's department was surer of its facts. They'd suspend the Infiltrator trial at once, of course – with accusations like Davenport's they couldn't do anything else – but with a company the size of Branium, with the minister's personal endorsements ringing in everyone's ears, they'd need to be very sure before going public. Take your time, she urged the unknown officials, make triply certain, do re-checks. Do nothing until Thursday – publication day.

Davenport swivelled in his seat again.

'Is that why they're after you?' she asked. 'They know you're the one who tipped off the minister?'

'Correct. Well, they don't *know*,' he emphasised the word, 'but they'll have a pretty good idea. That's why they locked me out of the system.'

He'd told her that before, but now the words rang in her head. 'So you've, er, been denied access to the information you've just told me? All of it?'

'Correct.'

She looked over at him. He was staring straight ahead. 'Did you, um, take a copy of any of it?' she asked.

'What d'you mean, on paper?' He sounded scornful. 'No.'

'Do you, in fact, have any evidence,' she said slowly, seeing the story swirl away down a drain, 'of what you've told me?'

'What? I don't see why it matters.' But he *was* seeing, she could tell by his voice. His word against Branium's. His extraordinary accusations of corruption and conspiracy and collusion in murder, against a hospital with the Mistletoe's reputation. 'Anyway, Mrs Tyler knows. I put it all down in the letter.' A short silence fell; in it Sasha heard him bite his nails. 'I'd have thought it would've been on the news by now, wouldn't you?' he asked after a moment.

'These things take time.' Of course, she thought, if Tyler hadn't got his letter, it gave her more time – but critically she needed that evidence.

'How about your report?' she said suddenly. 'Won't the results be in there?'

'Not the real ones. I reworked them.'

'Oh. I see. You wouldn't have left any notes, I suppose?'

'I . . . I erased everything when I finished it.' He was starting to sound panicky. 'I-it's the way I work. The thing is . . . the thing is, if Mrs Tyler didn't get it, I-I've got no protection, have I?'

'What d'you mean?'

'I-if there was a government inquiry, they couldn't touch me. But now . . .' He gulped. 'They know I've been snooping; they know I've f-found out about what West's been doing here.' He shuddered to a halt. 'Th-they're going t-t-to k-kill—'

'How about Tyler's letter?' Sasha felt inspired. 'Can't you just call that up?'

'I can't access it!' he howled. 'I sent it via the network, and now I'm locked out!'

'There's no way you can get in?'

'No! Access denied is like . . .' He was panting. 'It's like h-having your bank-card stolen. I can't use this account any more.' He smacked his hand on the laptop's casing. 'Oh God, oh God!'

'This account,' Sasha repeated to herself, accelerating round a bend in the road. 'What if,' she started carefully, 'there was another account you could use?'

'W-what d'you mean?'

'Your old laptop. Could you use that?'

'My old . . .' She could feel his eyes upon her. 'D'you know where it is?' He was suddenly wild with hope. It was as infectious as his panic had been.

She shot him a quick smile. 'I could take you to it. Could you use it to gain access to the data?'

'Of course I could!'

'They wouldn't have disconnected it from the network when it was stolen?'

'No point. Whoever's stolen it . . .' he delved into his pocket, 'wouldn't have one of these, would they?'

She glanced over. He was holding out a palm-sized mobile phone. 'Branium's security system,' he told her. He sounded almost proud. 'Even with the laptop, there's no entry to the network until the company's main computer has dialled the user's mobile and identified the machine.'

'Smart.' She meant it. She thought it was brilliant. They were going to get the data; the story was on again; Branium would be exposed. She saw with a start that Central London was only ten miles away and realised that automatically she'd been heading for home, not Surbiton. Not that it mattered now, she thought gratefully.

'This person who's got my laptop . . .' Davenport began tentatively, 'is he a scientist?'

'Um, no. He's a . . . I'll introduce you when we get there.' If she was lucky with the traffic, she estimated that they'd be back at the flat – and Charlie, Mike and the laptop – within thirty minutes. A traffic-light turned green as she approached, and she eased her foot down on the accelerator.

CHAPTER THIRTY-EIGHT

It was essential, Bernard Hall had told Anna, that the informant be found and dealt with as quickly as possible. The client had been most insistent. Hall had drafted in three extra men, sent two to Gatwick Airport and one to Ashford. Anna had despatched the Kent floater to an address in Surbiton, with orders that if the target failed to show up, there was an elderly relative close by who should also be visited.

Anna rose from the pretty but uncomfortable chair and walked slowly around the hotel room. Colin Davenport had been running for nearly ninety minutes. He could by now have reached Gatwick, the closest major airport. If he had, she estimated that his chances of escape were good: there were so many planes, so many people. He could be boarding a flight right now, and there was nothing that she or anyone else could do about it.

Later, of course, if the client wished to extend the hunt overseas – that was another matter. But she didn't think it would be necessary. From what she had learned about Colin Davenport – the way he'd left REDEV 'like a bat out of hell,' according to the guard at the gate – she considered it far more likely that he'd either caused a road accident or run for home. The cottage in Kent was being checked out, but she doubted he'd go there. Certainly he wouldn't feel safe enough to stay there.

The other possibility – that he'd go to the police – could for the moment be discounted, as apparently he was under the impression that the authorities were already involved.

Anna crossed to the table on which she had left Hall's fax. It comprised two pages: a 'background briefing' by Zodiac Securities, dated three months earlier. Then, Colin Arnold Davenport had been rated as a low security risk.

She raised an eyebrow, considering that at least part of the urgency in Hall's manner was a desperate need to save face.

'The client's very keen that you should handle Davenport personally. I don't know if that will be possible . . .'

She'd been mildly surprised. How was the client to know who had dealt with Davenport – and surely Hall could simply tell him whatever he wanted to hear?

She sat down in the window, felt the pull of sleep, but fought against it. She'd considered going over to the hotel in Floral Street in order to be on hand when Pearce and the journalist were taken. But prior to an action she preferred to be on her own, particularly when there was no immediate sign of the targets moving. They had eaten breakfast and were now, according to McMahon, watching television. In addition, the journalist had made some telephone calls.

'They can't stay inside for ever,' McMahon had said.

She knew that. But they could feasibly remain there until the journalist left for work again that night. Besides, though she respected McMahon, the prospect of being closeted with him (or anyone) in a state of tension for several hours was not appealing. He would call her as soon as the moment arrived. In the meantime she had to keep herself occupied and sleep at bay.

She glanced down at the briefing paper and picked up the telephone; McMahon could reach her on the mobile. She dialled a number, waited as it rang out, and was on the point of hanging up when a tremulous voice said, 'Hello?'

'Mrs Davenport? It's one of your grandson's colleagues here.'

'Oh yes, dear? N-nothing wrong, is there?'

'No. It's his day off and I need to get hold of him. He said that he might be visiting you.'

'Oh, that'd be nice!'

'You haven't heard from him then?'

'No, dear, not for a while. Not that I'm complaining – he's such a busy boy. If he comes, shall I give him a message?'

Anna mentioned a meeting that had unexpectedly been scheduled for the following morning. Colin mustn't miss it, she said.

'I'll tell him. And he's not in trouble or anything?'

Anna imagined the tinselly hair, the wobbly neck supporting the head. 'He's not in trouble', she said smoothly. 'Don't worry.'

The computer stood to the left on Stockart's desk. At the tap of a key he could summon up DAMR to see how the subjects were progressing, or he could monitor his e-mail to see whether Will West had replied at last to his messages, but both activities struck him as a fearful waste of time.

He knew what was going to happen to the subjects, if not in the next hour then that evening or in the morning. The only point in monitoring DAMR now would be to lay bets on who went first, and there was little fun in betting with oneself.

As for West . . . Stockart made a mirthless sound in the back of his throat. West had chickened out. To have actually been in the baby's room . . . Stockart felt a stab of pain in his guts and automatically reached for his pills, gulped them down without the need for water.

Gone to get a specialist, indeed. Stockart knew West, the weasly, lily-livered nature of the man; he'd be cowering in a corner somewhere, in the basement or the stock cupboard, those spidery hands wrapped around his head, whimpering, waiting for someone else to do his dirty work.

Stockart glanced at his watch. It was over an hour since he'd last called West's secretary. He'd been occupied with other matters. He acknowledged that there was a chance, albeit a remote one, that by now West had come to his senses, gone back to the room where the baby lay, done what he had to do.

He picked up the telephone – the handset was warm – and pressed the number for the doctor's extension. Steeling himself as the secretary answered, he put his question quickly.

'I'm ever so sorry, sir. Doctor's still not come up here. It's really not like him.'

'Have you checked the car-park?'

'Yes, sir. His car's there. He must be somewhere about. He's got a patient waiting.'

One of the pregnant ones, Stockart remembered. He felt momentarily sick. How much easier could it have been for the man? A helpless infant on one hand, a trusting woman on the other. Served up, ready and waiting.

'The Gilbert parents are talking about suing, sir,' the secretary said. 'They're ever so upset. They say they were promised a specialist, and the hospital's broken a verbal contract. To tell you the truth,' she went on in a lower and more confiding tone, 'Sister says it would be a relief if they went.'

'They're not to go.'

He'd barked it out as an order. He softened his voice. 'What I meant was, I've got an idea of which specialist he was referring to. Could you do me a favour, my dear?'

She stumbled. 'Er . . . yes, sir.'

'John. My name's John. Could you make sure that the Gilbert baby remains with us? I'd hate to have the specialist come over for nothing.'

'Oh, absolutely! I see what you mean . . . John. So I'll tell them to wait, what, another hour?'

He winced at the way she spoke his name, but he answered quite pleasantly. 'About that. Say two, to be on the safe side. Also,' he fingered his blotter, 'I've an idea of where I might find Dr West.'

'Really?' She sounded relieved. 'I've been so worried about him. He's been working so hard, and I think he was ever so upset about . . .' Her voice dropped to a whisper. '. . . that stillbirth yesterday. I don't know if you know about it.'

'Indeed I do. Will's deeply involved in new research, my dear, and it's just occurred to me which lab he'll probably be in. So if you'd also tell the lady who's waiting not to go?'

'Oh, of course! She'll be ever so pleased.'

'Good. Excellent. I'll be in touch, then. But of course, if Dr West should reappear with you beforehand . . .'

'I'll tell him to call you at once, John. No worries.'

Stockart replaced the receiver. He would make West pay for this, he promised. The ultimate sanction? He toyed briefly with the idea, the picture of West being hauled out of whichever hidey-hole he cowered in, the thought of . . . things . . . being done to that fleshless, medical body.

A movement in the windows opposite, a flash of colour, attracted his attention. Balloons and paper chains, plastic Santas and fancy dress. An early Christmas party in progress.

Stockart picked up a paper-clip. No, he decided, fingering it: West, for all his weakness, didn't deserve that. He hadn't set out to betray him. He hadn't turned like a viper, crawling into places where he had no business, hissing secrets into another's ear, hoping in so doing to destroy Stockart and everything he'd ever worked for. The paper-clip was yielding now, its bends becoming straight. No, West could be put away quietly. Albania, he thought. How appropriate.

But the other one . . .

Stockart looked down at the paper-clip. The destruction was complete; it lay unravelled in his palm. He set it quietly with the others in a line upon his desk. One for the boy who'd taken the laptop; one for the journalist – or two, he remembered; there was a girl too; then lots more (he counted them out carefully) for the babies, born and unborn; and, of course, the last one, the one he'd already broken in half. For Colin Davenport.

He set it a little apart from the others, at the front of the line-up.

As each one was dealt with, he'd flick it off into the aluminium waste-paper bin. He'd positioned it perfectly; it already contained one unravelled clip for the little Bristol boy. He'd despatched it almost twenty-four hours before.

It was high time for another one.

It was good to be by the river, but it was fearfully cold. When he'd run from the Mistletoe he had taken no thought for his comfort, his sole desire being to escape. At first he hadn't noticed the weather – or anything. It had only been the touch of a stranger's hand, the concerned enquiry – 'Are you all right, doctor?' – that had made him stop and look.

It was snowing, yet over his clothes he wore just his thin doctor's coat. He was sodden and cold.

'I . . .' He'd started and a tremor had shaken him.

'You look ill.' The stranger had spoken firmly. 'Which hospital are you from?'

And it had been then that West had seen the uniform.

'It's not me,' he'd blurted, stepping back. 'It's my . . .' He couldn't utter the word. 'She's the one who's sick.' And he'd moved away quickly, nodding and smiling back over his shoulder, increasing his pace until the puzzled look on the policewoman's face had blurred and she'd been no more than a shape behind him.

It seemed to him now that he'd been walking for hours. It had stopped snowing, which was a relief, but people still stared at him: people in cars, passers-by, no doubt wondering which emergency he was rushing to, open coat flying, whose life would soon be safe in his hands.

Truly, he'd wanted to save Mel's baby – for his sake, yes, he acknowledged that, but also for hers. He'd wanted so much for her to be happy, to have her perfect child, the one that he'd made whole for her, the replacement for when the boy died. He'd seen her joy so clearly, her lovely smile, her soft voice thanking him, her small hand pressing into his.

The wind came up from the river, hurt his face, made him cry. He wanted to be with her, to talk to her, to explain – but he knew now that it could never be. She wouldn't listen. She'd want to know only about the other matter, the silly white lie he'd told to make sure she came to him. He moaned aloud. Why did she know nothing of science? Why didn't she appreciate that the cure for a Duchenne's boy was still many years away?

He increased his pace. His hands, unmoving by his sides, were remote white objects that no longer belonged to him. His feet too, moving assuredly ahead on the pavement, seemed unconnected. He didn't like to look at them so he concentrated instead on the river, watching the small waves smacking against its boundaries, constantly sifting, rejecting and selecting those things it wanted before moving on.

He reached the end of the road, unsure where he was going, and stopped for a moment before turning left on to the bridge. On the other side St Peter's hospital loomed; a vast, ugly complex, he thought it, with its broken glass and stained sixties concrete. Stockart had told him only a few weeks before that if he wanted it, had a hankering for it to be turned into the William West School of Genetics, then it could be arranged.

'Just say the word, Will. I've got connections.'

He stopped again and the wind whipped round him. They – Branium, the government, Europe – would offer them the world, Stockart had said. West had been looking forward to that – not so much the financial aspect that had so excited Stockart, but the adulation, the books that he would be able to write, the papers that he'd publish, and after his death, or perhaps before, the memorials that would be erected to him. Doctor Will West, Creator of Perfect Life. Life more perfect than that given by God. What a glorious epitaph for any man! Who needed children to carry on his name?

He turned to the river and cried out in a great voice. He'd created nothing, save pain and false hope. He wasn't God. He was only . . .

The wind dropped suddenly and his cry was stilled. He whispered the words: he was a father, that was all.

He felt hot tears on his cheeks. He knew now what had drawn him to Mel, what had made him care so deeply for her, be so determined to find a cure for her unborn child. Mel – he wiped the tears away – was his daughter, and the baby she carried his grandson. Not genetically – he shook his head impatiently; that didn't matter – but she was the daughter of his ex-wife. He'd known it as soon as he'd seen her, at least part of him had. He'd seen the resemblance in the eyes, the full lower lip, the softness of her profile. A part of him had tried to suppress the recognition but it had been too strong a pull; the knowledge had kept breaking through in unguarded moments, in his dreams.

The night before, staring at the computer screen, he'd been tempted to do what he'd been thinking of for days now: to trace Mel's parentage back through DAMR. He could have done it – it would only have taken a little time – but in the end he'd turned away from it. He didn't need to see the facts; his heart knew the truth.

Mel was the daughter that he could have had – if his wife had not been so cruel to him, if she'd stayed and been patient with him. For Mel to be a DMD carrier his wife must be one too, although there'd been no trace of it in her family. Some people believed that there was a reason for everything; though he'd always scorned such drivel, now he could see that there might have been a purpose for this after all. To save his own descendants.

'Oh, Mel, my darling, my baby.'

He laid his hands on the cold parapet of the bridge. Down below him the water swirled; ahead he could see the Palace of Westminster. They world would judge him harshly. He prayed that she would not.

'It's wrong to hate your father,' he murmured out loud. 'Please don't hate me, precious. Look at what I tried to do, what I achieved. I . . .' he quivered, 'I only did it for you.'

The brown water rolled; it slapped against the vast uprights of the bridge. What he'd tried to do, what he'd achieved for Mel . . . He gave an ugly laugh. The result of his life's work, his fumbling attempts to intrude upon the blueprint of life, now lay dying like others before him on a hospital bed. In eight months' time West's own grandson would join him; his own daughter would be the mother at the bedside, crying and holding out her bundle to whatever doctor there was, begging whatever God there was: Please, save my baby.

His foot slipped on the ironwork. He'd engineered death into his own family tree. As if his own darling, his baby girl, hadn't suffered enough, wasn't already facing the death of a son in ten or fifteen years' time. His toes found a foothold and he climbed, his fingers clawing at the hard stone curl of the parapet's edge. Then he stood straight, his body moving freely in the wind.

'Mel,' he whimpered, 'what have I done?'

He'd meant to change the world to save her, to rearrange the pieces she'd been given, give her new ones. He'd have sacrificed anything – another dozen lives, a hundred other babies – he'd have broken any law.

But it was no use.

He howled, and the wind caught the noise and flung it back at him. Whatever went wrong with the Infiltrator was a mystery to him, and he hadn't had the time to look – not enough to save Mel's baby, which was all that mattered.

He gave another cry and stuffed his hand into his mouth. He tilted forward and saw his tears fall, dropping slowly before merging with the water below. A seagull flew up, hovered by his head for an instant, its cold eyes watching him, then cawed and flew away. He moved towards the centre of the bridge and his view was suddenly that much better. He could clearly see the muddy wash that an approaching boat left in its wake. He spread his arms wide like the gull's wings and rose up on the balls of his feet.

'Don't!' screamed a voice behind him, and he was tempted to look back. But he didn't, he went forwards. It was better this way, he thought, that he went now, before she hated him.

'Daddy loved you, darling,' he cried as he fell.

Davenport's cottage was empty. Jem had hammered on the door

and peered through the windows. Bennett, with little persuasion, had called his co-ordinator with the news and been told to await further orders.

'Did I sound all right?'

The wretched man had become quite desperate to please. He was gazing on Holland now with anxious, rheumy eyes. Coupled with the wet nose, Holland thought they gave him the appearance of a puppy – of an unappealing sort. 'Brilliant,' he said, and got out of the car, leaving him in the care of Jem and Julie.

It was perishing cold. The place was obviously one of those strange spots on the Weald where the weather was cruellest and where some people peculiarly chose to live. He found a semi-sheltered patch beyond a hedge and made a couple of calls on his mobile before the final one to his superintendent to inform him of Bennett's capture.

'You think he'll take you to them?'

'I think he's our best bet, sir. He's a minion, and a new boy. He doesn't know any details of who hired them, just that it was REDEV.'

'He's no idea of who's behind them?'

'No, sir. No names, just "the client".'

'His outfit's called Zodiac, you say?' Holland heard the scratch of a pen.

'He claims they work for MI5, sir. Or have done in the past.'

'Thanks, Holland. That gives me an excellent lead,' the superintendent said drily. 'Three dead people,' he continued hollowly after a moment – and Holland sympathised, it was a nightmare. 'Plus the Tenterden Four,' his superintendent went on. 'There's been no sight or sound of them for twenty-four hours. D'you think this Zodiac outfit's got to them?'

'No, sir,' Holland bowed his head against a particularly vicious gust of wind that had found him. 'I did think they were in danger, but it seems that Zodiac's not after them. It's the Pearce kid and the laptop they want.' He glanced up at the dark shape of the cottage. 'In addition to the REDEV man I told you about. Davenport.'

'The one you were monitoring?' There was a critical cut to the voice.

'Yes, sir,' Holland agreed quietly. The superintendent had been fully aware of the part-time nature of the surveillance, and had approved of it.

'And we've no idea where Pearce is. Or which journalists he's talking to, beyond "Charlie" or his side-kick . . .'

Holland's hands were freezing. He stuck the free one under his armpit.

'I don't suppose this female revealed to you which organisation she represented?'

Holland closed his eyes. Sasha Downey hadn't left him any numbers. 'No, sir,' he said evenly. 'She's a freelance.'

He heard a car door slam and footsteps approach. Julie's face appeared around the hedge. 'Sir?' she called anxiously. 'Bennett's been told to get to London, fast as he can. To a hotel in Covent Garden.'

Holland relayed the message to the superintendent, then hurried after her. She was in the back with Bennett; Jem was at the wheel with the engine already running. Holland got in beside him, blessing the car's immediate warmth, then flinching as Bennett leaned over and sneezed in his ear.

'It's where it's happening, Mr Holland,' Bennett said, thickly but eagerly. 'At this hotel. I asked Control what was going on. He wouldn't tell me, but he said they were down a man and needed me up there pronto. Didn't they, Jem?'

Jem was concentrating on a bend in the lane.

'Mr Holland,' Bennett clutched at his head-rest, 'd'you think we could, um—'

'What?'

'D'you think we could stop on the way? Get something to eat? I never finished my lunch, you know, and it'll be cold now.'

With a foot, Holland stirred the cartons beneath his feet.

'Just a sandwich.' Bennett snorted hopefully. 'Or a pasty or something. Feed a cold and starve a fever, Mr Holland.'

Holland turned round. Bennett was wiping his nose on the heel of his hand. Julie was looking determinedly elsewhere.

'Or a proper lunch, if you like,' Bennett said placatingly. 'I'm easy.'

Without a word, Holland resumed his prior position. London, he saw on a sign, was forty-seven miles away. A silence fell in the car, punctuated only by Bennett's sniffing.

*   *   *

Once on the South Circular, Sasha had called Charlie to tell him she was on her way to Floral Street with the laptop's owner.

'What?' He had sounded immediately alarmed. 'You're OK? You're not under any sort of duress?'

'No, no, nothing like that.'

'OK.' He'd sounded far from convinced. 'I'll, er, look forward to meeting him, then.'

When she'd finished the call, Davenport, who'd thawed considerably towards her, turned supercilious again. Fine, she thought, be moody, be anything you like, as long as when you get to Mike's laptop – she would always think of it as Mike's, not his – you do whatever you have to do in order to get that data. She glanced over at him. His head was turned away from her as he monitored the wing mirror on his side. In profile he looked very arrogant and disdainful.

Perhaps he was wrong about those little babies at the Mistletoe, she thought. Perhaps something could be done to save them.

'That car,' he said suddenly, turning in his seat.

'Which one?' She checked her rear-view mirror. There was a stream of cars behind them.

'The red Audi, two behind us.' He was ramrod straight now, eyes front. He spoke without moving his lips. 'It's been on our tail for the last five minutes.'

'Are you sure?' She looked in the mirror again, saw the one he referred to, and her pulse quickened. Then the car immediately behind them moved into the outside lane and the Audi closed the gap. She made out the shape of a woman at the wheel and what looked like a baby-chair in the passenger seat.

'I think they're OK,' she said diplomatically. 'You know what London's like. Everyone going in the same direction at once.'

Davenport sniffed. 'Just because it's a woman.' He crossed his arms. 'One of the worst ones – I think she's in charge, actually – is a woman. She always administers the *coup de grâce*, Stockart says.'

'Really.' She prayed that he wouldn't go into details.

'Anyway,' he sniffed again, 'how long before we get to my laptop? You said it would be an hour, and that was—'

'Minutes,' Sasha promised. They were coasting round the Aldwych now. 'I'm just going to phone Charlie so he can let the garage know we're coming.'

*　　*　　*

On his inspection of the apartment building that morning, McMahon had noted the presence of the tall metal garage doors, leading, he'd presumed, to underground parking for the residents. The opening of them now, heralded by a screaming scrape, gave him warning, and he was on his feet and in position in seconds, his eyes pressing hard into the binoculars' casing. Two vehicles came down the cobbled street. The first, a taxi, he ignored. The second he homed in on, saw the driver and recognised her instantly as familiar. She was one of the players. He hit the alert code on his mobile.

Both men answered at once.

'Intercept the BMW. Go.'

He could watch it unfold from where he stood. He could see one of the men, the biker, running – from the other end of the street, unfortunately, but he was closing fast – and the other . . . He bent forward. He couldn't see him. He scanned quickly, seeing as he did so that the girl had already entered the garage, that it was in fact a car elevator and that, although it was a tight fit, she'd got the car completely inside.

The doors started to move across, blocking her from sight.

'Come on,' he growled to his men.

The doors kept rolling. McMahon's body tensed, his hands fisted. He saw that his first man was there now, that he'd got his hand on the edge of the door, that he was trying to stop it moving, that he was trying to squeeze himself into the diminishing gap.

'Oi!' The porter's shout easily reached McMahon. 'What the hell d'you think you're doing? Get away from there!'

McMahon couldn't hear what his man replied, but saw him turn and put his hands up in a shrugging gesture, then move off.

McMahon swore softly. As he did so, he saw his second man emerge from immediately below him. Just for a split-second he was in view before sidling out of sight. He reappeared moments later, quickly crossing the road, shaking his head up at the window where he knew McMahon would be watching.

McMahon's stomach contracted. The man had been taking a break, *another* break, when he should have been on duty. It was the same man who'd been tucking into a leisurely breakfast that morning. He stared at his back as he moved with a rolling gait along the pavement. They were short on manpower right now, McMahon thought, calming himself. But afterwards . . .

He stepped back into the room to retrieve the slim folder in which he kept the paperwork. He examined the latest sheet that Control had sent over, 'just in case'. It showed the face of a man, faintly blurred by the fax process but with the features still quite recognisable. McMahon closed his eyes. He had trained his memory well, so it was not difficult for him to remember the glimpse he'd had of the girl's passenger.

He opened his eyes and glanced down into the flat opposite. The boy had his back to the window, but as McMahon watched, he straightened up and moved further into the room and out of sight. If he was not mistaken – and even as he thought it, McMahon knew he was not – four of the people that they sought were very shortly going to be in one place together, and ripe for the taking.

He dialled the number for Control.

'We're going.' Edward Gilbert, grim-faced, re-entered the room. 'I've had it up to here,' he hit his forehead, 'with their bloody excuses. They don't know where West's gone; they don't know which specialist he meant.'

Thank God, Rose thought, getting to her feet. She crossed over to the cot. Dr West had let them down badly; she'd been wrong to bring Jeremy here; and for the last hour or so, between Edward's outbursts, she'd been wondering whether maybe the other doctors had been right all along. There wasn't anything the matter with Jeremy except vicious older sisters.

'Get up, Lucy,' she told her daughter sharply. All day Lucy had been playing the silent child, huddling on the floor next to the cot, clinging to one of its metal legs. Edward had been taken in – 'It's all right, baby, Jeremy's going to be fine' – but then Edward, Rose reminded herself grimly, didn't know the truth.

Lucy cowered away from her now. 'I mean it,' Rose said warningly, but Edward sighed. 'Oh, leave her alone.'

She turned her back on them both, bent down to pick up Jeremy, feeling herself melt at the warm weight of him, at his struggle to focus on her face, and then, amazingly, he smiled. A tear trickled down her cheek. He loved her and she loved him, and he would never know – her Jeremy, her little boy – what terror he'd caused her. She sat down with him on the chair, cradling him close, breathing in his soft baby smell. 'Mummy's going to take you home, darling,' she whispered, brushing her lips against the down of his head. Carefully she began putting him into his snow-suit. 'Jeremy's going to sleep in his own little bed tonight, isn't he?'

'Mr Gilbert, Mrs Gilbert.' The head nurse stood in the doorway. She'd long since ceased to smile at them, and privately Rose didn't blame her.

'Dr West's secretary has just called me. The specialist has been located and will be on his way shortly. We apologise,' she stared fixedly at the wall behind them, 'for the delay, and we would very much like Jeremy to remain here until the specialist has seen him.'

'Oh, you would, would you?' Edward said belligerently.

Rose blinked. Her hand, in the process of getting Jeremy's arm into a sleeve, stopped in mid-air. But there's nothing wrong with the baby, she wanted to say. She knew that now, she'd accepted it.

'See?' Edward swung on her. 'If you speak to these people in a language they understand, you get results. How long before he gets here?' he demanded of the nurse.

Rose didn't hear the reply. She felt her heart grow cold. She understood now the reason behind Dr West's strange behaviour. He'd been able to see, just by looking, what was wrong with Jeremy – that it was something terribly wrong. That's why he'd refused to hold him, why he'd virtually run out of the door to get that specialist.

She heard a whimper and looked down, expecting it to be Lucy seeking attention again, but the child was staring silently up at her. Rose realised that it was she who had made the noise, and that Edward and the nurse were also looking at her strangely. She clutched Jeremy very tightly to her. 'I want to take him home,' she bleated.

'Don't be silly,' Edward said, but not harshly, and he came across and knelt down beside her. He stroked first her cheek, then Jeremy's, then (because she had thrust herself between them,) Lucy's too. 'You're tired, that's all, Rosie. Mummy's tired, LuLu. Don't be frightened.'

He transferred his gaze back to Rose. 'Should I take Jeremy, darling?' he asked in a falsely hearty way. 'He's going to get squashed in there!'

'No!' She clung tighter. 'No one's going to take him!'

'All right, darling.' Edward backed off instantly. She heard him at the door, muttering to the nurse, and wondered how they'd got so friendly all of a sudden. Then Jeremy sneezed and reclaimed her whole attention.

He was a bit pink in the face. At once her heart was in her mouth, but she calmed herself almost as instantly. It wasn't fever; he was simply a bit warm in his suit. She debated whether to take it off again, but that would be giving in to what the others wanted. She rocked him gently to and fro and, angel that he was, his eyelids fluttered shut once more in sleep.

No one else was going to hold him, she promised him, only her. No one was going to hurt him. Her love would make him well.

'Mummy?' Lucy put a hand on her knee.

'Get away from us,' she spat.

CHAPTER THIRTY-NINE

It had not been an auspicious beginning.

'That's him?' Davenport had said incredulously on entering Charlie's flat, and Sasha, who'd taken two seconds out to share a smile with Charlie, had been forced to transfer her attention.

She'd seen what Davenport meant. Mike, standing behind the sofa, was looking particularly youthful this afternoon; he seemed to have got gawkier and spottier in her short absence.

From his expression, he clearly didn't think much of Davenport either. It was a good thing, she'd told herself, making introductions, that no one was there to make friends.

Reluctantly, at her prompting, Mike had produced the laptop. Once Davenport had it in his hands his mood had improved. He was sitting now on the sofa with it open on his lap; Mike was on his left, and she and Charlie stood behind, watching.

Davenport switched it on. They saw the familiar file contents appear on screen.

'Still working,' Davenport muttered as if surprised. 'You didn't manage to break it then, Sonny Jim?'

'Course not!'

Davenport hit another key. One of the graphics came up – the red city landscape. He sniffed and pressed the function key to return to the contents box.

'Oh, please,' Mike started.

'What?' Davenport pulled out the mobile phone and set it down on the coffee-table.

'Can you tell me what that graphic means? How you get into that file?'

Sasha put a hand on Mike's shoulder. 'We don't have time. Colin's got to get into Branium's database and get some information.'

'Branium?' Charlie echoed. 'The Infutopin people? They're behind the glass womb stuff?'

Mike swung round. 'They're the ones who killed Gerry and the others?'

'I had to tell him,' Charlie put quickly.

She squeezed his hand, hoping it conveyed a fraction of what she felt – gratitude, love, longing – and nodded down at Mike. 'Yes, they're the ones. They've been trying to cover up what they've been doing. Awful things. Running medical trials without permissison. And everything's gone wrong and babies are dying—'

'*What?* Charlie said incredulously.

She nodded again. 'I'll tell you everything later. Colin's going to get the evidence we need, the list of names and the original notes.'

Davenport was tapping out a number on the mobile. She heard an electronic bleep, then a click, then a male voice pleasantly saying: 'Good afternoon. You have reached the internal database of Branium Pharma UK Incorporated. Please hang up.'

'It's a security thing,' she explained to Charlie.

'Yeah,' he nodded. 'For homeworkers.'

'Sorry.' She felt herself blush. 'Of course you'd know . . .'

He turned and kissed her on the lips, and for that moment she wanted nothing more but him – for the others to be gone, the story to be over, just the two of them together in that room.

The mobile was ringing. Davenport answered it at once. 'I'm in,' he said simply, and she saw that the second item on the contents file, the one marked 'Network' was highlighted.

Her throat constricted. 'You are?'

'Yes, but there's a queue.' He pointed at a small clock icon that had come up on the screen. 'There often is at this time of day.

People get busy after lunch.' He turned to Mike. 'What was it you wanted to know? What the graphics mean?'

Mike nodded.

'It's not very difficult.' He tapped the appropriate keys and again the city skyline appeared, the clock superimposed upon it in one corner. 'This is Turin.'

'Oh. Right.'

'You can recognise it by that dome over there.' He stabbed at a roof. 'It's the Santa . . . something. I forget. And it's red, isn't it?'

'Yeah.'

'So it's Red Turin. Which is an anagram for . . .' He pressed another key and a box appeared in the top right-hand corner of the screen. 'Intruder,' he said, keying it in. 'Which in turn is a synonym for Infiltrator. See?'

Sasha said nothing because she was too intent on reading over his shoulder what had just appeared on the screen.

'Branium Pharma UK Inc is on the verge of a medical miracle that will be of greater signifance than landing a man on the moon. Dr Will West has pioneered an amazing genetic technique which has been proved to eliminate the appalling disease of Duchenne's Muscular Dystrophy in young boys . . .'

If only she'd thought about word-games and anagrams, she told herself, but then remembered that the report was a whitewash. If she'd found it on the laptop and written a story about it, none of the truth would have come out. She glanced at the little clock, its second hand sweeping slowly. Come on, she urged it, let us in.

'I split the material into three sections,' Davenport said to Mike. 'Introduction, middle and end.' He exited from the page and another graphic appeared – the yawning Robin Hood figure. 'This is the second section. It's protected by my huntsman. He's yawning, isn't he? So he's the Tired Hunter.' Another empty box appeared, and Davenport started keying in letters.

'Another anagram?' Charlie queried.

Davenport nodded. 'The answer's based on the same thing: The Intruder.'

'And the champagne bottles?' Charlie asked.

'They stand for Third Neat Result, which refers to the third Albanian trial. Which, as I told her,' Sasha received a jerk of the head, 'was successful. The answer is: The Last Intruder. Easy when you know the answers, isn't it?'

'Very,' Charlie said, a fraction drily.

'We found the glass womb stuff, though, didn't we?' Mike said suddenly.

'Sure we did. In your safe,' Charlie added to Davenport. 'The amniocentesis test,' he continued in response to Davenport's blank look.

'The what?' Davenport's lip curled. 'What're you talking about? I never leave anything in my safe. It's not . . .'

'Safe,' Mike put in.

'Tidy.' Davenport gave him a cold look. 'If I pull stuff down off the network I don't leave it lying around.'

'Yes you . . .' Mike began, then caught Charlie's eye.

Davenport was already summoning up the icons. Sasha saw the little safe appear and the door opening. 'You see? Nothing,' Davenport said triumphantly. 'I don't know what you thought you saw,' he said scornfully to Mike, 'but as you can see there's—'

'It's right at the end,' Charlie interrupted. 'If you hit the "page down" key—'

'I know how to do it.' Davenport pressed two keys at once. 'And I know what I've got on my own—'

Sasha saw the embryos. There were two of them, suspended in pink. The latter had toes like stars and tiny hands that were spread out as if it were startled. The body was curled up, its back pushed against the round boundary as though trying to escape the needle.

'Oh my God,' she said. She felt sick.

'Ah.' Davenport cleared his throat. 'This must've been in an appendix. I never saw it before. Anyway . . .' He shrugged. 'It's only the illustrations, not the text.' Then he turned to face Charlie and Sasha with something of his old arrogance. 'And it's not amniocentesis. It's the harvesting I told you about, remember?'

Sasha stared at him as she started to explain to Charlie. 'To get Infutopin they, um . . .'

'It's all right, angel. Tell me later.'

'The clock,' Mike croaked suddenly. 'It's gone.'

Sasha stared again at the screen. 'Oh good,' Davenport said casually, but she saw that his hands were shaking. 'This shouldn't take a minute now.' He double-clicked on the second item. She saw a directory appear, a host of names and documents, then, in response to what Davenport keyed in, another box saying: 'SECURITY STAR ONE ACCESS. PLEASE IDENTIFY YOURSELF.'

'MIDAS,' Davenport typed in.

'Who's that?' asked Mike.

'Hang on a minute,' said Charlie.

Davenport was running the cursor down a new list of files. He was actually squeaking with excitement, Sasha realised. 'You wait, you bastard. Just you wait till I show Mrs Tyler . . .'

'What's wrong, Colin?' she asked. He'd stopped, hands in the air over the keyboard.

'I can't find . . . This doesn't make sense.' He stabbed another key, then another. He seemed to have gone into a frenzy.

'Colin?' Sasha said again.

He was still. From his lips came a low moaning sound. Mike looked round in alarm.

'What is it?' she said again.

'None of its there,' Davenport said tonelessly. He held up the laptop so that she and Charlie could see. The screen was blank.

'What does it mean?' she demanded more harshly than she intended.

'He's erased it,' Davenport said in the same dead voice.

'How about the UK trials?' she asked urgently. 'Maybe he hasn't had time . . .'

'I already looked. They're gone too. Everything.' Davenport slumped back. 'He's wiped the lot,' he whispered into the air.

Sasha gripped the back of the sofa. They couldn't prove anything. Branium had been too smart. The babies were going to die and Branium was going to slide out of any responsibility, sue anyone who suggested otherwise. Goodbye story, she thought – not for the first time. To know it was there, to be told everything; and then to know she couldn't use it, that Branium was going to escape . . .

'Are you all right?' Charlie whispered.

She took a deep breath. Davenport appeared to be coming apart, and Mike was looking increasingly frightened. It wasn't her place to crack up; she had to get control.

She skirted the sofa and sat down on the table in front of them. 'Colin.' Face-to-face he looked dreadful, completely colourless, and he was shaking badly. He pushed the laptop away and it clattered on to the table beside her. 'Wouldn't there be a back-up of that information anywhere?' she asked.

It was as if he hadn't heard her. 'H-he's going to k-kill me. H-he's going to come and get me.' He looked wildly around. 'He'll find me! You don't know him! He'll t-track me down here! He'll find me! Yes he will! He will!'

Mike flinched.

'No one's going to find you, Colin,' Sasha said firmly. She saw Mike get up and go to the window. She watched him worriedly for a moment, then turned back to Davenport. 'You're quite safe here. This is one of the safest apartment blocks in London. In the country. It's notorious, isn't it, Charlie?'

'Absolutely. No one gets past the guys downstairs.' He joined Sasha on the table. 'Would anyone else have downloaded the data into their own files?'

Davenport stared back. She thought he wasn't going to answer, then he said hopelessly, 'I don't know. Maybe the directors. But . . .' He trailed off.

'How about the authors of it? The scientists who discovered it?'

Sasha started. 'Dr West,' she blurted.

Davenport frowned at her.

She leant forward so that she was almost touching his knees. 'How about West? Surely he'd have all his original notes – and not just on the Albanian trials.' She was starting to feel excited.

Davenport blinked stupidly. 'Yes,' he said after a moment.

'Would they be on computer?'

He still seemed in a daze. She wanted to scream 'Wake up!' at him. 'Yes, they'd be on computer,' he said after another pause.

'Can you access his files on the laptop?' Charlie said.

'Laptop?' He frowned and seemed to recover slightly. 'Yes, I should think so. I'll have to find his password.' He picked up the computer again, bent over the screen and began tapping away once more. 'It'll be in personnel . . . Here it is. How original!' He said with something of his old disdain. 'Einstein.'

Sasha quickly glanced over at Mike, who stood with his back to them.

Davenport was keying quickly. 'They're gone too,' he said.

'Oh.' All at once she was exhausted, she could think of nothing else. She wanted to lean against Charlie and cry.

'Stockart's wiped every reference that's accessible on the network.' Davenport's voice was a flat monotone.

Sasha shut her eyes.

'What is it, Colin?' Charlie asked sharply, and she came to at once.

Davenport was staring off into space. 'West'll have what I had at REDEV.' He spoke dreamily. 'His PC'll be hard-coded.'

'What does that mean?'

'That no one else can access it except the password-holder,' Charlie said swiftly. 'Stockart won't have been able to use his own machine to wipe West's data.'

Sasha shook her head. 'But West's the doctor, Charlie! He'll have wiped the data himself.'

'Ah, yes. I'd forgotten about that.'

'I don't know, actually,' Davenport said in the same dreamy manner. 'It looked like he and Stockart were having words earlier on.'

'So – d'you think West would help us?'

Davenport shrugged. 'He might.'

Sasha stood up. 'Charlie, can I use the phone?'

'Course.'

She crossed quickly to his desk, found the number in the phone book and dialled.

'Who're you calling?' Davenport asked.

'The . . . Oh, good-afternoon. Could you put me through to Dr West, please?' Her heart was in her mouth. She saw that Mike had turned round and was watching her. She hoped that her smile was reassuring.

'Hello?' said a woman's voice rather breathlessly.

'Could I speak to Dr West, please?'

'He's, um, not here at the moment.' There was a pause. 'Can I take a message?'

Sasha debated briefly. 'No. No, thank you. When're you expecting him back?'

There was another pause that grew longer. 'Later this afternoon?' Sasha prompted.

'I hope so,' said the woman softly.

Sasha asked on which floor West worked, thanked the woman politely, and hung up. Everyone was watching her. 'I think we should go over there,' she said.

'And do what?' said Davenport. The dreaminess had gone.

'I don't know. Challenge Dr West.' She'd a sudden inspiration. 'Show him the Infutopin diagrams. Tell him we know what he's been up to.'

'He'll deny it,' Davenport said flatly.

'Well,' she swallowed, 'you can tell him what you know. Tell him what you've told Tyler.'

'Oh no you don't.' Davenport shook his head. He was smiling unpleasantly. 'I'm not going near that place.'

'Why not?'

'They'll be looking for me, that's why not,' he snapped. 'They could be out there now,' he flung an arm in the direction of the window and Mike flinched, 'and we wouldn't know anything about it until it was too late.'

'Colin—'

'So if you think I'm walking in there so West can get on the phone to Stockart's mob, you've got another think coming.'

'But Colin,' she said desperately. 'If there's no evidence, what's going to happen to the government inquiry?'

'I . . .' His mouth worked. 'There's nothing more I can do. M-maybe I'll call Mrs Tyler and ask her if she got the message. Tell her everything again . . .'

'Uh, well—'

'O-or I could have a look on the net, see if it got lost.' That thought seemed to inspire him, and he nodded his head vigorously. 'Yes! That's what I'll do. I'm not going out there.' He shuddered. 'They kill people, you know. That poor bastard, the first one . . .'

Sasha became aware of Mike's sudden stillness. 'Don't, Colin,' she said quietly.

'They frightened him to death. They told him what they were going to do to him. Burn his hands a finger at a time—'

'No,' Mike whispered.

'Stop it,' Sasha said more loudly.

'Then they were going to move down to – you know, his privates. But they didn't have to.' He sniffed. 'He gave them one name then he died. Dead before he hit the floor. That really pissed them off, you know.'

Mike turned his back again. She saw his shoulders heaving.

'Remember that car on the bridge?' Davenport demanded. 'I told you it was following us.'

'Sasha?' Mike croaked. He was trembling dreadfully. 'I-is that true?'

'No.' She shook her head. 'I think Colin maybe imagined there was someone.'

Davenport snorted.

'Shall we go?' said Charlie, getting up. 'Come on, Mike.'

'A-are you going to leave me here?' Davenport looked suddenly panicky.

'Well.' She felt rather helpless. 'You won't come with us . . .'

'You're safe here, Colin,' Charlie said patiently.

'B-but I don't like b-being on my own. S-s-suppose they get in?' His eyes flicked to the door. 'Th-there's no other way out, is there? Wh-what would I do?'

'It's not going to happen,' Charlie said.

Sasha had a flash of inspiration. 'I've got panic buttons in my flat. They're connected to the front desk and the police.' She wasn't entirely sure about the latter, but she sounded confident. 'Why not move down there?'

Davenport frowned. 'Your flat's in the same building?'

'Yes. Funny, isn't it? So what d'you think?'

'I don't know.' Davenport twisted his hands. 'I mean, I'm still going to be on my own, aren't I?'

God give me strength, Sasha prayed.

'I think it's a great idea,' Charlie said decisively. 'We'll stop off on the way down. You really couldn't be safer there.'

Colin rose hesitantly. 'I still don't like it.'

'You'll be fine, I promise.'

Sasha saw that Charlie had picked up the laptop and passed it behind his back to Mike, who was now sliding it inside his bulky jacket. She ushered Colin out in front of her. 'This place is known as Fort Knox. I'll roll down the window blinds so no one'll be able to see that there's anyone inside. Ready?' she said brightly to the other two. She opened the door and let Colin go first.

Initially, Mel had been quite glad when the secretary had gone off to her Chistmas party. After the dreadful waiting, the news that Dr West was finally coming had acted as a soporific, and the girl, though sweet, was incredibly talkative. Mel had urged her to go, promising to mind the phones, reassuring her that she was no longer hungry after the vending-machine lunch. As soon as the swing doors had banged shut she had phoned Patrick with the good news. Then she'd lain down on the banquette, closed her eyes and fallen asleep.

She'd dreamed of Ludi, but not as he was now. He was a teenager, eighteen years old, tall and strong. She'd been calling him to hurry, that he'd be late for school, and he'd run downstairs two at a time.

'I don't go to school any more, Mum.' His smile was her little boy's. 'I go to university now, remember?'

She'd woken with her cheeks wet. The Duchenne's counsellor had warned her and Patrick that in some cases the disease affects the brain. While that did not appear to be true in Ludo's case, they had to bear in mind that with his increasing disabiities he would lose a lot of school-time, and it would become difficult for him to use a pen or a keyboard. While a few boys did achieve good academic results they were the exception rather than the rule, and it was perhaps kinder for everyone concerned not to expect too much.

She'd dried her eyes and checked in her hand-mirror for smudged make-up. She should be laughing, not crying, she'd told herself. It was simply the suddenness of it, the gift of being able to dream in the knowledge that the dreams might come true. Of course, she'd continued earnestly to herself, Ludi didn't have to go to university or do A levels if he didn't want to. He could leave school at sixteen if he liked. He could be anything he wanted to be, fulfil his own dreams, not hers or Patrick's.

She'd checked the time, realised that West could be there at any moment, and had sat upright and composedly for a few minutes. Then, feeling a bit silly, she'd stood up and walked about. There'd been little, given the state of the place, to look at. Building works were obviously in progress. She'd stepped over some planks of wood to get to the window at the far end of the room, where she'd watched the Thames roll by, the cars clogging the roads, the people scurrying about. Then she'd heard the music, Christmas songs, seeping up from the floor below where the secretary's party was. In order not to disrupt the work of the hospital parties were being staggered that year, the girl had explained. Mel could have gone too, they could have left Dr West a note – but Mel had shaken her head.

As if she could go to a party when Dr West was coming!

But standing there forlornly, she'd almost wished that she had gone. She'd felt so very much on her own and rather exposed in that derelict place. She'd glanced again at the time. Where was he? she'd wondered. He was coming, wasn't he? He wasn't going to let her down, not help Ludo, was he? Had he decided to take on another boy instead of hers? She'd chewed her knuckle, seen the indentations of her own teeth-marks, heard in a burst of noise from below: 'It's going to be a sad, lonely Christmas without you . . .'

The telephone ringing on his desk had made her jump. She'd nearly tripped over a flex in her haste to answer it. She'd hoped that it might have been West himself, calling with an explanation, some reassurance, but no.

Now feeling chilly, she rubbed her arms. It had simply been someone else – another woman looking for him. Mel pondered briefly on who she might have been. A patient, a nurse, a doctor, another mother? She sat down in the secretary's chair, saw the pile of mail waiting to be opened, thought that if it had been her, she would have opened it and sorted it into categories for his urgent attention: business, personal, etc.

She flipped through the envelopes until she came across the one she was looking for, addressed in her own handwriting.

'I can't begin to tell you how grateful I am, my husband and me both. We would take it as a great honour to name our unborn child after you, as long as you don't mind?'

She pressed the paper to her cheek for comfort. She felt so lonely on her own. She wished that Patrick had accompanied her as he'd suggested. 'Not just for a chat,' she'd said, smiling. 'Later, when Ludi's treatment starts. Come with us then.'

She could feel her eyes watering, but she didn't want to cry any more.

'Please come quickly, Will,' she begged.

According to the street-atlas, Floral Street in Covent Garden was less than a mile away. Jem pulled into the kerb and swapped seats with Bennett. The man had become very quiet.

'Are you sure I've got to do this, Mr Holland?' he bleated.

'You'll be fine.'

Holland sincerely hoped that he would be. He was fully aware that Bennett ought to be wired up, but there'd been no time. The only means of communication they were going to have was one that Bennett had devised himself: into his mobile phone's memory he'd keyed the number of his spare, which Holland now had. If Bennett considered that anyone's life was in imminent danger he had only to press one key and Holland's phone would ring. He'd bragged that it would be 'a cinch; no problem, Mr Holland', but that had been during the journey, before reality had sunk in.

'McMahon's a real pro.' Bennett licked his lips now. 'Suppose he cottons on?'

'He won't.' Holland saw his sweaty palm marks on the steering-wheel. 'He's never met you before, so he won't know if you're nervous. If it's an emergency he's not going to be watching what you're doing.'

'You'll be downstairs?'

'Correct.' Once Control had told Bennett the hotel's name and address, Julie had called the reception desk and made some enquiries. 'We'll be in the bar on the ground floor.'

Bennett nodded uncertainly. 'And how long before – you know, back-up arrives?'

'Not long.' Holland shifted in his seat. He didn't know the answer to that one himself. Ten minutes? Fifteen? He hoped that his instincts were right: that to call in the Met now would be madness, that it would jeopardise everything – alerting McMahon and his men, warning off Zodiac, giving them time to flee. Leaving him with what? Three dead men, one lost boy – and Bennett.

He needed a lot more.

'All right?' He smiled with a confidence he wished he possessed and put his hand on the door-handle. 'You'd better be off. Just try to fit in with whatever's going on – but don't hurt anyone. Remember, if you see us in the hotel, don't acknowledge us. Good luck.'

He got out and stood on the pavement; Julie and Jem joined him. For a minute it looked as if Bennett wasn't going to move, then the brake lights went off, the indicator on, and the Sierra slid away. Watching it go, Holland had the same nervous sensation that he remembered from years before, when he'd seen his daughter walking away from him into the school playground for the first time.

'He's going to be OK, sir,' said Julie.

'Let's hope so.'

They had his name, address and passport. He had no criminal record, and he was terrified about going to prison. He believed that they would save him. But, away from them, would his nerve snap? Would he simply run off? Under stress, would he remember to use the phone?

The Sierra vanished out of sight. Holland saw a taxi on the other side of the road and waved at it. He and Julie would arrive first, as a couple; Jem would appear shortly afterwards, a young man on his own.

The taxi pulled up in front of them.

'I'll start walking then, shall I?' said Jem with a sigh.

Holland nodded and turned to the driver. 'The Heathman Hotel, please.'

In the distance, through the murky light, Sasha could see the green glow which indicated that the car-elevator was on their level and available.

'Charlie?' she said in surprise as he swung away from it.

With his eyes he indicated Mike sitting behind them. Since leaving Colin in her flat the boy had been extremely quiet; even the decision to take the AGN jeep had provoked little interest. 'I figure, why take the risk?' Charlie said casually. 'When there's another exit.'

'There is?' Sasha said.

'Sure.' They were swishing past empty spaces now. The car-park was far larger than she'd realised; she'd only ever used one of the visitor's spaces at the front. They reached what appeared to be a dead end, but Charlie turned sharply left and entered a narrow, unlit corridor. The headlights picked up raw, wet brick walls.

'Where on earth . . . ?' Sasha asked, then with another swing and a jolt they were on to a concrete upwards spiral. At the top Charlie stopped the jeep before steel gates, produced a plastic card from his wallet and swiped it through an old scanning machine. The gates folded smoothly to one side and they rolled out into the daylight.

'I told you,' Charlie said with a grin, 'it's an alternative exit.'

'But,' she swivelled in her seat, 'this isn't even Floral Street!'

'Nope.' Charlie changed up a gear as they bounced along the cobbles. 'We're in Long Acre.'

'Neat,' breathed Mike, the first word he'd uttered in a long while. 'So if Colin's right and anyone was out the front . . .'

'They're in for a long wait.'

'Brilliant.'

Sasha smiled at the relief in his voice. 'So how come you knew about that and not me?' she asked Charlie.

He gave her a teasing look. 'Alexander doesn't tell just anyone about it. Only his VIP residents.'

'I see.'

Charlie swerved to avoid a pedestrian. 'A few years back AGN had someone hot staying at the apartment. Some of our rivals got to hear about it and were camping outside, so Alexander – you know how he loves being in the thick of things – handed over a card for the overflow car park. It belongs to the building next to ours. We never got round to handing the card back. If there's a line for the elevator, I use it.'

They turned left into St Martin's Lane. It had been her suggestion to take a direct route to the hospital, but she'd forgotten about Christmas shoppers. She chewed her lip, hoping that they were going to be on time, that West wasn't one of those doctors who only called his office for messages. She ought to have left a message, she thought now, but what could she have said that wouldn't have warned him? Better to confront him in person, without giving him the chance to escape.

'Hey.' Charlie's finger gently stroked her cheek. 'I'm sure Alexander would give you a card if you asked him.'

'A what?' She laughed. 'Sorry. I wasn't thinking about that.'

Behind them, Mike cleared his throat. 'D'you really think this is going to work?' he asked.

'I sincerely hope so,' she said, sobering at once.

It was now twenty minutes since Anna had received the latest instructions from Hall. He'd sounded fully restored, no trace of his earlier panic – a change engendered, no doubt, by the news that Pearce, Davenport and both journalists were together in the flat. The client, apparently, was delighted.

'However, a previous matter has resurfaced, and expanded as it were. Again, the client's keen that you should handle it – and I think on balance he might be right. McMahon's got enough men for the other business. And this matter requires a considerable amount of . . . poise, shall we say?'

She'd listened, asked appropriate questions, jotted down the answers, and agreed to do it. Since then, she hadn't really moved. She stood in the window, one hand holding up the heavy brocade curtain so that she could see as much of the scene below as possible. Although only mid-afternoon the sky was dark, and down in the court-yard the lights of a large Christmas tree had been switched on.

She frowned and stood back, letting the curtain fall sharply, then crossed quickly to the wardrobe and examined herself critically in the mirror. She saw how tired she looked, but reasoned that it was in character for the person she was going to be; they often went for days without sleep.

She opened the wardrobe door, unsure about what such people wore. Her choice was limited. She selected a plain dark skirt and jacket and low-heeled shoes, added a pink silk scarf, and stood back to regard her reflection. It was good: unpretentious, feminine, but serious.

She wondered briefly about make-up. A little, she decided, going through to the bathroom. People were always reassured by an attractively turned-out person, and if they were reassured they were less likely to argue or ask awkward questions.

She inclined closer to the mirror, outlining her lips with care.

Bennett knew that he wasn't a brave man, and he considered what he was now doing to be so extremely brave – or foolhardy – that it was better not to think about it.

'You're absolutely sure?' McMahon asked him.

He nodded. The equipment that had been there in the hotel room, waiting for him to arrive and set it up, was the very best. If there had been anyone in the flat which McMahon indicated, the sound and heat sensors would have picked them up.

'Yeah, I'm sure,' he croaked, not looking up.

McMahon was standing beside him, to one side of the window, a pair of binoculars to his eyes. 'I can't see them either,' he said, puzzled. 'I don't understand it. They were there ten minutes ago and no one saw them leave.'

Bennett licked his lips. He didn't want trouble from anyone. He'd never meant to be a supergrass; he wasn't cut out for it. It was all that Holland's fault. 'They might've gone into another room and shut the door,' he suggested timidly to McMahon.

'Yeah?' The man glanced down.

'Yeah,' Bennett mumbled, immediately looking away.

'That explains it, then. Wonder what they're up to.'

Suppose, Bennett wondered, fiddling unnecessarily with a sensor, they – whoever 'they' were – stayed incommunicado for so long that McMahon told him to go? The police would have to find another stooge. He would be off the hook. He sniffed eagerly at the thought. He wouldn't have to sit here any longer, double-crossing a killer like McMahon – he was meant to be the worst – praying that the moment wouldn't come when he'd have to press the alarm button on the mobile. McMahon had eyes that were everywhere at once.

Bennett gave a little mew of fear.

'What did you say?'

'Sorry, just my cold.' On cue, he felt a sneeze coming, and with it the need to use the bathroom. He rose unsteadily to his feet.

'Not again?' McMahon grunted as he went.

In Sasha's flat, Davenport snooped casually. Her bedroom, he noted with a grimace, was very untidy: clothes and magazines everywhere, drawers wide open, make-up piled messily on the dressing-table. He liked his women to be tidy.

Not that she was his woman, of course, he told himself sourly. There'd been a period during the journey when he'd entertained the notion – she *was* attractive – but then hearing her on the phone to her boyfriend he'd thought, no. She was too young for him – and not his type anyway.

He entered the kitchen and opened a cupboard. Four tins of tuna and a packet of dried spaghetti met his gaze. Obviously no cook, he thought, which was another of his criteria. The fridge contained a bottle of wine and a carton of soup. 'Just help yourself to anything,' she'd trilled on her way out. Well, he thought meanly, he would. He found a corkscrew, extracted the cork and poured himself a generous glass.

He wandered with it back into the living room and sank down on to the sofa. She'd been right, he thought, taking a good gulp of the liquid. With the blinds down the room felt very safe and snug. And *he'd* been right, absolutely so, to let her and the other two go off on their own. He took another swig. They must be mad, all of them. He glanced at the laptop lying beside him and realised that they must have taken the old one with them. He shrugged. Let them. He'd lay bets that nothing on it would make Dr Will West talk.

He felt sleep tugging at his eyelids. He yawned, and caught sight of Sasha's ancient-looking PC on her desk, reminding him that he was supposed to be checking to see whether Mrs Tyler had received his memo. He took another mouthful of wine. He would do that in a minute; it had been a long day and he was very tired. The wine glass tipped forward in his hand, spilling a dribble on to the floor, his head eased back against the sofa, he fell suddenly and deeply asleep.

The sound of the telephone brought him awake in an instant. He didn't know where he was, didn't recognise anything. He jumped up in a panic, bringing down one foot heavily on the glass, then he saw the telephone on the desk by the wall, and the ringing stopped and there was the click of an answerphone.

He felt giggly with relief. There was a brief silence, presumably the outgoing message being played, and then . . .

Davenport listened intently.

No voice. He heard a man breathing, heavy and deep. Why didn't he speak?

Davenport swallowed quickly. His heart thumped in terror. The listening, waiting silence stretched on. This was exactly how Stockart had tortured him, day and night: clickings on the line and no one speaking, just the sound of slow, deep breathing, letting him know that the watchers were out there, waiting, and could come for him any time.

He jammed his fist in his mouth. Stockart knew he was there! He'd been right all along; they'd followed him there and now they were letting him know.

On the line, the man made a fearful sucking sound.

With a yelp, Davenport snatched up his laptop and ran for the door. Out in the corridor he sped for the lift, hit the call-button hard. 'Come on, come on,' he whimpered, hopping from foot to foot. He heard the lift approaching, the clunk as it came to rest, and he was struck by a new terror. Suppose they were in there? His chest tightened and he took a step back to run but it was too late, the lift doors were opening.

An elderly couple stepped out. He pushed in, gasping.

'I say,' said the man, affronted. 'There's no need to shove like that.'

'Oh sod off,' Davenport snarled, smacking the button for the ground, huddling himself into a corner as the doors slid shut.

Inside the flat, the voice of Sasha's father, fed up with waiting for the bleep on her answering-machine, curtly told her to buy a new one and added that her mother expected her home in time for lunch on Christmas Eve.

In the lobby bar of the Heathman Hotel, Tony Holland studied the notebook on his lap. It had come from Bennett's car. It was the one that contained Davenport's Kent address, but now it lay open at the previous page.

The writing was difficult to read but, idly flicking through some minutes before, Holland had seen the words 'Dark BMW' and paused. There followed a scrawl which Holland had taken to be a registration number, or part of one.

'Sorry, sir.' Julie, who'd been checking, finished her call. 'Nothing doing – there's too much missing.'

'OK. Thanks.' He remembered the type and colour of the car Sasha Downey had been driving the day before, but nothing of the registration. She didn't own it or any car – Julie had checked that out too. If she had they could have got her address that way, or if she'd left a phone number with him, if she'd told him who she was working for . . . He took a sip of coffee. He couldn't help remembering how he'd virtually ordered her to go to REDEV. He'd wanted her to stir things up.

He stared again at the readable letters on the page in front of him: 'F20S'. What if, he wondered, they didn't form part of a car's registration number at all, but a description of a female in her twenties?

He took another mouthful; the coffee was almost cold. The only man who could verify his suspicion was, he hoped, somewhere up

above him and incommunicado. He was nearby, definitely; he and
Julie had seen his car in the car-park at the back of the hotel.
Holland glanced at the mobile sitting on the table, wondering
again if Bennett would freeze at the vital moment.

'Would you like another drink, sir? Madam?'

Holland looked up at the smiling face of the barman. The staff
here seemed exceedingly pleasant, he thought. 'Have you any
conferences going on at the moment?' he asked. 'Any companies
holding meetings here?'

'No, sir. We're hosting two next week, but this week's clear.
We have excellent facilities. I could get you a brochure if you
like . . .'

Holland demurred, ordered himself and Julie more coffee, then
watched the barman move off in Jem's direction and heard the
request for another mineral water, no ice. Jem was sitting in the
body of the bar, facing the staircase, obstensibly reading a paper.
He'd be the first to see if Bennett appeared, whereas Holland and
Julie were closer to the front of the hotel and the entrance.

So far there'd been little activity beyond two American tourists
who'd come in asking if it was too early for afternoon tea. The
hotel was quiet and well ordered. What were Zodiac doing there?
Who were they monitoring, and why? And who exactly were they
working for? Holland removed two pencils from his jacket pocket.
World Med Inc in the Cayman Islands – that was obviously a front
for something else. Ashford was meant to be making enquiries, but
how long would that take? Was this – Holland glanced around the
comfortable, well-polished room, the little vases of flowers on the
tables, the discreet Christmas tree in the corner – really where
'something big,' in Bennett's words, was happening?

Where was Downey? And Charlie and Pearce? He glanced over
at his own mobile. Why didn't that damned boy call his mother
and tell her where he was and which paper he was talking to?

One of the pencils shot out from beneath his hand and fell on
to the carpet. Julie bent to retrieve it. 'Awful, this waiting about,
isn't it, sir?' she said sympathetically.

Out on the pavement, Davenport made little running movements
to and fro. He had to get away, had to run. Waterloo was nearby,
just over the bridge. He needed a bus or a taxi.

He whimpered in relief as down the cobbled street came a black cab with its 'Taxi' sign lit. He leapt in front of it, waving his arms, and flung himself inside as soon as it stopped.

'Where to, guv?'

'Uh, W-w . . .' He caught his breath. Waterloo, he thought suddenly: gateway to Europe. They'd think of that. They might already be there waiting for him.

He had another idea. The mere thought of it sent warm waves rolling over him. He leaned forward. 'Whitehall, please,' he said clearly to the cabbie, then he leant back against the shiny upholstery.

He was smiling, his eyes closed, his senses calmed. He didn't see or sense the motorcylist who emerged from the alley and tucked in behind him.

Having lingered in the bathroom for as long as he dared, Bennett opened the door and emerged regretfully into the room. McMahon looked up. His eyes were brighter than before.

'You've been a long time,' he commented.

Bennett bit his thumbnail. 'Sorry, McMahon.'

'You missed all the action. We're tailing a player out there.'

'We are?' Bennett sidled past him, resumed his position on the floor to the left of the windows.

'Yes.' McMahon cracked his knuckles. 'And about bloody time too.'

CHAPTER FORTY

The Mistletoe stood on the north side of the Thames, within easy walking distance of Westminster. Its golden bricks gave it a mellow appearance, its wards situated to the rear and side of the building, so that from the front it didn't look like a hospital at all. Previously, driving past, Sasha had rather admired it, had thought how much more pleasant it must be to be a patient there than in most NHS hospitals.

Now, approaching it along the Embankment, she thought how looming it was, how impersonal its discreetly blinded windows, how sinister the three steel chimneys that rose above its roof, their metal glinting in the security lights. Chimneys for burning up debris, for doing away with that which was not perfect. The word that Davenport had used about the Albanian trials came to her. 'Duff' babies, the pitiful products of Branium's illegal experiments. She stared again at the chimneys as the jeep swung into the main entrance. How exactly was Branium going to dispose of the evidence this time? How, she thought numbly, had the Nazis done it?

'Are you all right?' Charlie asked.

'Fine.'

They were driving down the side of the building. Sleet had obliterated the last remnants of daylight and the headlights picked up pools of spitty rain. Looking up, Sasha saw a fire-escape and, beside it on the second floor, a nurse drawing a curtain across a window.

They left the jeep in a visitor's space. No one said much as they got out. Mike handed her the laptop and they set off, heads bent against the weather, for the main entrance. Words would come, she assured herself as they mounted the stone steps. Once she faced that doctor she would know what to say.

They reached the top and entered through revolving doors. Inside, piped music was playing, gentle uplighters cast a creamy glow, and a semi-circular reception desk faced them.

One of the two female receptionists looked up. 'Good afternoon.' She smiled pleasantly. 'Can I help you – or do you know where you're going?'

'We know, thank you,' Sasha said, equally politely. 'If you could just direct us to the lifts, please?'

They were round to the right, beside a flight of stairs. Sasha pressed the button to summon one and Charlie brushed her hand. 'Do you want me to come?' he asked quietly. 'I can wait down here, Mike too, if you like.'

She shook her head. 'I want you with me,' she said.

Seeing the quantity of traffic in Whitehall, Davenport had asked the cab-driver to drop him off and he'd covered the last few metres on foot. The look of the building enchanted him. Set back slightly from the main drag, it had miniature turrets, like a medieval castle, on each corner. Fit for a queen, he told himself, walking in confidently.

He stated his purpose, without stumble or stammer, to a man behind a desk.

'I'm afraid the minister doesn't see members of the public without an appointment,' the man said, cheerfully enough.

'She'll see me. Tell her . . .' He glanced around, then muttered, 'Tell her I'm the one who sent her the memo today.'

'The memo?' The man raised an eyebrow.

'Concerning a highly confidential matter.'

'I see.'

'Tell her I'm . . .' Davenport thought hard for inspiration. 'The Butterfly man,' he said, triumphantly.

The man's mouth twitched. 'She'll know what that means, will she?'

'Oh yes.'

The man exchanged a look with one of the commissionaires, then picked up the telephone. 'If you'd like to wait over there, sir . . .'

'I'll wait here.'

'As you wish.' He dialled a number. 'Sebastian? There's a gentleman down here who wants to see the minister. Claims he's the Butterfly man . . . Butterfly, yes.'

That would do it, Davenport thought, and felt excitement wash over him again. She'd take his hand; there'd be tears in her eyes. How could I ever thank you enough? she'd say.

'Sir?'

Davenport came to.

'The minister's office says she's very busy at the moment, but they're sure she'll be reading your memo soon if she hasn't already. They'd like to thank you very much for coming in.'

'But I've got to see her now!'

'I'm sorry, sir, that's not possible.'

Davenport gripped the desk. 'Try her again!'

Some of the amusement left the man's face. 'I'm sorry, I can't do that, sir.' He raised his voice slightly and a commissionaire materialised at Davenport's elbow. 'As you don't have an appointment, sir, I'm afraid I'm going to have to ask you to leave the building.'

'But . . .'

Outside, he stood glaring in at them for a moment. Then, clutching the laptop to him, he strode off in search of a telephone-box. The man hadn't called the minister's office at all, he thought; he'd probably reckoned Davenport was a nutter, had dialled a mate or the talking clock. Davenport scowled. He'd been having fun at his expense. Well, he'd be laughing on the other side of his face once Davenport had called the minister's office himself, got through to her private secretary, told him what the oaf at the front desk had done.

The pavement was teeming with people. He kept his head down, using his body as a battering ram, cursing them all. As he crossed a small street in a mass of pedestrians he felt someone shove him from behind, turned angrily and saw a man in a motorcyclist's helmet.

'Watch it,' he snapped, then gasped as the thin blade entered between his ribs.

'Sorry, mate.' The voice was muffled through the helmet as the man drove the knife home into Davenport's heart.

For a time the weather had held Mel's attention. From her lofty, cosseted vantage point at the window she'd watched the sleet fall, seen the trees throw themselves at the wind, the world turn wintry. Then she'd considered whether it would be worse at home, whether there it would be proper snow and Ludo would be out in it, making a snowman.

She hoped that, whatever the treatment was for Ludo, it wouldn't be too painful. From the little she knew of gene-therapy, it involved a procedure similar to a blood transfusion. How long would it take? she wondered. Would there be several sessions?

Ludo didn't like needles – and he hated hospitals. She thanked God that, so far, apart from the splints at night – and they were more uncomfortable than painful – Ludo hadn't suffered any physical pain. Mentally, though, God knows what having Duchenne's had done to him. She took a deep breath. But that was in the past now.

She stared out into the darkness. If the cure was to be painful, then she and Patrick would have to be strong, promise Ludo whatever it took – a dog, a bike (he'd always wanted a bike) – to make him go through with it.

The sleet was turning to rain on the window. Mel put out a finger and traced one drop's quick descent. She pressed her face to the glass. She'd take Ludo's place, she vowed, if she could spare him the pain. She'd do it for him now for a cure. But until now – although she'd told no one and had never before verbalised it, even to herself – she would not have swapped places with him. No. Never that. Not his dying life.

Her hand went to her mouth. Was she a terrible mother? She thought of the tiny life growing inside her. Perhaps she didn't deserve him – or Ludo. She felt a shaft of terror, then dizziness, and she steadied herself against the glass. From below came the sound of the party.

Mel made up her mind. Stepping carefully, she returned to the secretary's desk and found a pad of yellow stickies. Not knowing which of the two doors was the doctor's office, she stuck a note on each.

Turning to go from the second one, she thought that she'd heard a noise, something distinct from the humming sound of the lab equipment. She stared at the door for a moment. It was well sealed; she could detect no light or movement coming from within. All was silent now. She must have imagined it, she told herself, and headed off in search of the secretary to remind her of her promise to contact the doctor if he'd failed to arrive by now.

Immersed in his work, the noise at the door had made Stockart jump, causing him to bang his knee on the desk. He didn't know if he'd been heard. He stared at the door, feeling rather than hearing someone on the other side. Then came the sound of light footsteps moving quickly away.

He waited for the creak of the swing-doors at the far end of the floor, then distantly heard the footsteps again, this time moving along the corridor behind him. They sounded like a woman's steps. They paused (and he imagined her waiting for the lift), then moved off once more. She had opted for the stairs.

Only when the last sound had completely died away did he get up. He listened at the door, then very quietly turned the lock. The floor was empty, shadowy, half in darkness. In the stillness he heard Christmas music.

He turned back, saw the note on the door, tore it off and read it. Damn, he thought: it had been Melanie Alder out there all along, and not (as he'd assumed) West's secretary. He grimaced. So, Mrs Alder had gone looking for West. Good luck to her. He glanced at his watch. If only she had waited there a little longer . . . He screwed up the note and stuffed it in his pocket. No matter – she could be dealt with later, at her home.

At least, now that he had the floor to himself, he didn't need to worry about making a noise.

He returned to the task that had brought him to West's office – entering stealthily by the corridor door – in the first place. The man's absence from the room (and the adjoining lab) had only confirmed what he now accepted as the truth: that, like Davenport, West had turned traitor and would talk. The revelation had come to him in a flash after his last telephone call with Bernard Hall, when he'd been hearing the excellent news that both journalists, Pearce, *and* the viper Davenport were together in the Covent Garden flat.

'It can only be hours now, sir,' Hall had said and Stockart had laughed shortly before replying. 'This time, Bernard, I think I *do* believe you.'

He'd delivered his new orders and put down the telephone.

And then he'd seen it plainly: West, not in hiding at all but sitting in an interview room, his pink head gleaming, his dry lips parted in a sneer, his spidery fingers counting as, point by point, fact by fact, he set out to betray him. Names, places, dates, times, data – all presented neatly for the superintendent. Of course he could hardly deny his own involvement, but Stockart knew exactly how he would play it: West the coerced genius; Stockart the ruthless mastermind who'd made him conduct the UK trials before he'd been ready and without legal permission.

Stockart had seen those long white hands twisting, heard the flutey voice mewling that none of it had been his fault, just Stockart's. Stockart was to blame. And he could prove every word of what he said; it was all on his computer.

Stockart's flesh had crawled. While he'd wiped every trace of the Infiltrator and Infutopin material from the network – including the back-ups in the security archives – he'd forgotten about West's computer. He couldn't erase anything on that unless he did so in person.

On his way over he'd briefly envisaged the hospital surrounded by police, SWAT teams breaking down doors, SOCO men seizing evidence – but when he'd reached it the place was quiet. Perhaps, he'd thought, West hadn't mentioned the data part yet; or perhaps the police were telling him to make a statement first, assuring him that the evidence on the computer could wait.

It had occurred to Stockart when he'd first entered the room to snatch up the machine, run out into the corridor and fling it from the window, but that would have drawn attention to himself. Besides, he wasn't sure that computer's memory-boards, like black boxes in crashed aircraft, couldn't be retrieved and made to divulge their secrets. No, he'd reasoned, deletion was more discreet, and it would look so much worse for West. When the police burst in and found nothing, they'd see the doctor's story for what it was: a cowardly attempt by a Mengele to crucify an innocent man. As evidence: the dead babies, their altered DNA; West's own words. He would be hoist by his own petard. How glorious, Stockart had gloated. West would die in prison, utterly villified, his life's work on the bonfire.

He'd worked quickly, starting with the Infutopin material, erasing one file after another. Then he'd moved on to the Albanian data. At first he'd been concerned that the noise of the computer would be heard outside, but there'd been no tap at the door, no enquiry as to who was there, so he'd assumed that the whirrings from the fridges and the DNA machines in the labs drowned out any sound that he was making.

He was on the last Infiltrator file now, marked INFL. ALD. He called it up – it was Subject Eighteen's case history – and pressed the 'delete' button. Then he heaved a great, contented sigh. As ever, when a problem presented itself, he had solved it. He'd think of a story for himself and the other directors to tell the police. Blank astonishment would do at first, but later, in the morning, something along the lines of how they'd all been worried about West, how he'd become so withdrawn, refusing to tell anyone what he'd been doing. Stockart yawned. He'd give it proper thought later.

He ran the cursor back up the screen, preparing to exit, and saw the DAMR icon: the tiny stethoscope. He wondered how they were doing, whether the first one had succumbed yet. He knew that he ought not to tarry, but it wouldn't take a moment – and he'd always liked living on the edge. He felt his stomach burn, gulped down two tablets, and summoned up the latest on Subject Two, the one who'd been transferred to the Bristol hospital.

'Leukaemoid picture clearing,' he read. He stared: that couldn't be. The fools must have made a mistake. Cretinous, half-witted—

He froze. Behind him, the elevator had announced its arrival with a gentle ping. He'd left it too late. The police were here already. West would be leading the way, throwing open the door, pointing the dramatic finger. 'This is the man!'

He had to move, run, hide himself – but where to go where he wouldn't be found? He heard the lift doors open, footsteps on the floor behind him. Any moment now the door would click open. In dread, he turned to face them.

'There's a door,' exclaimed a young voice.

'It's by entry-card only,' said an older male.

'Look,' a woman exclaimed, 'the entrance is along at the other end.'

The footsteps moved off. It sounded like several people. Stockart knew that he had only moments. He crept to the outer door and paused, pressing his body against it. When he heard the doors at the far end creak open he opened his own and, on tiptoes, headed for the stairs.

Would there be more police down there?

He descended the first flight quiet as a whisper, his body close to the wall. Then the second. Then he knew that they had missed him, and he ran.

They stood just inside the double doors, letting their eyes adjust to the dimness and the sight of the deserted floor.

'This doesn't look too good,' Sasha murmured, gripping the laptop tightly. 'I wonder if it's the right floor.'

'You said the fifth, and this is the fifth,' Mike whispered.

'There's a light on down there,' said Charlie, also keeping his voice low. They moved carefully towards it. As they got nearer the signs of building work lessened until, reaching the uplighter by the secretary's desk, it all looked as it should be: the computer with a telephone beside it; glossy magazines laid out on a low table for visitors or patients – but no sign of a patient or a secretary or, Sasha had the growing suspicion, a doctor.

'Look at this.'

She turned round. Mike was standing in front of a door on the right. He peeled a yellow note from it. '"Dr West,"' his voice trembled slightly, '"I've gone to see if someone can locate you. Melanie Alder."' He looked up. 'So we're on the right floor. This is West's office.'

But if people had gone looking for him, Sasha thought uneasily, it meant that he wasn't there. She saw another door, a little further along: there was no name on it. She was about to turn away when she saw a crack of light at the bottom. The door wasn't quite shut.

She tapped it softly. 'Dr West?' she called, and went in.

The anglepoise lamp was on; so was the computer. She took another step inside.

'Sash?' said Charlie, coming in quietly behind her.

'I don't think there's anyone in here,' she whispered back. She saw a connecting door in the opposite wall. Again, when she pushed, it opened. She called the doctor's name a second time, and hearing no reply, went cautiously inside. This room was long and thin, L-shaped, and lit only by a pink glow that none the less illumined what was there. In the short part of the L, immediately on the left, was what appeared to be ordinary office equipment – a photocopier and, behind it, a printer – although on a grand scale. There was also a very large white fridge. Around the rest of the room ran steel-fronted cupboards topped by work-benches that supported various machines, all of which seemed to be switched on and humming. But there was no sign of the doctor.

'Let's go back and have a look at that computer,' Charlie said softly.

Sasha recollected herself. He was right: it looked as if whoever had been using the computer had only left the room temporarily; he or she might return at any moment.

She went to close the door to the main floor as Charlie sat down at the desk. She felt no qualms about what they were doing; her only fear was of discovery before they found the evidence.

She joined Mike, crouching in front of the computer.

'This looks like some kind of medical record,' Charlie said, scanning down the screen. He stopped, looked over at her. 'Leukaemoid picture,' he read out.

She swallowed. 'Does it say which baby?' she asked.

'Uh . . .' Charlie's finger moved to the 'page up' key, then hovered. 'Hang on,' he said. 'The last entry says, "Leukaemoid picture clearing. Blood film normalised."' He looked up with a grin. 'It says the infant was removed from the intensive care baby ward.'

'What?' She peered at the screen, read the words too, felt the tug of hope. 'He's got better?'

'Looks like it.' Charlie smiled at her.

'But babies don't get better from Leukaemia, do they?'

'This one has.' Charlie ran up the page. 'He's from Frome in Somerset. Aged eight weeks and three days.'

'But Davenport said they would all die,' she said slowly, then shook herself. If one baby had survived, that was fantastic – but it didn't alter what Branium had done. There were other babies, other pregnant women. And they didn't have much time.

'Charlie . . .' she started, then saw that he'd already exited from that baby's notes and called up a directory. He scrolled down slowly.

'There! Look!' She stabbed in excitement at the glass. '"INFL. INS"! What'll that be? Insertion? And there; "INFL. PRE; INFL. PR." Those must be it!'

'OK, OK!' Charlie waved her away lightly. 'Let me at it.' He tapped a key and the disk-drive hummed. Sasha stared so hard at the screen that her eyes hurt. The file names vanished. The screen went blank.

'What the . . . ?'

'Oh no,' whispered Charlie.

'What?' She stared at him. He looked sick. 'It's been wiped too?' she ventured.

Charlie nodded.

'But the names are still there in the directory! Isn't there some way that we can get the data back?'

'It's the shell directory,' he said quietly. 'It holds the names even when the contents have been erased.'

Blood pounded in her head. With an effort she stood upright. She saw the filing cabinet behind the door and went over to it.

The first drawer was empty.

Mike joined her, yanking open the second.

'Hush,' she told him urgently.

'It's bloody empty.'

The third drawer contained a doctor's white coat; the fourth was empty like the rest.

'How about the desk?'

Charlie was already rummaging through a few papers on the top. 'There's nothing,' he said despairingly, holding them up. 'Doodles. Dates. A name: Mel. "Baby". That's all.'

'Aren't there any discs anywhere? Back-ups?'

Charlie pulled open the only desk drawer. 'Oh shit.' It contained a quantity of used plastic cups and stale sandwiches. 'I don't know what else we can do. Wait for whoever was in here to come back?'

Sasha shook her head. She felt suddenly very calm. 'There's no point. If West's wiped everything it means he's covering his tracks. Sweeping clean.' She took a deep breath, recalling part of her conversation with Davenport. 'That's what they did in Albania when the babies started dying.' She shuddered. 'He's not going to want to talk to us. We'd better go. Oh!' She paused, remembering something. 'D'you think we should take a copy of that baby's medical notes? It's not much, but at least it shows he was ill.'

'Sure.' Charlie nodded. 'We'll take a quick copy.' He tapped at the keyboard. 'The printer's in the lab, isn't it?'

'In the corner,' said Mike. 'I'll get it.'

'I'm so sorry, Sash,' Charlie said softly.

'Me too.' She tried to smile. 'I'll think of some other way of proving this, but just at the moment we don't even know who the sick babies are. Apart from this one, that's got better . . .' She broke off. Mike was standing in the connecting doorway, holding a sheaf of papers. He looked very strange. 'What is it, Mike?' she asked.

'It's . . . I think it's the stuff you need.'

'What?'

He nodded jerkily. 'It was in the printer.' He held out the papers. 'It's still printing out.'

Now she heard the soft swish of paper. She took the pages from him. The first one was headed 'Same World Hospital. Clinical Trial of the Infiltrator Retrovirus.'

She gasped. 'Oh my God! Charlie, look!'

'That's it? That's really it?'

'Yes! Yes, look at all this stuff!'

Mike re-emerged from the lab with a thinner pile. 'It's stopped printing now.'

He gave the last pages to Sasha. She flicked quickly through, her hands trembling. 'Here! "Subjects Selected for UK Programme".' It was a list of eighteen names and addresses.

She leafed over, saw 'Case Histories', stopped at Subject One, read: 'Rose Gilbert, 17 Holydale Lane, Clapham. Infiltrator inserted on 28 March.'

'Oh my God,' she breathed.

Charlie was reading over her shoulder. 'Jeremy James Gilbert, born October eleventh. Dystrophin gene present and working . . .'

Sasha flicked over a page, skimmed quickly down. 'It's his medical record,' she said. A shiver ran through her. 'He was admitted here last night. Given a blood-test. It was clear.'

'He's OK as well then,' said Charlie.

The words jumped in front of her eyes. 'No he isn't,' she whispered. 'West went to examine him this morning. That's the last entry.'

Her hand was suddenly trembling so badly that she could hardly hold the page. 'I've just realised what Davenport meant.' She heard the conversation again in her mind. 'He said the Syndrome babies got Leukaemia. I asked him if they'd all died of it; he didn't reply, so

I asked him again. He said he'd heard me the first time.' She turned to Charlie. She had tears in her eyes.

'What's wrong, hon?'

'He said, "They all died. Let's just say that." Charlie,' she seized his arm, 'he meant they'd killed some of them!'

He shook his head. 'You don't know that.'

'I do! He said it in such an odd way – but I was driving, we were on the motorway, I had to concentrate.'

'So you're saying this baby . . . ?' Charlie shook his head again. 'They wouldn't do that,' he said.

'Wouldn't they?'

'They've done loads of other stuff,' Mike said.

Sasha's mouth went dry. With an effort she stilled her hands. 'He's in Clare Ward. It's probably too late, but we've got to try!'

The secretary was clearly drunk. She thrust her own wine glass into Mel's hand and insisted that she join the party.

'But I need to find Dr West,' Mel yelled above the uproar.

The girl smiled tipsily back. Mel doubted that she'd heard or even recognised her. She felt pure despair.

'D'you know where I can reach him?'

'Sorry?' the secretary giggled at a young man standing next to her. The Santa earrings that Mel had helped her put on danced dangerously.

'Please. It's about my little boy, you remember?'

'Oh.' The girl turned back. Mel saw her focusing hard, saw the tears spring to her eyes. 'Hasn't Doctor come yet?'

Mel shook her head. Silently she appealed with everything she had.

The girl frowned deeply. 'Try . . .' She stabbed at Mel's shoulder and the wine slopped in the glass. 'Try Clare Ward.' She hiccuped. 'Doctor's special . . . specialist's going to see the Gilberts.'

Clare Ward, Mel repeated desperately to herself. She'd beg that specialist to locate Dr West; she'd scream and cry if she had to. 'Thank you,' she bawled, but the girl had already gone.

Mel fought her way out, depositing the glass on a table. On the landing by the lifts she found the hospital's directory. Clare Ward was two flights below. She hit the call button but couldn't bear to wait. She would walk down, she decided.

*   *   *

Anna had two tasks to perform at the hospital. Until she'd reached the foyer she hadn't fully decided which one to tackle first, but facing the receptionist's polite enquiry she'd instantly made up her mind. The directions had been straightforward; the elevator very quick.

She stood before the nurse's station in Clare Ward. When one of the two women looked up, she said with calm authority, 'I believe I'm expected. In connection with Jeremy Gilbert.'

'You're the specialist?'

Anna inclined her head.

'Oh, thank goodness! I . . . I mean, the parents have been very anxious.' The nurse glanced at her colleague before continuing in a quieter voice, 'The mother's been given a sedative. She's sleeping in Room Nine, just across from Jeremy. Mr Gilbert's in there with her; I'll go and tell him you're here.'

'That won't be necessary,' Anna stopped her swiftly. One of her chief concerns had been how to handle the parents. 'I'll examine the baby first. I've got his notes.'

'Oh.'

The nurse looked taken aback, but her colleague murmured, 'That's probably best.' She smiled at Anna. 'You don't want Mr Gilbert screaming at you while you're trying to work. Jeremy's in Room Ten, right at the end on the left.'

'Thank you.'

Anna set off. The black briefcase in her hand was the sort of thing doctors carried, though hers was almost empty and quite light. She told herself not to hurry, not to look back to see if the nurses were watching her. They wouldn't be; they suspected nothing.

She walked steadily. She'd heard that the method she was going to use took only a few minutes and that it was virtually impossible to detect. She passed Room Four on her left. The door was slightly ajar; she didn't look in. Behind her came the sound of the second nurse's voice, raised and rather bossily addressing someone else. Anna didn't listen to what she said. She kept going, her eyes fixed upon her goal.

CHAPTER FORTY-ONE

The lift had stopped on the fourth floor but no one had entered. They'd been on the point of taking the stairs when the doors had closed.

They reached the second floor. Clare Ward was straight ahead, the nursing station immediately on the right. A woman was standing in front of it. It struck Sasha that she had a supplicating air. She turned at their approach; so too did the nurse to whom she'd been speaking.

'Yes?' the nurse said.

'I was wondering, is Jeremy Gilbert . . . ?' Sasha swallowed.

Charlie put in quickly, 'Is he still here?'

'Yes.' The nurse raised her eyebrows expressively. 'Are you relatives?'

'Could we see him?' Sasha blurted.

She shook her head. She looked bored. 'There's a doctor with him at the moment.'

'A specialist,' the woman next to Sasha added gently.

'Oh.' Were her fears unfounded? she wondered. Had she misinterpreted Davenport's remark?

She saw that Mike was leaning over, trying to read things on the nurses' desk.

The nurse didn't notice. 'You can probably see him if you'd like to wait. Over there,' she nodded meaningfully at some sofas, 'with this lady. It might be a little while. Doctor's only just arrived.'

'I'm sure she'll find he's quite all right,' the other woman said comfortingly to Sasha.

'She?'

'The specialist.'

'Oh. Yes.' Sasha turned to the woman. She'd such kind eyes, but they were also sad. 'Thank you.'

'Shall we sit down?' Charlie said. 'Coming, Mike?'

There was no reply. Sasha looked round for him, and saw him walking quickly down the corridor away from them. 'Mike?' she called softly after him. 'What are you doing?'

'Room Ten!' he shouted, and broke into a trot.

'Mike!'

'What's going on?' demanded the nurse, peering over the desk after him.

Mike started to run.

Time stood still. Anna had slid in and closed the door behind her before she'd raised her eyes to look for the cot. It stood to the right. She saw the baby in it, registered that he was sleeping, that this would make it easier. Then her eyes moved on to the small girl standing over him, a blanket in her hands big enough to swamp her.

'Let me do it,' Anna said softly, and took the blanket from her.

Mike skidded to a halt. He didn't care if he was wrong; he couldn't risk it. He seized the handle and opened the door. She was standing there: the woman who'd driven Gerry away, the killer who'd haunted his dreams. And she was bending over the baby, doing something to him.

'Don't,' he gasped.

The woman spun round. The faraway look on her face vanished as the blanket dropped from her hands.

The baby started to cry.

'Pearce,' the woman said. In one swift movement she stooped for her briefcase and picked it up, her eyes never leaving his, pinning him to the spot, turning him into lead.

'Mike!'

He heard Sasha and Charlie call but he couldn't turn his head.

He saw the gun in the woman's hand, knew what she meant to do. He heard the others coming, but they were so far away, almost in another world. The real world was here, in this room, in doing what the woman willed . . .

Her gaze skewed to his left and then above his head.

He turned. Charlie and Sasha were there, behind him in the doorway. 'It's OK, Mike,' Charlie said.

'Don't move.' The woman spoke softly, moving her gun between them, trying, Mike saw, to cast her spell again.

'What the hell's going on?' A man's voice erupted from behind them. 'Let me in! My children are in there!'

The woman stiffened.

'Give me that laptop,' she said to Sasha.

'No.' Sasha said firmly. She wrapped both hands around it and Charlie drew her against him.

'I said let me in!' shouted the man again. 'Call security, someone!'

'Get out of my way,' the woman hissed suddenly, pushing them aside. Mike fell back against the man.

'What the hell . . . ?'

'I've got a gun.' The woman waved it. They were out in the corridor now, and there were other people there, frozen against the walls. A door opened and a man in a white coat came out then went back in again quickly. 'I'll use it!' the woman cried and, turning, kicked open the fire-door and was gone, her heels clattering on the steel staircase.

For a moment no one moved. Then someone yelled, 'I've called security!' and someone else ran to the fire-door and shouted, 'She's in the car park! She's headed for the road . . . She'll be gone!'

The man Mike had fallen against pushed him away and dashed into the baby's room.

'Daddy!' came a child's voice.

'Lucy! Oh, baby, are you OK? Is Jeremy OK?'

'Mike?' Sasha said shakily. 'How about you?'

A shudder ran through him, a need to cry. 'I'm fine,' he muttered, ducking his head.

'You saved that baby's life,' Sasha said.

'He did *what?*' The man emerged carrying the small girl in his arms.

'Are you Mr Gilbert?' Sasha asked.

'Yes I am. Look, what's going on here?'

'I'd like to know that too,' said the woman who'd been standing by the nurses station. 'Is your wife one of Dr West's patients?' she asked the man.

'Yes. Who're you?'

'Melanie Alder. Another of his patients. Have you seen him this afternoon, by any chance?'

Mike became aware that Charlie and Sasha were signalling to him. They had their backs to the fire-door. He sidestepped the man and woman, deep in conversation now, and joined them.

Sasha said very quietly, 'We're leaving, OK? We can't get caught up here, and they're safe now. No one else is going to try anything.'

'But the police are coming! They'll want to talk to us.'

'Which is why we're going. Come on, now, before anyone notices.'

They eased slowly through the door and followed each other down the fire-escape.

CHAPTER FORTY-TWO

It was four o'clock in the afternoon. It had been, Philippa reflected, a very long day, possibly the most challenging in her life to date.

In half an hour she was expected at a lobbyist's firm for pre-Christmas drinks. She'd no intention of cancelling it; in fact, she told her reflection in the mantelpiece mirror, she felt charged with more energy, more confidence than ever before.

There was, however, one small matter about which she wished to make completely sure before descending to her car outside. She picked up her handbag and opened the door.

Sebastian, at his desk, looked up.

'Did security deal with that man downstairs?'

'The Butterfly man?' Sebastian gave a brief nod. 'He scarpered.'

'Jolly good.' She put on her coat. 'One feels sorry for such people, but . . .' She gave a little shrug. 'Don't work too late, Sebastian.'

'I won't. Have a good party, Minister.'

The first sound that Bennett heard through his headphones, was the door opening. The second was a young woman saying, 'But Davenport was so nervous, Charlie. Why would he just take off? Where's he gone?'

Bennett swallowed miserably. He could tell her the answer to that last one. McMahon had wanted to know all the grisly details of how and where, and then he'd relayed them twice: once to the man on his way to Davenport's Surbiton home, calling him off that surveillance and telling him to come here instead; and then once more to Bennett's unwilling ears.

The girl sounded nice. He wished he didn't have to tell McMahon about her. He knew the police were downstairs . . . but the men outside were such evil bastards, and as time went on and his fear of McMahon grew, he seriously doubted whether he'd be able to alert Holland on the mobile.

'Ah,' said McMahon, putting the binoculars to his eyes. 'I think I see movement. Our friends have resurfaced, have they not?'

'Just this minute, yes, McMahon,' Bennett said hurriedly. 'I-I think they've been out. From the sounds of it.'

'We'd have seen them go out, Bennett. They've obviously just been in a room with the door shut.'

Bennett wasn't going to argue.

'What're they saying?' asked McMahon.

There was no point in dissembling. McMahon might rewind the tape and catch him out. 'That they've got everything now. The medical data, the names of the babies, all the background on the Infiltrator. She can do the story now.'

'Wonder where they've got their information from.'

Bennett said nothing.

'No matter.' McMahon turned cheerfully from the window. 'I'll let Control know we've got sound now. Give me a bit more, will you? And remember, if they say they're going out . . .'

'I'll tell you at once, McMahon,' he promised.

After finding Davenport missing, they'd decided on Charlie's flat because of the greater floorspace. Sasha and Charlie, on their hands and knees, were sorting the papers into different piles.

'Mike,' Sasha said. He was standing in a space that she wanted. 'Could you move, please?'

'Sorry.' He skipped out of the way.

'OK.' She smiled up at him. She thought he'd been amazing, and had told him so. She recalled the face of that woman at the hospital. She could understand now how Mike had been haunted by those eyes: completely merciless. Sasha didn't like to think of the alternative scenario that could have taken place in that baby's room: the baby dead in his cot, Mike dying on the floor.

'That's me done,' Charlie said.

She tidied her final pile. 'Me too.'

Charlie sat back on his heels. 'I don't know who this lot was intended for,' he said, 'but it's every cough and spit that we need. Infutopin and the glass womb data's over there.' He nodded to his right, where Davenport's laptop sat on a pile. 'The Albanian trials are under the desk in three separate piles; the stuff on the diagnostic blood-testing's by that lamp; the letter to GPs asking for pregnant DMD carriers is by Mike's foot . . .'

'Sorry,' said Mike again.

'That's OK, just don't stand on it. I've put the list of subjects on top of the Yellow Pages, and the Infiltrator insertion dates under that chair-leg.'

'Great.' Sasha surveyed her own work. She'd separated out the case histories, first into born and unborn and then into individual subjects: six in the former category, twelve in the latter. 'I'd better start going through this lot and making notes.'

'I'm going to make us some coffee. I think it's going to be a long night.' Charlie stood up carefully. 'Come on Mike, I'll show you how it's done.'

'Wait a minute,' Sasha said slowly. Her eyes had fallen on her last stack of papers, Subject Eighteen's case history. 'Can you remember what that woman at the hospital said her name was? The nice one who spoke to us?'

'Melanie Alder,' Mike said promptly.

Sasha bit her lip. 'She's one of the patients.'

'Yes, that's what she said to that Gilbert man,' Mike said.

'Was it?' Sasha remembered that Mike had been much closer to the man and woman; at that stage she and Charlie had been at the fire-escape. 'She – or rather her fetus – was injected with the Infiltrator last week.'

'Oh.'

Sasha chewed at her thumb. The woman had been so sweet to them, thinking they were the baby's relatives and trying to comfort them. 'She's going to give birth to a baby who's going to get Leukaemia.' She took a deep breath. 'And my story's going to alert her to that fact.'

'No it isn't, Sasha.' Charlie stepped over the papers and squatted awkwardly beside her. 'She and Gilbert were locked in hard when we left. They're going to figure a few things out between them.'

'Yes, maybe you're right.' She nodded uncertainly. 'But the Gilbert baby doesn't have Leukaemia, does he?'

'That's right.' Charlie frowned. 'And neither did that one we read about on West's computer.'

'He's Subject Two, from Somerset.' Sasha leant over to retrieve a pile, and flicked through to the last page. There it was again: Leukaemoid picture clearing.

'Davenport said all the babies in that second trial got Leukaemia?'

Sasha nodded, wishing Davenport hadn't gone. He might have been able to explain things.

Charlie picked up the subject list. 'The Gilbert baby's Subject One; Subject Two we know about; Subject Three . . . Where's he?'

'Here.' Sasha picked up another pile. She leafed through to the last page. 'He's fine,' she said, surprised. 'Of course, he mightn't have contracted it yet. But he's A1 at the moment.'

'Great. Subject Four?'

Her optimism died. The three-week-old boy was in the intensive care baby unit of his local hospital in Northampton. Her eyes skimmed over his haemoglobin and platelet count and came to rest on the clinician's diagnosis: Leuakaemoid picture worsening.

'Oh hell,' she said, and set his notes behind her on the sofa.

'Subject Five?'

'He's by the telephone directory. Mike, could you . . . ? Thanks.' She leafed through the pages: the blood-test that had diagnosed the fetus as a DMD boy; the insertion of the Infiltrator carrying the healthy gene; the subsequent pregnancy scans; the birth; the quick heel-prick test, which showed the Dystrophin gene present and working; two visits from the midwife . . . Sasha got to the last sheet.

'What is it, Sash?'

Shakily, she handed Charlie the page. 'Oh God,' he said.

'What?' Mike demanded.

'He, um . . .' Sasha swallowed. 'He was killed yesterday in a road accident.

'No.' Mike shook his head. 'Wh-why'd they kill a little baby?'

'We don't *know* they did it.' Sasha closed her eyes. That was true

– but when that baby's death was put in context with everything else . . . She scrabbled on the floor for Subject Six. A stillbirth, she read with a tremble, and put it down again. Babies did die that way; it might not mean anything conclusive. Of five live births, then, she thought, one was healthy; three were in hospital (although two looked as if they were going to be all right), and one baby, only nineteen days old, had been killed.

'I think we need to make some telephone calls,' she said quietly.

When he sat down, Stockart felt better. Upright, he felt a little strange: light-headed, sleepy, not like himself at all. Seated, he was in control again. He closed his eyes to appreciate the smell of the whisky fumes from the tumbler in his hand.

'Davenport's dead, Mr Stockart.'

Stockart smiled, savouring those words again. They improved on recollection and also now that he was calm. The first time he'd heard them, when he'd been pulling away from the Mistletoe in his Jaguar, he'd still been in a panic about the police and his own narrow escape.

When his car-phone had rung he'd almost screamed. But it had been Bernard Hall. He'd been trying to reach him with some good news.

'You're sure he's dead?'

'No question.'

He would have preferred the agony to have lasted longer, for the woman to have done it, but she was elsewhere about his business and at least the snake was dead. Stabbed through the heart. The body left in the gutter to be trodden upon by others.

Stockart put the tumbler to his lips and sipped, allowing the glow of the liquid to warm his throat, to settle the slight queasiness he felt. But no pain; his stomach had ceased to trouble him, which was amazing, considering.

Davenport's death had been the good news. The not-so-good (by the tone of Hall's voice Stockart had understood at once that it must be pretty bad) was that the journalists and Pearce seemed to be putting together a story for publication.

'And?' Stockart had barked.

'And they appear to have got hold of a lot of very detailed information. They're talking about the Infiltrator – I don't know if that means anything to you . . . ?'

Stockart had ground his teeth. Davenport must have told them quite a bit. 'What else?'

'Diagnostic blood-testing, GP's letters – and, er, the Bristol infant's death.'

He'd nearly hit the car in front. Davenport hadn't known any of that!

Before erasing the material on his computer at Branium, Stockart had checked to see which of the sensitive files Davenport had looked at. The only trace of him had been in Stockart's own directory, in his memos to West earlier that day. In a way, that made the betrayal worse: to have used those pathetic snippets to sell him out! But if Davenport hadn't told those journaliststs about the UK trial data, who had?

Hall had gone on quickly, 'They're also talking about Leukaemoid pictures clearing, although quite what that means . . .' He'd made a feeble attempt at a laugh.

Stockart hadn't joined in; a horrible suspicion had been dawning. 'I'll call you back,' he'd snapped.

He'd driven on then, but not back to Branium or even to his apartment in Pimlico, but to a small one-bedroom flat in Victoria which he'd acquired several years before for office dalliances. Women could be vindictive; he'd no wish for unpleasant scenes outside his own front door. His stomach had been troubling him again; he'd taken another dose of pills, swallowing them before remembering that he'd already taken some and not very long ago. But he had pushed the thought aside – drugs companies always err on the side of caution in their prescription advice.

He'd sat down on the sofa and briefly buried his face in his hands. West's visitors, who had caused him to panic and run, hadn't been the police: they'd been the journalists and Pearce. 'No matter, no matter,' he'd whispered to himself. He'd erased everything.

But how, then, to explain their knowledge?

Then he'd nearly gagged as he realised exactly how.

Some of Branium's employees, the forgetful variety – and, cliché though it was, the research scientists and doctors were among the most forgetful – had an automatic failsafe mechanism built into their computers. When the computer was on, the printer was on, and if someone deleted a file, perhaps by accident, a print-out was automatically made. If the user had intended to delete the file, then all he or she had to do was throw away the paper copy. But if not, if the erasure had been a mistake, the data was still there – the ultimate back-up.

Stockart had trembled. West had one of those printers, a huge one, so that if ever he pressed the 'delete' button, his years of research wouldn't be lost. Stockart even vaguely remembered authorising its inclusion with the rest of the equipment, when West's rooms had been kitted out a year before. The printer would have been on in the lab while Stockart had been busy in West's office, chugging away – except it wouldn't have chugged; it was too expensive to make much noise, its gentle hum would have been lost amidst the whirrings of the other machinery in there.

Stockart had cried out loud. He'd spoon-fed them the documents: the Infiltrator data, Infutopin, the super-fast diagnostic blood-test. All they'd had to do was pick it up. Davenport might be dead, Philippa silenced, West . . . He wasn't sure where West was, but he didn't appear now to be a threat. But the journalists and that bloody boy had the lot. Courtesy of John Stockart.

When would American Global News – it *would* be global too, beamed around the world – run it? He'd whimpered. He couldn't quite envisage the depth and suffering of this final nightmare. In spite of everything he'd done, all his cleverness, a couple of hacks and a snivelling kid were going to best him.

He'd patted his pockets. His passport was in one, West's back-up discs in the other. He had his credit-cards.

He'd simply have to run.

Then he'd paused.

The three of them were back in that flat. Somehow – and he'd sneered – Hall's superb operators must have missed them slipping out to the Mistletoe. But that didn't matter now.

What mattered was that they were back, with the laptop, *and* all those documents . . .

The plan that had then occurred to him was quite beautiful in its simplicity.

He inhaled, took another mouthful of whisky and was suddenly overcome with a yawn.

He bent down and picked up the telephone, set it on his knee, and dialled Hall's number.

Succinctly, he outlined what he had in mind.

Hall spluttered. 'You cannot be serious!'

'Oh, I'm serious,' he said quietly.

'Then I'm afraid we must terminate our contract, sir.'

'What?'

'I cannot carry out those instructions.'

Stockart breathed, slow and deep. 'You'll do what I say,' he said with emphasis.

'I'm sorry, sir, but I won't.'

Stockart smiled. As he explained to Hall exactly why he would, his words seemed to slur slightly. He must be a great deal more tired than he'd thought, he realised.

'You've done *what?*' The smooth veneer had slipped from Hall's voice, revealing a pronounced South London twang.

'Mm. By a device that you sold me yourself. An excellent little thing, easily fitted into the mouthpiece; and, as you told me, it picks up every word.

'You've got everything on tape?'

'Oh yes.' And it was true: his orders, Hall's reports, everything stored on tiny cassettes. They were neatly stacked in his safe at work.

'But you'll be on it too!'

'Oh yes.' Stockart closed his eyes. 'Loud and clear. But what I'm saying is, if I'm caught,' he took a gulp of whisky, 'you will be too.'

Hall fell silent. A minute went by. Stockart smiled to himself.

'Very well,' Hall said curtly. 'You leave me no other option.'

Stockart grunted. He was glad that Hall had finally come to heel. 'How long'll it take?' he asked.

'Not long. I'll call you. You'll be there?'

'Oh yes. I'm not going anywhere,' he said. He replaced the receiver. For a moment the room seemed to spin. It was probably a touch of the flu, he thought, nothing serious. Later he'd be quite able to take to the road.

But for now he was determined to stay for the finale.

CHAPTER FORTY-THREE

Every fifteen minutes, Bennett made a rush for the bathroom. It wasn't pretence; it was a genuine need to relieve himself – brought on, he'd no doubt, by the appalling circumstances in which he found himself. McMahon eventually stopped saying 'Gangway' and merely stood aside to let him pass.

He flushed the toilet again and peered in the mirror. It helped, of course, that he looked so horrible, greeny-white with red-rimmed eyes. McMahon obviously believed him to be sick, didn't suspect for a moment what was actually making him run. What would he do if he did? Some of the things that Bennett had been told came back to him in a rush. He watched his own eyes grow wide in fear, then stopped himself. He mustn't frighten himself. If he got too scared it would show.

It helped now that he had something to listen to: Sasha and Charlie and Mike (he knew their names now). He wished he was over there with them, or downstairs with Mr Holland, or – best of all – at home with his girlfriend and the babies. Anywhere, he thought, but here.

He opened the door. He could hear McMahon on the mobile at the other end of the room, idly watching the flat as he talked. Why didn't Sasha close the curtains? Bennett thought peevishly. At least then McMahon wouldn't be able to spy on them.

McMahon snorted. 'He wants *what?*'

Bennett stopped where he was and listened. McMahon had his back to him and he wasn't speaking very loudly, but Bennett quite clearly heard: '. . . bloody big bang, I can tell you!'

Bennett froze, then took a step back into the bathroom.

'Wipe Covent Garden off the map, eh?'

Bennett let out a gasp; he couldn't help himself. But McMahon hadn't heard him. He was actually laughing.

Bennett closed the bathroom door again and withdrew the mobile from his pocket. His fingers were slippery with sweat. He stared at the machine, unable to think clearly. He had no idea what to do. He reopened the bathroom door.

'Wild,' McMahon was saying lovingly. He was still out of sight. Bennett emerged once more and a terrible roaring sound filled his head, his vision blurring. He took a step towards the door to the corridor, waiting to hear McMahon call his name, but all he heard was, 'Yeah. A Jiffy-packet job. Seen it done.'

Bennett turned the handle, cursed the tiny click it made, then was outside, sliding down the hallway, fingertips against the wall, whimpering to himself. He could still hear McMahon's voice, but not the words. Then came another burst of that crazy laughter.

He reached the staircase. The elevator was round to the right, but Bennett didn't hesitate. He took the stairs in great elongated leaps, jabbing the 'send' button on his mobile as he did so.

They knew now that the Bristol mother and her nineteen-day-old son had been killed in a hit-and-run accident the day before. The local paper, who had run the story as their splash – 'Tragic Mum in Double Death Horror' – had faxed them the copy.

'What's your interest?' the reporter had asked curiously, and Sasha had replied vaguely that she was looking at infant death statistics, which had satisfactorily doused his interest.

'It's no coincidence,' she'd said after reading the story.

'No.' Charlie had nodded. Mike had gone very quiet again.

'Monsters,' Sasha had murmured. 'Don't worry, we're going to get them, Mike.'

'Are you going to write the story now?' he'd asked.

'We've got some calls to make first.'

For the next two hours she and Charlie had used the telephones.

After a great deal of effort they'd tracked down a geneticist within the London area who was sufficiently approachable, and who agreed – intrigued – to see them in the morning. Charlie had arranged another meeting with the embryologist for early lunchtime, and they'd both tried to find an expert who could explain how a baby who'd had Leukaemia one day could suddenly recover from it the next.

The last had proved the most difficult. Everyone appeared to be in meetings. At six-twenty, when Sasha had been about to give up for the night, a clinician who was also the press officer of a children's Leukaemia charity called her back.

'Tell me what the figures are,' he said.

She did. She had Subject Two's case history in front of her.

'The clinician's diagnosis is right. Leukaemoid picture.'

'But he got better today – without treatment.'

'Ah. You do know that "Leukaemoid picture" doesn't automatically mean Leukaemia?'

'Er . . .' She hadn't. But presumably West had.

'Blood-films of very young babies are notoriously nightmarish. It might look like Leukaemia one day – or any one of a host of infections and the next there's nothing amiss.'

Sasha stared at the notes before her. 'Perhaps, if someone was expecting Leukaemia,' she suggested slowly, 'and they saw these figures, might they jump to the wrong conclusion?'

'Could do, yes. But very few people *would*. Leukaemia in babies that young is just about unheard of.'

Unless it had been engineered into them, Sasha thought. Unless the man looking at those results was the engineer. Unless he'd had a previous batch whose Leukaemoid pictures had all heralded the real thing.

She thanked the press officer and replaced the receiver as if in a trance. The British babies *didn't* have Leukaemia; West had only assumed they had. Which was fantastic for all the babies in the study, of course – apart from Subject Five from Bristol and his mother. She looked round. Mike was dozing on the sofa. He'd wanted to phone his mother at six, she remembered, but he looked so exhausted that she decided against waking him yet.

She went in search of Charlie, found him in the kitchen making yet more coffee, and told him everything.

'Wow,' he said. He stared at her. 'If you're right, you're going to be telling those parents and parents-to-be one hell of a piece of good news.'

'D'you think I ought to phone the hospital in Northampton? That baby's still in the intensive care ward. I don't know what I'd say exactly, but it would be awful if they went on thinking the worst when he's going to get better.' She broke off. Charlie was smiling at her. 'What?' she asked, smiling back.

'I think you're wonderful.'

'You do?'

'I do. Come here a minute.'

She went willingly, felt herself dissolve. 'Charlie, I really ought to go, and—'

'Ssh,' he said, and kissed her on the mouth.

'Oh, Charlie,' she breathed.

'Where're you sleeping tonight?'

She pressed herself against him. 'Here,' she whispered.

A terrible noise rent the air, making her jump back. She covered her ears.

'What the hell?' she saw Charlie mouth.

The noise stopped for a second, then started again. It was like something from the war.

Mike ran in. 'What's that?'

'Some kind of alarm?' she shouted.

It stopped. 'Thank God for that,' said Charlie. 'It must be the apartment's alarm system being tested.'

'This is the police!' boomed a voice from outside. 'We have reason to believe that there's a suspect package in the near vicinity of Floral Street.'

'A bomb?' Mike whispered.

'Oh my God,' said Sasha, clutching Charlie in one hand, Mike in the other.

'Would everyone please clear the area immediately!' the voice continued. In spite of the distortion caused by its magnification, Sasha could hear the urgency. 'Do not stop to take possessions! Please follow police directions and proceed at once to designated places of safety!'

'Come on,' said Charlie, snatching up his keys from the counter. 'This is no rehearsal. Let's get out of here.'

*   *   *

It had been a wise decision, Stockart congratulated himself, to have kept the flat looking reasonable, cleaned once a week and the sheets changed on the double-bed. The furniture, admittedly, had seen better days, but under subdued lighting it didn't look too bad. And the music system was entirely passable. 'The Way We Were' was playing softly now.

He bent to plump up a cushion on the sofa and felt light-headedness seize him again. Mind over matter, he told himself, straightening up. He had a visitor coming, a lady visitor. He had to be on top form for her.

He grinned. Hall's woman.

She had called twenty minutes before, waking him from a strange, muddled sleep. Her voice had been purring like a cat's. A wild cat's. He'd detected the trace of a foreign accent – oh, how he loved foreign women!

She had just set in motion his final instructions, she'd told him. And Mr Hall had mentioned that he wished to meet her . . .

'Wh-why, yes.' His own voice had sounded thick and slow to him, but she hadn't appeared to notice.

'May I take down your address?' she'd asked huskily.

'Please do!'

She wasn't far away, she'd said; she'd be there at any moment.

He walked with concentration into the kitchen, found another glass, poured her a whisky – it was the only alcohol in the place – and added, for good measure, a splash of water. Everything was going to come right, he thought, steadying himself against the sink. Davenport already dead, the journalists, Pearce and the data about to be blown to smithereens. He belched. The only loose end was West, but Stockart was convinced now that he'd been wrong, the old man hadn't gone to the police. He'd still be quivering in a corner somewhere; he wasn't a problem.

He returned to the sitting-room. The flat was on the sixth floor, looking east. The explosion ought to be visible from here. He and the woman could stand there together, watching, touching – it would be so exciting – and then afterwards, on the floor, against the wall, in the bed, he'd have her.

He heard the doorbell chime.

He set out to answer it. It rang again. 'Coming, coming,' he cooed. She was keen for him, hungry. He giggled in anticipation. With difficulty – the latch was stiff – he opened the door.

'My dear,' he said, smiling. His eyes were playing up but she looked good to him, dark and slim, demurely dressed. Underneath, she'd be a tiger. 'Come in, do.'

She entered, her right hand hidden in her handbag.

He closed the door. 'I don't even know your name. Oh!' His eyes focused suddenly on the revolver in her hand, its long, thin silencer pointing straight at him.

'It's Anna,' she said, shooting him twice through the heart.

Out in the street the night was filled with blue and red flashing lights and police everywhere. Sasha, Charlie and Mike joined a tide of people surging to the top of the street. No one seemed afraid, there was more a mood of excitement. Sasha grabbed hold of Mike; Charlie was right behind them.

'Keep to your left, please!' a policeman shouted every few paces. 'Keep moving!'

At the top of Floral Street where it joined the market, they were funnelled through a police barricade into a single lane. Some people tried to stop, intent it seemed on staying to watch, but they were pushed forward by the police and the people behind them.

A policeman shouted in exasperation. 'If a bomb goes off, glass will come flying straight through here! Move on, please!'

A bomb, Sasha thought. It didn't seem real. But then, on the far side of the market-place, she saw the fleet of ambulances and fire-engines waiting.

'Sasha Downey?'

She jumped at the sound of her name.

'And Michael Pearce.' Tony Holland stood on the other side of the barrier. 'I take it that that's Mr Davenport's laptop you're holding. And you must be Charlie,' he added. 'Will you all come through here, please?' He shifted the metal barrier to one side. 'I've got some questions for you.'

EPILOGUE

The bomb proved not to exist, although belief in the threat had been so high that it took POLSA (specially trained Police Search Advisers), using sniffer dogs and sophisticated electronic equipment, most of the night to establish that fact.

Sasha, Charlie and Mike were questioned by Tony Holland for several hours. They surrendered the laptop to him, but not the papers which Sasha, in spite of the bomb-warning, had gathered up before leaving the flat. The only one that she did volunteer – as soon as they got to the police station – was the list of patients' names and addresses, in case they were in danger from the bogus specialist or anyone else.

But as the night passed, that prospect became more remote. It had taken less than twenty minutes from the time that Bennett had first hit the panic button for a team of armed police officers to enter the hotel bedroom. McMahon had gone, although Bennett's equipment was still there. In the street, in the pandemonium of the bomb alert, it had been impossible to detect who might have been McMahon's men.

Shortly afterwards, another team of armed officers raided Zodiac's registered premises in Moon Street, Paddington. The building was deserted. There'd been no sign of Bernard Hall or of the man Bennett knew only as 'Control'.

Bennet had tried to give an adequate description of McMahon

but failed, as he'd spent most of his time trying not to look at the man. Mike, on the other hand, provided an excellent E-fit picture of the woman, which was issued to all airports, ports and railways stations. Unfortunately, it did not result in her detention.

Davenport's body was discovered in a road off Whitehall; West's was fished out of the Thames. West's secretary had been tearful but not surprised by his suicide.

Holland rang Branium himself. At that time of night the telephone was answered by one of the company's security staff, who were busy dealing with a burglary within the building itself: the safe of the special projects director had been opened and emptied, although no force had been used.

'Mr Stockart's office?' Holland had queried.

'That's right, sir. We've been trying to locate him.'

He was found eventually, lying sprawled against the radiator in the hall of his Victoria flat with a surprised look on his face.

Branium's chief executive did not return Holland's call until after midnight. When he did, he sounded truly shaken. John Stockart and Dr West had always been held in the highest regard within the company. Of course the police were welcome at his offices in the morning.

Sasha, Charlie and Mike were held in protective custody over-night then released, although Mike's release was conditional upon police bail. In spite of his protests he was escorted home by his brother.

Sasha and Charlie returned to the apartment and resumed work. Sasha only just made the deadline for *Comment*.

Her story was reported around the world.

Charlie interviewed her for AGN. She spoke simply, but the effect was the more shattering for that. Not only had two senior Branium employees colluded in conducting illegal experiments on human subjects, many of whom had died; not only, when they faced exposure, had they sought to cover their tracks by extreme measures, including murder; but their last desperate panic had been based on an utterly false premise.

'The babies in the UK trial do not, and never have had Leu-kaemia,' Sasha said into the camera. 'They've got a mild form of glandular fever which clears itself in a few days. Dr West was expecting Leukaemia, and that's what he saw. Apart from that, they appear to be absolutely healthy.'

Her information had come from a haematologist at the Northampton Hospital who, by the time of her telephone call, had already seen the similar case on DAMR and spoken to the Bristol hospital that treated the first sick infant. With the knowledge that Sasha had been able to provide, he'd understood what appeared to be a new medical phenomenon, of such tiny babies contracting the disease at all.

Sasha went on: 'These babies' DNA patterns had been altered by the Infiltrator retrovirus. That made them particularly susceptible to the glandular fever virus.'

'But why,' Charlie asked, 'did the British babies contract the virus when the Albanian babies hadn't? Had Dr West made a mistake with the Infiltrator in the British cases?'

'No, he just thought he had. He'd forgotten about the different environment. Apparently the glandular fever virus isn't prevalent in Albania in the way it is here. Not yet, anyway. Albania's been a closed country for so long.'

'So the Infiltrator is a genuine medical breakthrough?'

'Yes. It's the way that the tests were conducted, without permission from either the government or the patients, that was illegal and so morally wrong.'

Charlie turned to the second guest in the studio, the Branium spokesman.

He, too, was quietly spoken. Branium was as shocked as anyone else, he said – and he did look pale – to discover what Stockart and West had been doing. The company had been assured that the processes by which Infutopin was discovered and the Infiltrator Technique perfected had had full government approval 'all the way along the line.' It was only now that they realised, much to their horror, that Stockart and West had been falsifying data, reports and papers for years, including government letters giving permission for the Infiltrator trial to go ahead in the UK.

'I have one here to show you,' the man said, holding it up.

'If we have erred,' he went on, 'it was in allowing our tremendous excitement at the potential of West's discoveries to blind us to the true natures of the two men. Perhaps we should have asked more questions, perhaps we should have challenged what they told us, carried out spot-checks on the laboratories. But we ask: how were we to have known? We wanted to believe them; we *did* believe them. And it cannot be forgotten that, however distasteful and illegal the means of discovering Infutopin might have been, the drug is now in the process of eradicating infertility throughout the world. In addition, the success of the Infiltrator with the Duchenne's babies indicates the most exciting development in the history of medicine to date.

'We ask the public to remember the goodness that has come – and has yet to come – out of the evil that Stockart and West did.'

Dead men, Sasha thought, make wonderful scapegoats.

The spokesman then announced that, although there was no proof that the Bristol baby and his mother had been killed on Stockart's orders, Branium wanted to express its grief and horror at everything that had happened by offering the widower and the other members of the UK trial compensation.

Charlie turned back to Sasha. The government, he said, had just announced that there was to be a full inquiry into the Branium affair. 'Mrs Tyler has repudiated the allegation in the *Comment* article that she was "tipped off" about the illegal Infiltrator trial. In view of this, do you believe that the inquiry will be unbiased?'

'I have to,' Sasha said. 'It looks like it's the only inquiry there's going to be.'

That was the unsatisfactory conclusion that Tony Holland and his superiors were also beginning to reach. Branium appeared to lend its full co-operation to the police investiation, allowing technical officers complete access to its records, but all that was discovered was the falsified data about Infutopin and the Infiltrator. They suspected the company of a great deal more than they could prove.

Whatever their suspicions, the guilty parties were either dead or gone. Talking of being gone, Holland's superintendent had continued grimly, the Tenterden Four hadn't been seen for four days. He wanted Holland to get over to Europe and find them.

However, the following morning they effectively gave themselves up. They'd been living and sleeping in the back of a rusty Renault camper-van, bought at an extortionate price at a car auction outside Brussels. Caroline had cut off Mary's hair and dressed her as a boy. They'd lost themselves in the watery hinterland north-east of the capital; at times they'd trailed into the Netherlands without being aware of it. They'd dared to travel only at night, finding woodland in which to sleep during the day. Their money had run out; they were hungry, exhausted and sick of each other. It was Caroline's idea to return to the Belgian capital to seek out the office of one of the British newspaper correspondents based there.

No one argued with her. They'd lost all will-power.

The young British journalist they went to became very excited indeed. Then he made the mistake of taking them out to a restaurant frequented by other journalists. An unpleasant scene ensued, the police were called, and the Four were taken into custody, then, later in the day, extradited.

Mike and Mary, after some deliberation on the chief constable's part, were simply cautioned. At the trial of their elders two months later, the prosecution did their best to emphasise the seriousness of the offences, particularly the psychological impact upon the security guard. However, other factors succeeded in undermining the case. On the eve of the trial, Branium let it be known that they would have preferred the three not to have been charged. 'We owe them,' a Branium source was quoted as saying to a newspaper. Then Tim Dacre, the chief prosecution witness, declared under cross-examination that he hadn't really been scared. He'd seen it was just a little girl who'd damaged his car.

The Henshaws were acquitted. Stuart Richley was given a two-year suspended sentence for threatening with an imitation firearm. They were released amid cheers, giving victory salutes to the TV cameras as they left the court.

The item had just ended on the early-evening news when Mel's telephone rang. She guessed who it would be – and she was right: Rose Gilbert, asking if she'd seen it.

Mel kept the conversation short. Although initially she and Patrick had clung to the Gilberts as fellow victims, Mel had found Rose's preoccupation with Jeremy to the exclusion of her daughters hard to stomach. Also, she wanted to forget; whereas the Gilberts, along with some of the other parents, seemed determined to remember. But then, she told herself as she replaced the handset, she had more to forget than many of them.

The police had told her that, judging by notes found on West's desk, the doctor appeared to have had an obsession about her, possibly to have believed – dates had been checked and verified as birth-dates – that he was her father. She'd been incredulous, actually hysterical, at this revelation, coming as it had on top of her own realisation that, if the gunwoman hadn't been stopped by the journalists, Mel would probably have been her next target.

Mel shut her eyes tightly. She cried less often now than she had at first, but still there were times when it became unbearable to remember what it had been like to believe in a cure for Ludo.

She leaned back against the dividing wall, out of sight of the hatch which was open on to Ludo's room.

'Mummy?'

She knew that if she spoke he would detect the thickness in her voice. She heard him coming – stiffly on his new, more supportive splints – and quickly rubbed at her eyes, hoping to dry them in time.

'Poor Mummy.' He held on to the door. 'Does your tummy hurt again?'

Not trusting herself to speak, she nodded and gave a quick smile. Ludo laid his head softly against her stomach. 'Don't hurt Mummy, naughty baby,' he said reprovingly.

'Oh, Ludi.' She put her hand on his head and her tears fell hotly. 'I love you so.'

Coming awake, Sasha turned her head to see that Charlie was watching her.

'You're beautiful when you're asleep,' he said, smiling at her.

'Only then?'

'Some other times too.' He leaned over and kissed her and, as she responded, came nearer and kissed her again, more slowly. 'Will you have my baby?' he murmured in her ear.

'What, now?'

'Maybe.' His lips brushed her nose, then her cheeks. He stopped, pushed her hair back from her face and regarded her seriously for a moment. 'D'you think she'd have your eyes?' he asked.

'Might be a boy.'

'No, I want a girl, just like you.'

Sasha remembered what her dream had been about.

'Why so sad suddenly?' Charlie asked.

'Oh . . .' She took a deep breath and smiled. 'I don't mind if it's a boy or a girl, so long as its healthy,' she said.

'Come here then.'

Eight months later, the research team who'd been largely resited from REDEV a week before the break-in, to a more desolate spot in the Scottish Highlands, celebrated their latest findings wildly.

They gave the brightest beagle puppy (that they'd selected as a pet) champagne too, but he wouldn't touch it. 'Too smart,' the head of the team praised him, stroking his ears.

Later, when things had calmed down slightly, she went into her office, closed the door and dialled the number in London. It went straight through to the chief executive's office. He was delighted to hear from her, and even more delighted at her news.

'You've cracked it?'

'Yes, sir, we have.'

'Bloody well done, girl!'

The research scientist smiled. She raised her eyes to the window that separated her room from the sterilised lab next door. The two surviving fetuses lay side by side in their glass worlds. 'Thank you, sir. Once we'd got enough of the IQ genes, it was just a matter of knowing which bit of the DNA to put the Infiltrator into.'

'But trial and error has won the day again, eh? Your old boss would have been proud of you.' He cleared his throat. 'If all goes well we can start in utero trials within the next six months.'

'That's excellent, sir.'

He chuckled. 'I think I can say we won't have much problem finding candidates for this trial. I'd put my own wife down if she was still of childbearing age. Mind you, the day isn't far off, I wager, when age won't be relevant any more. When you'll be able to *watch* your baby grow – the baby of your choice, that is – and open its lid on delivery day.'

The scientist smiled. She wondered whether to share with him the latest results that her team had achieved with one batch of the glass womb fetuses. They'd broken the previous survival record of twenty weeks – only by four days, it was true, but they were obviously on the right track with the new combination of ingredients in the nurturing culture. Perhaps – and her eyes strayed again to the fetuses – they'd try it on them. For now, she decided against telling the chief executive. It was well known that he was liable to become too enthusiastic too soon.

After the call ended he poured himself a large vodka. Later, he would notify the other GO members – the legal director, and the exciting young man who'd replaced Stockart – but for now he wanted to enjoy the news from Scotland himself: babies that could be *made*, that was the word (and he repeated it aloud), with IQs of 180 guaranteed.

Neither the break-in, nor the journalist's revelations, nor West's and Stockart's deaths had prevented it. And with the contact that he had made at a lobbyist's Christmas party on that fateful day, Branium's future had never looked rosier.

The very charming secretary of state for health had kept him informed of the progress of her department's inquiry into his company. She'd been behind the government's decision to allow Branium to continue with its Infutopin treatment centre at St Peter's – 'Why punish the public?' had been her cry – and he'd known five weeks before that Branium would be effectively cleared in one month's time by the inquiry chairman.

'A little rap over the knuckles for allowing your brilliant scientist a touch too much freedom, that's all.'

'That's wonderful news! If there's ever anything that I can do to assist you . . .'

'Just continue making sure your scientists get there first. And I'll make sure Branium gets all the help it needs.'

The chief executive smiled and reached for his secure phone. Before telling anyone else, he had to tell Philippa about the latest application for the Infiltrator Technique.